TORRENT OF PASSION

"Oh, yes, my little hellcat," Devlin whispered throatily, "I shall have you."

Kyra fought valiantly, but the remaining threads of her composure snapped and suddenly she was confronted with an altogether different enemy—her own blossoming desire. Appalled by her body's traitorous response to the array of overpowering sensations Devlin had skillfully summoned within her, Kyra tried to push away—to no avail. She was forced to contend with an inner mutiny even more devastating than the stranger's advances.

This is madness! her reason shouted. *Your conduct is shameful, despicable. You should be screaming or swooning, not . . .*

With a horrified gasp, Kyra realized that the scream she had fully intended to release had somehow taken the form of a rapturous moan of unmistakable pleasure.

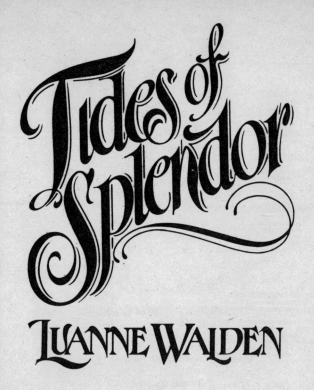

Tides of Splendor

LUANNE WALDEN

CHARTER/DIAMOND BOOKS, NEW YORK

TIDES OF SPLENDOR

A Charter/Diamond Book / published by arrangement with
the author

PRINTING HISTORY
Charter/Diamond edition / August 1990

ISBN 1-55773-375-9

Charter/Diamond Books are published by The Berkley Publishing
Group, 200 Madison Avenue, New York, New York 10016.
The name "CHARTER/DIAMOND" and its logo are trademarks
belonging to Charter Communications, Inc.

PRINTED IN THE UNITED STATES OF AMERICA

10 9 8 7 6 5 4 3 2 1

To Darryl and Jane, my very good friends, who let me tag along on their vacation to Savannah, enabling me to undertake much of the research for this book. Thanks for your support, the laughter, and the good times, but especially—thanks for your friendship and for caring.

To Constance O'Day-Flannery, a fellow writer and kindred spirit who would not let me give up on myself. For that, and so much more, your friendship is deeply appreciated.

And once again to Adele Leone, my agent, who—against all odds—made this book a reality. Thanks for not throwing in the towel.

PROLOGUE

Charleston, South Carolina
April 1853

It was a perfect day for a wedding. At least that was the consensus of the friends and relatives whose carriages crowded the narrow roadways leading to the Cookson plantation outside Charleston where Miss Carolly Cookson and Mr. Robert Latham would presently exchange marriage vows. There was, however, one member of the growing assemblage who could have cheerfully wished the bride-to-be in perdition, and the lady would have done precisely that had it not been for the tempering hand of restraint placed upon her arm.

"Fanny, you promised not to make a scene!" came the stern reminder from the young woman at Fanny's side. "Carolly is, after all, your cousin."

"Humph! That did not stop Carolly when she set her cap for my Robert," Fanny wailed.

"Not again," sighed her less-than-sympathetic companion.

"Kyra, you don't understand. I loved Robert. I thought he loved me," whined the jilted Fanny.

"Yes, well . . ." Kyra's violet eyes shrewdly considered the betrothed couple. "You were apparently mistaken." Then, out of patience with her childhood friend and

1

confidante, Kyra blurted, "Honestly, Fanny, I think you
have gone soft in the head. Will you just look at them? Do
they look like a truly enraptured couple?"

Fanny settled her gaze grudgingly on the wedding party,
but when she turned once more toward Kyra, the frown that
had previously marred her pretty face had been replaced by
a self-satisfied smile. "No, they look positively miserable.
Is it wicked of me to be happy about that?"

"A little, perhaps," Kyra said, laughing as she hooked
her arm with Fanny's and led her away from the gathering
crowd. "I overheard Papa telling my brother that this is to
be a marriage of convenience," she whispered confidentially.

"No!" Fanny gasped, horrified.

"It's true," Kyra vowed. "It seems that Robert needs the
financial security this marriage will afford. And Carolly?
Well, it would appear that your uncle has endured quite
enough of her peccadilloes—remember the scandal she
created last fall with that drummer from Richmond?—and is
determined she will settle down and be a good wife."

"But why does it have to be with my Robert?" Fanny
cried.

"Must you forever go on about that man? You are better
off without him, believe me. Why, any number of gentlemen in Charleston would be honored to court you. You
needn't go all the way to Atlanta to find yourself a beau."

"Hah! The men of Charleston don't give me a thought
when you're around," Fanny accused.

"Fanny, you know I cannot be bothered with a beau right
now; I am much too busy taking care of Papa and Andrew.
I assure you I have no interest in men and romance and such
nonsense. You may have them, one and all."

They stopped at a huge gnarled oak tree and Fanny,
heedless of the possible damage to her dress, settled on the
blanket of spring grass. Intrigued by her friend's earlier

comment, she said, "Very well, then. Suppose you just tell me the names of some of my would-be sweethearts."

Kyra bit her lower lip in thoughtful contemplation. "Well," she mused aloud, settling in a swing that dangled from a sturdy limb. "There is Timothy Butler."

"Timothy!" Fanny shrieked, thoroughly pleased with this revelation. "Who else?"

Kyra grasped the ropes on either side of her and allowed the swing to glide forward. "I have it on good authority that Henry Wilcox is quite taken with you."

"No—not Henry! Why has he never spoken to me?"

"Because you've been so preoccupied with your precious Robert," Kyra admonished, planting her feet firmly on the ground in order to pump the swing more forcefully. "Oh, and then there is—"

But this potential suitor's identity would remain an enigma, for as Kyra swung forward, one of the wedding guests stepped directly into her path. Kyra issued a throaty cry of warning to the gentleman, but it was to no avail. In the next instant, Kyra sailed into the unsuspecting man. The force of the impact dislodged her from her perch, pitching her headlong into the hapless passerby and knocking them both to the ground in a mass of entwined limbs and wrinkled muslin.

"Oh, dear," Kyra eventually mumbled. Now that the initial shock of the collision had subsided, she had the presence of mind to extricate herself from her embarrassing position—sprawled across the stranger's broad chest. Planting her hands on either side of her unfortunate victim, she pushed herself up and found herself staring into a pair of the darkest brown eyes she had ever seen. "Oh, dear!" she repeated somewhat breathlessly.

"Hmm, yes." The gentleman chuckled wryly.

"I'm so *very* sorry, sir!" Kyra apologized. "I fear I caught you unaware. I—"

"No time for apologies," the man said brusquely, jumping lithely to his feet and extending his hand to Kyra. "The ceremony is about to begin, and Robert must be searching frantically for his best man. Come along, miss." When Kyra did not take his arm, the stranger bent forward and pulled her to her feet. "You haven't hurt yourself, have you?"

Kyra shook her head numbly. "No, I just need a moment to tidy myself," she explained, indicating her sadly mussed skirt. "Please don't wait for me if Robert is expecting you. Fanny and I will be along in a moment."

"Suit yourself." His broad shoulders moved in a shrug, and he strode off toward the mansion.

Fanny, who had scrambled to her feet, stood beside Kyra and watched in bewilderment as the man walked away. When he was out of hearing range, Kyra whirled on Fanny. "Who is he?"

"I thought you couldn't be bothered with a beau right now," Fanny taunted her friend.

"Fanny!" Kyra cried in exasperation. "I nearly knocked the man senseless! I'm not interested in him as a beau. I would simply like to know who he is, so that I can make my apology."

"Of course," came Fanny's skeptical reply. "I don't know who he is, Kyra, but I'll find out."

The ceremony was over, an early wedding supper had been served, the guests had gathered in the second floor ballroom to continue the day's festivities, and still Kyra was no closer to learning the identity of the mysterious stranger. With a disheartened sigh, she settled in a chair in an alcove just off the dance floor and took a sip of iced champagne. The drink was refreshing but did little to assuage her tempestuous thoughts.

"Here you are!" Fanny's voice invaded Kyra's reverie. "I thought I'd never find you. How can anyone ask you to dance when you insist on hiding like this?"

"I am not hiding, and I don't care to dance this evening," Kyra replied shortly.

"Don't take that tone with me, not if you expect me to tell you what I found out about your new friend."

"Sit down, Fanny, and lower your voice," Kyra hushed the excited girl. "People are starting to stare."

"Oh, forget the busybodies—I'm too excited to sit!" Fanny exclaimed, taking the seat next to Kyra in the same breath. "He and Robert were at the university together and became the best of friends. That's all I could find out from Robert before Carolly whisked him off to dance"—she made a face—"but I spoke to Aunt Helen about him. Oh, Kyra, just imagine! It appears that he is a *perfect* scoundrel. Aunt Helen says he's very private and doesn't talk much about himself, but she says a man only acts like that when he has something to hide. She is positive he's led a depraved life and is trying to conceal a sordid past, although she is not quite certain what that might entail. But Aunt Helen is usually right—*ouch!*" Fanny screeched when Kyra soundly pinched her arm.

"Why did you do that?" she demanded, but a cursory glance at her friend's face prompted Fanny to follow the direction of Kyra's worried look. She suddenly ascertained the reason for Kyra's expression—the object of their discussion was approaching, a purposeful air about both his features and his gait.

"There you are." He paused before Kyra. "I have been searching everywhere for you," he said as though he were addressing a servant. "My carriage is waiting, but I was hoping you might honor me with this dance before I depart for Charleston."

Kyra stared dumbfounded at his outstretched hand until Fanny prodded her with a well-aimed elbow. "Go on, ninny!" came Fanny's raspy whisper of encouragement.

Kyra could have said any number of things. She could have reprimanded Fanny for coaxing her into the arms of a man whom she herself had pronounced a perfect scoundrel. She could have denied the man's request with the excuse that they had not been properly introduced—Kyra did not even know the man's name. She could have, and probably should have, informed the stranger that she did not care to dance. What she said, however, was "Thank you, sir. I would love to."

The man inclined his head slightly toward Fanny, then escorted Kyra to the dance floor, and as the orchestra struck up a popular waltz, he drew Kyra into his embrace, and they began to sway in perfect rhythm with the romantic music. Kyra tried to concentrate on the heady melody and the intricate steps of the waltz, but time and again her attention was drawn to the man's face, especially to his eyes. Eyes that revealed a captivating range of moods from mysterious and brooding to calculating and yet were clouded with a hint of sadness.

Presently those dark eyes, the color of rich sable, were twinkling with merriment, and when Kyra glanced about her, she fully understood the reason for his amused expression. Not only had the music ended, but her partner had somehow managed to maneuver her out onto the terrace with Kyra none the wiser. She looked about her wildly, and her worst fears were realized. They were completely alone on the moonlit terrace.

Kyra's escort took one look at her frightened face and quickly resolved to put her fears to rest. "There's no need for you to worry. My reputation might be that of a rogue, but my plans for tonight do not include ravishing an innocent maiden. Would that I had the time," he whispered, with a mischievous wink. "Alas, my carriage," he explained, nodding toward the waiting conveyance.

"I thank you for the dance, miss." He stepped away from Kyra and, bowing grandly before her, turned toward the stairway that led down to the veranda. He had taken no more than two steps, however, before he muttered some unintelligible oath and wheeled to pull Kyra back into his arms. "Damn it all!" he swore, his dark eyes staring into hers.

For one fantastic moment, Kyra thought he intended to spirit her away with him. But he just stood there, those incredible brown eyes boring into hers.

She stood transfixed, too dazed to think about speaking, much less removing herself from a potentially disastrous situation. Panic swelled in her breast, for she suspected that this man was contemplating the daring notion of soundly kissing her and the ensuing repercussions should he give in to the impulse. Buy Kyra's misgivings proved unfounded, and she was, quite frankly, disappointed when he merely lifted her hands to his lips and pressed a parting salute upon each of them.

"Good-bye," he whispered, turning once more to take his leave.

This time it was Kyra who was provoked into action, and she scurried after him. "Wait!" she cried.

The man had already descended a few steps, but the desperation in her voice delayed his departure. Kyra paused at the top of the staircase, one hand clutching the railing, the other pressed against her heaving bosom. "Your name?" she asked hopefully.

He considered her question for several moments. Then, having reached a decision, he squared his shoulders and shook his head, saying, "No, little one. It is better for one to pine for what might have been than to know for certain that it could never be." With that, he was gone.

Kyra remained on the terrace long after he had disappeared into the dark, even after the crunching of the carriage wheels had ceased to echo down the dogwood-lined driveway and the glow of the vehicle's lamps had faded into the black horizon. She had no idea how long Fanny had been standing beside her, but Kyra sensed her friend's presence and did not so much as blink when Fanny placed a comforting arm around her shoulder.

"It's like a fairy tale, Kyra. He didn't dance a single dance with anyone else—only you," Fanny sighed dreamily. "All of the guests are talking about it."

"Are they?" Kyra murmured.

"I know his name, Kyra," Fanny whispered, thinking this might console her dispirited friend.

"No," Kyra mumbled glumly. "He's right, you know. I am better off not knowing. Don't worry about me." She forced a smile and patted her companion's hand. "Go inside, Fanny. I'll join you in a moment."

Several minutes passed before Kyra rejoined the wedding celebration. She remained on the terrace, the jasmine-scented breeze cooling her flushed cheeks, and struggled to restore a sense of order to the evening, realizing all the while the futility of such an exercise; her life would never be quite the same again for having met him.

Finally Kyra exhaled a heavyhearted sigh and, turning away from the balustrade, found her way back to the ballroom. Though she affected the appearance of a young lady passing a pleasurable evening with friends, Kyra knew inwardly that her thoughts and dreams in the coming days and nights would be haunted by the memory of a certain mysterious gentleman and a pair of unforgettable sable-brown eyes.

PART I

The Arrangement

1

Savannah, Georgia
July 1853

The agitated young woman paced the deck of the yacht, her hands clasped behind her. The sultry summer breeze and the spray from the river washed over her, leaving her cheeks flushed and wreaking havoc with her carefully arranged coiffure. As the seaworthy vessel made its way toward Savannah harbor, Kyra Ann Raybourne abruptly ceased her aimless ambling to stand by the railing, focusing her gaze on the landscape.

Completely absorbed in thought, she barely noticed the moss-draped live oaks and colorful wildflowers that dotted the distant horizon. It was not until a gust of wind sent her skirts billowing above her ankles that she was distracted from her reverie. With a malcontented shrug, she let go of the railing and turned to make her way to the master cabin, which was located below the main deck, far removed from the crew's quarters. But as her slender fingers reached for the door latch, the portal was swung open from within.

"There you be, Miz Kyra!" exclaimed the servant girl through the aperture. "I was just comin' to git you. I figgered you'd want to freshen up before we git to Savannah."

Kyra favored her maid with a gentle smile. "Yes, Biddie,

11

those were my exact thoughts. I must look a sight, and I cannot roam the streets of Savannah looking like a hoyden," she admonished herself good-naturedly, allowing the maid to assist her out of the damp gown and into a fashionable walking dress.

Kyra seated herself before the dressing table mirror and waited patiently while Biddie endeavored to restore some order to her wayward, windswept tendrils. As the maid went about her task, Kyra contrived to assume a more cheerful countenance, for although she normally possessed a sunny disposition, her brother's most recent indiscretion had caused her temperament to suffer.

Kyra was the high-spirited twenty-one-year-old daughter of a wealthy South Carolina plantation owner. She was slight of stature with a slender yet enticingly proportioned figure and waist-length gold-brown hair. Her eyes were an unusual hue—almost violet—and, depending on her mood, could sparkle with uninhibited merriment or darken with intense anger. Perhaps Kyra's most charming attribute, however, was her infectious laugh, which seemed to emanate from her toes and bubble upward, creating a delightful, rippling sound that had captivated many a masculine ear.

Kyra did not consider herself a great beauty, albeit her mirror belied this critical self-appraisal. Though her comely expression and winsome personality had captured the hearts of a great number of would-be suitors, Kyra scarcely acknowledged their attention; her devotion lay with her father and brother and the management of the family plantation, Raybourne.

Kyra's present state of unrest was due to the unprincipled antics of her brother Andrew. Though he was four years her senior, Kyra oftentimes found herself playing the role of mother hen, especially when Andrew besmirched the Raybourne name with his outrageous behavior and thereby incurred their father's wrath. It was fortunate for Andrew that the elder Raybourne could be so easily swayed by his daughter, for many a time Andrew had been spared a thrashing due to his sister's intervention on his behalf. But now, as Kyra contemplated Andrew's latest devilment, she doubted the wisdom of her unconditional loyalty.

Kyra's brow contracted into a pensive frown. "Perhaps I *have* been too protective of Andrew," she reflected aloud.

"You always did take up for that boy," Biddie agreed, nodding.

Hardly aware that she had spoken her thoughts, Kyra was reminded of her immediate purpose by Biddie's candid rejoinder. She fidgeted uncomfortably on the chair and glanced at herself in the mirror. "That will do nicely, Biddie. Now please go and ask Captain Wilkes when the *Driftwood* will be docking."

"Yes'm." The servant bobbed a curtsy and scurried from the cabin.

As the door closed behind Biddie, Kyra's thoughts reverted to the subject that had plagued her since the previous morning when Silas, the Raybourne butler, had presented her with a note from her father. Colin Raybourne had been in New Orleans for the past month on business and, during his absence, had placed his son in charge of the family estate. In reality, Kyra had seen to the day-to-day management of Raybourne while Andrew had amused himself with a variety of pursuits that included drinking, wenching, and gambling with his boisterous acquaintances.

But Kyra's amiable disposition had been tested when she learned that Andrew had accompanied his friends to Savannah to continue his escapades. When she learned of her father's imminent return, Kyra's ire had grown particularly acute; certainly he would be anxious to question Andrew about his handling of the plantation.

Kyra shivered as she envisioned her father's fury when he discovered that his only son had demonstrated a complete lack of responsibility. She had to find Andrew and persuade him to come home before their father returned from New Orleans. These turbulent thoughts were abruptly interrupted as Biddie reentered the cabin to inform Kyra that they could disembark at once.

The two women emerged on deck just as the *Driftwood*'s gangplank was being positioned against the pier. Preoccupied with issuing instructions to the captain, Kyra failed to notice the equally impressive yacht that was moored beside her own. When Captain Wilkes informed her that she could depart, Kyra tucked her reticule under her arm and descended the ramp, calling out to her maid, who had already disembarked and awaited her on the pier. "Run along and hail us a carriage, Biddie."

There was a marked determination in the set of Kyra's jaw as she progressed down the narrow plank, confident that Biddie would secure them a vehicle. But as she neared the end of the ramp, the toe of her leather walking boot caught the edge of an uneven floorboard, throwing her off balance. An instinctive squeal of surprise issued from Kyra's throat as she plummeted forward in an awkward configuration of flailing arms and swirling skirts. But, happily, she was spared a debilitating injury, for a passenger from the neighboring yacht was passing by at that precise moment, and Kyra literally fell into the man's arms.

Kyra was stunned by the mishap, but as capable hands set her aright, she realized that only her pride had suffered from the experience. She quickly smoothed the wrinkles from her gown and straightened her bonnet, which had been knocked askew, then lifted her face to the gallant, prepared to express her gratitude for his timely intervention. She was ill prepared for the sight that greeted her eyes, however, for before her stood the man she had encountered at Carolly Cookson's wedding—the very gentleman who had frequented her dreams and preoccupied her every waking thought for the past three months.

He was more devastatingly handsome than Kyra remembered. Finding herself suddenly incapable of coherent speech and heedless of the awkward situation developing on the pier—a result of her prolonged silence—Kyra set about a cursory inspection of the stranger. She was impressed with what she saw.

Kyra allowed her inquisitive gaze to wander over him, refamiliarizing herself with this man. He was tall, very tall, with broad, muscular shoulders that were enhanced by the cut of his expensive coat. His solid chest tapered to a lean, narrow waist, but Kyra refused to permit her eyes to stray any lower should the color in her cheeks betray her maidenly curiosity. With some difficulty, she refocused her attention on the man's face and, though his twinkling brown eyes gave him a youthful appearance, the lines that creased their outer corners gave her reason to believe that he was well into, or perhaps slightly past, his thirtieth year.

Kyra was so engrossed in her examination that she did not realize her rescuer was engaged in a similar scrutiny. The sable-brown eyes quickly assessed the lovely vision before him and, though they were presently clouded with a mixture of amused indifference and a disturbing sense of familiarity, the man found himself oddly stirred by this young lady's innocent beauty. His haughty, aristocratic nose detected the faint scent of rosewater, and his mouth involuntarily twisted into a cynical grin as he waited for the enchantress to address him.

Unaware that she had been the object of a thorough inspection, Kyra stared fascinated, at the stranger's wide chest. She had a vague recollection of being briefly crushed against that imposing barrier, and the memory caused her pulse to quicken and brought a beguiling flush to her cheeks. With a start, Kyra realized she was actually gaping at the handsome stranger, and pressing her hands to her blushing face, she averted her eyes.

"Wh-where are my m-manners?" Kyra stammered,

glancing about to see if anyone had noticed the collision. To her profound consternation, Kyra discovered that the exchange had attracted the attention of a number of stevedores and curious passersby, all of whom seemed mildly amused.

Swallowing the gulp that constricted her throat, Kyra forced herself to continue. "Thank you for coming to my rescue, sir. You spared me a nasty fall." Kyra offered him her most engaging smile and extended her hand in a friendly gesture.

She fully expected the man to grasp her hand for an instant, murmur some offhand remark comparing this incident to their initial meeting, and then be on his way. But Kyra suffered a painfully rude awakening when she discovered that he apparently had no recollection of their earlier encounter. Perhaps more disheartening was the fact that the dashing hero of her fanciful dreams bore little resemblance to the rake who now clasped her fingers and stepped boldly toward her.

"Yes, it would appear I happened along at a most propitious moment," he drawled in a deep voice, his lips parting in a mocking smile.

For all of her twenty-one years, Kyra's knowledge of the opposite sex was sadly lacking; therefore, the man's aggressive stance immediately put her on guard. Affecting a wary countenance, Kyra favored him with a disdainful look and withdrew her hand.

"Sir," she began patiently, choosing to ignore his blatant display of bad manners, "I *am* grateful. If you would care to leave your name and direction, I shall send my maid around with a personal note of thanks at the earliest opportunity," she said coolly, masking her disappointment.

But the menacing stranger had a very different notion in mind, and Kyra suddenly found herself enveloped in an unyielding embrace. She was taken aback by the man's impudence, yet even as she began to struggle, she knew that her feeble attempts would be ineffective against the man's superior strength. Still, she was outraged that this reprobate possessed the nerve to disgrace her on the public docks, and she was prepared to give the presumptuous scoundrel a much-deserved reprimand.

Before she could utter a scathing retort, however, Kyra was distracted by a throaty chuckle, and to her shock, she felt his warm breath along her cheek. As if reading her thoughts, the man ran his thumb under her chin and forced her to look at him, his taunting expression defying Kyra to resist.

"There is no need to waste your time scribbling some inconsequential message," he said breaking the awkward silence. "I find myself sorely tempted to collect my reward now, lest fortune not grant me a second opportunity."

Kyra stiffened at the man's infuriating speech, but before she could wriggle from his grasp, he matched his actions with his words. She grew deathly still as the stranger's mouth descended upon hers, and despite her strict upbringing, Kyra felt an unexpected tingle of excitement as his surprisingly gentle mouth moved slowly against her own.

Her bemused state dissolved rapidly, however, when the blackguard unashamedly coaxed Kyra's lips apart, clearly intending to sample the sweet-tasting treasure within. It was then that Kyra regained her senses and, with a genuinely frightened cry, summoned the strength to push her captor away. Without pausing to consider the repercussions of her actions, Kyra raised her hand and delivered a resounding slap across the villain's cheek.

She watched in guarded anticipation as a variety of expressions crossed over his face; Kyra assumed he would be enraged by her outburst. Therefore she was more than a little annoyed when a sardonic smile turned up his mouth.

"How . . . how dare you!" Kyra shouted at him when she could again find her tongue. "If I were a man—" She faltered, pressing her fingers against her lips, which still throbbed pleasurably from the pressure of his mouth.

He regarded Kyra thoughtfully, once more suffused with the uncomfortable feeling that he had encountered this charming beauty on another occasion. He promptly discounted the notion.

In her present state, Kyra resembled a wild animal, what with her large, frightened eyes and the fingers that trembled slightly against those wondrously full lips. Amazingly, the man discovered he had to repress the instinct to draw this vulnerable woman back into his arms to resume the gratifying interlude. But the tolling of a church bell in the distance reminded him that he did not have time to dally on the pier, regardless of this enticement. Clearing his throat, he favored the flustered young woman with a disinterested expression.

"My dear woman," he began dryly, "had you been a man, I would not have wasted the effort to forestall your tumble." He casually brushed a fleck of dust from his otherwise immaculate sleeve and said no more.

Kyra breathed a sigh of relief, thinking that the rogue was finally going to leave her in peace, but her deliverance was brief. Just as the relentless pounding of her heart began to subside, the man took a step toward her. Fearing he meant to continue his plundering, Kyra squared her shoulders proudly and prepared to defend herself. She was puzzled however, when the stranger merely began to speak.

"May I suggest," he intoned, his eyes carelessly scanning the topmast of a ship that was heading out to sea, "that in the future, when you experience this impulse to fling yourself into a man's arms, you refrain from doing so until you have made his acquaintance?"

Kyra's fine complexion grew uncommonly pale as the implication of the man's speech struck her with full force. For the second time since stumbling upon this insufferable miscreant, Kyra found herself at a loss for words. This time, however, her silence was the result of fury rather than fascination.

It was inexcusable for this arrogant monster to presume she had intentionally thrown herself into his arms to attract his attention. With an indignant gasp, Kyra again flung out her hand to repay him for the insult. But she was ill prepared for his lightning-quick reflex as his hand shot out to grasp her wrist. Thus immobilized again by the rake, Kyra instinctively began to struggle for her release, but one look at the ominous flicker in those brown eyes was enough to dampen her adventuresome spirit.

A terrified squeak rose out of Kyra's throat, for the man's grip on her arm was so fierce that she feared any sudden movement on her part could provoke him to snap it. Kyra's pulse accelerated as the man drew her to him, and his lips were a mere whisper's breath from her own when he began to speak in low tones that made her shiver despite the warmth of the noonday sun.

"You will, I think, understand that while I might be willing to suffer one outraged reprisal for my conduct, I cannot passively endure another. Unless, of course, I find myself guilty of a crime befitting such harsh retribution." He cast a glance toward his yacht, which bobbed gently in the calm water, and made a halfhearted effort to tug her in that direction.

Kyra had not thought it possible, but she grew even more angry. Favoring the man with her coldest glare, she rasped between tightly clenched teeth, "You, sir, are a dreadful creature. And now I shall joyfully take my leave of you!"

Kyra sent the toe of her boot crashing against his shin, which caused him to release her from his bruising grip and let out a painful howl, but Kyra thought it unwise to tarry lest the rogue act upon his lascivious intentions.

Drawing herself up to her full height of five feet four inches, Kyra pointed her nose high in the air and trudged off in unladylike haste. She half expected the irksome man to follow her, but was relieved to note that his footfalls did not echo against the wooden planks behind her. Only his mocking laughter drifted down the pier to taunt her, spurring Kyra into a swifter gait that she did not ease until she reached the safety of the waiting carriage that would forever deliver her from this despicable man.

Devlin Joseph Cauldwell's gaze settled upon the provocative hips that swung furiously beneath the folds of the fashionable skirt as the young woman hurried away from him. A low, appreciative whistle sounded from his lips as he casually leaned against a wharf post and watched the agitated lady execute a clean escape. A wistful gleam sparkled behind his brooding eyes as he envisioned a more satisfying conclusion to the fleeting interlude.

He had ascertained by the young lady's indignant reaction to his kiss that she was completely ignorant of men and romance. But Devlin had recognized the faint stirrings of a timid response before reason had intervened and the lovely young woman had spurned his advances. Despite her display of righteous fury, Devlin had sensed a surging undercurrent of awakening passion and knew instinctively that this ravishing innocent could—with a little gentle coaxing—be persuaded to respond to his lovemaking.

Even as he mulled over the diverting notion, Devlin ran a tentative hand along his cheek, which still smarted from Kyra's less than endearing caress and a thoughtful smile curved his lips. Oh, what pleasure a man could derive from taming that willful termagant, he mused, his eyes never wavering from the proud back that hurried toward the waiting carriage.

Devlin continued to loiter along the pier long after the object of his thoughts had disappeared from view. Then, with a purposeful shake of his head, he resolved to put the young lady from his mind; she was obviously of superior breeding and not the sort one could hope to engage in a casual flirtation. Not that Devlin would allow that insignificant obstacle to dissuade him, if he truly desired her. But dwelling on the subject was useless, he reasoned, for it was highly improbable that he would encounter the enchantress again.

With a careless shrug, Devlin filed the memory of this latest escapade with his somewhat extensive repertoire, so that he might savor it at a later date. Then, deciding that enough of his valuable time had been wasted, he sauntered toward the line of vehicles that waited at the end of the pier. As he walked, Devlin was reminded of the reason for this excursion to Savannah, and his countenance grew positively grim.

The coachman was understandably leery of the imposing gentleman who arrogantly claimed his carriage, but the gold coin that was unconcernedly tossed in his direction quickly dispelled any doubts the cabbie might have nurtured. Pocketing the coveted payment, the driver made a great to-do in seeing that his passenger was comfortably settled before commencing the journey. Then he clambered atop the carriage, cracking his whip behind the ear of the lead horse.

Unbeknownst to Devlin, the scene on the wharf had been witnessed with keen interest by a man who loitered by a lamppost nearby. But as Devlin's carriage merged with the other wharf traffic, the man collected his horse from the tethering post in front of the tavern and, after mounting, began to follow the coach at a discreet distance.

Completely unaware of this covert surveillance, Devlin leaned back against the worn squabs and tipped his hat forward to cover his eyes. He was jostled against the seat as the carriage progressed through the congested city streets. A less determined man would have been lulled to sleep by the soothing motion. Instead, Devlin folded his arms across his chest and mentally devised an effective stratagem against the most intimidating person he knew—his mother.

* * *

The highly perturbed occupant of another carriage that trundled through the same crowded thoroughfares was similarly preoccupied in the plotting of a scheme meant to disengage her brother from the clutches of his irresponsible comrades. Unlike her villainous assailant, Kyra had promptly consigned the distasteful wharf incident to a secluded corner of her mind. After all, she was a sensible young woman and she reasoned that she did not have time to dwell on unpleasantness. Her paramount concern was to locate Andrew, a task that could very well require all of her attention for the remainder of the day.

But later, much later, ensconced in her cabin on the *Driftwood*, she would find solace in a leisurely dissection of the brutish lout who had dared to treat her with such disrespect. Yet even as she resolved to force her concentration on more pressing matters, the memory of a waltz on a spring evening and a pair of expressive brown eyes suddenly flooded her memory, prompting the fingers of one hand to climb to the lips that still burned from the stranger's uninvited kiss.

Biddie sat on the opposite seat, her vivid brown eyes glued on her mistress. The servant had witnessed the unhappy encounter, but she had been reluctant to discuss it with the distraught young lady. She did not fear being punished, for Miss Kyra was usually most pleasant. However, she could, when provoked, become a raging hellcat, and Biddie, wise beyond her years, recognized the telltale warning signs that her mistress was consumed by smoldering anger.

But the dark look that distorted Kyra's face filled the young servant with concern, causing her to ask, "Miz Kyra, is you all right?"

Kyra's glower became even more pronounced when she raised her thick eyelashes to reveal incredibly lovely violet eyes that glittered with fury. Her expression softened, however, when she saw Biddie's concerned face.

"I am fine, Biddie," Kyra reassured the anxious servant. "It's been a hectic morning, and I fear that my nerves are somewhat frazzled, that is all. I shan't rest until this matter with Andrew has been settled," she confided to her loyal servant, resting her head against the side of the coach.

Biddie regarded her closely, thinking that she had never seen her mistress in such a state. Even though she realized that Kyra's mood could be attributed to that unfortunate episode on the wharf, she could not forestall the shiver of apprehension that tingled along her spine as she pondered the impending encounter between brother and sister.

Poor Master Andrew, Biddie lamented silently. He was in for a rare scolding this time. Why, Miz Kyra hadn't been this out of sorts since the time Andrew locked her in the icehouse all night, causing her to take a chill.

The servant chanced another look at her disgruntled mistress and was chagrined to see that Kyra's temper had not waned, causing Biddie to reaffirm her earlier supposition. She did not envy young Master Andrew the forthcoming confrontation with his sister.

2

Kyra's disposition had shown no visible sign of improvement when the carriage rolled to a stop before a stately mansion on Barnard Street minutes later. As she waited for the driver to assist her from the vehicle, she silently applauded her decision to deposit Biddie at the residence in which the maid's grandmother served as cook before initiating her search for Andrew.

Kyra kindly thanked the coachman as he let down the steps, so that she could alight from the conveyance and, dropping the required payment into his outstretched palm, she scurried across the sidewalk to the house. The Monteith residence was perhaps the most elegant dwelling on the square, but Kyra barely noticed the impressive structure as she hastened up the steps and rapped sharply on the door. It took the servant only a few seconds to respond, but Kyra had already set one foot to tapping out an impatient rhythm on the doorstep when the portal swung open to reveal Keating, the Monteith family's butler.

The staid English retainer did not so much as bat an eye when the unchaperoned young lady in the entranceway requested an audience with Richard Monteith.

Keating regarded Kyra with a critical eye beneath a severely arched brow and, after clearing his throat, said, "I fear that Master Richard is unavailable. Should you care to leave a message, I shall see he is made aware of your visit at the earliest possible moment."

"But—" Kyra attempted to voice an objection, only to be brought up short by the butler.

"I fear my instructions were quite explicit; the master is not to be disturbed for *any* reason," Keating stated in a droll monotone.

"That may very well be," Kyra returned, her voice rich with determination, "but I've come to discuss an urgent matter with Richard, and I will not leave until I have done so!" She swept past him and assumed a dauntless stance in the foyer just a few feet away from the nonplussed butler.

"Miss—" Keating uttered in exasperation.

"Raybourne," she announced to the servant, whose aloof facade was beginning to crumble under Kyra's unwavering persistence.

"Miss Raybourne, I shouldn't think—" Keating began diplomatically, only to have his entreaty dashed aside.

"You're quite right, you should *not* think. I would, however, be much obliged if you would tell Richard that I desire a word with him." Thus dismissing the domestic, Kyra strode down the corridor to pull open a door at random—luckily happening upon the library.

Pausing on the threshold, she favored Keating with her most expressive look, saying, "Ten minutes, my good man. If Richard has not joined me by then, I shall seek him out personally."

Keating watched as the outspoken young woman disappeared within the chamber, and he stared dumbfounded at the door for nearly a full thirty seconds before spurring himself to action. Ordinarily, the task of delivering messages was one that Keating would have delegated to a lesser staff member. But the reserved butler decided that he would derive enormous satisfaction in announcing the arrival of this infuriating female to his benefactor.

The butler mounted the staircase slowly, his wounded

mien growing more intense with every footfall. By the time
he arrived at the top landing, a sneer could be seen on the
old man's lips. With a fleeting glance toward the corridor
that led to Richard's bedchamber, Keating turned and strode
determinedly in the opposite direction.

"Humph! Who does the chit think she is? No well-bred
English lady would conduct herself in such a shameless
manner, forcing her way into the house and making all sorts
of demands," he muttered sourly. "We'll just see how the
lady"—Keating snarled the term as though he seriously
doubted its authenticity—"enjoys a taste of her own sauce."

Kyra sat stiffly in an upholstered armchair as she awaited
the entrance of her brother's friend. Despite the chair's
plump softness, she soon abandoned the comfortable seat to
wander about the library, absently admiring an exquisite
leather-bound volume or a figurine as she tried to suppress
her spiraling temper. She reasoned that she needed to
maintain her composure if she hoped to achieve her purpose.

Yet when the clock on the mantel chimed half past the
hour, Kyra found herself fraught with frustration. She had
not truly thought she would be forced to carry out her threat
of rousting her prey, but she was left with no other choice.
Summoning her courage, Kyra marched straightaway to the
door and wrenched it open. She came up short on the
threshold, however, when she found her pathway blocked
by a pair of broad shoulders.

Startled, Kyra stumbled backward, nearly tripping over
the hem of her gown, but she was spared an awkward
tumble when a hand shot out to steady her. Kyra, temporarily stunned by the man's unexpected appearance, tried to
gather her wildly scattered thoughts. Composure restored,
she prepared to greet her host, but her carefully rehearsed
speech died on her tongue when she beheld the man's
unfamiliar face.

"You're not Richard!" she blurted.

"Indeed!" a masculine voice chuckled, and Kyra found herself staring into a pair of vivid blue eyes, eyes that glittered with unbridled merriment. "A blessing for which I am extremely grateful, for while my younger brother lies abed—the victim of excessive indulgence in whiskey and sport—I am permitted the opportunity to make your acquaintance, charming lady." He bowed over her hand, murmuring politely, "May I know your name?"

"You mean that impossible old relic didn't announce me?" Kyra demanded loudly, positive the butler had returned to the foyer and would overhear her deliberate slander.

With a genuine laugh, the gentleman entered the library and closed the door behind him. "No," he drawled slowly, carefully mulling his reply. "Keating said only that an encroaching sort of female had descended upon the house," he mimicked the aging retainer. Then, noting the flush that dotted Kyra's cheeks, added, "He failed to mention that the lady is also quite the loveliest creature to have adorned this humble dwelling in many a day." His smile broadened, causing Kyra to feel more at ease, and her ire began to subside.

"Thank you," she said shyly.

"Not at all," he replied and, taking her hand, directed her to the chair that she had earlier vacated. Then, after selecting a seat opposite Kyra, he settled his quizzical expression upon her. "How may I be of service to you, Miss . . . ?" He paused expectantly.

"Raybourne. Kyra Raybourne," she answered.

"Raybourne?" He looked surprised, pleasantly so. "Then you must be Andrew's sister."

"Yes, I fear that I must. And you are . . . ?"

"Christopher Monteith."

"Richard's brother," she said.

"None other." He laughed good-naturedly. "Well, that explains it, then."

"What?"

"Your reason for turning my household topsy-turvy. You've no doubt come to inquire after Andrew." Christopher crossed one leg over the other and, as he awaited her response, allowed his eyes a leisurely inspection of his visitor's graceful figure; he was not disappointed with his findings.

Kyra, however, was so obsessed with locating Andrew that she did not notice Christopher's assessment, else she would have had just cause to feel wary of him. Leaning forward, she extended her hand in a pleading gesture. "It's imperative for Andrew to return home at once. Is it too much to hope that he, too, lies abed in an upstairs chamber?"

"I'm afraid he does not."

"I feared as much." She heaved a desolate sigh. "Now what am I to do? I was so hoping Andrew would be with Richard. I haven't an inkling as to where I should go next." Kyra sank back in her chair, her slim shoulders slumped in defeat.

"You needn't be so gloomy, Kyra." The man chose to forgo formality and addressed her by her given name. "Andrew *is* here—at least he's in Savannah. He and Richard have been . . . uh . . . carousing together this past fortnight."

"Then you do know Andrew's whereabouts?" she asked hopefully.

"I think so. You see, they accompanied me to an . . . er . . . exclusive card game Wednesday evening. Richard finally stumbled home at dawn. I assume that Andrew remained behind to continue testing his luck," Christopher informed her.

Kyra was dumbstruck by this revelation. She had grown accustomed to plucking Andrew from close scrapes, and she had learned to accept many of the friends with whom he chose to associate. At least Richard was the same age as her brother. She could not, however, like the fact that Andrew had somehow become entangled with the older, more worldly Monteith brother—a man who had not only assisted in Andrew's debauchery but apparently encouraged it as well. Several moments elapsed before Kyra could again move her tongue, but the use of it returned with a flourish as she sprang to her feet before her bemused host.

"Andrew has been gambling for two entire days *and* nights?" she cried incredulously.

Christopher's perceptive gaze took in Kyra's fiery splendor. The hands pressed tight against softly rounded hips, the shapely breasts that rose and fell temptingly, and the unfettered anger that enlivened her eyes all served to bolster his feeling that fate had delivered an undeniably ravishing creature to his door. Christopher could merely nod a response to her heated inquiry, for his bold scrutiny had left his throat parched, and he did not yet trust himself to speak. But Kyra's harsh invective was to remedy his plight and temporarily douse the amorous reflections dancing about in his head.

"And you did not attempt to dissuade him from such a foolish stunt?" she said accusingly.

Christopher's eyes narrowed at the implication that he had behaved in a less than honorable fashion, and he grew defensive. "Miss Raybourne," he droned icily, "I am not *my* brother's keeper, much less *yours*. You cannot presume to hold me responsible for Andrew's actions, foolhardy though they may be," he informed her, in no uncertain terms.

Thus chastised for the unfairness of her indictment, Kyra became instantly contrite. "Of course I don't hold you responsible. I apologize, Mr. Monteith. I don't usually exhibit such shocking manners, I assure you. It's just that my father is returning home shortly, and he expects to find

Andrew in charge at Raybourne. Father will not tolerate such irresponsible behavior from Andrew. I simply *must* find him. Could you . . . *would* you help me?"

Kyra met his inscrutable face for a brief instant, then lowered her gaze to the floor, dreading the forthcoming answer. But her fears proved to be unwarranted when Christopher rose and stepped across the carpet to stand before her. He placed a finger under her chin and tilted her head up until their eyes met, and Kyra was thankful to see that a smile again played over his lips.

"I can never resist a lady in distress," he admitted laughingly, and Kyra knew that her plea for assistance would not be denied.

"Thank you, Mr. Monteith," Kyra murmured gratefully.

"Think nothing of it. Wait here while I have the carriage brought around," he said, stepping to the door. Christopher paused as his fingers firmly grasped the doorknob and turned to address her once more. "Kyra?"

"Yes?"

"Do you think you could call me Christopher? I'm not much older than you, and your last 'Mr. Monteith' is still ringing in my ears."

"Yes, Christopher." Kyra returned his smile and watched him slip through the doorway.

In the corridor, Christopher issued instructions to a footman and then sprinted up the staircase to his chamber to freshen his appearance. Having sensed the lady's dislike of gambling dens and the men who frequented them, he had not admitted that he had returned from the card game himself only moments before Keating summoned him to the library.

When he descended the stairs a quarter of an hour later, the carriage was rolling to a stop in front of the house. Christopher arrived at the library door just as it was flung open from within and Kyra rushed into the hallway.

"There you are!" she exclaimed in relief. "I thought you were going to leave without me.

"To be honest, that was my intention. The river district is hardly the place for a young lady," he explained, but Kyra would have none of it and, assuming a rigid stance, prepared to make her thoughts on the matter crystal-clear.

Even before she spoke, Christopher regretted his decision to help her find her accursed brother. She might be a beauty, he conceded, but it had been his experience that even the most perfect blossom possessed some hidden flaw. With Kyra it was her sharp tongue and annoyingly willful disposition. Her declaration merely served to confirm Christopher's assumption.

"Nevertheless, I'm coming with you," Kyra stated unequivocally and, stepping past him, advanced toward the exit where Keating stood as sentry.

The loyal retainer did not immediately open the door, eager though he was to be rid of the irksome female. But Keating, ever mindful of his responsibility to his employer, glanced behind Kyra to witness Christopher's begrudging nod before pulling the door ajar.

Christopher might have derived some measure of amusement from Keating's sullen demeanor had he not been experiencing similar feelings toward his uninvited guest. He was unaccustomed to having his wishes ignored, especially by presumptuous young ladies; it was the anticipation of collecting Andrew and relinquishing his role as escort that prompted Christopher to check his rising temper and join Kyra on the doorstep.

As Kyra placed her hand on Christopher's arm to be led down the steps to the carriage, she chanced a parting glimpse over her shoulder at the butler, who continued to glower at her. The servant's insolence persuaded Kyra to inquire, "Is Keating always so sour?"

"Only when provoked," Christopher replied tersely, adopting a formal air. "Miss Raybourne, you must realize that Keating is seldom confronted by unescorted, head-strong young women who threaten to dislodge the male members of the house from their bedchambers. Tell me, do you always behave so shamelessly?"

Kyra bristled at his insolence, and her tone was stilted when she inquired, "And how, sir, does my conduct concern you?"

"It doesn't, but I would curb my reckless tendencies were I you—if you harbor any hope of ever finding yourself a *willing* husband," he ruthlessly admonished her.

Kyra responded by jerking her hand from Christopher's arm and favored him with a less than endearing look. "I came to Savannah to find my brother, not a husband, Mr. Monteith!" Kyra snapped and, ignoring his proffered hand, climbed into the carriage unassisted.

Christopher heaved a small sigh of frustration. Then, satisfied that the day's end would render him free of this menacing wench, he joined Kyra inside the vehicle.

At the exact moment Kyra was entering the carriage on Barnard Street, a discontented gentleman was alighting from one on State Street. Devlin Cauldwell presented an awesome visage as he crossed the sidewalk to mount the steps three at a time. His thunderous knock was still echoing throughout the expansive dwelling when a flustered servant jerked the door open seconds later.

"Master Devlin!" the butler exclaimed in surprise. "Miss Mandy didn't say nothin' 'bout you comin' to pay us a visit."

"There is a perfectly reasonable explanation for her oversight, Josiah," Devlin said, stepping across the threshold. "Mother is not expecting me. Is she home?" he inquired blandly, as if the answer was of no great interest to him.

"Yes, sir. She's in the courtyard havin' tea with some of her lady friends," Josiah explained, aware that the young man's countenance grew more forbidding with this revelation. "Do you want me to fetch her?"

"That won't be necessary, Josiah." A third voice joined the exchange. Devlin glanced behind the servant to see his mother striding regally toward them.

Amanda Cauldwell was an imposing lady, a little taller than most women, and she carried her slender frame with a self-assurance and dignity that had been the undoing of many of her male business associates. She had been widowed at a young age, and her friends had urged her to sell her husband's businesses and remarry so that her three children might enjoy the full-time companionship of their mother as well as the strong guiding hand of a father. Although she was an attractive woman with bright green eyes and shimmering ebony hair, Amanda had chosen not to marry. She had a shrewd business mind and in no time at all had turned her husband's paper and textile mills into flourishing enterprises. She saw to it that the profits from these endeavors were wisely invested, thereby making herself an extremely wealthy and powerful woman.

As a result of so many long years of hard work, her hair had lost a good deal of its luster and wrinkles now marred her once flawless face. But Amanda Cauldwell was still a handsome woman. Her green eyes sparkled with intelligence, and her winning disposition ultimately charmed all those who had damned her unpopular decision those many years past. It was only when she came face to face with her rebellious son that Amanda felt a pang of remorse.

She was the first to admit that she had not been the best of mothers, but neither had she been an indifferent parent. She had provided a good life for her children—given them a home, food, clothing, and educated them at renowned schools. But there was no substitute for a mother's attention, and that, sadly, was the one thing she had not always been able to provide.

Poor Devlin, she thought as she walked toward him. *How*

much longer will you allow this resentment to fester? Better you should air your feelings and have done with it.

"Hello, my son," she greeted him cordially, offering him her cheek. But when Devlin failed to respond to the gesture, Amanda pressed a fleeting kiss of welcome against his cheek, and then turned to Josiah. "Tillie is serving my guests in the garden—see that she brings some refreshment to the blue salon."

Before Josiah had taken his first step to carry out Amanda's request, Devlin intervened. "That won't be necessary." He stepped around the pair and walked straight to the designated chamber. "I won't be staying long enough to accept your hospitality. I do request, however, an audience with you, Mother . . . alone and without interruption." He arched one eyebrow in the direction of the courtyard. "Surely your friends will not feel neglected if I take up a few moments of your precious time."

"As you wish," Amanda acquiesced and, ignoring Devlin's sarcasm followed her son into the salon.

The click of the door had barely sounded when Devlin turned on his mother, demanding furiously, "Where are they?"

"What?" Amanda gasped, taken aback by his outburst.

"Do not play coy with me, madam." Devlin's sable-brown eyes narrowed forbiddingly as he strode across the room to stand before Amanda. "You're perfectly aware of the reason for this visit. I repeat: *Where are they*?"

Many a stalwart man had crumbled beneath Devlin's fierce countenance, but Amanda did not so much as flinch. Instead, she assumed a comparable demeanor and swept past her son to perch stiffly on the edge of a plush chair. "How like you to waltz in here making all manner of accusations and demands."

"You know I don't give a damn what you think about my actions," he replied coldly.

"Yes, I know, and more's the pity," she whispered, the

anger absent from her voice. "The children are with Emily." Amanda unexpectedly provided Devlin with the answer to his question.

"Hah! So, you don't deny you spirited my children away from Cauldurae during my absence!" he barked accusingly.

"How dare you charge me with the abduction of my own grandchildren," she snapped at him with renewed pique. "Sit down, Devlin! We can hardly discuss this civilly with you pacing about like a caged animal." Amanda waited until he had grudgingly heeded her advice, then explained, "Emily and I seldom get to see the children since you insist upon isolating yourself on that godforsaken island. So when I received your note saying that you were going away on a lengthy business trip—no doubt accompanied by that *hussy*—I decided the children would enjoy a holiday here."

"My note?" Devlin echoed.

"Yes. Why should that surprise you?"

"It's nothing." He dismissed the matter with a shrug. "I don't recall writing you a note, but I have an excellent secretary. He no doubt took it upon himself to apprise you of my plans, and you are correct in presuming that Elyse accompanied me—she often does," he informed her without a trace of compunction.

"So Nicholas has said."

"Yes, well, Nicholas is an impressionable five-year-old who is given to exaggeration." Devlin drummed his fingers impatiently against the arm of the chair and adopted a brusque tone. "May I remind you that my private affairs are precisely that, and no concern of yours?"

Amanda regarded her son with a solemn expression and found herself so infuriated by her son's attitude that she could not immediately formulate a reply. Realizing that a cool head must prevail if she was to make her position clear, she swallowed the angry retort that lingered on her tongue and faced Devlin calmly.

"Not insofar as my grandchildren are involved," she told

him matter-of-factly. "Nicholas and Sarah are very much my concern, Devlin, though you would have it otherwise."

Devlin became unusually contrite as he considered his mother's remark. In all honesty, he conceded that he allowed the tenuous relationship between himself and his mother to influence the amount of time his children were permitted to spend in Savannah. With an uncharacteristic pang of guilt, Devlin realized that he had been unfair to his children, and vowed that in the future he would strive to be more sensible in this matter. His present objective, however, was to collect Nicholas and Sarah and take his leave of his mother without further discussion.

Devlin released a conciliatory sigh and, leaning forward, addressed his mother in a more subdued tone. "Where has my darling sister taken the children?"

"For an outing in the country, a picnic. I really could not tell you their exact destination."

Devlin cast a mildly irritated eye toward the mantel clock. "When do you expect them to return?" he queried, a hint of annoyance creeping into his voice.

"Not for several hours, I should think. In fact, you will no doubt be well on your way back to Elyse before they return." His mother's cynical gibe caused the hairs on the back of Devlin's neck to bristle.

To be truthful, Devlin was exercising remarkable self-restraint—the whitened knuckles of the hands that gripped the arms of the chair were the sole indication that something was amiss—but his voice was taut with repressed anger and his eyes darkened warily when he spoke. "What is that supposed to mean, Mother? You are sadly mistaken if you believe for an instant that I intend to leave Savannah without my children."

Amanda did not shrink from her son's hostile glare. Indeed, she had realized when she removed her grandchildren from Devlin's lavish island estate that a confrontation was inevitable, yet she was loath to make her son aware of her decision regarding his children. The barrier that separated her from Devlin was already insurmountable, and continued provocation on her part would merely serve to aggravate their already precarious relationship. But the happiness of two dear and precious children remained in the balance, and it was her concern for her grandchildren that spurred her on.

Amanda did not offer an immediate rejoiner, however, for she discovered that her throat was unusually dry, and she could not summon the desired words. Lowering her eyes, she stood and proceeded to the crystal decanter that sat upon a table near the fireplace. She poured herself a generous portion of sherry and, when Devlin declined her offer, returned the vessel to the tray and gazed out the window.

After swallowing a fortifying draft of the wine, she turned to face her son. "Nevertheless, you shall be leaving without them. You see, Devlin, your capricious behavior during the past two years has prompted me to arrive at a somewhat awkward decision."

"Oh? And what might that be?"

"The children will remain here in Savannah with Emily and me."

"*The hell you say!*" Devlin thundered, leaping to his feet.

"Calm down!" Amanda hastened to clarify the rest of her ultimatum. "I'm not implying that you will never see Nicholas and Sarah again."

"Hah!" Devlin snorted. "Then what the hell *are* you suggesting?"

Amanda considered her son thoughtfully, realizing that the most unpalatable condition had yet to be revealed. Releasing an apprehensive breath, she continued, "You've grown unrelentingly bitter since Lynette's death. In fact, I sensed there were problems long before her tragic accident."

"Yes, well, our marriage was conceived a few feet short of heaven," Devlin grunted, stalking across the room to pour himself a hearty portion of the sherry he had earlier refused.

"The two of you seemed so well suited," Amanda murmured.

"Appearances can be deceiving," he drawled. Then, with an impatient gesture, Devlin quaffed the contents of his glass and turned to face his mother. "What does this drivel have to do with my children?"

Amanda deposited her glass on the mantel and, lacing her fingers together in front of her, looked at her son. "It's my conviction that Nicholas and Sarah need the love and gentle guidance of a mother. Succinctly put, Devlin, it's time you started behaving like a responsible parent instead of galli-vanting about the globe whenever the whim strikes you.

"You are going to remarry," she stated firmly. "You're going to find a nice, respectable girl and make her your wife. Then when you go off to—well, wherever it is you go, at least I shall know that my grandchildren will not be left in the care of servants."

With considerable effort, Devlin controlled the anger that flared within him. He was embroiled in a potentially explosive situation, and he knew that nothing would be accomplished if his composure failed him.

"Mother," he growled, between tightly clenched teeth. "I think you've finally taken leave of your senses, for you are quite mad if you truly believe I will leave my children with you or marry to suit your fancy." Thoroughly disenchanted with the proceedings, Devlin decided the time had come to end this disagreeable interview, and he stalked to the door. "I shall return this evening for Nicholas and Sarah." He prepared to leave the room, but his mother's stern voice stayed his departure.

"They won't be here, Devlin," she informed him calmly. "I shall make arrangements to keep them elsewhere until I am satisfied you will abide by my terms. Carefully consider all I've said, for I warn you that you are powerless to thwart me in this matter. I have both the position and the finances to squelch any counterplan you might devise. It will be better for all concerned if you heed my advice.

"Go now," she said abruptly. "And do not return until you're willing to accept my decision. Josiah will be advised that you are not welcome in this house until you've agreed to comply with my wishes."

Amanda's voice quavered slightly as she delivered this final edict, but she was not to be subjected to a scathing retort, for Devlin was far too enraged to speak. The lethal glare he leveled at his mother served to convey his feelings on the matter, and his departure was punctuated by the deafening slam of the salon door.

Devlin was grateful he had possessed the foresight to instruct the coachman to await him, for in his present temper he would have been hard-pressed to locate a cabbie who would take up such a fierce-looking character. He threw a deadly parting scowl toward the house, then bolted down the steps to the conveyance and jerked open the door before the driver could leap down from his perch to accommodate him.

Devlin paid no heed to the driver's oversight. Instead, he barked out the name of a waterfront tavern, then climbed inside the vehicle, satisfied that a soothing drink would quickly obliterate his mother's threat.

The coach had traveled less than a block, however, when a lone figure rose from a bench in the square across the street, climbed astride his horse, and fell in behind the carriage.

3

On the doorstep of a once-grand mansion a few blocks from the waterfront paced a decidedly fretful young woman. Kyra's anxiety gradually succumbed to outright frustration as she whirled on her escort. "Christopher, why doesn't someone respond to our knock? Is it possible the game ended and Andrew returned to your home, passing our carriage en route?" she asked hopefully.

"I doubt it," Christopher answered, remembering the pile of winnings he had seen earlier on the table before their host. A generous portion of that money had been won from Kyra's hapless brother, and Andrew had been determined to recoup his losses. The game was still in progress; of that Christopher was certain.

"Have patience, Kyra." He reached for the tarnished brass knocker a third time. "Clayton Fairchild recently leased this . . . uh, house"—he regarded the dilapidated building disdainfully—"and hasn't had time to have it properly staffed." The knocker slipped from his fingers as the door creaked open to reveal a pair of beady eyes, cautiously scrutinizing the newcomers.

"Yes," inquired the owner of those shifty orbs.

"Open the door, Wilson, it's Christopher Monteith. I've come to fetch young Raybourne, and I've brought his sister with me. She has an important matter to discuss with her brother. Step back, man!" he ordered gruffly and, before the servant could respond, shoved the smaller man aside.

With a reproving glance at Christopher, Kyra offered Wilson a thin smile as she preceded her escort across the threshold. She came up short, however, as the pungent odor of the long-uninhabited dwelling attacked her nostrils.

"As I explained," Christopher murmured at her elbow, "Fairchild has been in residence but a short while."

Kyra waved the matter aside, focusing her attention on the rotund servant who cowered in the shadows of the dimly lit foyer. Stepping toward him, she said, "Mr. Wilson, I believe?"

"Yes, ma'am."

"I'm Miss Raybourne. Would you please inform my brother that I have arrived?" Kyra asked without demur, her apprehension having waned now that her quarry was so close at hand.

The unassuming servant appeared on the verge of acquiescing when the sound of raised voices from a room at the end of the corridor captured her attention. Recognizing her brother's agitated voice, Kyra marched determinedly toward the door from behind which angry shouts emanated, casually tossing over her shoulder, "Never mind. I'll announce myself."

The occupants of the room did not notice their visitor's arrival; they were enmeshed in a heated discussion. Kyra understood little of their discourse, since it dealt with the mechanics of the game they played. She listened for a moment and had decided to make her presence known when Andrew's offhand comment induced Kyra to check herself on the threshold and observe their exchange a while longer.

"I'm telling you, Clayton," the sandy-haired young man said pleadingly, "the watch is worth a fortune! It belonged to my grandfather—"

"And *I* told *you* that I already have a watch," the blond man opposite him replied wearily. "If you wish to call my hand, I suggest you produce the appropriate ante. If not . . ." The man's voice trailed off, and he leaned forward to rake the pile of coins from the center of the table.

"No, wait!" Andrew cried. "Just *look* at the watch," he persisted and, reaching into his pocket, withdrew the timepiece and thrust it across the table.

The older man regarded the jewel-embellished bauble with mild interest, turning it this way and that to catch a glimmer of fading sunlight that filtered through the thread-bare draperies. Then, with a careless shrug, he tossed the watch onto the table.

"So?" he grunted.

"*So!*" Andrew shouted. "This would more than cover the wager!"

"So it would," Clayton conceded smoothly, "*if* I agreed to the substitution, which I haven't. The pot remains five hundred dollars light, Raybourne," he reminded the restless youth. "How do you propose to sweeten it?"

"I don't know. Let me think," Andrew muttered, raking his fingers through his hair in a desperate gesture.

"It's obviously a good deal too late for that," a feminine voice admonished. "Had you been *thinking*, you would not be in this predicament."

Andrew, who had expected a rebuke from Clayton, was thoroughly shocked to hear his sister's accusation flung at him from the doorway. The blood drained from his face, giving his pale complexion an even more ashen pallor. He sprang to his feet to confront Kyra and nearly toppled his chair in the process.

"What the devil are you doing here?"

"I shall tell you everything during our carriage ride to the *Driftwood*," she informed him. "Regardless of my purpose, it is apparent that I've arrived too late to prevent you from behaving like a complete fool. Oh, Andrew, why do you insist upon acting like an unprincipled schoolboy? Will you never grow up?" Kyra sighed dismally, advancing from the entranceway to stand beside him. "How dare you gamble away Grandfather's pocket watch!" She plucked it from the table and deposited it in her reticule.

"Now, hold on!" Andrew cried angrily. "That belongs to me!"

"Not anymore. It was a gift, Andrew, meant to be cherished, not thrown away on some ridiculous game of chance. Come along," Kyra said impatiently. "We must return to Raybourne without delay."

"No, you don't understand!" Andrew wailed. "Kyra, there are thousands of dollars on this table and there's a sporting chance it can be mine, if only . . ." He paused, lost in thought, but his eyes took on a brilliant luster as an idea occurred to him. Without warning, he grabbed Kyra roughly by the shoulders. "How much money do you have with you?"

A fulminating expression darkened Kyra's pretty face as she jerked out of her brother's harsh grasp. "You disgust me," she rasped. Then, deciding that facing her father alone would be a great deal easier now that she had witnessed her brother's deprivation, Kyra turned and walked toward the door. "I'll be in the carriage, Andrew. If you care to join me, I suggest you do so promptly; I shan't wait." She was about to leave the stuffy room when Andrew lunged for her reticule, knocking her off balance.

"Raybourne!" Clayton Fairchild leaped to his feet and sprinted around the table to assist Kyra. After assuring himself that she had not been injured, he whirled on Andrew. "Sit down!" he commanded, his temper such that Andrew dared not defy him.

"Pardon me, miss," Clayton addressed Kyra warmly. "I don't usually meddle in family squabbles, but I felt the situation warranted my intervention. Could you tell me how you learned your brother was here?"

Kyra stared in fascination at the stranger who had come to her rescue. Within a chamber that reeked of chaos—what with the clutter of empty whiskey containers, dirty dishes, and plates of neglected, half-eaten food—emerged a veritable gallant. A stunned Kyra glanced at her brother to fully appreciate the sharp contrast.

Andrew was a picture of complete dishevelment. His clothes were hopelessly wrinkled from days of wear, his hair was mussed, and sleeplessness had left its mark on his unshaven face. By contrast, Clayton Fairchild gave every indication of having recently stepped from the hands of a worshipful valet. His coat showed nary a smudge or wrinkle, every hair was neatly combed in place, and even though he had in all likelihood consumed a liberal portion of the pungent whiskey, he did not reek of the stuff as did her brother.

Suddenly aware that the man's green eyes glistened with amusement as he awaited her answer—he obviously enjoyed the effect he had on her—Kyra devoted her full attention to the matter at hand.

"Christopher brought me."

"Monteith, of course! He'll lend me the money I need!" Andrew exclaimed, bolting from his chair and starting for the door. But Clayton's angry voice stopped him in his tracks.

"Raybourne, if you leave this chamber, you'll forfeit the hand. Now, sit down while I see that your sister is comfortably situated. We'll continue our discussion presently." Clayton strode to the door and, taking care not to step over the threshold, called into the empty corridor, "Jim, come here."

Kyra observed silently as the small, nondescript Wilson scurried into the room in response to the summons. She continued her discreet surveillance while the two men conversed, not unimpressed with what she saw.

Clayton Fairchild was of medium build and stood only a few inches taller than Kyra. He was scrupulously, almost foppishly dressed, a man who took obvious pride in his appearance. Yet the harsh outline of his jaw and the authoritative sound of his voice belied his meek demeanor. He was attractive, she decided—but not as appealing as a certain mysterious stranger, a little voice in the back of her mind impishly reminded her.

Kyra found her thoughts ruthlessly dominated with the image of that handsome scoundrel and, though she shook her head to clear her mind of the annoying vision, she could not deny the sudden wave of gooseflesh that tingled along her spine at the memory of his face. Her reprieve was not a lengthy one—to Kyra's dismay, she discovered another man attacking her consciousness, but this rogue did not have the decency to disappear when she closed her eyes.

"I told you this was no place for a lady," came Christopher's smug observation.

Kyra chose to swallow the bitter retort that lay on her tongue and, turning from Christopher, focused her attention on Clayton.

"I apologize for the confusion," he said amiably. "Wilson will show you to the upstairs sitting room. We'll join you once we've concluded our transaction." Clayton guided her to the door while, unbeknownst to Kyra, he permitted his eyes to wander wantonly over her shapely figure.

Christopher remained behind to lounge against one wall. He, unlike Kyra, had not missed the gleam of passion that brightened Clayton's eyes, and he found himself observing the proceedings with increasing curiosity.

Clayton tarried beside the door to assure himself that their conversation would not be overheard by the lady, then sauntered across the room to reclaim his seat, a coy smile spreading over his lips.

"Raybourne," he began shrewdly, casting a lustful glance at the door through which Kyra had departed, "I think we can arrange something after all." He collected his cards and carefully fanned them out.

A suspenseful silence enveloped the room as purposeful green eyes met expectant, and surprisingly insightful blue ones across the table. Andrew's voice was calm and calculating as he said, "I see. Would you care to discuss the particulars?"

Kyra found the upstairs sitting room more to her liking. At least someone had tried to make it suitable for human occupation. The dustcovers had been removed, the carpets swept, the furniture dusted and—she breathed gratefully— the room aired. As she casually scanned her surroundings, Kyra decided the chamber was still badly in need of a woman's touch. Shabby curtains hung at the windows, worn and faded carpets lay at her feet, and not so much as a vase of fresh-cut flowers adorned the drab room.

"Oh, well," she sighed, removing her bonnet and depositing it on a table, "I won't have to endure the discomfort for very long."

Kyra continued her pensive study of the gloomy chamber until the thunderous crash of a door downstairs wrested her from her reverie. Assuming the card game had finally reached its wretched conclusion, Kyra relaxed and sat back, content to await the arrival of the gentlemen. The slamming of another door brought a perplexing frown to her brow. However, Kyra did not become unduly anxious until some ten minutes had ticked away and she was still alone in the sitting room.

It was then that Kyra began to suspect some mischief was afoot. She stood up, intent upon thwarting any scheme Andrew might be plotting. Kyra found herself thinking more than a few unkind thoughts about the rogues ensconced in a downstairs chamber, no doubt swilling whiskey and enjoying a good laugh at her expense. Her anger thus sparked, Kyra resolved that Andrew would receive a rare trimming for ignoring her express wishes.

She marched to the door, only to come up short when it

did not respond to her insistent tug. Realizing the door had been locked from the outside and thinking Andrew to be the culprit, Kyra began to pummel the wooden plank, loudly demanding her immediate release. She was unsure of the results her tantrum might produce, but she did not anticipate an instantaneous response to her summons. During her outburst, Kyra heard the rattle of a key in the lock and jumped back, prepared to vent her spleen at her jailer.

Clayton was pleased to discover that the lovely enchantress looked even more beautiful after their brief separation, for Kyra's anger had caused her cheeks to flush scarlet and her chest to heave invitingly beneath her fashionable traveling ensemble.

Kyra, on the other hand, was far from pleased to see the meticulously plumed peacock who swaggered into the chamber, looking for all the world as though he was about to entertain an adoring sweetheart. Her disdainful gaze did not miss a single affectation as her stare swept from his costly silk dressing robe to the silver tray laden with bread, wine, and cheese.

"Where is my brother, Mr. Fairchild?" Kyra demanded before this insufferable dandy had a chance to speak.

Clayton observed Kyra's impassioned state with interest. She stood in front of him, a veritable bulwark of determination, arms akimbo and nostrils ever so slightly flared in anger. *Lord, what a magnificent spitfire she is,* he thought, envisioning the various methods he would use to tame her willful spirit.

"Give me a moment and I'll explain," Clayton answered.

Without ceremony, he pushed the tray into Kyra's hands, indicating she should place it on the table beside the sofa. While an unwitting Kyra responded to this unspoken request, Clayton closed the door, locked it, and pocketed the key before turning a smug grin on his guest. But Clayton's comments were not to be immediately heard, for Kyra's ire had simmered long enough.

"Explain what?" she demanded, rounding on the man. "How do you intend to explain how you stood idly by while Andrew left without me, for I seriously doubt he remains within these halls." Her violent eyes challenged his green ones across the dingy room. His haughty smirk confirmed Kyra's suspicions. "You, sir, are a cad!" she informed him baldly, and the fact that Clayton seemed genuinely un-moved by her denunciation only served to inflame an already burning temper.

"So I've been told," Clayton replied dryly, taking a seat on the faded brocade sofa, "but never by anyone quite so lovely."

Kyra was not the least bit flattered by the man's banter. "You will regret your decision to help Andrew, Mr. Fairchild. I assure you that my father will not take your interference lightly." Kyra marched to the exit, intending to take her leave of him.

"I do wish you'd stop this nonsense," Clayton said petulantly. "Andrew left with Christopher, and I could not have stopped him even if I had been inclined to do so—which I wasn't. Young men will do what young men will do, Kyra, regardless of what their meddlesome sisters may wish. Now, have done with your tantrum and come share this delightful repast with me," he purred sweetly, crossing his legs as he painstakingly attended a wrinkled sleeve that marred an otherwise perfect appearance.

Kyra's hand froze in midair as she reached for the doorknob, and she turned to confront Clayton. "I have not given you leave to address me by my Christian name," she reminded him.

"No?" Clayton drawled, a devious grin on his face. "I believe you will feel differently come morning," he added vaguely, paying an inordinate amount of attention to one impeccably manicured hand.

"Morning!" Kyra choked incredulously, her hand encir-cling the knob. "You've taken leave of your senses if you think I intend to remain in this house an instant longer," she cried bitterly, giving the handle a fierce jerk.

Kyra's eyes widened in surprise when the barrier did not yield to her, and she whirled to face her host once more. "What is the meaning of this?" she demanded.

"A necessary precaution, I fear. You see, I'm to keep you tucked away until Andrew is safely on his way out of Savannah," he explained. Only an astute observer would have detected the faint twitch of his jaw—a reliable indication that there was little truth in his remark.

"Andrew need no longer concern himself with me," Kyra assured Clayton. "I'm returning to Raybourne without him. I have decided that Andrew may henceforth wage his own battles with our father."

"An admirable decision, to be sure. But a promise is a promise, and I am not a man who reneges on a vow to a friend. Besides, you cannot set sail before morning," Clayton reasoned, patting the cushion beside him. "Come sit by me," he murmured suggestively.

Kyra was tempted to inform the wretch that she would sooner sit beside a deadly viper. She had the presence of mind, however, to note that the unsavory man possessed the key to her freedom, and she resolved to humor him until she could escape. Thus, she grudgingly swallowed a crisp retort and stepped across the room to occupy a chair that sat a considerable distance from her host.

After making herself as comfortable as circumstances would allow, she asked, "Where is the key?"

Clayton had busied himself with pouring wine and did not immediately respond. "I'm certain we'll come across it in due course," he said eventually. "Never mind that now, my dear." He held a goblet toward her.

"Thank you, no."

"Very well." Clayton gave her a negligent shrug. "Perhaps you'll change your mind when you discover that continued impertinence will gain you little ground with me."

The room was awkwardly silent while Kyra pondered the various places in which her jailer might have hidden the key. Haunting shadows of twilight flickered through the ragged draperies, causing her eyes to dart anxiously toward the window. Kyra was dismayed by what she saw. Nightfall was nearly upon them, and though she was not timid by nature, Kyra did not relish the idea of traipsing through the darkened streets of an unfamiliar city unescorted.

Clayton, too, was aware of the hazy shadows, for the sudden dimness had clouded his vision, denying him a clear view of his lovely guest. This prompted him to rise and step to the fireplace where he lit the matching porcelain lamps on either end of the mantelpiece. Kyra watched as he paused to admire his reflection in the mirror that hung above the mantel. Given different circumstances, Kyra would have been mildly amused at such excessive vanity, but her little voice reminded her of the precarious situation, and she wisely stifled the urge to laugh.

When Clayton finished preening, he turned to Kyra and, adopting a casual stance, asked, "What do you know about poker?"

"Merely that it's an idiotic game of chance that induces men to make complete fools of themselves," she replied promptly.

"I see." Clayton mulled over her response. "Then you know nothing of the application of the game—how wagers are placed, what constitutes a winning hand?" he inquired, tipping his glass to his lips, savoring the wine's delicate flavor.

"No, nor do I care to suffer an explanation now," she snapped impatiently, jumping to her feet. "Mr. Fairchild, I am weary and wish to return to my own lodgings. I *demand* you hand over the key at once!"

"You do make such pretty speeches." Clayton chuckled

at her temerity. "I'm afraid, however, you must resign yourself to the fact that you're destined to remain with me until I choose to release you. Sit down, Miss Raybourne!" he barked.

Kyra was not accustomed to being ordered about, but the evil glint in the man's eyes frightened her, and she peevishly obeyed his command.

When she was once again perched on the edge of her chair, Clayton continued. "Do you recall any portion of my conversation with Andrew?"

"Only that he appeared flustered because he did not have enough money to continue playing," she answered, wishing desperately that he would reveal his purpose and put an end to this charade—a wish she would quickly come to regret.

A sly grin appeared on Clayton's lips as he leaned back against the mantelpiece and folded his arms across his chest. "How do you suppose he was able to remain in the game?"

"I don't know. Perhaps Christopher loaned him some money," she suggested, her lack of interest in the tale plainly registering on her delicate features.

"You obviously don't know Christopher," Clayton scoffed. "He does not readily part with his cash, especially when he sees no chance of recovering his investment." He leaned away from the mantel and ambled over to the table to refill his glass. "As it turned out, Andrew and I were able to reach an amiable agreement of our own. Care to know more?"

"Much it would matter if I said no—it would seem you're determined to acquaint me with all the boring details," Kyra snapped testily.

"Yes, but only because the outcome of our little venture concerns you, my dear," he said and, after draining the glass for a second time, discarded the goblet and went to stand by her chair. "You see, Kyra, your brother wagered a night of your . . . shall we say, *favors*, in lieu of the cash needed to finish the hand." Clayton placed a finger under Kyra's chin and forced her head up. He could tell by her aghast expression that she understood the implication of his statement. "Well, I could hardly refuse such an engaging challenge." His green eyes boldly raked over Kyra, sending a shiver racing down her spine.

She shoved the man's hand aside. "Liar! Andrew would not do such an unspeakable thing!" she blurted, though she was no longer wholly convinced of her brother's integrity. Surely not even Andrew could sink so low as to barter her virtue to this . . . this vermin!

"Perhaps not—under normal circumstances," Clayton admitted. "Unfortunately, when the gambling fever strikes, it often blurs a man's reason." Clayton's hand returned to caress the softness of one exquisitely high cheekbone.

"Be that as it may, my 'favors' are not Andrew's to wager," she informed him brusquely.

Kyra had grown increasingly wary of the man, and in an effort to avoid more of Clayton's groping, she stood and began to pace before the fireplace. Knowing that she was hopelessly trapped, she willed herself to remain calm as she frantically searched her mind for some means of escape.

"You mustn't think unkindly of your brother." Clayton helped himself to a third glass of wine and, after quaffing the drink, advanced toward Kyra. "I assure you, he didn't make the wager with the intention of losing. One never does, but neither could I afford to allow such a titillating opportunity to slip through my fingers."

"What are you saying?" Kyra stopped pacing and stared at him.

"That the hapless Andrew didn't have a chance. The cards were . . . stacked in my favor."

"You cheated?" Kyra deciphered his coy reply, no longer shocked by the man's revelations.

"Guilty."

"Andrew did not suspect as much?"

"Your brother is a gullible young man. Besides, I'm *very* good at what I do," he whispered meaningfully, allowing his eyes to play over Kyra's form.

"You're revolting," Kyra said from between taut lips. "You cannot seriously expect me to spend the night with you!"

Clayton now stood before her, and Kyra was helpless to prevent him from pulling her into his arms. "I certainly do," he drawled thickly, thoughts of the evening ahead sending his passions flaring.

Kyra stood rigid as his hand stroked her cheek. "You must relax," he whispered throatily. He somehow managed to loosen the topmost buttons of her gown, and his eager fingers slipped beneath the material to fondle the firmness of her youthful breasts.

"*No!*" Kyra shrieked, jerking away from the hands that sought to defile her. "I . . . I don't even know you! How can you expect me to . . . to—"

"Pleasure me?" he interrupted. "I promise you, my lovely innocent, this sort of thing happens frequently."

"*Not to me!*" Kyra screamed. "You don't understand. I . . . I've . . . *never*—" she stammered, shaking her head wildly as she backed away from him.

Clayton was not to be denied the prize he had so cleverly won, however. With little effort, he recaptured Kyra and dragged her back into his embrace. "I know. Your brother assured me of that before I agreed to accept his wager. Now, I can be as gentle as the next man, but you must not provoke me," he warned, brushing his mouth against her forehead.

Kyra had never felt more terrified, and she cringed as the man's moist lips traveled across her flesh. She struggled to remain collected, realizing there was no one to save her from the lecher—she had to depend upon her own cunning. Summoning her strength, Kyra broke free of Clayton's grasp and sprinted for the door, managing only a few steps before he jerked her back into his arms. Outraged, Kyra delivered a vicious slap to his cheek, but her resistance did not dissuade Clayton. Indeed, her high-spirited struggle merely served to arouse him further.

With a wicked laugh, he pushed Kyra onto the sofa and threw himself on top of her. Despite her disadvantageous position, Kyra fought him until, no longer amused by her efforts, Clayton seized her face between his hands. He derived immediate satisfaction as he watched her eyes widen in terror. Purposefully he lowered his head to take Kyra's lips in a savage, brutal kiss—one that was meant not to give pleasure but to demand her submission.

Kyra found it impossible to endure the wet, demanding tongue that Clayton tried to thrust between her lips as she faced the startling realization that this was but a prelude to the ultimate humiliation he intended for her. Kyra felt a knot of revulsion begin to churn in the pit of her stomach, and she doubted her ability to fight back the nausea, should Clayton persist. She did not consider herself weak-willed, but Kyra had never been subjected to such abuse, and she could feel her strength waning. Then just before she yielded to exhaustion, she heard the clank of the key as it fell from Clayton's pocket onto the floor, filling her with renewed hope.

Clayton was oblivious to this; his concentration lay in the exquisite creature writhing beneath him. When at last he tore his mouth from hers, he was surprised to see the defiant gleam that still shone in her eyes—his captives usually succumbed to him by this time. Undaunted, Clayton left a trail of kisses from Kyra's lips to the pulse that pounded frantically in her throat. Then, consumed by his mounting passion, he groaned and began fumbling with the heavy folds of her skirt.

Kyra's fear knew no bounds by this point, but she had the presence of mind to recall the tray Clayton had brought into the room—it was on the table behind her. If she could reach the wine bottle, perhaps she could stun him long enough to retrieve the key and flee to safety. Even as the thought occurred to her, Kyra stretched her hand high over her head and groped for the bottle.

She was conscious of Clayton's hand as it caressed the softness of her inner thigh, and her probing hand located the wine bottle at the exact moment Clayton pulled her more intimately against him, causing her to knock the weapon from her reach. Her hastily contrived plan thwarted, Kyra's basic instincts prevailed and she raked her nails across his face.

Clayton howled painfully and jerked away but Kyra did not stop to gloat over her victory, for opportunity was at hand. Rolling onto the floor, she located the key, then scrambled to her feet and flew to the door. Her fingers trembled as she tried to slide the key into the lock and, although the two seemed destined never to meet, Kyra's efforts finally proved successful. With a cry of relief, she wrenched the door open, but her triumph was short-lived, for Clayton sprang unexpectedly from behind to hurl himself against the barrier.

"*No!*" Kyra wailed, slumping against the closed portal and burying her face in her hands. "Oh, *please* let me go!"

Clayton responded by grasping her wrists and forcing her hands from her face. "Look at me, bitch! Look what you've done to me!" he shouted deliriously, and before Kyra could react to this command, Clayton delivered a savage blow to her unprotected cheek.

Kyra was dazed by the assault, but when her vision cleared and she saw Clayton's enraged face, she was given reason to fear him all the more. She was hard-pressed to account for his violent reaction; her impulsive act had left him with the merest scratch. But the lethal glare he leveled at her gave her reason to believe he considered the wound to be a permanent blemish to his flawless appearance.

"I . . . I'm sorry. I didn't mean to hurt you. I just

wanted you to . . . stop," she said lamely, knowing full
well that Clayton was not sympathetic to her plight.

"Shut up! I'm not interested in your meaningless apologies. You'll pay dearly for your rash conduct, my sweet,"
he promised. Without warning, his hand flew up and struck
her rapidly swelling cheek again.

Kyra's head fairly reeled from the impact, but now more
than ever she was determined that this despicable creature
would not have his way with her. Correctly anticipating
Clayton's next move, she sidestepped him and ran to the
window, hoping to attract the attention of a passerby, but
the street was deserted. When Kyra again faced her assailant, she was horrified to find him advancing toward her, a
sneer curling his lips.

Although the passionate gleam had vanished from Clayton's eyes, the unbridled fury that presently distorted his
face gave Kyra little reason to feel reassured. If anything,
she felt more vulnerable than ever—not only was she in
danger of losing her virtue, but now she feared for her life
as well. She glanced around her, wildly searching for
something to use for protection.

On impulse, Kyra seized a poker from the fireplace and
swung it with all her might as Clayton lunged at her. He
managed to deflect the blow, but was thrown off stride and
sent sprawling headlong into the mantel. The collision left
Clayton dazed and disoriented and knocked one of the
porcelain lamps to the floor.

Kyra noticed only that Clayton was incapacitated, and
thus presented with a second chance at freedom, she hastily
discarded the poker and dashed across the room to fling
open the door. Without a backward glance, she bolted into
the corridor and scurried down the stairs, completely
oblivious to the wall of fire that had consumed the thread-
bare draperies.

She exited the house seconds later and glanced about,
looking for a landmark or street sign that would guide her

back to the *Driftwood*. But the sound of scuffling footsteps from within the weather-beaten house prompted Kyra to scamper down the steps and across the street to disappear into the night.

In her zeal to elude pursuit, Kyra did not notice the carriage parked opposite the house. The same, however, could not be said of the occupant of the conveyance; a pair of calculating eyes observed Kyra's flight with rapt curiosity. In fact, the owner of those eyes remained inside the coach for several moments after Kyra had fled, thoughtfully pondering all that had been witnessed. Those perceptive orbs were glistening with anger by the time the inhabitant of the enclosed vehicle entered the house from which Kyra had just escaped.

4

In a secluded corner of a crowded Savannah taproom sat a brooding gentleman, oblivious to the coarse reception he would soon receive. Devlin looked forbidding in his present state, and his size, coupled with his aura of a pent-up storm about to unleash its wrath upon an unprotected village, had spared him the companionship of tavern regulars inclined to strike up conversations with newcomers.

Devlin had arrived in midafternoon, selected a back table for privacy, then ordered a bottle of the establishment's best whiskey. After his request had been seen to by a pretty serving girl, he quickly tossed down a brimming glass of the liquid. Then he refilled his glass and settled back in his chair, a pensive frown wrinkling his handsome features as he contemplated the various stratagems he might use against his exasperating mother.

Thus the afternoon had passed, and as day faded into evening and one whiskey bottle was drained to be replaced with yet another, Devlin's disposition gradually improved. It was then that he noticed Polly, the buxom tavern maid who had gone out of her way to attend to him during his sojourn in the taproom. It was unfortunate that Devlin did not likewise take heed of the solitary figure who had followed him into the tavern; that man had remained throughout the afternoon as well and had wasted little time in making Polly's acquaintance.

As a result of the excessive quantity of whiskey he had consumed, Devlin eventually allowed his passions to override his customary good judgment, and though it was the image of a gold-brown-haired beauty with astonishing violet eyes that haunted him, he invited Polly to accompany him back to his yacht, the *Windjammer*. They had barely moved away from the table, however, when Devlin began to lament his decision, for the girl proved to be little more than a nuisance as she guided him from the taproom and beckoned him to follow her down a dark passageway, explaining she was leading him to a back exit.

Then she playfully wrested the whiskey bottle from Devlin and, running her pink tongue across her lips, drank thirstily of its contents, ignoring the excess that dribbled down her chin. Polly then shoved the container back into Devlin's hands, gave a most unladylike belch, and began prancing around him. Her shrill laughter set the vein in Devlin's left temple throbbing mercilessly, and he was more than a little relieved when she scampered off and was swallowed by the darkness.

Devlin suspected that the girl—Molly . . . Holly . . . her name eluded him—had hidden in the shadows, intending to carry out some childish prank. But as he inched along the unlit corridor without encountering her, he became irritable and realized that were his restless passions not in need of a bit of release, he might very well have sent her on her way despite the compensation he had already settled on her.

As he stumbled around a corner, Devlin detected a shadowy figure before him. Assuming he had come upon his lively companion, he extended his arms and, with slightly slurred speech, said, "Come here!"

He was unprepared for what occurred next. Instead of his arms being filled with Polly's voluptuous curves, his head suddenly exploded in a thousand brilliant lights that were instantly replaced by total darkness. Seconds later he lay motionless, oblivious to the club that thudded to the floor next to him as Polly stepped over his stricken body.

She stretched out her hand to accept the payment the lurking figure bestowed upon her. "Get him out of here, quick! Take him through the tunnel that leads to the river," she ordered as the man reached down to grasp Devlin's shoulders. "He's a big one, all right. I'm almost sorry you came along with a better offer." The woman regarded Devlin with a regretful sigh. "Funny, he don't look like a sailor."

"He ain't," the man snapped. "This ain't one of your regular shanghais, lady. Now, suppose you git one of your men to help me with my cargo here afore the 'thorities come nosin' about."

That spurred Polly into action, and within moments a swarthy youth appeared to help carry Devlin through the tunnel that led to the wharf. Less than a quarter-hour later Devlin was carelessly dumped onto the deck of a yacht that lay at anchor in Savannah harbor.

It was some time before the victim of this base assault began to stir. Devlin gradually regained consciousness, though he did not immediately realize where he was, and he couldn't recall how he had come to leave the tavern. He was keenly aware of an ache that throbbed at the back of his head, but disregarded that trifling discomfort when he heard the scuffle of footfalls along the deck. He now realized that he had somehow managed to find his way back to the *Windjammer*.

He glanced up in time to see a woman board the yacht and scurry toward the companionway. Guessing that the tavern girl had wearied of her childish games and was now ready to commence with their sport, Devlin staggered to his feet and slowly and painfully made his way toward the master cabin.

* * *

Kyra sat before the mirror in her cabin, silently recounting the unbelievable events of the day. Upon reflection, she realized it to have been an absolute miracle that she had managed to repel her attacker. Her ordeal had not ended with her timely escape, for after she emerged from Clayton's house, she had faced the additional dilemma of finding her way back to the *Driftwood*.

During her hasty departure, Kyra had left her reticule behind. She was virtually penniless, and her hair and clothing were in disarray following her brutal mauling. Thus, without funds and not wishing to draw attention to herself, Kyra had started walking in a direction she prayed would lead her to the waterfront. She had traveled no more than three blocks when she realized she was going the wrong way. Heaving a sigh, she had wheeled around and retraced her steps.

She did not want to return to the street where Clayton resided, so she turned left and walked a few blocks, then right again, and just as she was about to abandon all hope of ever finding her way, she heard the faint sound of music and laughter in the distance. Encouraged by the noise, she began to walk faster, and just as she hoped, the din grew louder, prompting her to realize that she had arrived at the bawdy waterfront district at last; the safety of the *Driftwood* was but moments away.

Kyra did manage to curtail the shout of pure glee that collected at the back of her throat, but she could not refrain from breaking into a perilous gallop across the final thoroughfare and down the steep embankment to the street that ran parallel to the river. It was then that her boot caught the edge of an uneven cobblestone, and she fell forward, stumbling ungracefully before coming to rest in a heap, but she did not dawdle or fuss over any possible injuries. She climbed up on wobbly legs and resumed her treacherous gait, not slowing her pace until she arrived at the yacht—breathless and exhausted, but relieved.

Kyra winced at the memory of the final stages of her journey as she glanced down in dismay at her scratched hands. Lifting her skirt to inspect her wounds, she discovered one badly scraped knee. Her stockings were ruined, her skirt was hopelessly soiled, and she ached all over. She longed to soak in a tub of hot, soapy water, but the crew had already settled down for the night. She would not disturb them, deciding instead to make do with the pitcher of cold water on the washstand.

She stripped down to her chemise and scrubbed her sorely abused body until it was pink and tingling all over. The ablution concluded, Kyra sat down before the mirror to attend to her mussed hair, but as she reached for the first pin, she noticed that her hands were trembling. In fact, her entire body was a tightly coiled bundle of nerves, and she reasoned that she must do something to relieve her tension if she hoped to enjoy a restful night's sleep.

Her father often drank a glass of whiskey before retiring, she remembered. She paused in mid-conjecture and began rummaging through drawers and cabinets.

Fortunately, Kyra did not have to conduct a lengthy search, and once she had located the sought-after beverage, she again sat down and carefully measured a dram into a glass. Then, giving her shoulders a careless shrug, she filled the container to the rim. Kyra had never tasted whiskey before, but she recalled that her father could consume a great quantity of the stuff before suffering any ill effects.

She quickly altered her opinion on that score, however, for a generous sip of the fiery brew left her sputtering, choking, and gasping for breath—all at once. The whiskey evoked a similar reaction when it fell into her empty stomach, causing that region to rumble noisily. Promptly putting the half-empty glass aside, Kyra redirected her attention to her coiffure.

She effortlessly dismantled the elegant style over which
Biddie had toiled that morning, then carefully brushed the
tangles from the silken waist-length tresses. Had Biddie
been present, the dutiful servant would have braided the
gold and brown tendrils to ensure they did not become
tangled during the night, but considering the harried day
she had experienced, Kyra was not concerned with combing
out a few tousled curls come morning.

Instead, her thoughts were preoccupied with Andrew and
how she would explain his latest predicament to her father.
She was similarly concerned over the yellow and purple
bruise that discolored her cheek and the unsightly swelling
that marred an otherwise flawless complexion. The skin
was sensitive to the touch, and Kyra knew she should do
something to diminish the swelling before giving in to the
exhaustion that tempted her to seek the comfort of her bed.
It was when she stepped toward the washstand to prepare a
cold compress for her smarting cheek that she heard
footsteps in the corridor, and her heart all but thudded to a
halt as the sound caught her off-guard.

She promptly told herself it was probably one of the crew
coming to see if she had returned safely.

Perhaps Clayton followed you, her inner voice chimed in
cruelly.

"I'm letting my imagination get the better of me," she
whispered, for Clayton had not struck her as one to venture
far from the protection of his own house.

Kyra cocked an ear toward the door and, when she heard
no further sound, began to breathe more easily. Her reprieve
proved momentary, however, for just as she dipped the
washcloth into the porcelain basin, the cabin door behind
her exploded open with a thundering crash. A startled
scream was torn from Kyra's throat. Clutching wildly at the
washstand for support, she whirled to see the one responsible for giving her such a fright. She gasped in surprise as

her eyes settled on the huge frame that filled the entranceway. It was the stranger from Carolly's wedding.

Devlin braced his forearms against either side of the
narrow doorway and struggled to steady himself; the physical exertion required to break open the locked portal had
caused him to lose his footing. When he righted himself, he
leaned against the doorjamb and folded his arms across his
chest. The expression that came over his handsome face
was undecipherable as he set about a routine inspection of
the cabin. In the depths of Devlin's whiskey-saturated brain
a vaguely disquieting sensation stirred, almost as if the
setting were unfamiliar to him, and his vision clouded ever
so slightly in confusion.

His sable-brown eyes continued their casual surveillance,
but it was not until Devlin's indifferent glance fell upon the
fetching young woman standing motionless in the center of
the cabin that his befuddled frown gradually transformed
itself into a sensuously wicked smile. With a grunt of
approval, Devlin pushed away from the entrance and, after
kicking the door closed, began to swagger—though somewhat falteringly—toward the lovely vision.

"Damn it," he grumbled crossly. "What is your purpose
in running off like that and barring the door to my cabin?
Can it be you think to make me *work* for my pleasure?" he
whispered, his warm breath caressing Kyra's cheek.

He was in front of her now, and Kyra remained numbly
rooted to the floor as he stretched out his hand to fondle a
tendril of hair that tumbled across her shoulder. His
questions went unheeded, for Kyra was disconcerted by this
devastating spectacle that towered over her. Though she
had not mistaken the man's identity, in his present disheveled state he only vaguely resembled the stranger she had
encountered at Carolly's wedding and, more recently, that
morning on the pier.

The expensive coat that fit him to perfection was sadly

rumpled and smudged with dirt, his neckcloth hung loose about his throat, his snow-white shirt lay open to his waist, revealing an abundance of dark, curly chest hair, and his hair was mussed. Kyra gazed warily into the man's face and guessed that her uninvited visitor was well into his cups; there could be no other explanation for his slovenly appearance. Although he carried his tall, athletic frame with aplomb, he could not disguise the glassy cast of his eyes or the mingled stench of tobacco smoke, cheap toilet water, and strong spirits.

With a shudder, Kyra correctly interpreted the passionate gleam that twinkled in his dark brown eyes as they continued to scrutinize her face, and she felt herself grow panicky. She had observed a similar expression on Clayton's face, and though she had managed to fight off that wretched man's advances, she realized that Fairchild was not as formidable as her present adversary.

Kyra swallowed, and she searched for the words to convince the stranger that he had mistakenly boarded the *Driftwood*. Given his inebriated condition, Kyra could allow for such a blunder, but she was not inclined to allow him to continue the dalliance he had begun that morning. Yet from the looks of him, that was precisely what he had on his mind. Kyra shivered as she recalled the brief amorous moments spent in his arms, and she was suddenly aware of a blanket of gooseflesh along her spine.

Without warning, Devlin released the silken wisp of hair he had been fondling and moved his hand along her shoulder to gently stroke her bare arm, serving to remind Kyra that she was clad in only the scantiest of undergarments. With a shriek of genuine mortification, she jerked away from him and thrust an indignant finger at the door behind his head.

"*Get out*!" she screamed. "This is *not* your cabin! I—"

Kyra broke off abruptly as Devlin, annoyed by her abrupt outburst, stepped forward and seized her wrist in an unrelenting grasp. *Impudent baggage*, he thought dryly. *She will no doubt hum a different tune come morning.* An arrogant smile twitched at the corners of Devlin's mouth as he considered the night to come, and he was about to enfold Kyra in his embrace when his eyes fell upon the whiskey glass. His curiosity piqued, he stepped to the dressing table, dragging Kyra along behind him.

"What's this?" he asked, his eyes glistening mischievously. Grasping the glass, Devlin turned his deliberate scrutiny to Kyra's face. "So, you started without me. No matter." His magnificent shoulders rose in a negligent shrug and he held the glass to Kyra's lips. "Drink," he ordered.

But Devlin was to discover that this young lady would not readily heed his commands; she shrank away from the proffered drink and gave her head a stubborn shake. Not easily dissuaded, Devlin roughly pulled her against him and, holding her in check with one hand, pressed the glass to her lips with the other. Kyra reacted by closing her mouth in defiance.

"Come, come, pretty one," he purred softly. "Why have you suddenly grown so contrary? You were more agreeable at the tavern, else I never would have sought your company." Then comprehension sparkled in his glazed eyes and he added, "So that is your game. You wish to haggle for more money." A chuckle rumbled in the broad chest and echoed in Kyra's disbelieving ears. His next conjecture, however, caused her to tremble with fury. "Perhaps I can be persuaded to be more generous, but much will depend upon your performance tonight," came his suggestive whisper.

Kyra grew stiff with rage, and her countenance could have warned Devlin that the sudden dark hue of her eyes did not bode well for the one responsible for her foul mood. She did not think it possible, but her rancor was even more intense than it had been when she was obliged to suffer his caress that morning. For not only had this drunken scoundrel forced his way into *her* cabin, but he possessed the gall to believe her to be the trollop with whom he had arranged an assignation. Was the man so completely absorbed by drink that he could not see she was the same gentle young woman he had met in Charleston and not some doxy who was destined to warm his bed for the night? The notion was not to be borne!

"You wretch!" she spewed hotly.

In her fury, Kyra forgot about the whiskey, and Devlin took advantage of her memory lapse by swiftly pouring the liquid into her open mouth. Caught unaware, Kyra swallowed a generous portion of whiskey before she could respond. Her spontaneous reaction was a mistake, for when she slapped his hand aside, the liquor sloshed over the side of the glass and spilled onto her skin, trickling in a diverting path down into the valley between her breasts.

Kyra's chagrin turned to panic when she heard the man's satisfied chuckle, and he slowly lowered his head to her breast and began to flick lightly at the whiskey with his tongue. Kyra bristled, but as she started to push him away, Devlin tossed the glass aside, swept her into his arms, and strode toward the bed. Kyra began to struggle in earnest. She pummeled Devlin's face and chest with her balled-up fists, and she kicked and squirmed in a frantic attempt to escape his grasp, but her efforts proved futile.

Devlin was beginning to fall completely out of charity with this troublesome girl. By the time he reached the wide berth, his pique was of such proportions that he released her unceremoniously onto the bed. Gratified to note that his companion appeared momentarily docile, Devlin took advantage of the welcome respite and swiftly removed his clothing. When he turned toward the bed again, he found that the girl had scrambled to her knees, fists clenched at her sides. As he watched, Devlin saw the resistance drain from her beautiful face, although he mistook Kyra's new reticence for the desire to be in his arms.

Kyra was dumbstruck—as any self-respecting girl would

have been—when her innocent eyes beheld a man's un-·
clothed body for the first time. Try as she might, Kyra could
not look away from this remarkable exhibit, and her
curiosity compelled her to embark on a thorough scrutiny of
this masculine phenomenon who flaunted himself shamelessly before her.

Kyra's breath gathered in her throat as her inquisitive
eyes moved along the broad, muscular shoulders, down the
powerfully sculptured arms, and across the wide expanse of
chest that boasted a sea of dark hair. She was denied an
inspection of his well-developed thighs, however, for when
her wide-eyed gaze slipped below his tapered waist, she
became mesmerized by a rather intimidating sight.

Kyra did not hear the smug laugh her dazed expression
elicited from Devlin. Indeed, she was deafened by the pulse
that thundered at her temples, pounding out a desperate
warning, urging her to flee before the situation became
more grave. But some alien force commanded her to remain
frozen to the spot, staring with fascination at the essence of
his masculinity. It was not until that part of him began to
undergo a dramatic transformation that Kyra managed to
tear her eyes from the startling sight. Unfortunately, she did
not possess the presence of mind to plan an escape; her eyes
flew to the stranger's face and she was alarmed by the lusty
gleam in his sable-brown eyes.

Precious seconds ticked away before Devlin himself
provoked Kyra to action. Given the advanced state of his
drunkenness, he misinterpreted the reason behind Kyra's
lingering perusal of his manly attributes, prompting a
haughty chortle and vain riposte.

"Is madam pleased with her discovery?" he drawled
teasingly.

Kyra's breath came in a rush then, and though she
yearned to deliver a blistering retort, a more logical course
of action prevailed, and she sprang like a cat in the direction
of the cabin door. She had hoped to catch her tormentor

off-guard and scurry through the door before he recovered.

Devlin—who was finding his temptress's behavior more vexing with each passing moment—had anticipated such a maneuver. Therefore, when Kyra vaulted sideways, Devlin's arm darted out to encircle her waist and he hurled her backward onto the mattress, the impact leaving her breathless and gasping for air. In the next instant, he was straddling her, his large hands gripping her slender wrists, pulling them above her head to pinion them there while his passion-inflamed manhood pressed unmistakably against her lower abdomen, boldly taunting her.

"Let's have done with this coy display, shall we? We both know what you are," he callously told her, ignoring her frantic denials. "Lest you forget, I paid to have you, and have you I shall."

His whiskey-impaired vision settled upon the swell of Kyra's breasts as her labored breathing caused the crimson peaks to strain against the diaphanous chemise and fall away, only to quickly rise again in a maddening motion that exacerbated Devlin's already heightened passions. When next he spoke, his voice was thick with unbridled desire.

"Oh, yes, my little hellcat," he whispered throatily, "I shall have you."

He was leaning so close that Kyra could feel his breath as it touched the silky smoothness of her throat. She turned away from him to bury her face in the pillow, vainly struggling to avoid the kiss that she knew was imminent. But her efforts were useless, for when Devlin grew weary of nibbling at her perfectly formed neck, he merely placed a finger beneath her chin and forced her to look at him.

Kyra was startled by the expression clouding those wondrous eyes as they bored hungrily into her frightened face. They were brimming with desire, radiating a heat that seared her flesh in a way she found far more threatening than the hardened scepter that was thrust impatiently against the softness of her thigh. But Kyra noticed something

else flickering behind those great brown eyes—a need, a
longing so great that she experienced a fleeting sensation of
being suffocated by its intensity, a hollow, haunting loneli-
ness—and she once again sensed a trace of sadness in his
eyes.

Unwittingly, Kyra worked her hand free and lifted it to
gently stroke his austere brow. Too late, she realized the
folly of her impulsive gesture; Devlin interpreted it as
encouragement, and his mouth immediately descended
upon hers.

This kiss was infinitely different from the one inflicted
earlier that morning. During that encounter, Devlin had
been rude and abusive, bent on asserting his dominance
over her, but she was permitted no opportunity to reflect
upon the incident. Indeed, she could think of little but the
pressure of Devlin's mouth as it moved leisurely and
possessively over her lips, teasing, tantalizing, demanding
an enthusiastic response rather than passive submission; a
kiss not unlike those she had received again and again in her
dreams of recent months.

Nonetheless, Kyra fought valiantly to curtail the unexpected upheaval that this sensual assault wrought on her
normally temperate emotions. She knew that she had to
keep a clear head if she expected to thwart this stranger's
seduction, but that glimmer of hope was dashed in the very
next instant as Devlin's hard, inquisitive tongue slipped
between her lips to explore her mouth.

The remaining threads of Kyra's composure snapped as a
result of this attack, and she found herself confronted with
an altogether different enemy—her own blossoming desire.
Despite her efforts to the contrary, Kyra could not disregard
the curiously pleasant tingling in the very depths of her soul
as his tongue flitted playfully across her lips, then retreated
to tease one corner of her mouth, and again darted inside to
skillfully fence with her own. She tried again to push him
away, to no avail, and when she thought to disengage her

tongue, his was there to fondle, coax, and manipulate her own, assaulting her senses in a way no man had ever done before.

She was appalled by her body's traitorous response to the array of overpowering sensations he had skillfully summoned within her. Kyra's conscience screamed at her to voice her outrage, but she was finding it increasingly difficult to fend off the stranger's uninvited advances and to contend with an inner mutiny that was even more devastating.

This is madness! her reason shouted. *Your conduct is shameful, despicable! You should be screaming or swooning, not . . .* Rational thought was swept aside as Devlin again molded his pliable lips against her own.

With a horrified gasp, Kyra realized that the scream she had fully intended to release had somehow taken the form of a rapturous moan of unmistakable pleasure. Scandalized by her body's betrayal, Kyra gathered all her physical resources and wrenched her lips free.

"*No!*" she shrieked wildly. "Let me go *at once!*"

But the notion of releasing her never penetrated Devlin's besotted brain. Instead, he pulled her more tightly against the length of his muscular physique, and his lips caressed hers briefly before they began to press a trail of fleeting kisses along her cheek. He paused to consider the bruise that discolored her exquisite cheekbone and, after murmuring some muffled endearment, brushed his lips across the afflicted area and continued to trace a haphazard pattern along her shoulder and down her throat until he encountered her singularly annoying chemise.

Grumbling an inarticulate oath, Devlin swiftly gathered the offensive undergarment in his strong fingers and, in a single motion, tore the delicate fabric from neckline to hem, freeing Kyra's ample breasts. Ignoring her sharp intake of breath, he lowered his head to her breasts and began to taste her alluring flesh. Devlin reveled in her immediate response as the pale pink crests grew rigid beneath his insistent caresses.

When at last he lifted his dark head, and met her violet eyes, Kyra was staggered by the expression of primitive lust on his rugged face, and with a choked sob she realized that nothing short of divine intervention would save her now. Still, she had to try, for the sake of her own sanity.

"*Oh!*" Her cry of surprise split the air as Devlin's tongue returned to tease the hardened tips of her breasts, and his next maneuver quashed the plan she had begun to formulate in the confused recesses of her mind.

Kyra felt his hand skirt across her stomach and move down to the triangle of hair that gave way to her slender thighs. Here his hand paused, and his nimble fingers began to fondle the sensitive place, purposefully sliding into the supple crevice to expertly stroke the very core of her womanhood. Never in Kyra's wildest dreams involving him had she imagined this! With a pang of self-reproach, she tried to ignore the tremors of delight that were shaking her body, even going so far as to press her legs together, thinking that might discourage him.

Guessing her motive, Devlin laughed and simply persisted with this maddeningly sensuous motion until, as if possessed of a will of their own, her legs parted in a welcoming gesture. With a horrified cry, Kyra realized she had unwittingly provided him with the opportunity he had been waiting for. He positioned his manhood at the opening of the silken passageway that had never before been violated.

"No! Please don't!" Kyra whimpered, bracing her palms against his shoulders in a vain attempt to push him away. "Not . . . not like this!"

Devlin captured her hands in his and coaxed them to her sides as he lowered his torso until the hair on his chest tickled the tips of her breasts. Brushing his lips against her quivering mouth, he murmured, "Shh, my lovely. I can't help myself—I'm mad with passion for you." Then as if truly sensing her anxiety, he whispered, "Don't worry, little one. I'll be gentle."

Kyra tasted blood the next instant, as she bit into her lip to keep from crying out when Devlin's sudden penetration took her by surprise. The initial stab of pain quickly subsided, to be replaced by a peculiar, and not altogether unpleasant, sensation of fullness as he thrust himself deep inside her. Tears gathered in the corners of Kyra's eyes, but before they could slip down her cheeks, Devlin was there to kiss them away.

Despite her humiliation, Kyra was perplexed by this tender gesture. Feeling compelled to look at him, she was more than a little surprised to note a flicker of sympathy in those brooding eyes.

In a conciliatory gesture, Devlin pulled her close and, gently stroking the silky brown hair that cascaded across one shoulder, he murmured against her throat, "I'm sorry if I hurt you, little pet."

Kyra stifled a tearful sob and moaned beseechingly, "Please, now that you've finished, would you just go away?"

"*Finished*?" he mumbled vaguely, the dark eyebrows arching up incredulously, the broad chest shaking with mirth. "Foolish child," he breathed huskily, touching his lips to the pulse that pounded in the hollow of her throat. "I assure you I've barely begun."

Kyra experienced an unbelievably pleasurable sensation as he began to move within her, establishing a measured and leisurely motion meant to provide them both with the ultimate satisfaction. Although she was forced to contend with this monumental assault on her senses, Kyra put forth a valiant effort to disregard the lips that tugged playfully at the stiff points of her breasts, the hand that slid beneath her hips to draw her as close to him as possible, and most of all, that great sword of lust that plunged deeper inside her with every commanding thrust of his hips.

Kyra was at war with herself, and even though she gripped the sheets and tossed her head from side to side to avoid Devlin's persistent kisses, she realized with a sinking heart that she was losing the battle that had erupted between reason and her own budding passion. She realized the extent of her body's perfidy when her courageous struggles were eclipsed by a natural eagerness to enjoy this new experience to the fullest. She felt perplexed, for her mind cried out for a swift conclusion to this shameful ordeal while a part of her wished quite fervently that these delightfully intoxicating sensations might never end.

By now it was impossible for Kyra to ignore the crescendo of her own awakening desire, for Devlin cast a dizzying spell as his blade of passion relentlessly pierced her, banishing all coherent thought from her head. Driven to the edge of insanity, she flung her arms about his neck in sheer desperation and buried her head in his shoulder as she struggled to ride out the raging storm that whirled all around her.

The maddening interlude seemed interminable, and just when Kyra thought she might be able to collect her scattered thoughts and formulate some plan of escape, she was introduced to an extraordinary feeling. For one fleeting moment it felt as if the exhausting conflict had ended and the very life within and around her had ceased to exist. But in the next instant she was overwhelmed by a series of sweet, exquisite sensations that culminated in one glorious, spellbinding explosion that left her clinging breathlessly to Devlin. The scream she had been unable to release came out in a rush—a mingled cry of pent-up anger, emotional release, and pure sensual delight.

Several moments later Kyra felt the hard, rippling flesh beneath her fingertips shudder as Devlin, his passions spent, came to rest atop her. With a sob, Kyra fought back the tears of humiliation that glistened in her eyes and slowly removed her arms from Devlin's neck. Her fingers trembled as she pressed her hands against his shoulders and pushed him away from her.

"Now will you *please* go?" she mumbled tearfully, but she was frustrated yet again. Now that Devlin's desires had been satiated—coupled with the disabling effects of the whiskey he had consumed and the blow to the head he had sustained earlier—he promptly succumbed to an impenetrable sleep.

Kyra resolved to remove herself from the man's presence, but when she would have suited her actions to her thoughts, her plan was neatly thwarted by a pair of sinewy arms that reached out to enfold her in a tight embrace. With a disheartened sigh, Kyra decided to bide her time, reasoning that the opportunity for escape would surely present itself again during the night. But with her ear pressed against Devlin's chest, she eventually fell victim to the rhythmic beating of his heart and, without being truly aware of it, was lulled to sleep.

5

Kyra awoke at daybreak, jostled from her dreams by an unfamiliar snore and bedeviled by a nagging sense of gloom. She was momentarily confused by her surroundings, but the restless stirrings of the roomy berth's other occupant quickly cleared the cobwebs from her head as recollections of the previous evening flooded her thoughts in glowing detail. Kyra fought the instinct to jerk away from Devlin, not wanting to disturb him until she herself was fully awake and prepared with an adequate defense lest he attempt a second sensual onslaught.

She painstakingly removed the hands clasped intimately beneath her breasts and wriggled from under the weight of the leg her unwelcome bedmate had flung across her during the night. Then Kyra inched away from him, her watchful eyes trained on his sleeping face. She had reached the comparative safety of the far side of the bed and had sat up when Devlin suddenly moved. Her heart in her throat, Kyra squealed in alarm, but he merely shifted to a more comfortable position and continued snoring.

Kyra fastened a cold, steely glare on his muscular back. At first she had felt nothing more than humiliation at the disgraceful events of the preceding evening, but with the dawn of a new day, Kyra found herself consumed by an altogether separate emotion—anger. She was positively livid with the thought that this *brute* had simply waltzed into her cabin and . . .

He introduced you to the single most thrilling sensation you've ever experienced, the naughty voice in her mind ruthlessly interjected. *You've thought of nothing else for weeks,* her conscience reminded her.

Kyra gasped, averting her gaze in staunch denial of the accusation. The very idea that she could have been plea-. sured by this blackguard's actions was outrageous! But before she could convince herself of this, her eyes returned to the impressive body of the man who slept just inches from her, and her memory was flooded with visions of the night she had spent in his arms.

I doubt that Fairchild would have been as tender, nor could that great lout have transported you to such heights of ecstasy, her impish inner voice tormented her.

Kyra grudgingly acknowledged the absurdity of these observations, though her concession did little to dispel her mounting frustration and self-incrimination. She stared gloomily at the stranger's broad shoulders until the din of hungry gulls swooping around the *Driftwood* interrupted her reverie and she was reminded of the unpleasant chore still facing her.

Her thoughts reeled with sobering possibilities. It was morning and the crew would soon be up and about. And Biddie, concerned that her mistress had not returned for her, might arrive at any moment. Therefore, though she was reluctant to rouse this menacing intruder, Kyra knew that he would have to leave the *Driftwood* without delay—the events of last night must never be discovered by anyone.

With the greatest trepidation, Kyra leaned forward and thrust a tentative finger between his shoulder blades. Anticipating an immediate response, she snatched her hand away and huddled near the wall, only to discover that her actions had no visible effect. Swallowing hard, Kyra poked him again, more vigorously and, when she again encountered defeat, grabbed his arm and gave it a vicious tug. Still he did not stir.

Kyra slumped against the wall with an indignant huff. *Isn't this just like a man?* she asked herself. *When I wished him unconscious, he remained awake to torture me, and now by refusing to awaken, he persists in his torment. Well, he will soon learn that while I was at a disadvantage last night, I am a more worthy opponent this morning.*

With the growing light of day, Kyra was experiencing a resurgence of her fiery spirit and felt less intimidated by the stranger. The fact that her nemesis was in no condition to defend himself did not bother Kyra, who toyed with the notion of employing any number of painful methods to rouse him, mulling over each idea with wicked and shameless enthusiasm.

It was not until the nagging little voice of her conscience reminded her of the urgency of the situation that she sprang into action and, drawing her knees up to her chest, kicked Devlin, catching him squarely in the back. This tactic produced the desired result when he was sent tumbling, limbs flailing wildly, from the bed, landing with a thud on the floor.

His cry of surprise and indignation was enough to inform Kyra that her stratagem had worked, the intruder was awake. But the string of coarse expletives that split the air only served to remind her of his explosive personality, and her triumphant smile soon withered into an uncertain frown.

Kyra was spared an immediate confrontation with the rogue, for Devlin made no prompt attempt to rise from the demeaning position into which he had tumbled. Indeed, he barely took a breath for the longest moment. As he lay there on the cold, unyielding floor, the events of the preceding day began to penetrate his murky thoughts, causing him to swear again.

"Damn it, Polly!" he roared, finally recalling the serving girl's name.

Kyra bristled at the harsh oath, prepared to endure the forthcoming onslaught, but the stranger grew unaccountably silent. Curiosity temporarily prevailed over better judgment and Kyra crawled across the bed to determine Devlin's condition. She was within inches of peering over the edge of the mattress when she recalled an old saying about "the calm before the storm," and clutching the sheet to her bosom, she retreated.

Meanwhile, Devlin struggled to achieve some semblance of inner calm, for his exertion had sent an incredible, blinding flash of pain coarsing throughout his body. Though the discomfort gradually subsided, there remained a persistent throbbing at his temples, a drumming that would have tested the patience of the most docile man. Convinced that his suffering had been brought on by the unconventional manner in which he had been awakened, Devlin was determined to make the brazen female pay dearly for her wretched behavior.

Summoning every ounce of self-restraint, Devlin willed himself to ignore the crippling pain that ravaged his head as he groped for the edge of the bed. With a firm hold on the mattress, he pulled himself up to his knees. But the invective he had been prepared to unleash died abruptly on his tongue when his bloodshot eyes focused on the thoroughly disheveled vision who sat shooting daggers at him from the most captivating pair of violet eyes he had ever encountered.

Taken by surprise, Devlin hesitated and reorganized his thoughts, he was not so incapacitated that he could mistake this enchantress for the barmaid. This was no common tavern girl, but a lady of breeding and quality.

But what the devil was this beauty doing on the *Windjammer*? he wondered, his head now whirling with confusion as well as unrelenting pain. A hint of recognition flickered in Devlin's sable-brown eyes as he conducted a deliberate scrutiny of the young woman.

His gaze fastened on the luxurious gold-brown hair that cascaded in disarray across her shoulders and down her back. From there his eyes traveled to her mouth, the lips drawn in a taut white line as though she could barely contain her wrath. The next sight his bleary eyes perceived caused his breath to catch in his throat; his gaze traveled to where she clutched the sheet to her breasts, the rosy tips of which were clearly visible beneath the thin material.

He paused to take an unsteady breath before forcing his eyes back to her face. Without a doubt, she possessed the most exquisite features he had beheld in a long while. Her complexion was nearly flawless, with the single exception of the bruise that discolored her cheekbone. Puzzlement creased his brow when he next met her unwavering stare.

It was the unusually vibrant color of her bewitching eyes that ultimately triggered something in Devlin's foggy memory, and with a groan he remembered when he had first confronted them. They belonged to the unfortunate young woman who had knocked him over—literally—at Robert Latham's wedding. He had been so preoccupied with thoughts of fetching his children when he arrived in Savannah that he had failed to make the connection when he encountered her on the pier. But here she was again. Just who was she and why was she in his cabin?

Thoroughly bemused by this unlikely coincidence, Devlin could not contain his surprise. "*You!*" he cried, cringing as the top of his head throbbed painfully with his outburst. He added more quietly, "What are you doing in my cabin?"

This was Kyra's moment, and she promptly mounted her attack. "*Your* cabin!" she shouted, ignoring the grimace that contorted his handsome face. "Look around you, you stupid lout! This is *my* cabin, and I would consider it a great kindness if you would remove your loathsome, mangy hide from my yacht at once!"

"Your yacht? Your cab—" Devlin's voice faltered as a cursory glance around the room confirmed the girl's claim.

"Yes!" Kyra hissed, glancing nervously toward the door, fearful that she might be discovered with this unsavory rogue. "Now will you please go?"

Devlin did not immediately respond to her request. Now that his initial surprise had subsided, he found himself plagued by curiosity concerning the previous evening and decided that he would not take his leave until the girl had made him privy to the circumstances that led them to spend the night together. And though Devlin could not even claim the girl as a passing acquaintance, he knew intuitively that any further discussion would be pointless.

Thinking that he could better converse with Kyra from a less humbling position, Devlin slowly raised himself to perch on the edge of the berth. Since she had confiscated the sheet, he nonchalantly covered his nakedness with a pillow before meeting her fulminating stare.

"I'll leave in due course, but first I want you to tell me what happened last evening. My memory fails me this morning, and to my embarrassment, I cannot recall how we met," he frankly admitted.

Though Kyra did not wish to encourage him to prolong his stay, she could not resist the temptation to give him his due. In a voice dripping with sarcasm, she said, "That's not surprising, considering your shameful condition when you forced your way in here. I assure you, sir, I do not make a practice of sharing my quarters with . . . with the likes of you!" She stared down her nose at him in obvious dislike.

"Ah, I behaved that badly, did I?" A devilish grin parted his lips in spite of the unnerving glare she leveled at him.

"You were positively oafish, pawing me with your hands and sickening me with your foul whiskey breath!"

Devlin pondered this revelation, then reached out to thoughtfully fondle a silken curl that tumbled over her shoulder before he issued a scandalous rejoinder. "I can state, without fear of contradiction, that no woman before you ever had cause to pitch me from her bed. I trust you were dissatisfied with my performance?" he drawled, cocking one eyebrow at an angle that Kyra found infuriating.

Without thinking, she slapped his hand aside and, snatching the remaining pillow from the bed, lashed out at him, pummeling his head and chest with savage blows. "You vile, wretched man!" she cried, affronted by his haughty manner, but when she would have delivered an especially devastating punch, her opponent sprang into action.

The swiftness of the girl's assault caught Devlin unaware, and he attributed his sluggish response to his weakened condition. Under normal circumstances, he might have considered Kyra's antics diverting—a playful prelude to more pleasurable things to follow. In truth, he was rapidly losing patience with this impertinent female, for with each relentless blow, his head reeled and his stomach churned. Deciding that his retaliation should be equally merciless, Devlin thrust out a hand to ward off her attack.

Before Kyra knew what was happening, he had jerked her arm away and captured her wrist in a bone-crushing grip. She tried to pull free, but when his grip proved steadfast, she struck out at him with her unencumbered hand, only to have him seize that hand, too. When she grappled for her freedom, Devlin threw her to the mattress, pinned her hands above her head, and straddled her stomach with his hard, overpowering body.

Kyra bit back a frightened scream when she beheld the victorious gleam twinkling behind his sable-brown eyes; she had seen a like expression only hours earlier, and the memory of his subsequent plundering still burned in her brain. Hoping to discourage him, she managed to wrench one hand free, and grasping a lock of hair that tumbled across his forehead, she gave it a savage yank.

"*Ouch*!" came his startled cry, and though Kyra did not gain her freedom, she rejoiced in the knowledge that she had caused him considerable discomfort. "Damn, you little hellcat!" he swore, the expletive sounding very much like a frustrated groan.

In a pure reflex action, he drew back his hand to repay the offensive vixen in kind. It was then his eyes again beheld the unsightly bruise that disfigured her perfectly defined cheekbone. A troubled expression clouded his eyes, and with the hand that he had intended to use as an instrument of punishment, he gently stroked the bruise.

Devlin was uncharacteristically contrite and his voice was edged with concern when he asked, "Did I do this?"

"No," she mumbled, averting her gaze, more than a little confused by this unexpected reversal in his disposition.

As he rubbed his fingers along his smarting hairline, Devlin's lips slowly curved into a boyish grin, and he responded glibly, "Perhaps I should have."

Then, weary of his sport, he rolled away from Kyra to look for his clothing. Finding his trousers, he climbed out of bed, but the exertion proved too great for his aching head, and he had barely pulled the garment on before he was forced to sit down again, desperately praying that the cabin would cease spinning.

Realizing that the man was no longer a threat to her and that he was obviously making an effort to effect his departure, Kyra decided to remedy her own state of undress. Gathering her ruined chemise about her, she began to crawl toward the dressing gown that she had draped across the foot of the bed the night before. She had traveled only a few inches when she was given reason to abandon her goal.

"Have you no heart, woman?" Devlin bellowed, lowering his aching head into his hands and moaning pitifully. "Must you make nauseating motions while I am trying to compose myself?"

"I'm sorry," Kyra whispered and was instantly angry with herself for appeasing the provoking man. Precious little she cared if his head fell from his shoulders. Nevertheless, she made no further attempt to retrieve the dimity robe.

Devlin turned in time to see her crestfallen gaze and, with an agitated gesture, motioned for her to carry on. "Go ahead. I suppose I won't expire from this malady."

"More's the pity," Kyra muttered under her breath, retrieving the robe and quickly draping it about her shoulders. Exhaling a grateful sigh, she started to get out of the bed when Devlin once more gestured toward her.

"Wait, please. I need your answer to a particularly nagging question." He paused to deliberate how to go about posing his inquiry. "I cannot truly believe I am about to ask this, but since I cannot recall last night's events, I have no alternative." He shook his head, not believing that he had been reduced to such humiliating circumstances, and taking a deep breath, forged ahead. "Did we . . . that is to say, did I make love to you last night?" he asked casually, as though inquiring if she cared for a cup of tea.

Kyra had not expected such a forthright question, but from the moment it pealed in her ears, she knew what her response would have to be. No one could ever know what had taken place on the *Driftwood*! She would never be able to bear the shame.

She swallowed hard before lifting her eyes to meet his probing gaze. "No, you did not," she whispered hoarsely, and thinking that he would not be satisfied with so brief an answer, she continued, "You attempted to do any number of repulsive things, but you were so encumbered by drink that you fell unconscious before . . ." Her voice trailed off meaningfully, and she lowered her eyes as if embarrassed by the conversation.

Devlin studied the girl closely, silently considering all she had said. He was unconvinced of the veracity of her declaration, for despite his malfunctioning memory, the image of a pair of soft, pliable lips and a fresh rose scent mushroomed inside his head. He favored Kyra with one last penetrating look, but found that he could ascertain nothing from her impassive expression. Then, giving his broad shoulders a shrug, he dismissed the incident, reasoning that no rational female would allow a man to compromise her virtue and then walk away scot-free.

"I see." He stood up carefully, his bloodshot eyes scanning the cabin for the remainder of his belongings. When he located his shirt, he made an earnest endeavor to pluck the garment from the floor, but when he bent over, the room whirled precariously.

Fearing that the man would keel over in a dead faint, Kyra scampered from the bed to assist him. She retrieved the elegant lawn shirt and held it out for him as he eased his broad shoulders into it. This task accomplished, she started to move away, but the scoundrel captured her hands in his and Kyra knew that his next statement, though obviously difficult for him, was nonetheless sincere.

"Thank you. Your kindness is appreciated and unexpected, considering the distress you have no doubt experienced because of my presence here." He tilted Kyra's head back until he was permitted a clear view of her face. "Please allow me to apologize for the inconvenience I have caused you." He lifted her hand to his lips and pressed a gentle kiss against the soft flesh.

Kyra stood transfixed, unsure of what she should do. Before she had the presence of mind to remove her hand from his, the cabin door flew open and Biddie rushed across the threshold.

Kyra snatched her hand free at once, but the damage had been done: She had been discovered in the most compromising of positions.

But perhaps all was not lost, she mused, a glimmer of hope beginning to warm her anxious heart. Biddie had always been loyal to her mistress and would wish her no harm.

Kyra was confident she could explain everything to the

maid and persuade her to hold her tongue—provided, of course, she could get the servant to calm down long enough to listen to reason. Biddie presently stood in the doorway, screeching at the top of her lungs, her brown eyes large and round as she gaped at the couple who stood motionless in the center of the cabin.

"Lordy, Lordy!" she wailed. "I knowed somethin' terrible was gonna happen if I left you by yourself. Why did I let you go off like that?" Biddie groaned. "Now look what this awful man done. Did he hurt you, missy?" She chanced a tremulous glance at the forceful stranger whose baleful expression only served to make her tremble all the more. "Just wait till your papa hears about this. Your poor, poor papa!" Her mournful squall grew even more strident. "What's he gonna do when he finds out what happened? Oh, Lordy!" She wrung her hands in front of her.

Kyra finally regained her composure and ran forward to pull Biddie into the room. Devlin, whose tortured head had begun to thump even more vigorously as a result of Biddie's high-pitched ravings, was eyeing the servant with a menacing scowl. Kyra correctly interpreted the look of raw savagery that filled his eyes and, fearing for Biddie's safety, completely forgot to close the door in her zeal to protect the young maid and dispose of her unwanted guest. She arrived at Biddie's side as Devlin's carefully gauged temper reached its boiling point.

"Hell *and* damnation!" he thundered, startling Biddie so that she paused in mid-shriek, her mouth slightly agape as she stared at this raging spectacle. Then, settling a murderous glare on Kyra, he thrust a warning finger toward the frightened servant and the cabin reverberated with his shout: "Tell this ill-bred, loudmouthed shrew that if she cannot cease her infernal caterwauling, I shall wrench her tongue from her head and feed it to the buzzards. Then I'll fling what is left of her into the river." He ended on a deafening note, winded and clutching a straight-backed chair to steady himself as the room began to surge again.

Kyra rushed to the maidservant's defense. Placing a protective arm about the shaking girl's shoulders, she satisfied herself that Biddie was all right before turning a scathing look on the surly blackguard.

"The fact that you were foolish enough to drink yourself into a stupor last night does not give you the right to bully my servant with your ridiculous threats." She glowered at him, her violet eyes deepening to a vibrant hue.

"I assure you, madam," Devlin began stiffly, his knuckles turning white on the back of the chair, "that I would have cheerfully carried out those threats had the wench not possessed the good sense to cease that damnable squawking."

"Well, it's all over now, so your tantrum was quite wasted," Kyra chided, hurrying about the cabin to collect the remainder of his possessions in an effort to initiate his departure. Pressing the items into his unsteady hands, she directed him toward the door.

"What about her?" Devlin suddenly recalled the scandalous implications of being found in this clandestine fashion, and as he made his way across the floor—a maneuver that was accomplished only by the grace of Kyra's supportive arm about his waist—he experienced a slight twinge of guilt that the girl should be left on her own to make explanations for his deeds.

"Don't trouble yourself," Kyra said, guiding him toward the door. "Biddie has been with my family for years and will wish me no harm. I'll think of something to satisfy her."

"I wonder if you would be so good as to include me in your tête-à-tête?" inquired an unfamiliar feminine voice from the doorway. "My curiosity has been piqued, and I should very much like to know how my son came to be a part of this charming little adventure," Amanda Cauldwell stated candidly. Without waiting for an invitation, she stepped across the threshold, her curious gaze enveloping the couple who stood like statues before her, comparable expressions of horrified disbelief marring their faces.

Several tension-filled moments elapsed before Kyra and Devlin recovered enough composure to deal with this catastrophic development. Kyra glanced back and forth between mother and son, her confused gaze taking in Amanda's imperious expression before looking up to see Devlin's thunderstruck grimace gradually evolve into a cold and hardened scowl. She could not repress a chilling shiver as she observed the angry glare the pair exchanged, and she vaguely wondered how two such closely related kin could be so openly hostile to each other.

The implications of this latest discovery finally wormed their way into Kyra's consciousness, and on this sobering thought she pushed away from Devlin and stumbled to a chair to sit down, no longer trusting her quaking knees to support her. With a befuddled shake of her head Kyra watched as the duo continued to glower at each other, and she was besieged by a perplexing thought: How had the woman known her son was on the *Driftwood*?

As the initial shock of seeing his mother in the cabin began to subside, Devlin's bitter countenance dissolved until his face was masked by a totally bland and unreadable expression.

As Kyra watched the drama unfold before her, she was puzzled by the man's apathetic demeanor. He merely gave his head a stoic shake, muttered some offhand malediction, and sat down on the edge of the bed to pull on his boots. This task completed, he stood and, with considerable effort, shrugged his broad shoulders into his whiskey and smoke-scented jacket. But when he started to leave the cabin without so much as a by-your-leave, Devlin found his way impeded by an immovable obstacle: his mother.

"Where do you think you're going?" Amanda demanded, laying her hand on his arm.

Without truly considering his actions, Devlin wrenched his arm free and hissed, "*Anywhere*, as long as it is away from you!"

"I am well acquainted with your sentiments," Amanda offered dryly, giving no outward indication that his retort had dented her impenetrable armor. "Surely you realize that I have no intention of allowing you to skulk off without giving me an explanation." And in the event that this chastisement did not produce the desired results, she added, "Lest you forget, you stand to lose a great deal if you persist in behaving like a pigheaded jackass."

The look Devlin fastened upon his mother was filled with resentment, for he well understood her innuendo: he must yield to her demands if he hoped to regain custody of his children. Knowing that he would eventually succumb to his mother's wishes, Devlin decided that he would do so at *his* leisure, not hers. "How the devil did you know where to find me?" he blurted, changing the subject, much to Amanda's irritation.

"I heard you as I was walking along the pier toward your yacht. In fact, your vulgar threat against this poor child"— she nodded at Biddie—"was heard throughout Savannah.

"I had a change of heart and thought we could resolve our differences," Amanda said, explaining her visit to the waterfront. "It appears, however, I was mistaken. You are hopelessly corrupt—therefore, yesterday's ultimatum stands." With a sad shake of her head, she concluded in a scolding tone, "Will you never outgrow your disgraceful ways?"

"Perhaps—that is, *if* I gave a damn about what you or anyone else thinks of my conduct," he snapped. "You should realize by now that my behavior is none of your concern, Mother," he continued bitterly, the muscle in his jaw beginning to twitch. "If you're determined to poke your nose where it's not welcome, I suggest you interrogate this young woman"—he jerked his head toward Kyra—"but I won't be staying. I cannot abide being here an instant longer." He pushed past Amanda and stalked toward the cabin door.

He was within inches of the threshold when the doorway again was obstructed by a curious observer. This time the caller proved to be an attractive woman. At first glance, Kyra suspected she was her unwanted overnight guest's sister, for the similarity in coloring and facial characteristics was striking. But as Kyra's eyes fell to the small blond child the woman held in her arms, then to the boy of five or so who clung to the woman's skirt, she was persuaded to reevaluate her hasty supposition. There was no denying the parentage of the little boy—he was an exact replica of the awesome man who towered over the other occupants of the cabin.

My God! came Kyra's first hysterical thought. *He's married and has children! Oh, why did I not stay at Raybourne where I belong*?

But this silent agonizing was of little consolation to Kyra now. She sat in a daze and watched as the room again became a whirlwind of activity. The rafters quaked as angry voices stirred the air, making Kyra feel like a spectator at some poorly staged drama.

Mother and son locked horns again as the young woman stepped inside the doorway, beseeching someone—*anyone*—to tell her what was happening, while the younger child stretched her arms toward her father, her shrieks of "Papa, Papa" echoing in Kyra's ears like an artillery's cannonade. The ultimate shock came, however, when the little boy broke away from the woman and marched over to Kyra.

"Are *you* going to be my new mama?" he demanded in the authoritative tone of voice that Kyra had by this time come to expect from this odd family.

Kyra started to laugh. It began as a lilting warble in the back of her throat, but as the absurdity of the child's query registered in her mind, the laughter grew to a frenzied pitch, causing her to double over as streams of tears flooded her cheeks. Try as she might, Kyra could not suppress her convulsive shrieks, which became so strident that the others ceased bickering and turned to stare at her.

It was not until Kyra noticed yet another shadow lurking in the doorway that she was able to smother her delirious titters. Her violet eyes filled with horror as she realized with numbing dismay that the deep blue eyes which scanned the faces in the room before returning to her belonged to Colin Raybourne—her father.

Kyra's initial thought was that she was witnessing a strange and eerie apparition—or that she was the victim of a cruel deception. Her father could not be here; he was en route to Raybourne from New Orleans, or perhaps he had arrived at home by now, but it was inconceivable that he was in Savannah. Kyra blinked in an effort to shake the alarming vision, but the "hallucination" remained firmly rooted in the doorway.

Then, confirming her worst fears, the mirage stepped toward the little boy and, in a voice that Kyra recognized instantly, said, "Offhand, young man, I'd say you can safely assume *that* to be a distinct possibility." His meaningful gaze traveled from his daughter to meet and hold a pair of smoldering brown eyes that returned his calculated scrutiny.

As Kyra watched the two formidable men exchange dangerously composed expressions, she was overcome by a stifling premonition of disaster. The unfortunate situation was rapidly deteriorating, and for the first time in her life, Kyra felt as if she might faint. But fate was not to be so obliging, and during the ensuing confrontation, she rued the fact that she had been denied unconsciousness as a means of escape.

When Kyra next summoned the courage to look at her father, she was not surprised to find his accusatory gaze fixed squarely on her. Though she knew those normally compassionate eyes would soon be clouded with disappointment, she also realized that the moment of truth was at hand. She must somehow explain this delicate situation to everyone's satisfaction. Swallowing the great lump that had lodged in her throat, Kyra squared her shoulders and bravely faced her father.

"Papa?" she said tentatively, unsure of where and how to begin.

Before she could proceed, Colin raised his hand. "Come, now, magpie," he said, using the pet name he had coined when she was an infant, "where are your manners? You have neglected to introduce me to your friends." His speculative gaze swept over the group crowded inside the small cabin before it returned to Kyra's panic-stricken face. Although Colin's own face remained composed, Kyra knew that in a matter of moments her father would be given reason to lose control of his temper.

Dreading the confession she was about to make, Kyra gulped, threw a glance at Devlin, then raised her head to meet her father's steadfast gaze. "I cannot introduce you, Papa. You see, I"—she swallowed again, lowering her eyes in shame—"I don't know their names." This admission emerged as little more than a choked whisper, but it was heard as clearly as if she had shouted it on the wind.

"*What!*" came the shocked cry from Amanda and Colin, whose shared outburst prompted the little girl to break into boisterous sobs.

Amanda turned to the woman holding the child. "Emily, take Sarah and Nicholas to the carriage and wait there while I sort this out."

"But—" the young woman started to protest.

Amanda was adamant. "Do as I say, Emily—*at once!*"

Her command was gruff, though her anger was directed at her son.

"Yes, Mother," Emily murmured, crossing the room to pull Nicholas away from Kyra and usher him toward the door. At the threshold she turned to bestow an encouraging smile upon a fuming Devlin before whisking her young charges from the yacht.

"You may leave as well, Biddie." Colin dismissed the maid, and sensing the development of a very ugly scene, the domestic bobbed a curtsy and promptly disappeared.

There was a lengthy pause while the four remaining occupants of the cabin contemplated their next maneuver. Just when Kyra began to think she would be driven mad by the silence, Amanda began to rail at her son.

"Devlin Joseph Cauldwell!" she began angrily, enunciating each syllable with a deliberation that grated on Devlin's nerves. "You've given me cause to lament your behavior many, *many* times in the past, but this . . . *this*—" She faltered, at a loss for the words that would have expressed her feelings. "How do you explain this shameful incident?"

Everyone's attention was focused on Devlin, and his willful disposition prevailed. "Mother, I thought I had made my position clear: My actions are none of your bloody affair!"

Devlin favored Amanda with a look completely devoid of feeling, and though it might not have produced the desired effect upon her, it sufficed to send a shiver of foreboding slithering down Kyra's spine. A strange sensation, almost as though he were being smothered by the confines of the minuscule cabin, enfolded Devlin. He thought that if he did not shortly gain his freedom, he would very likely do mischief to the nearest unlucky bystander.

Devlin breathed a harried sigh and, between gritted teeth, said, "I will not endure another of your insufferable quizzings. I'm not a puling adolescent in need of a meddling mama's supervision. I have no need of your maternal concern. Now, if you good people will excuse me, I shall adjourn to my yacht. Have the children brought to me immediately, Mother; it's my intention to leave this godforsaken city without further delay." Concluding his tirade, he stomped toward the door.

While Devlin's caustic speech momentarily rendered Amanda silent, it incensed Colin, who promptly halted the headstrong young man. "This situation cannot be resolved that simply, young man," Colin informed him matter-of-factly. "I don't know why you harbor such resentment toward your mother, but you will not leave this cabin until I give you leave to do so. You have compromised my daughter, sir, and you are damned well going to account to me for your conduct." Colin folded his arms across his chest and pinned Devlin with a challenging look.

On impulse, Kyra placed herself between the two imposing men, hoping to prevent an out-and-out brawl. "Please, Papa," she began fretfully, "this is nothing more than a wretched misunderstanding. I can explain everything." She glanced back and forth between the two men. Then, taking a fortifying breath, she hurried on, "You see, this gentleman . . . Mr. Cauldwell, was not in command of his faculties last night . . . that is to say—"

"I was drunk," the masculine voice behind her interjected flatly. Then, leveling a haughty stare at Kyra, Devlin said, "I appreciate your efforts to absolve me of any wrongdoing, but I assure you that I hardly need a *woman* to defend my actions."

"*Defend you*!" Kyra turned on the scoundrel furiously, all apprehension having fled the instant his condescending speech exploded in her ears. "Why, you overgrown bully!" she snapped at him and angrily thrusted a finger into his chest, catching him unaware and causing him to stumble a few steps backward.

Glorious in her fury and oblivious of the effect she was

having on the onlookers, Kyra raged on. "Believe me, the notion of absolving you never entered my head, for if the finger of blame is to be pointed at anyone, it must surely be you! You alone are responsible for becoming so encumbered by drink that you behaved like a . . . a half-witted jackass!

"Defend you? Not likely! But neither will I condone your behavior. Indeed, I would shout my story throughout Savannah if it would ensure that I never again had to endure the sight of your wretched hide!" Turning to her father, she cried in complete frustration, "Oh, Papa, what are you doing here?"

Colin's rigid countenance softened when he beheld his daughter's distraught face. He maintained an inflexible stance before the closed door, however. "Later." He brushed her query aside with a wave of his hand. "We have more pressing matters to discuss. For instance, I am curious to know how Mr. Cauldwell proposes to atone for his shameful actions." Colin redirected an intimidating glare at Devlin.

"But there is no need for atonement," Kyra insisted. "I assure you that nothing happened, absolutely *nothing*! He fell unconscious soon after forcing open the door. No harm has been done, and this is hardly the place to conduct a long and tedious discussion. Can we not talk this over at Raybourne?"

"Were this one of Andrew's childish pranks, I would yield to your request, but this is far more serious, Kyra. Regardless of your claim, a great deal of harm has been done," Colin said gravely. "Your reputation has been hopelessly tarnished, and I know of but one way to protect your good name."

"But if we are discreet—" Kyra began, only to encounter her father's hand as he impatiently waved her protest aside.

"You forget Biddie."

"Biddie?" she echoed hollowly.

"You know how the servants talk. I cannot think she would deliberately malign your character, but Biddie loves gossip, and this"—Colin gestured around the cabin with a broad sweep of his hand—"is too great a temptation for even the most loyal servant to resist."

"But nothing happened," Kyra repeated weakly.

Colin's gaze wandered over the powerful physique of the man in question, then returned to skim over his daughter's womanly figure, and his tone was clearly skeptical when he said, "That does not matter. The fact remains that you and he spent the night alone together in this cabin. Regardless of what you say, there is but one solution to this dilemma." Colin leveled his frosty gaze at the man who simmered in the middle of the cabin. "Cauldwell, I believe a marriage proposal is in order."

"*Marriage!*" Kyra's horrified shout made the room quake, and she bolted forward to grasp her father's sleeve. "No! Oh, Papa, *no*! You cannot be serious!" she wailed. "You cannot expect me to wed a man I do not know."

"Nevertheless, you shall."

"But you saw that other woman," Kyra said, on impulse. "His affections are obviously otherwise engaged. *They must be.* A marriage between us is quite impossible." She noted that a disturbing frown wrinkled her father's brow as she silently applauded herself for her quick thinking.

Her jubilant mood was short-lived, however, for Amanda said, "That young woman is Devlin's sister. My son has been a widower for nearly two years. There is no reason a marriage cannot take place. In fact, I am in complete agreement with your father; it is the only way to preserve your reputation."

"But . . . but I don't want to marry *him*!" Kyra blurted wretchedly.

"Nor is it my wish to become leg-shackled to a willful, ill-tempered virago," countered the would-be bridegroom. "I've already sampled marital bliss and found it to be singularly wanting. It's not likely that I'll willingly entertain the notion of attaching myself to another of your kind." His contemptuous gaze washed over Kyra.

A muscle in Devlin's face began to twitch ominously as he delivered this passionate speech, and though he would have relished the opportunity to air his opinion of the female sex at length, he abruptly terminated his caustic address and concluded by offering Kyra a heartfelt piece of advice. "Go home," he said bluntly. "Surely your reputation can survive this peccadillo, and I assure you that you'll be far more content at home with your papa than marooned on a West Indian island with me."

"That suits me just fine!" Kyra answered peevishly, her anger rekindled by his offensive speech. Unthinkingly, she took a step toward the abusive man as if to resume the argument, but further debate was made impossible by Amanda, who wisely intervened.

"Children, children!" she said, clucking her tongue. "We're all overwrought by this awkward business, but there is no need to bicker. Nothing will be resolved by exchanging insults." Turning to Kyra, she said, "You were quite right, my dear, when you suggested that we sort out the complexities of our little problem in privacy. It appears we may be deadlocked for quite some time. Therefore, I would like to extend the hospitality of my home to you and your father. I'm confident we'll reach an amicable solution once everyone has had a chance to reconsider the consequences of last night's unfortunate occurrence." She directed this statement at her son, then turned to Colin. "If you would be so good as to step outside with me, Mr.—"

"Raybourne."

"Yes, Mr. Raybourne. I will give you directions to my house."

She waited patiently for the fierce-looking man to relax his stance before the door. Noticing the untrustworthy look he had fixed upon her son, Amanda reassured him, "Please do not think for a moment that my son will fail to accommodate us. Though his shabby appearance may suggest otherwise, Devlin *is* a gentleman, and you may depend upon him to behave honorably."

Colin mulled over her words, then with a grunt of acquiescence opened the door. "Madam, I will not leave Savannah until this young man either agrees to do right by my daughter or grants me an opportunity to defend her good name." He fastened a deadly glower on the accused man.

Devlin's response to this challenge was to cram his sadly disheveled hat upon his head and stalk from the cabin. Colin then escorted Amanda across the threshold, but before closing the door, he turned to observe his daughter. She looked so vulnerable, standing in the middle of the cabin, the voluminous folds of her dressing gown making her appear smaller than she was. Not wishing to cause Kyra further distress, he simply announced that he would send Biddie to her, adding that he would return to escort her to the Cauldwell house in an hour's time.

With a grateful sigh, Kyra heard the click of the door that granted her a moment of solitude before being subjected to a barrage of questions from Biddie. Sinking down onto the edge of the bed, she was thankful for the opportunity to collect her thoughts. She needed to think of a way to dissuade her father from pursuing this abominable notion; under no circumstances would she agree to wed that man. . . .

6

Kyra's determination to avoid marrying the scoundrel had not waned by the time she and her father arrived at the Cauldwell mansion. It was with a conflicting mixture of dismay, relief, and surprise that she observed Devlin's arrival late that afternoon from an upstairs window. With a pang of guilt Kyra found herself wishing that Devlin had made good his threat to leave the city, thereby solving all her problems. Yet before that thought had grown cold, she felt a small sense of relief when she saw the handsome gentleman emerge from a hired carriage on the street below.

Kyra had heard the restless stirrings from her father's adjoining room and realized that he was only moments away from announcing his intent to go and fetch the young upstart himself. At least for the time being, Kyra would be spared the worry of her father forcing a confrontation with the younger man.

With a desolate sigh, she returned her gaze to the powerfully built man who strolled across the sidewalk, through the iron gate, and up the narrow path that led to a divided stairway. As if from habit, Devlin selected the right staircase, but before beginning his ascent to the porch, he halted and directed a taunting glare toward the upstairs window where Kyra's lovely face could be plainly seen.

Her every instinct commanded her to retreat from that withering look, but determined not to be intimidated, she returned his scowl in full. As if reading her thoughts, the provoking man offered a condescending smile and bowed mockingly before resuming his leisurely progress toward the entrance.

With considerable effort, Kyra suppressed the irresistible urge to greet Devlin at the door and scratch the arrogant expression from his face. She turned from the window and began to pace about the room, her thoughts racing. Yet despite her agitation, Kyra was surprised that he had so easily yielded to his mother's wishes. It had taken no great genius to sense their strained relationship, and Kyra had suspected that he might ignore Amanda's summons out of pure spite.

A small frown wrinkled her brow as Kyra wondered exactly what hold Amanda had over her son that enabled her to bring him to heel like a well-trained dog. Although Kyra had scarcely made his acquaintance, she realized that Devlin was very much his own man, and she knew it must gall him to be manipulated by Amanda. Further speculation became impossible when a knock sounded at the door and a maid announced that the evening meal was about to be served.

The repast proved to be even more unpleasant than Kyra had imagined possible. Amanda endeavored to mollify the disgruntled guests who graced her table by chatting about the delicacies her chef had prepared and about the interesting sites of the city, but the stilted nods and detached murmurs from her visitors made her dispense with further attempts to draw the group into friendly conversation. The room reeked of tension that could have been sliced with a knife.

Kyra sat in subdued silence, her father seated at her right elbow. Her hostess sat at the head of the table to her left, and the gentleman who was the source of all her woes occupied the chair opposite her. Having very little appetite, Kyra ate sparingly of the endless array of dishes placed before her, merely tasting a few of the tantalizing servings so as not to offend her hostess. She was beginning to think they might progress through the interminable evening without a recurrence of the morning's bickering when Devlin began to speak in a most disparaging way, his manner suddenly truculent and insulting.

Kyra was taken aback by Devlin's attack, for his barbed comments were directed either at her directly or at females in general. She was at a loss to understand his behavior, for she had done nothing to warrant his condemnation.

Kyra had been so absorbed in her own thoughts that she had failed to notice that Devlin, too, had eaten little. Unlike her, however, he had demonstrated no aversion to the various wines that accompanied the meal and, heedless of the castigating looks his mother threw at him, consumed a liberal quantity of the stimulating drink. It was the wine—coupled with Kyra's irritatingly innocent femininity—that goaded Devlin.

Determined not to be provoked by the man's remarks, Kyra threw him her most chilling look and selected an apple from the fruit bowl. Picking up a paring knife, she began to peel the fruit with meticulous precision. When she inserted the razor-sharp blade into the delicate skin, the apple underwent a gratifying transformation and, in her mind, took on the features of the abrasive gentleman. Though Devlin's harangue continued, Kyra no longer paid him any attention; she was lost in fantasy as she plunged the knife into the apple.

Amanda, cognizant of the wicked gleam twinkling in Kyra's eyes and the perverse smile that curled her lips, turned a quizzical stare upon the girl, but Kyra was engrossed in her activity and did not notice the woman's curious scrutiny—Kyra was to remain thus entranced for several minutes. Indeed, had one of Devlin's cruel gibes not interrupted her concentration, she could have whiled away the evening engaged in this gratifying activity.

"Even the most virtuous of the female sex will adopt the practices of a harlot if it serves her advantage," he drawled smoothly, reaching for the goblet that had only seconds earlier been emptied and refilled. "Take the lovely Miss Raybourne as an example. Only this morning she announced—quite emphatically, mind you—that she was not the least bit interested in having me as a husband. Yet look at her this evening, clearly attempting to seduce me with this alluring display of her . . . *charms*."

Kyra glanced up expectantly and was chagrined to discover that his rakish gaze had settled upon the swell of her breasts where they rose above the décolletage of her gown.

"Tell me, ma'am"—he regarded her closely—"is this your coy way of communicating to me your intent to yield to our parents' request that we wed to salvage your sullied reputation? For if that is your purpose, I warn you that, even though the lures you have cast out are enormously enticing, my conviction remains unchanged. You do not suit me. In fact, there isn't a woman alive who would suit me, so you may abandon your ploy; it is highly unlikely I will succumb," he concluded on a wry note and leaned back in his chair, hoping that he had shattered any romantic notions the young lady might be nurturing.

Devlin need not have concerned himself with the matter, for Kyra was more resolved than he to prevent this travesty of a marriage. Dropping the mangled apple onto her plate, she plunged the knife into the delicate fruit, imagining it was the scoundrel's black heart. Then mustering her pluck, she sprang to her feet. With hands on hips, eyes blazing, one foot tapping impatiently, she prepared to deliver the overbearing brute a blistering dressing-down.

Realizing that an altercation was at hand and wishing to prevent a scene, Amanda stood and raised her hand. "I think it is time for us to withdraw so the men can converse openly." She took Kyra by the arm and gently coaxed her toward the door. "I promise you shall be granted the pleasure of a rebuttal before the evening ends, my dear."

Amanda offered Kyra a halfhearted smile as she ushered her from the room, but her expression grew solemn when she paused to address her son. "Devlin, when you and Mr. Raybourne have concluded your discussion, I should like a word with you. I'll wait for you in the library."

Though Devlin's expression clearly indicated he was loath to attend her, the curt wave of his hand implied that he would not deny his mother an interview. Acknowledging his gesture with a slight tilt of her head, Amanda followed Kyra into the corridor and closed the door behind her.

With the gentlemen sequestered in the dining room and Amanda gone off to attend to a household matter, Kyra was left to her own devices in the sitting room. She welcomed the solitude; it allowed her time to think of a way to divert her father from the drastic course he seemed set upon. But as she began to compile a list of arguments, Kyra's concentration faltered and her thoughts turned to the tall, provoking rogue who was presently conversing with her father. Filled with renewed pique and finding that she could not remain docile in her agitated state, Kyra rose and began to prowl about the room.

"How dare he!" she spoke aloud to the portrait of a staid-looking ancestral Cauldwell hanging on the wall. Under normal circumstances, Kyra would have taken note of the elegant room, but in her present humor the intricate design of the handwoven Oriental carpet was a blur in her mind as she stormed up and down the length of the chamber, the rug's myriad colors fanning her temper.

"*How dare he!*" she repeated furiously. This time she directed her speech to an antique porcelain figurine of scantily clad lovers entwined in a passionate embrace. "How dare he suggest that I would stoop to such vulgar tactics! Lure him into marriage, indeed!" she scoffed.

Her rancor momentarily spent, Kyra turned her attention to her reflection in the corner window. The servants had lit the candles but had neglected to draw the draperies. Thus, with the room aglow and her likeness reflected in the glass, Kyra embarked upon a self-scrutiny.

She had not known how many days she would be spending in Savannah when she instructed Biddie to pack her valise, and not until this morning had she discovered her woefully limited wardrobe. Kyra reddened with shame as she recalled the ruined bloodstained chemise she had guiltily stuffed beneath the mattress to be destroyed at a more convenient time.

As she studied her reflection, Kyra allowed that her ensemble was perhaps a trifle recherché for a somber occasion such as this, but in no way could the dress be construed as indecent. The chintz gown was styled in the current fashion, the bodice closely fitted to Kyra's shapely bosom. The bell-shaped skirt was embellished with a multitude of dainty peach and pale yellow flower petals. A wide ribbon of deeper yellow circled her waist and was tied in an elaborate bow at her back, the streamers gently fluttering nearly to the floor. Rows of peach and yellow flounces extended from midway down the skirt to the hem. The lace-trimmed capped sleeves were set slightly off the shoulder, exposing a generous expanse of alabaster skin. And though the low neckline did reveal a good deal more of her flesh than Kyra considered prudent in this particular setting, she thought the yellow lace of her chemisette served as an adequate barrier to masculine eyes.

Kyra then recalled the sensuous gleam sparkling in Devlin's brown eyes as they took in the generous curve of her breasts, and she was reminded of what a reprehensible man this Devlin Cauldwell was. Having settled this in her mind, Kyra relaxed and, smoothing her skirt, returned to her chair and contented herself with envisioning various methods of torture she could inflict upon the villain while awaiting the arrival of her father.

She did not have to wait long, for Colin arrived while she was in the midst of a rewarding fantasy in which a skewered Devlin was being roasted over an open flame. The appealing vision faded as the click of the sitting room door interrupted her reverie, and she turned toward the sound. Judging from the tired expression on her father's face, Kyra concluded that his debate with Devlin had been arduous, but she could not guess who had won.

Kyra watched in silence as her father crossed to a table bearing a crystal decanter and selected a glass. He filled it with cognac before taking a seat on the brocade sofa, and several moments passed as Colin seemed unusually engrossed in the intricate pattern of the goblet. Then, swallowing a liberal draft of the cognac, he lifted his haggard eyes to his daughter's face.

His lips parted in a wan smile when he observed her pout. "What a day this has been," he commented.

"Yes," she murmured distantly.

Then, casting her carefully rehearsed speech to the wind, Kyra moved to the tapestry-covered stool at her father's feet and sat down before him. When she gazed up at him, Colin was surprised to see that her bright violet eyes were brimming with tears—his daughter rarely succumbed to histrionics—and he was taken aback by her anguished cry.

"Oh, Papa, why do you hate me so?" she blurted, burying her face in her hands.

Colin placed the glass on a table and sat back, visibly shaken. Leaning forward, he gently forced her hands from her face and, cupping her chin in a firm, fatherly grasp, he tilted her head until their eyes met.

"Hate you?" he repeated incredulously. "What a thing for a daughter to say to the father who has cherished her and doted on her since the blessed moment she came into his life!"

Seeing that his declaration had not alleviated her distress, Colin coaxed Kyra onto his lap, as he had done when she was a small child. When she was comfortably settled, Colin said solemnly, "I don't hate you, magpie. Indeed, of all the things in this world, you and Andrew are the most precious to me. How can you accuse me of such malice?" he demanded, the hurt in his voice apparent.

"Because you're going to make me marry that . . . that *man*!" As always, whenever Kyra made reference to Devlin, her voice took on a rankled tone and her eyes glittered wrathfully.

Colin somehow managed to swallow the chuckle that rose in his throat; he knew that Kyra would take offense if he appeared amused at her indignation. He had always thought his daughter favored her mother in looks, but now it was obvious that Kyra had definitely inherited her mother's fiery temperament as well.

A wistful, nostalgic smile flitted across his face before he returned his thoughtful gaze to Kyra. He was sorry that she was enmeshed in this unfortunate mess, but he could think of no other way to save her reputation. Suddenly the echo of a door being slammed somewhere in the nether regions of the massive house interrupted his musings, and Colin returned to the problem at hand—soothing Kyra's ruffled feathers.

"Aha," he murmured. "It would seem that Amanda's conference with her son has ended somewhat precipitately." He shook his head, recalling his recent stormy encounter with the headstrong young man and, rubbing a hand across his brow, mumbled wearily, "I'm too old for this sort of thing."

"Nonsense! You're not old," Kyra insisted, folding her arms and sticking out her chin defiantly. "But *he* must be nearly *forty* . . . much too old for me!"

"He's thirty-two," Colin informed her, laughter illuminating his deep blue eyes.

Kyra gave her head a careless toss. "Well, that is neither here nor there, for in any case he is positively dreadful. I will never understand how you can condemn me to a lifetime with that miserable man!" she cried in frustration, springing from Colin's lap to stand before him.

Colin reached out to still the slender hands that she wrung in front of her, and as he lovingly stroked the silken flesh he said softly, "It's for the best. Listen to me, magpie, for I love you dearly. That is why I came to Savannah when I arrived home to discover that you had donned your suit of armor again and come here in search of your wayward brother.

"It's because I love you that I insist you marry young Cauldwell, for I can think of no other way to preserve your reputation." He paused for a moment to consider Kyra's sullen expression and squeezed her hands affectionately. "You know, on the surface he appears to be a bitter man, but through the years, I have discovered that people are not always as they seem."

Kyra snorted doubtfully.

"Do you remember the stories your mother told you when you were a little girl—about how she and I met and about the early days of our courtship?" He acknowledged her stilted nod, and as he rose from the sofa, his serious blue eyes locked with her rebellious violet ones. "Then you know that your mother and I were less than enamored of each another in the beginning . . . much like you and young Cauldwell."

"I know, I know!" she snapped impatiently, pulling away from him. "That's different!"

"How so?"

At a loss for a plausible explanation, Kyra spread her hands in a helpless gesture. "Because it just is!" she shouted in exasperation, realizing with a sinking heart that her father remained unswayed.

Hearing his deep chuckle, Kyra looked up into her

father's aging face, and her brow wrinkled into a puzzled frown.

"You look just like your mother when you're angry," he told her.

As Colin stroked her cheek, a concerned expression clouded his eyes when he again noticed the ugly bruise. When he had quizzed her about it earlier in the day, Kyra had insisted that Devlin was not responsible for the unsightly mark, but she had steadfastly refused to reveal the name of the one who had dared to treat her so callously.

"Kyra," he murmured thoughtfully, "are you certain Cauldwell had nothing to do with this?"

"Yes, Papa," she muttered, grimacing slightly as he fingered the sensitive area.

Growing suddenly weary, Colin realized that he and Kyra had reached an impasse in their discussion. He pressed a fatherly kiss against her forehead and announced his intention to retire for the night. At the door, he turned to offer a parting comment. "Kyra, you've never disappointed me. I am convinced you are a victim of circumstance in this instance, but I shall not waver in my conviction that marriage is the only way to solve this problem. Believe me when I say that I will not permit you to ruin your life because of your stubborn Raybourne pride.

"Therefore, my willful magpie, if Cauldwell comes to his senses—as I suspect he will—and offers marriage, make certain you accept." His probing cerulean eyes searched her face to determine if she accepted his terms, and seeing her glum expression, he felt certain that she would not fail him.

Kyra stood for a long time in the center of the room, staring at the door her father had just closed behind him. Feeling completely helpless, she resolved to avoid a confrontation with Devlin for as long as possible. After all, she could hardly accept a proposal of marriage if the offer was never made, she told herself.

With a beleaguered sigh, Kyra ambled over to the

decanter and poured herself a small glass of sherry, hoping the wine would soothe her shattered nerves. She knew it was folly to think she could avoid Devlin indefinitely, but she reasoned that she just needed a little time to convince her father of the absurdity of his solution.

She was about to sit down and reevaluate her approach when she spied the evening newspaper on the mantel. One headline caught her eye, and Kyra picked up the paper and read the account of a fire that had destroyed a house near the waterfront the previous evening. The charred remains of a man had been found in the rubble, and since a Clayton Fairchild had recently leased the residence, the authorities assumed him to be the unfortunate victim.

The authorities were assuming the blaze had started accidentally, but an eyewitness reported seeing a woman run from the house moments before it was consumed by flames. The article went on to state that the identity of the mysterious woman was unknown, but she was being sought for questioning in connection with the fire. The balance of the story was to remain unread, however, for the paper slipped from Kyra's stunned fingers as she collapsed on the sofa to absorb the horror of what she just read.

Devlin meandered aimlessly along a footpath in the square opposite his mother's house. His hands were shoved deep inside the pockets of his close-fitting, immaculately tailored trousers, and he was lost in thought. He remained engrossed for several minutes, oblivious to the other people who had sought a rejuvenating stroll in the summer night before retiring.

Devlin remained deep in reverie as he paused on the path to pull a jeweled case from his coat pocket. After selecting a cigar, he puffed it to life and inhaled deeply, savoring its mellow flavor. He remained transfixed, staring blindly at the haphazard patterns of evening shadows that danced around his feet. However, his serene expression belied the tempestuous thoughts that whirled through his head. In an effort to end his trance, he shook his head and heaved a disconsolate sigh before resuming his walk. Devlin continued in this manner, walking and thinking, for several minutes, furiously working the cigar between his lips. The thick, steady cloud of smoke hovering above his head was a clear indication that something grieved him.

The walkway before him suddenly forked, forcing Devlin to choose one of the paths that branched off in separate directions. Although this was not a particularly difficult decision, it was one that Devlin appeared loath to make, and in frustration he threw himself down onto a bench beside the footpath to consider his situation at length.

"Damn it all!" he grumbled, recalling his meeting with Colin Raybourne and his interview with Amanda.

The former had ended predictably, with the girl's father insisting that Devlin wed his daughter and Devlin steadfastly refusing to take such an archaic measure merely to prevent the girl's name from being dragged through the mire a bit. She could surely weather the tempest, and he was not about to allow a purely unintentional indiscretion to condemn him to a lifetime of misery by bucking himself to that quarrelsome female.

Devlin had concluded that session feeling quite charitable with himself, but the confrontation with his mother had quickly dispelled all hope for a swift and complete victory. His mother had been succinct and to the point: Devlin would marry Kyra, or Sarah and Nicholas would remain with her indefinitely. With her ultimatum of the previous morning thus reaffirmed, and having been given no opportunity to dispute her, Devlin had adjourned to the square.

"*Women!*" he spat disgustedly. "The *gentle* sex." That certainly was a myth.

His mother had been a plague to him since the day he arrived home on vacation from the university, determined to assume his rightful place at the head of the business empire his father had built. Amanda had found his temerity amusing, suggesting that he postpone his impetuous move until he had completed his studies, traveled abroad, and seen the world. In truth, Amanda had her son's well-being at heart, but Devlin possessed a stubborn streak, and misinterpreting her suggestion as an attempt to prevent him from assuming control of the family business, he had stomped off in a huff to seek his own fortune.

It was during his travels that he met Lynette.

A murderous expression darkened his handsome features as the memory of his wife flooded his thoughts. She had been a rare beauty, and he had loved her with the kind of passion a man could hope to experience only once in a lifetime. Lynette had beguiled him with her innocence and guileless charm, and then had played him for a fool. Now that one conniving temptress had exited his life, he had not the slightest desire to be saddled with another.

Devlin's ponderings progressed until they focused on Kyra. His brow puckered into a contemplative frown as he endeavored to assess the fiery-tempered young lady who had abruptly entered his life. She was not a classic beauty, but there was something there to attract a man's interest.

If a man was so inclined, he conceded grudgingly.

Perhaps it was the arrogant slant of her nose, the defiant set of her chin, or the infuriating little smirk that graced her lips whenever one of her precisely aimed barbs struck its mark. While Devlin found himself oddly stirred by these musings, he admitted that he was most fascinated by her eyes, those wondrous pools of violet that mirrored her every emotion—eyes so large and inviting that a man might drown in their splendor if he was foolish enough to be seduced by her wiles. Well, he would not succumb to the coquettish charms of a mere slip of a girl!

"The little wretch!" he muttered irascibly, his anger stemming from his inability to dismiss Kyra from his thoughts.

A look of uncertainty continued to cloud his usually vibrant brown eyes as he pondered his dilemma. If the girl's tale was a truthful one, she had successfully resisted his passionate onslaught. He raised one eyebrow doubtfully, and his lips formed a thin line as he conjured the pathetic vision of Kyra frantically attempting to shield her nakedness with her tattered chemise. Still, she insisted that he had not dishonored her.

Devlin's head began to ache with this contradiction, and crushing the cigar beneath his boot, he rose and breathed deeply of the fresh air, which made him long for the breezes of his island home. With an acquiescent sigh, Devlin offered a mock salute to his mother's house as he grudgingly acknowledged his defeat. Surrender was a completely unfamiliar experience for Devlin, and the fact that he had been forced to accept Amanda's terms left a particularly bitter taste in his mouth. But as he retraced his steps along the footpath, a tiny glimmer of hope began to flicker behind his eyes.

After all, Miss Raybourne appeared to be a sensible girl, and she had already voiced her displeasure with the notion of taking him for a husband. An idea mushroomed inside his shrewd mind: He would propose to the girl, she would refuse his offer, and Amanda . . . well, his mother could not expect him to *force* the girl to accept. He smiled despite himself, but his self-satisfied grin vanished as abruptly as it had appeared, prompting him to halt in mid-stride as he was about to step down from the curb. A disquieting thought had ruthlessly wormed its way into Devlin's head: What if the girl's father had convinced her that marriage was the only solution to her awkward predicament?

Devlin pushed the thought aside and proceeded across the street, his heart made lighter by the decision he had impetuously made. Perhaps it would be amusing to have the lovely Miss Raybourne at his mercy for a time. He would break her spirit and set her in her place. She would be utterly miserable—he would see to that.

"She will scamper home to Papa within the week," he predicted gleefully.

A wicked smile transformed his handsome face as he savored the notion of making the redoubtable Miss Raybourne cower before him. Indeed, his step became lighter and a decidedly sinister gleam sparkled in his piercing dark eyes as he made his way toward the courtyard behind the spacious house.

Kyra stood motionless on the back porch of the Cauldwell mansion, gripping the iron railing in desperation. To an outside observer, it might have appeared that the young woman was inordinately engrossed in the view of the moonlit gardens. In reality, a very different scene was being enacted before Kyra's rapt gaze, for her lively imagination was busily engaged.

In her mind, the shimmering garden was transformed into a dreary, dismal courtroom. Kyra, pale and wan in a plain gown of gray muslin, stood trembling before the magistrate, who was about to announce the punishment for the grisly crime of which she had been convicted. This reverie progressed at a feverish pace, and in the following scene her hands were bound behind her back and a cruel-looking guard was forcing Kyra to climb a crudely constructed wooden staircase.

Kyra imagined the anxious buzz of the crowd that had gathered in the street, and with a heavily pounding heart she realized that the steps led to a gallows. With a startled gasp, she glanced up to see a hangman's noose swaying gently in the balmy morning breeze. Her eyes widened in horror, and her quivering hand crept to protectively finger the smooth flesh of her throat.

"It was an accident. I didn't mean to harm anyone," she

mumbled weakly, blinking rapidly in an attempt to expel the terrifying spectacle from her mind's eye.

But her inventive imagination triumphed, and Kyra was obliged to witness the conclusion of the bizarre dream. She watched in numb silence as her fantasy self stumbled dazedly up the steps. Her feet became tangled in the hem of her gown, sending her sprawling clumsily to her knees. The unsympathetic guard bent down and hoisted her to her feet, but before continuing up the steps, Kyra turned to face the crowd, searching frantically for a compassionate face—one face in particular.

He was there, standing near the outer edge of the eddying throng, his powerful physique and superior bearing easily distinguishing him from the others. With an unblinking stare, he watched the proceedings, his distaste obvious, but when those haughty eyes came to rest upon his daughter's panic-stricken face, Kyra was devastated by her father's cold, dispassionate expression. She was completely undone, for never before had she experienced a look of such steely contempt, as the one her father leveled at her. She did not have to long endure this scornful scrutiny, however, for Colin's interest in the hanging quickly palled and he turned to take his leave.

"*Papa!*" Kyra cried piteously and would have held out her hands to him had they not been behind her back. The tall figure seemed to hesitate for a fleeting moment upon hearing her anguished outcry, but then he strode away, leaving his disgraced daughter to suffer the consequences of her gruesome crime.

In the next instant, the burly guard pushed Kyra up the few remaining steps and delivered her into the hands of her executioner. She gulped convulsively as her tearful eyes took in the large, imposing figure clad entirely in black. The only visible indication that this great hulking creature was human was a pair of glittering brown eyes that ridiculed her through the narrow slits in the black hood that covered his head. Kyra's gaze flew to the tiny openings in the hood, but when she heard the sinister laugh, she knew the hangman's identity.

"How fitting!" she choked out, musing over the exquisite irony of her situation.

Kyra was convinced that no one would derive more pleasure from settling the ghastly noose about her throat and drawing it taut. It was true that she knew very little about Devlin Cauldwell, but she was certain that he nurtured an unnatural dislike for the whole of her sex and would not think twice about lessening its number by one.

The pounding of Kyra's heart mounted in a thunderous crescendo as the incredible drama unfurled before her. She was suddenly turned around by brutal hands and thrust forward, the cynosure of the murmuring crowd. The noose was carefully secured around her throat. Kyra's mouth went dry with an indescribable fear, her legs trembled, and she felt faint. Her ardent prayer was that she would be rendered unconscious.

But her entreaty went unheeded, and Kyra—the insistent demands of the restless throng echoing in her ears—was compelled to address her executioner in one final attempt to escape her fate.

"Please!" she beseeched him, raising her horror-filled eyes to the hooded man. "It truly was an accident. Won't you please help me?"

He responded by snatching the black hood off his head and pulling her roughly against him to claim her mouth in a passionate kiss. He released her abruptly and his cruel, mocking laughter was still echoing in Kyra's ears when the trapdoor beneath her feet gave way. Her shriek of terror was muffled by the din of the crowd, and the face of Devlin Cauldwell swam before her wide, staring eyes as she was swallowed by a merciful sea of darkness.

7

As Kyra stood alone on the back porch, she did not hear the creak of the unoiled gate to the courtyard; she was deep in her own distressed thoughts. But as her worries began to fade and her pulse gradually slackened, she was able to calm her overworked nerves. Even so, she could not find the courage to ease her hold on the railing, not trusting her unsteady legs to keep her from sinking to her knees.

Suddenly, Kyra sensed that she was no longer alone, and tensed as a large hand steadied her elbow while another patiently disengaged the fingers that gripped the railing. The next instant, Kyra turned to face the interloper, and she could not forestall a startled squeak when she beheld Devlin's handsome face curiously studying her in the moonlight. Her squeamish reaction was not unfounded, for his deep brown eyes sparkled with mischief, and save for the snowy whiteness of his shirt, he was clad entirely in black.

Kyra blinked wildly, hoping to eliminate the offensive vision, but knew her efforts were in vain when she heard his sardonic chortle. The initial shock of his appearance passed, and Kyra, shaking off his unwelcome grasp, took a guarded step backward. Indeed, she had to forcibly repel the cowardly instinct to turn tail and flee from him. Before she could think of a way to take her leave without appearing completely bereft of backbone, Devlin addressed her.

"Miss Raybourne, are you all right?" he began, his manner more phlegmatic than solicitous. "I saw you when I entered the garden and thought you looked distressed. You did not answer when I called, and when I came to offer my assistance, I saw that your face was white with terror. Won't you tell me what you've seen in Mother's garden to give you such a fright?"

"A snake!" She blurted the first thought that entered her mind. "I . . . I know it's silly, but I'm quite frightened of them."

"Then point out the nasty creature's direction, and I'll see to it," was Devlin's chivalrous rejoinder, though Kyra detected a taunting resonance in his deep voice.

"Oh, n-no," Kyra stammered faintly, lowering her eyes lest he suspect her of lying. "I should not like you to take the chance of being bitten and, besides, it will not be necessary. I watched him slither beneath the shrubbery." She gestured vaguely toward the courtyard. "I feel much safer now, thank you."

"I see," he murmured, thoughtfully rubbing his chin. "Perhaps I should alert the gardener to watch out for it. After all, we can't have him lurking at one of Mother's garden parties, can we?"

Despite the fact that the snake was a figment of her imagination, Kyra could not help but smile at the chaotic scene that came to mind. "No, I suppose not," she murmured, sidling toward the entrance to the house. Devlin, however, laid a firm hand on her wrist.

"What's this? Surely you don't mean to desert me so soon."

Kyra looked up in time to observe the playful twinkle in his eyes before it was replaced by a hard, unreadable expression she found far more disturbing. She shuddered and, praying that her companion did not sense her unease, rushed into an explanation.

"Mr. Cauldwell, as you well know, I have had a fatiguing day. I can well imagine the path our discourse would take, and I need time to compose myself before engaging you in a battle of wits."

"Then by all means, let us converse at once," Devlin crowed, a rakish smile curving his lips. "With a slight advantage, I may stand a sporting chance against your eloquent tongue," he said not unkindly, entwining her arm in his and escorting her down the steps to the courtyard.

"But—" she started to protest, suddenly very much aware of his nearness and the fact that she was alone with him in the secluded, moon-drenched garden.

"Ah, you're still bedeviled by thoughts of your pesky reptilian friend." Devlin chuckled in a way that made Kyra doubt he believed her. "You can depend upon me to protect you from him."

"And who is to protect me from you, Mr. Cauldwell?" The saucy question was out before Kyra thought to check it.

He guffawed, genuinely amused by her candor. "Your clever tongue has a sting to it despite your harrowing day. That will serve you well, for I anticipate a heated discussion. You may, however, allay your fears of ravishment, for even an infamous rogue such as I would not seduce a woman beneath his mother's bedroom window." He smiled down at her, an indolent lopsided grin that did not quite reach his eyes.

They strolled along the brick pathway in silence, each wondering about the other's thoughts and speculating on the outcome of the imminent tête-à-tête, until they came upon a stone bench in a corner of the garden, where Devlin motioned for Kyra to sit down.

Kyra made herself as comfortable as possible on the hard seat and, smoothing down her wide skirt, gestured for Devlin to share the bench with her. To her surprise, he accepted the invitation, but he seemed reluctant to begin the conversation. Devlin's reticence did not last long, however, for the sound of carriage wheels on the cobbled street just beyond the courtyard wall coaxed him from his reverie, and he suddenly turned to her.

"May I ask, Miss Raybourne, why you have chosen this particular time to fly into my eye?"

Kyra's puzzled expression clearly implied that his question was not what she had expected. "I beg your pardon?" she said, her brow puckering.

He noticed her confusion and, with a casual wave of his hand, explained, "Ah, I see you are not familiar with the expression. It was purportedly first used by some English king after a bug flew into his regal eye. I have taken the liberty to paraphrase the speech. It means, Miss Raybourne, why have you come to Savannah?"

"To fetch my brother. I intended to take him back to Charleston before Father returned from his business trip." She provided him with a brief account of Andrew's antics without mentioning her encounter with Clayton Fairchild.

"Sounds like quite a scamp," he commented, "but then, all young men sow a few oats before they settle down. Am I to assume you located him?"

"Yes, only . . ."

"Yes?"

"Everything went awry." Kyra sighed heavily. "First, Andrew refused to accompany me; then you came along to complicate matters." Kyra avoided his eyes as she voiced this sentiment. "If that wasn't enough to test the patience of a saint, Papa arrived unexpectedly and discovered that I was embroiled in a scandal. Now Papa has learned that Andrew ran off to Atlanta with some friends, conveniently removing himself from the situation so that Papa can focus all his attention on me," she muttered glumly.

It was on the tip of Devlin's tongue to suggest that she might be unfairly casting the blame on her brother; there was little doubt in his mind that hers was the more critical dilemma facing Colin Raybourne. Before he could voice this shrewd observation, however, Kyra continued, having taken exception to Devlin's earlier mention of the fly in his eye.

"While you find me to be an irritant in your eye, *you* have been a thorn in my side ever since our unfortunate encounter on the wharf yesterday morning!"

"That was bad of me," he agreed, an irrepressible gleam flickering in his eyes. "But what would you expect from a gentleman who unexpectedly found his arms filled with such . . . um . . . alluring bounty?" His eyes lowered to the swell of her breasts, enticingly bathed in moonlight.

"A *gentleman* would have behaved honorably," she responded curtly, and noting with dismay the direction of his gaze, she favored him with a look that plainly told him he was in no danger of being regarded as a gentleman.

With some difficulty, Devlin managed to avert his eyes, and she noted that the playful gleam was gone, supplanted by a haughty, scornful look that openly mocked her. "You're doubtless right; a gentleman would have engaged in all kinds of tedious activities."

Then as if anxious to lend substance to her judgment, Devlin withdrew a slender cheroot from his jacket and, without asking her leave, casually lit the cigar. "As you can plainly see, *I* am no gentleman. In fact, I am generally considered a rag-mannered scoundrel," he boasted, "certainly not suited for a gently bred young woman like you.

"Since you obviously have your heart set on a gentleman, I assume you won't have me and we can dispense with this preposterous charade," he concluded on a questioning note. He pretended to focus a contemplative eye on the starlit heavens, but a surreptitious glance at Kyra's lovely face confirmed his worst fear: Her father had convinced her that an immediate marriage to her defiler was the only way to salvage her good name.

Damn it all to hell! Devlin swore silently and, thrusting the cigar into his mouth, stood and began to pace about the garden.

Kyra observed his actions ruefully, realizing full well that he had expected her to be his salvation. Devlin's assumption was far from the mark; Kyra did not fear those gossipmongers who might besmirch her reputation. Had she not learned about the death of Clayton Fairchild, she would have resisted marriage to the bitter end. But the fact remained that she was a wanted criminal who needed a place to hide. What better refuge could she hope to find than an isolated tropical island?

It will only be for a short while, Kyra promised herself. *Just until I can think of a way to convince the authorities that the fire was a dreadful accident.* She glanced up at Devlin, who had ceased his pacing, and was not surprised to find his hostile glare fastened on her.

"So that's the way it's to be," he growled bitterly.

"I'm sorry," Kyra whispered, looking away, for she could not long endure his scowl. With a forlorn sigh, she added, "It would appear that neither of us has control of our destiny."

"Destiny!" he spat resentfully, discarding the cigar and crushing it beneath his boot in an impatient gesture. "I shudder to think what the future holds for me with you as my helpmate, Miss Raybourne. But we are at a crossroads, you and I, and must yield to the dictates of others.

"Well, I see no reason to prolong this ordeal any longer than necessary. Tomorrow is Sunday, but Mother is forever rattling on about her influence. Therefore, I shall present her with the fitting challenge of procuring us a license so that the ceremony can take place without delay. I've been away from Cauldurae far too long as it is. We shall wed Monday morning and set sail at once," he concluded, his face alive with raw determination now that the unhappy decision had been made.

He began to pace again while he informed Kyra of his recklessly formulated plans, but the disheartened expression that shadowed her pretty face gave him pause. "Is something wrong? I don't understand. I thought you were in agreement about all this."

"I am. It's just—" How could she explain to this stranger

that she had always envisioned a different kind of proposal from the man she would marry? Tears gathered at the corners of her eyes as she considered her hopeless predicament and the tiny droplets sparkled on the tips of her lashes when she again looked at him.

Devlin immediately guessed her thoughts, and a cynical smirk twisted his sensuous lips when he stepped near her. "I see," he said with disdain. "You had contemplated a *romantic* proposal from an enraptured beau.

"Well, no doubt you deserve one, but I cannot see how our bleak circumstances would be altered if I went down on my knee before you thus"—he knelt before her—"clutched your hands to my heart"—he pressed her hands to his chest in an exaggerated, passionate motion—"and proclaimed that you would make me the happiest of men if you would agree to be mine." He ended his taunt and would have released Kyra's hands had she not jerked them away.

The tears that had clouded her eyes vanished and were replaced by a fiery gleam of resolution. Kyra leaped to her feet, nearly toppling Devlin. He had barely enough time to regain his balance and rise before Kyra launched into battle.

"I did not mean to appear maudlin," she began, "but I am no more pleased with this arrangement than you are. I have consented to this . . . *travesty* to suit *my* needs, sir, not yours. I have listened to your suggestions as to how we should proceed with the . . . nuptials"—her throat constricted at the ludicrous notion—"and before you initiate your plans, I think you should be aware of my thoughts on the subject."

"Of course." He immediately adopted an air of sublime indifference, but Kyra would have been surprised to learn that Devlin's demeanor was merely a facade; he was curious to discover what the little spitfire had on her mind. With his arms folded across his chest and one eyebrow raised skeptically, he prompted in his most mellifluous voice, "By all means, have your say."

"Very well, then, this is what I propose." Kyra clasped her hands behind her back in a businesslike manner and, squaring her slim shoulders, faced him, looking far more confident than she felt. "I will marry you, manage your home, and be a loving and caring mother to your children, but—"

"Ah, yes, the obligatory conditions," Devlin drawled flippantly.

"*But,*" Kyra repeated and, though her voice remained steady, her gaze wavered uncertainly as she delivered the remainder of her homily, "we shall have a marriage of convenience." She suddenly developed a keen interest in the buttons that adorned his vest and focused her nervous stare in that direction while she awaited his reaction.

Devlin bristled at Kyra's words, and his smoldering brown eyes raked over her resentfully. So he was to be fettered to another female who would shun his advances. Swallowing the bile that rose in his throat, he placed a stern finger beneath her chin and forced her to look at him.

"Is this your way of telling me that you do not intend to share my bed?" he demanded bluntly.

"A gentleman would have phrased it more politely, but yes, that is what I am telling you." Kyra held his unnerving gaze for several moments; had she not been so distraught by the day's events, she would have noticed that the frown that marred those provocative eyes went beyond simple bruised masculine pride.

But Kyra could vividly recall the passion-filled night spent in the arms of this volatile man. He had been drunk beyond all reason—a total stranger—and yet he had evoked a rapturous response from her that still made her blush scarlet at the memory. Devlin, fortunately, had no recollection of the encounter. But she was not foolhardy enough to imagine that he would be so incapacitated a second time, and if he could drive her to such frenzied abandon when he was inebriated, just think—

No! She immediately expelled the unsettling thought from her head. Above all things, she must not think of that!

"Good night, Mr. Cauldwell," she said abruptly, her voice trembling despite her attempt to appear nonchalant. She had taken but two steps toward the house, however, when he caught her wrist in an iron grip and whirled her around to face him.

"A moment or two more of your time, if you please," he drawled in a way that clearly indicated he did not care whether or not it pleased her. "Since you are obviously a woman who does not mince words, perhaps you will appreciate my candor. You are to be my wife—a dubious honor that gratifies neither of us, but my wife nonetheless. And as your husband, I promise you this." He pulled her against his rock-hard chest and, clasping her about the waist with one hand, he forced her head up with the other so that they could exchange glares in the moonlight. "*If* I decide to warm your bed, you'll damn well welcome me into it or be prepared to suffer the consequences!"

This declaration hung between them like an ominous threat. Kyra, angered by his arrogance, prepared a rebuttal. Her bitter retort died on her lips, however, when she saw the knowing gleam in Devlin's eyes. Feeling suddenly vulnerable, she struggled for her freedom, to no avail; he held on to her steadfastly. His chuckle made her shiver, but whether her anxiety stemmed from fear or anticipation, Kyra could not tell.

Common sense ultimately prevailed. "Let me go at once!" she demanded.

"But we are betrothed," he protested smoothly. "Surely you won't be so heartless as to deny your fiancé a token kiss to seal our engagement."

Kyra tensed, expecting him to be vindictive and brutal, and that was Devlin's intention. There was no time like the present, he decided, to initiate his plan to frighten the girl back to her father. His purpose had been to teach the sharp-tongued female a lesson, but the instant his lips touched hers, his stratagem quickly went awry.

Kyra discovered that if she entwined her fingers about Devlin's neck and tilted her head at a certain angle, she might find his kiss pleasant—quite pleasant indeed. She parted her lips ever so slightly as a soft moan of contentment escaped and promptly found that Devlin's tongue had skillfully maneuvered its way inside to sample the sweetness behind her lips. Kyra stiffened at first, for she was still unaccustomed to being kissed in such a way, but the gentle motion of his tongue against hers gradually coaxed her to relax, and she began to return the caress with a shyness that produced a tortured groan from Devlin.

She felt a twinge of disappointment a moment later when he removed his lips from hers, but he did not release her from the grasp that held her against the length of his lean, hard body. For this, Kyra was thankful, since she did not trust her quaking knees to support her. Devlin seemed reluctant to release her at all and, instead began to press feather-soft kisses along her cheek while one hand slid inside the bodice of her gown to boldly fondle her soft flesh.

Hearing her startled intake of breath, Devlin kissed the bruise on her cheek and recaptured her lips before she could protest. As his tongue deftly sought hers, his hand massaged the sensitive peak of one breast with maddening skill until it rose brazenly against his palm.

Their sighs of pleasure mingled, and Kyra abandoned herself to the potent sensation of Devlin's hand against her breast. She might have succumbed once again to his masterful seduction had he not chosen that moment to murmur against the silken column of Kyra's throat, "So you will not have me in your bed?" He chuckled huskily, his lips moving to nibble at an earlobe. "I think perhaps you spoke prematurely, for you promise to be a most satisfying bedmate, Miss Raybourne."

Kyra managed to extricate herself from his stifling

embrace, but the angry denial she longed to hurl at him would not come forward on her tongue. After all, how could she deny that she had been a willing party to his kiss?

As her eyes were drawn to his face, Kyra was overwhelmed with the realization that she would soon be at the mercy of this insufferable man and subject to his every whim. She nearly choked at the thought of a lifetime spent dodging Devlin's lecherous advances, and she gathered up her heavy skirts in trembling hands. Without a parting word or a backward glance, she sprinted past him to seek the sanctuary of her room.

Had she glanced over her shoulder, however, Kyra would have been surprised to find that a glib expression no longer occupied Devlin's handsome face. Instead, a meditative grimace wrinkled his austere brow as he watched that splendidly provocative creature disappear inside the house. The normally detached Devlin Cauldwell had been quite affected by that tempestuous embrace as well.

After the highly emotional scene in the courtyard, Kyra found sleep elusive. She dozed fitfully, and her fleeting moments of slumber were haunted by a daunting pair of sable-brown eyes and a deep, cold chuckle. The faint, flickering shadows of the coming sunrise had begun to filter through the window when Kyra flung the bedcovers aside in frustration. Thinking that an invigorating ride might revive her dwindling spirits, she walked straight to the clothespress to select a riding ensemble.

She did not summon Biddie to assist her, thinking that the servant would only attempt to discourage her from embarking on such a capricious jaunt. Instead, Kyra rummaged through the press for something suitable to wear. Biddie had not thought to pack any of Kyra's riding habits, and so she was forced to settle on an ordinary walking dress. The gown was thoroughly unfit for riding, but the hour was early and Kyra doubted anyone would see her.

She reached for the dress, but as she tried to remove the garment, it became entangled, prompting Kyra to investigate the clothespress. Indifferent curiosity grew into genuine interest when her exploration uncovered a Cauldwell family portrait.

"How odd," Kyra muttered. "Why would Mrs. Cauldwell store a family heirloom in such an unlikely place?"

Her interest now fully aroused, Kyra positioned the painting so that the images were illuminated by the candlelight. She immediately recognized three of the four likenesses that an accomplished artist had rendered. In the painting, Amanda Cauldwell sat on a rose-colored satin chair with three children around her. Even though the canvas had been painted several years ago, Kyra had little difficulty recognizing her husband-to-be. Even as a child, she noticed, Devlin had possessed an awe-inspiring air—not to mention the most captivating pair of brown eyes Kyra had ever seen.

Kyra ignored that unbidden thought as she settled her gaze on Emily, who resembled an angel dressed in pink frills and lace. But a question furrowed Kyra's brow when her eyes moved to the remaining figure in the portrait. He looked a year or two older than Devlin and was less powerfully built, but the distinct family resemblance led Kyra to believe him to be Devlin and Emily's brother.

She thought it strange that no mention had been made of another Cauldwell son, but with recent events so trying for all those concerned, it might have slipped everyone's mind. With a shake of her head, Kyra started to return the portrait to its storage place, but her eyes were drawn once more to the unknown youth. There was something sad about the young man, and Kyra's heart swelled with sympathy for him.

She stood thus engrossed until the crowing of a rooster in the distance reminded her that precious time was slipping away, and she hurriedly replaced the painting. She donned her gown and, after tying back her heavy tresses, left the mansion without disturbing the rest of the household.

She had not given much thought to preparing a mount for her outing; she was merely enthralled with the notion of enjoying a few carefree moments away from the trouble-filled mansion. But as luck would have it, one of the grooms in Amanda's service came to her aid. The boy was just returning to the stables from an early morning visit to the outhouse and was in the process of hitching up his suspenders when he came upon Kyra. She explained her desire for a ride and the boy promptly readied a mount.

Kyra held the feisty mare to a sedate pace until they cleared the city limits. But when they reached the open road, she gave the animal its head, and horse and rider were soon bounding along the roadway as one. In no time at all, the exhilarating sensation of the wind in her face and hair began to soothe Kyra, and for a brief time she forgot her problems.

She continued to urge the animal to a rigorous gallop until, sensing that the mare's stamina was beginning to wane, Kyra tempered their pace and guided the horse off the public road and through a stand of trees to a clearing beside the river. There she coaxed the mare to a halt and slid from the saddle, permitting the animal to graze as she strolled along the riverbank. Kyra's wandering led her to the foot of a gigantic oak tree, where she sat down to revel in the tranquillity of this place. Her mind temporarily at peace, Kyra was lulled to sleep by the gentle morning breezes and the softly rippling river.

The pounding of hooves on the roadway eventually jolted her from her dreams. Thus awakened from a heady slumber, Kyra was momentarily disoriented, but her confusion swiftly changed to apprehension when she heard heavy footfalls coming toward her. Kyra lay on her side facing the river, and just as she pressed the palms of her hands against the grass to push herself up to confront the interloper, a pair of dust-covered boots appeared in front of her, halting any further movement.

Kyra's breath caught in her throat as her eyes traveled up along a pair of lean, muscular thighs to the powerful hands that clutched a leather riding crop. But when her gaze spanned the commanding torso to encounter a pair of virulent brown eyes, her misgivings vanished.

"Oh, it's only you." Kyra breathed a sigh of relief. "For a moment, I feared I might be in danger." Again she made as if to rise from her subservient position, but Devlin clasped her shoulders in a viselike grip and roughly hauled her to her feet.

"I suggest that you not abandon your fears prematurely," he advised grimly.

Just when Kyra thought that he was about to mete out some horrible punishment, he abruptly released her and stalked away to pace along the riverbank, impatiently tapping the riding crop against one brawny thigh. It occurred to Kyra that he dared not trust himself to speak lest he be tempted to do her a mischief, so she tactfully held her tongue while Devlin grappled with his raging temper. Her reprieve proved brief, as the formidable though considerably more subdued gentleman soon returned to loom over her.

"You realize, Kyra," he said, addressing her by her given name for the first time, "that I have two small children who require almost constant supervision. I can but pray this morning's escapade is not an indication of how our life will progress once we reach Cauldurae, else I shall be obliged to employ a nanny to watch over you as well," he informed her, a sarcastic inflection tainting his voice. "Have you any idea of the commotion that ensued when we all gathered around the breakfast table to find that you were not among us?"

Kyra had listened to his restrained tirade in mild amusement until this reminder that her impromptu ride had caused others to be concerned for her safety, and she was instantly contrite. "I'm sorry. I did not mean to be a bother; I just needed a little time alone. Had I not fallen asleep, I would have returned before anyone missed me." As she started to move toward her mount, Devlin laid a restraining hand on her arm, causing her to regard him questioningly.

"Did you give no thought to your fate had I not been the one to discover you in your charming state of repose?"

"No, I only wanted to——"

"Be alone," Devlin finished for her. "Yes, I can sympathize with your feelings," he added cryptically, his expression thoughtful as he considered her upturned face. "There is still time to change your mind if that is your inclination," he offered casually, hoping she had not detected the eager lilt that crept into his voice.

Kyra felt an unexplainable pang of remorse for this rogue who had caused her so much grief, and for one fleeting moment the thought of releasing him from his obligation flitted through her head. But the very next image she saw involved the lifeless form of Clayton Fairchild, herself with a noose around her neck, and a man shrouded in black, and she knew what her response must be.

"I'm sorry, Mr. Cauldwell," she whispered hoarsely, lowering her eyes to avoid his stare, but if he was disappointed with her reply, Devlin was not about to allow her the pleasure of observing his chagrin.

The tapping of the leather crop against his thigh was the only indication that he had heard her softly spoken words. With a melancholy sigh, Devlin turned and strode toward his horse, calling over his shoulder as he departed, "Since you are determined to rivet yourself to me, I suggest you begin addressing me by my Christian name. I don't usually concern myself with others' opinions, but I confess I might find it a trifle embarrassing if the servants questioned why the new mistress of Cauldurae was ignorant of her husband's name." He cast a glance in her direction and was irritated to discover that she had not budged an inch.

"Come along, Kyra. When I left, Mother was insisting she could not make wedding arrangements on such short notice. I'm confident, however, that she will contrive to do so," he said with a wry twist of his mouth, "for I informed her that I shall leave tomorrow with or without my bride. It is imperative that I return to Cauldurae immediately," he added in a serious undertone, a worried frown briefly crossing his brow. But his expression changed to one of annoyance when he realized that Kyra had made no move to follow him.

"Damn it, woman, are you hard of hearing? I said we must make haste." He beckoned Kyra forward so that he could assist her to her mount, but Kyra's shyly murmured question caught him unawares, and he momentarily lost sight of his purpose.

"What happened to your wife?"

The query was as much of a surprise to the person who had voiced it as to the one at whom it was directed, but Kyra was consumed by an overwhelming desire to learn more about this man she was being made to marry, and thinking it a reasonable question, she had not checked it. Yet as the imposing man slowly turned and, with measured strides, returned to stand in front of her, Kyra cursed her impulsive tongue.

He gave off a commanding essence as he towered over her, but his expression was unreadable and his voice oddly bereft of emotion when he spoke. "So, your curiosity has been piqued at last, and you would know something about your husband-to-be. I suppose that is only natural."

Devlin focused his contemplative gaze on a stand of trees that spanned the crest of a distant hill, and just when Kyra thought he had forgotten her existence, he shrugged in nonchalant resignation and favored her with a cynical grin. "Which version of the tale would you care to hear?"

"What do you mean?"

"Merely that the 'official' report states that Lynette died of an accidental drowning. You see, my foolhardy wife took a small craft out during a treacherous thunderstorm. The boat capsized, and she perished," he explained perfunctorily in a dull monotone as he thoughtfully considered the back of one sun-browned hand. "There are those on the island, however, who contend that I did away with her." A smile of inestimable pleasure spread across Devlin's face as he observed Kyra's horrified reaction to this disclosure. "I thought that would get your attention," he added with a wicked chuckle.

"Why would anyone say such a thing?" she blurted, her eyes wide with astonishment.

"Perhaps it had something to do with the fact that I threatened to kill my wife on any number of occasions," he replied offhandedly.

"And *did* you . . . murder her?" Kyra asked, valiantly trying to maintain an indifferent air.

"Now, I would hardly make such an admission to you, would I?" He barked in amusement before his tone became abruptly subdued, and he continued bluntly, "The truth is, my wife committed suicide. Lynette was not a good swimmer, and she knew nothing of boats. You see, Kyra"—his voice grew hard and there was a mix of hurt, guilt, and anger in the gaze he turned on her—"the simple truth is that Lynette preferred death to living with me. Perhaps you should reconsider your decision before it is too late and you find yourself contemplating a similar fate."

Devlin continued to regard her beautiful face, looking for some sign of disgust at what he had told her. He had anticipated any number of reactions, but when Kyra slowly lifted her hand to compassionately stroke his cheek, he was genuinely surprised.

Kyra experienced a similar sensation, but she could not control her actions; she was inexplicably drawn to him. The tale of his first wife had been difficult for him to relate, she realized, though he would have been loath to make such an admission. But the anguish was plainly written on his face, and Kyra had felt compelled to smooth away the lines that distorted his features.

"I'm so very sorry for you," she whispered gently.

"Don't be. I am well rid of her," Devlin snapped. "I'd long since grown bored with her, and I daresay that if I had to relive those times, I would have sent her back to her family in France long before her tragic demise."

Not for an instant did he consider telling Kyra that he had been sorely shaken by his first wife's death. He did not understand what had prompted Kyra to express such sympathy, but he could not truthfully say that her interruption had been unwelcome. For Devlin was acutely aware of her soft scent, the bright color of her eyes, and the enticing beauty of her upturned face. All of these combined to swathe her in a vulnerable aura that almost persuaded Devlin to throw caution to the wind and pull the bewitching woman into his arms to kiss her sensuous mouth, which was begging him to do so.

But the image of another alluring beauty wheedled its way into his thoughts. Lynette's philandering had schooled him well in the ways of women—they were not to be trusted. He would not give Kyra the satisfaction of knowing he could be tempted by her charms. If he decided to take her, it would be on his terms—to satisfy his desire or to frighten her back to her father. He would never fall victim to her feminine wiles.

Aware of the tension in the air between them, yet completely unaware of her narrow escape, Kyra endeavored to make light of the moment. "I see, and do you deal so harshly with everything that bores you?"

"Yes," was his prompt and unequivocal response, "and I am frequently bored, so you are forewarned," he concluded on a menacing note, and sensing Kyra's reluctance to comment on his candor, Devlin took advantage of her indecision by placing his hand under her elbow and coaxing her toward the horses.

"Are there any other dark, lurking secrets you would like to know about?" Having asked the question in jest, Devlin was genuinely confounded by her response.

"Yes. Who is the boy in the picture?"

Devlin halted abruptly in his tracks. "Boy? Picture?" he repeated hollowly, an odd inflection in his voice.

Kyra felt a sudden chill, despite the morning sun that warmed her like a blanket. "I came across a family portrait quite by chance," she explained, though she knew that he no longer listened to her; he was transported to some distant memory in his mind. "I thought perhaps he might be your brother," she offered weakly, her voice trailing off.

Kyra was not encouraged by the dark scowl that crossed Devlin's face when he next looked at her, causing her to shrink away from him. "Must all women be alike? Busybodies, the lot of them," he muttered to no one in particular, then said gruffly, "Yes, the boy in the picture is—or rather *was*—my brother. Your snooping, however unintentional, has led you to a subject that I do not care to talk about—with you or anyone else," he informed her stiffly. "Suffice to say that he was my older brother; his name was Gareth, and he is dead—no!" He threw up a warning hand to forestall the question that he read in Kyra's eyes. "I am adamant about this, Kyra. It is not a topic I care to discuss," he cautioned her.

With that, Devlin hoisted Kyra into the saddle and instructed her to follow him to the highway. They made the return trip to Savannah in virtual silence, and though thoughts of Devlin's brother did intrigue Kyra for a time, they did not plague her for long. For as they approached the Cauldwell mansion, Kyra was reminded of her impending fate, and all other considerations promptly flew from her head.

PART II

~

The Tempest

8

Less than a week following her ill-fated excursion up the Savannah River, Kyra again found herself on the deck of a yacht, her gaze focused on the distant shoreline. Her perturbed expression that fateful day did not begin to compare with the look of utter desolation that now darkened it. Days earlier Kyra's thoughts had been dominated by Andrew and his contretemps, whereas now her musings were riveted on her recent wedding and the disheartening state of her young life.

Amanda Cauldwell had managed to complete the wedding preparations—procuring a marriage license, recruiting a minister, and having one of Emily's elegant dresses hastily altered to serve as a wedding gown. The ceremony was attended by the couple's immediate family, Biddie, and a few Cauldwell servants. And much to Kyra's dismay, it took place in the courtyard not far from the spot where Devlin's passionate embrace had awakened her to her folly in thinking that she could expect him to grant her request for a loveless union.

The garden was in full bloom and made an enchanting setting for the "romantic" ritual, but the circumstances surrounding this travesty of a ceremony so haunted Kyra that she barely paid any heed to the minister's tedious recitation of the wedding vows. Such was the depth of her reverie that, during a critical point in the proceedings,

Devlin had been forced to give his bride's arm a pinch to remind her that her undivided attention was required.

Following the whirlwind service, the principals adjourned to the dining room to partake of a wedding breakfast that had been hurriedly, though superbly, prepared by Amanda's kitchen staff. And if anyone noticed the grimace on the minister's face as he watched the newly wedded couple with frank skepticism, no one commented on it. Had anyone bothered to consult him, he would have told them that in his twenty-five years of service to the Lord he had never joined a more inimical pair in wedlock.

The groom had not even thought to provide a ring for his bride, an oversight that resulted in confusion and raised voices until Devlin finally removed his signet ring and slid it onto Kyra's finger to pacify the outraged onlookers. But it had proved too large for her, and rather than risk losing the ring and incurring her husband's wrath, she had returned it after the ceremony, an act that did not go unnoticed by the stunned clergyman. The minister was still shaking his head in wonder when he took his leave.

Kyra was unable to do justice to the lavish array of foods that had been prepared in her honor—the eggs tasted like sawdust, and the sumptuous pastry fillings looked curdled and unappetizing. The unpalatable meal ended when Devlin, having made quick work of his food, informed his bride that they would depart within the half-hour.

When she had absorbed this grim news, Kyra excused herself and made her way up the curved staircase to her room to change from her wedding gown into a traveling dress. The remainder of her meager belongings, along with Biddie and the children, had already been dispatched to Devlin's yacht. So, with a final melancholy glance in the mirror, Kyra had resigned herself to her fate and descended the stairs to bid farewell to her father and the only life she had ever known.

Kyra lifted her hand to wipe away the tears that had

begun to trickle down her face as she recalled her father's tender good-bye. She could still feel his firm grip on her wrist as he held her away from him to address a parting word of caution to Devlin.

"Take care of my little magpie, son," was all Kyra had heard before the men moved aside to conduct their conversation in private. Afterward, Devlin had helped her into the open landaulet, and they sped to the harbor where his yacht lay at anchor. Colin, Amanda, and Emily had followed in a second open carriage and remained on the wharf until the *Windjammer* was under sail.

Kyra had not immediately sought out the comfort of her cabin, preferring instead to stand by the rail and stare plaintively at the tiny spot on the distant horizon that was her father. She continued her vigil long after the port of Savannah had disappeared from view, and it was not until the vessel had left the mouth of the river and headed out to sea that Devlin exhibited any real concern for Kyra's welfare.

He was aware of the watch she had maintained since boarding the *Windjammer*, but he had been preoccupied with getting the yacht under sail, and a good amount of time had passed before he felt it was safe to turn the vessel over to his men and devote his attention to Kyra. She was standing in the same spot, and he knew she must be exhausted. Not only had she withstood the rigors of their hasty marriage, but she had also been standing in the sweltering July sun for some time with only a bonnet for protection.

Not that he harbored any great affection for the girl; Devlin's motivation was purely selfish. If Kyra continued to be so reckless, she would surely succumb to heat prostration. And the very last thing the reluctant bridegroom wanted was to be saddled with an indisposed female on the journey home. With this thought in mind, he strode across the deck to stand behind her.

"Kyra," he said sharply. When she did not respond, he placed his sun-bronzed hands on her shoulders and turned her to face him. "It's time you went to the cabin. You've been out in this treacherous sun far too long, and you will become unwell if you continue to do so."

"I prefer to remain here," she mumbled laconically and made as if to resume her former stance, but Devlin would not permit her to turn away.

Devlin was moved by the sadness that distorted her pretty face. Unthinkingly, he stroked her cheek with the back of his hand, and his voice was unusually soft and tender when he spoke.

"I realize you're feeling downcast, but you will see your father again. In fact, I expect him to visit Cauldurae in the not too distant future to make sure I'm not mistreating his 'little magpie,'" he added dryly and, dropping his hand from her cheek, tugged her toward the narrow companionway.

But Kyra was in no mood to be cajoled, and she angrily pulled away from him. "How can you possibly understand what I am feeling at this moment? I'm utterly and completely miserable!" she shrieked at him, oblivious to the crew members who observed the proceedings with interest. Kyra nearly gave in to the pent-up sobs that swelled in her bosom and asked defiantly, "Why should it matter to you if I choose to while away the afternoon on deck?"

"Under normal circumstances, my pretty and infuriatingly obstinate wife, it would not concern me in the least." He flicked a speck of dust from his sleeve to demonstrate his disinterest. "Your health stands to suffer from your mulish behavior, however, and I assure you that I would not make a congenial nursemaid during the course of this voyage.

"Now, will you allow me to escort you to your quarters like the gentleman you know me to be, or must I toss you over my shoulder and carry you below like a bundle of cargo?" A wicked gleam began to sparkle in his dark eyes as he contemplated the alternative, and he leaned forward to whisper, "I'll allow that such a tactic might serve as a prelude to more . . . ardent endeavors, but I had not thought you yet prepared to embark upon that marital path." His sensuous eyes slowly lowered to skim over her trim figure, returning to feast upon the voluptuous swell of her bosom.

"I'm not!" Kyra snapped and stepped away from him; his nearness had provoked a reaction in her that she did not like. "I have reconsidered your suggestion," she stated more calmly, her composure restored now that she had placed some distance between them, "and have decided to repair to my quarters and lie down for a while before dinner. I suddenly feel quite weary."

She held up a hand to dissuade him when she realized he intended to accompany her. "You needn't trouble yourself. I'll manage, thank you." Without waiting for his response, Kyra hurried toward the companionway, completely unaware of the appreciative gaze that followed the enticing sway of her skirts.

Despite Kyra's resolve to doze for an hour or so before facing Devlin's maddeningly distracting physique across the dinner table, her efforts proved fruitless. Every time she closed her eyes, her mind was filled with the likeness of the man. It troubled Kyra more than a little that she was unable to instantly dismiss Devlin from her thoughts—but the plain fact was that she could not.

The most insignificant occurrence reminded her of him. The solid, powerful motion of the ship as it cut through the ocean's current was reminiscent of his lithe, athletic stride. And Kyra found it ironic that Devlin had thought her in danger of being felled by the sun's rays when in fact she had felt far more threatened by the rapturous flame glowing in his brown eyes than by the scalding July sun.

Even now the recollection of his intimate perusal of her womanly figure sent a heady flush to her cheeks, and she grew uncomfortably warm at the memory. It was as though she could feel those piercing orbs searing her flesh, as if Devlin could strip her bare with a single passionate glance. Completely shaken and feeling considerably more confused by her reaction to him than she cared to admit, Kyra abandoned her efforts to sleep and climbed out of the narrow berth.

Thinking she would change from her wrinkled gown into a suitable dinner dress, Kyra stepped across the floor to where the crewmen had placed her portmanteau. Biddie had been given the responsibility of looking after the children during the voyage, thereby leaving Kyra to fend for herself. Not that she considered the inconvenience bothersome; Kyra much preferred tending to her own needs to being subjected to Biddie's inquisitions.

Biddie had readily accepted the news that she was to be uprooted to accompany her mistress to a West Indian island. The servant looked upon the excursion as the beginning of a great adventure, an attitude that escaped her mistress, who viewed the future with considerably less enthusiasm.

With a small sigh, Kyra selected a gown, laid it across the bed to press out the wrinkles, and started to remove her crumpled traveling ensemble. But in the next instant, Kyra lamented the absence of her very efficient maid, as the yacht suddenly lurched sideways, pitching her off-balance and causing her to become hopelessly entangled in the dress.

Kyra stood in the center of the cabin in a state of dishabille, with her skirts above her head and her arms flailing wildly as she endeavored to recover from her plight. But her efforts merely served to worsen her absurd situation, as her frantic movements caused the lace-trimmed bodice to become ensnarled with the pins that anchored her painstakingly styled coiffure. Mercilessly ensnared and frustrated with her thwarted attempts at freedom, Kyra unthinkingly sent her toe crashing into the bed frame. This induced a squeal of genuine pain, and she hopped and pranced about the cabin in an effort to assuage her smarting foot.

Kyra heard the click of the door and, assuming that Biddie had come to inquire after her or request her assistance with the children, breathed a sigh of relief. "Thank heavens you've come!" she cried. "I cannot manage even the simplest task on my own. Help me out of this infernal gown!"

"With pleasure," came the reply from Devlin, who stood there, his broad shoulders resting against the closed door, taking in the enchanting scene before him.

Kyra's instinct was to hurl any number of unpleasantries at his head, but she grudgingly swallowed the first oath that sprang to mind. Like it or not, Devlin was her only hope of deliverance from this humiliating situation; yet her great pride prevailed, and she refused to humble herself by requesting his assistance. With a disgruntled huff, Kyra turned her back to him and resumed her struggle with the dress.

"Stubborn, willful wench," Devlin muttered, pushing himself upright, and crossing the room. He grasped Kyra's shoulders and whirled her around. Devlin was finding it increasingly difficult to maintain a straight face, so great was the urge to laugh, especially when he beheld the exasperated face that peeked out at him from amid a wreath of crumpled lace and muslin.

"Tell me, Kyra," Devlin began glibly, managing to suppress the chuckle that swelled in his chest, "is this some sort of ritualistic dance that Charlestonian brides are instructed to perform for their husbands on their wedding night?"

Kyra's irritation knew no bounds by this time, but her arms were growing stiff and weary from being held at such an awkward angle, and she knew that she must behave rationally. There would be time to bandy words with him once she was in a more advantageous position.

With a genuinely pleading lilt in her voice she said, "Do stop being ridiculous, Mr. Cauldwell." She turned away from him again. "I'm terribly uncomfortable. Won't you set aside your boorish witticisms long enough to help me?"

Devlin's next maneuver filled Kyra with chagrin; he circled her waist with his muscular arms and pulled her against his hard body. Even through the weighty material of her gown, Kyra could feel the warmth of his breath caressing her cheek and neck, and she shivered in spite of her determination to ignore him.

"I could perhaps be persuaded to give you some assistance," he drawled slowly. "I must, however, make a request prior to the execution of this chivalrous deed."

"What?" Kyra asked tentatively, bristling in anticipation of his request."

"My name," was his unexpected response.

"What?" she repeated incredulously.

"You have been Mr. Cauldwelling me to death for the past two days," he answered and, pulling her closer, he added, "I want to hear my name from your lips, Kyra, else I shall have to explain to your father how his little magpie perished while divesting herself of her clothing. A trifle awkward, to be sure, but who is to say what misfortune might befall a blushing bride on her wedding night?" Then, more seriously, he whispered, "Say it."

Kyra could feel the tension in the sinewy arms that held her to him, but she attributed the sudden giddy sensation that swept over her to the fact that she was near the point of collapsing from lack of air. Self-preservation being her sole motivation, Kyra brushed her wounded pride aside and muttered his name aloud.

"Again," Devlin prompted, and this time, her response was more to his liking.

"Devlin!" she cried angrily. "Stop behaving like a brute

and help me. I'm suffocating, and you cannot imagine how ghastly it feels to be held in your arms."

"Really? This may surprise you, Kyra," Devlin drawled smugly, "but a number of women would welcome my caresses."

"They are welcome to them" was the muffled retort from beneath the folds of crinkled muslin.

Her words, intended as a blow to his ego, clearly fell far from the mark as he chortled heartily. Turning her once more to face him, Devlin commenced the diverting task of liberating Kyra from her self-imposed prison. As he carefully disengaged the gown from the hairpins so as not to damage the garment's exquisite lace or wrench her hair, Devlin continued with his taunt.

"May I be the first to compliment you on such liberal thinking? I daresay not many of your sex would grant their husbands leave to seek comfort in the arms of another woman. However, I think there may come a time, Mrs. Cauldwell," he offered thoughtfully, "when you will regret your magnanimous gesture.

"You'll grow weary of lying abed alone and your natural curiosity about the rapturous delights men and women experience in the throes of passion will begin to gnaw at you, causing you to toss and turn in your lonely bed. And then . . ." His ministrations completed, Devlin yanked the sadly mistreated gown over her head and let it fall to the floor between them. "Then," he continued, his voice husky with desire as he permitted his eyes to roam freely over Kyra's shapely curves, "I shall derive inestimable pleasure from introducing you to all the wondrous mysteries of lovemaking. The process will no doubt require many, many lessons."

"Never!" Kyra backed away, thinking he intended to match his actions to his threat. She was relieved when Devlin merely walked to the door.

"Never, you say?" He paused at the threshold. "We shall

see. After all, you displayed a similar reluctance to call me Devlin, but you were brought around with minimal persuasion, and with such charming results. I'm certain my name has never sounded quite so melodious." He eased the door ajar and was about to take his leave when Kyra's bold denunciation made him pause.

"Devlin." Kyra rolled the name on her tongue. "It suits you. That's precisely what you are—a heartless, unfeeling *devil*! I wish . . . I wish I'd never met you!" she cried bitterly.

Devlin remained silent a moment longer, pensively considering Kyra's impassioned speech. From his tense expression, Kyra expected him to hurl a vile oath at her. She did not, however, anticipate his wry retort. "Yes, well, this is what comes of a young lady hurling herself at a gentleman's head, be it from a swing or a yacht." Having achieved his purpose—Kyra was so taken aback by his candid observation that she could not find her tongue to lash out at him—Devlin exited the chamber.

The evening meal progressed smoothly—as smoothly as could have been expected with two small, excitable children in attendance, but at least Devlin did not provoke Kyra. Indeed, he seemed blissfully unaware of the proceedings, engrossed as he was in reading some nautical journal. He glanced up only occasionally to instruct a servant to refill his glass or to correct the children's table manners. It was on the tip of Kyra's tongue to inform Devlin that his were sadly wanting, but she bit back the remark in order to avoid another squabble.

With a shrug of resignation, Kyra favored the youngsters with the most cheerful smile she could muster and focused her attention on her food. Devlin took his leave of them immediately following the meal, and Kyra accompanied Biddie and the children back to their cabin so that she might become better acquainted with her ready-made family.

Kyra did not know what sort of reception she might receive from the children. She realized it must have been perplexing for Nicholas and Sarah to suddenly have her thrust upon them as their stepmother—Lord only knew she was floundering in a similar state of confusion. Kyra also knew that it was natural to expect a certain amount of aloofness until they grew accustomed to having her around, but in no way was she prepared for the look of pure mistrust that Nicholas bestowed upon her when she followed them into the cabin.

"What do *you* want?" he demanded in an angry little voice.

Kyra was taken aback by his verbal assault, but she quickly masked her startled expression and offered the child a warm smile, responding softly, "I thought we could visit and get to know each other. I'm to be your new mama, after all."

"My mama's in heaven," Nicholas replied.

"Mama hebben," echoed the little girl, whom Biddie still held in her arms.

Kyra released a disheartened breath; this was not going to be easy. "I know, Nicholas, and I'm truly sorry that she can no longer be with you. But I *am* here, and I want so much to be your friend," she whispered affectionately, before turning her attention to Sarah.

Thinking that the little girl might be more easily swayed than her surly brother, Kyra stepped over to Biddie and held her hands out to the child. "Won't you come sit with me, Sarah? You could introduce me to your dolly, and I could tell you a bedtime story," she offered temptingly.

Kyra saw the myriad emotions that played across Sarah's face. The little girl clearly longed to accept her offer, but a glance in her brother's direction promptly banished the notion. With a saddened heart, Kyra saw Sarah's eager expression wither as she jerked away, giving her head a determined shake as though convincing herself of the decision as well.

Kyra did not miss the look the two children exchanged; they were obviously very close. Indeed, all they had was each other; while it was clear that Devlin did not mistreat his children, neither did he lavish attention upon them. It was not likely that Sarah would risk losing the affection of the one person in this world on whom she could depend.

Poor darlings, Kyra thought. They had been through so much in their young lives—losing their mother to a violent death, being ignored by the father they both adored, being stolen away from their home by their grandmother, and now they were embroiled in a bizarre custody dispute. It was little wonder that they regarded Kyra with such mistrust.

"Very well," she said resignedly. "You are tired. We'll postpone our acquaintance session for another time."

"You don't understand—we don't want you!" Nicholas blurted.

"Not want you," Sarah parroted her brother.

The barb stung, but Kyra was determined that Nicholas would never know how easily he could upset her. Therefore it was with a stern yet gentle tone that she next addressed the boy. "You are nevertheless stuck with me, and we must somehow contrive to make the best of this situation."

She turned to make her way toward the door. "I'll leave you in Biddie's care and we can begin anew tomorrow, for I believe I will like both of you very much, and I think you could grow to like me, too, if you will give me a chance," Kyra said in parting. She paused in the doorway to see if her words would elicit a response from the boy, but when he made no reply, she moved to exit the cabin.

"Wait!" Nicholas called. "What are we s'posed to call you?"

Kyra regarded the defiant little face, which was so like his father's, for several seconds before replying. "I don't know. I haven't given it much thought," she answered truthfully. "What would you like to call me?"

"Don't know," Nicholas responded gloomily before shoving his hands in his pockets and giving her a disinterested shrug.

"Well, you could call me Kyra, or perhaps Mama Kyra," she suggested casually, praying that Nicholas would not detect the hopeful lilt in her voice. "The decision will be yours. Sleep well, little ones," she called in farewell, and as she closed the door behind her, Sarah's cries of "Mama Keewa" echoed in her ears.

The smile that those delightful words brought to Kyra's lips was short-lived. Once in the corridor, she found herself faced with an even greater dilemma—Devlin's unexplained detachment from his children. Kyra released a heavy sigh as this fact wormed its way into her head, for she understood her enigmatic husband enough to know that he would not appreciate any charges she might level at him regarding his treatment of Nicholas and Sarah.

Kyra likewise knew that Devlin would interpret any advice she might offer as interference; therefore, she could not leap headlong into the fray with him—her strategy must be carefully planned. The frown that distorted her lovely features became more intense, and her head began to ache as she pondered the mystery in which she had become involved.

"What have I gotten myself into?" she mumbled as she walked along the corridor toward her cabin. "Why should Devlin listen to my complaints about his conduct when I am utterly without experience in child rearing?"

You know enough to love them, came the unbidden response from her inner voice that had been unusually silent until now.

Kyra's face brightened and her head began to swim with plans for the following day—how she would earn the children's trust and make Devlin see the error of his ways.

Several ideas sprang to mind, only to be cast aside an instant later when she opened her cabin door. An unexpected movement caught her eye as she stepped across the threshold, filling her with a sense of impending doom.

"Come in, Kyra," said the menacing voice that could so readily intimidate her. "Tell me what has occurred to provoke such a forlorn look. I expected a decidedly more *eager* expression from my blushing bride."

Thinking to stop him before he could taunt her any further, Kyra closed the door and faced him. "What are you doing in my cabin?" she demanded bluntly.

One of Devlin's dark eyebrows shot up in mock surprise, and Kyra prepared herself for the derisive comment she knew was forthcoming. "What a singular question for a bride to ask her husband on their wedding night! Tell me, dear wife, where would you have me sleep?"

"I would gladly condemn your mangy hide to perdition were it within my power," she retorted as she walked over to a chair and sat down.

Devlin guffawed at her candor. "So you would cast me out of the only available cabin and force me to pass the night on deck, exposed to the elements, where a sudden lurch of the *Windjammer* could deposit me on Neptune's watery doorstep?"

Kyra could not suppress a tiny smile at this picture of righteous indignation, nor could she contain her reply. "I think you make too much of the situation, sir."

The room grew eerily quiet while they studied each other. Kyra was the first to break the awkward silence, for his statement had ignited a spark of concern in her heart. "Are you being truthful? There are no other cabins?"

"On my honor as a *gentleman*." He bowed grandly before her, a mischievous twinkle in his dark brown eyes.

"Humph!" Kyra scoffed. "That hardly reassures me."

She looked from him to the small bed in the corner of the

room and sighed heavily. Then her eyes found his again, and she was not surprised to discover that the twinkle had burgeoned into a lustful gleam. Determined to douse any amorous ideas Devlin might be harboring, Kyra walked to her valise.

"I suppose it cannot be avoided, then," she addressed him offhandedly as she began to rummage through the case in search of her dressing gown. "I'll prepare a pallet on the floor; you may have the bed."

Devlin closed the distance that separated them in three long, powerful strides and, impatiently snatching the garments from her fingers, cast them to the floor and twirled their aghast owner around to face him. "Do you truly think you can dismiss me that easily—or safeguard yourself from my advances by avoiding my bed?"

Kyra grimaced painfully as Devlin's fingers dug into her shoulders, but he was oblivious to the discomfort he caused her. Lost in his anger, he continued to rail at her. "I fear you don't know me very well, madam wife, else you would realize that I am apt to carry you above and take you beneath the starlit heavens. So what is to prevent me from tumbling you here on the floor of our cabin?"

Kyra attempted to quell the frantic tempo of her heart, which had been quickened as much by his threat of ravishment beneath the stars as by his cavalier attitude. "You . . . you would not dare!" she challenged him, praying all the while that the sound of her knees tapping out a frightened rhythm would not reach his ears.

"Wouldn't I?" Devlin's haughty laugh reverberated throughout the cabin. "When we have become more intimate, you will realize that I am inclined to do as I damn well please. Besides, we are husband and wife, and it is within my rights to bed you," he callously informed her.

"And what of *my* rights?" Kyra demanded, shaking off his hurtful grasp. "We agreed that ours would be a marriage of convenience. You promised!"

"I agreed to nothing of the sort," Devlin answered irascibly, wheeling to take an agitated turn about the room. "This marriage-of-convenience nonsense sprang from your ridiculous mind." He thrust an accusatory finger at Kyra. "I hasten to inform you that I have yet to encounter a less convenient situation!" He punctuated his declaration by smacking a fist into his other palm.

Kyra stood motionless, staring at him, wide-eyed. It was just as well that her mouth was dry, leaving her bereft of coherent speech, for Devlin was in no mood to attend her. Impervious to Kyra's daunted expression, he raged on, airing his pent-up thoughts, but his ravings were wasted on his bewildered wife. His tirade concluded, Devlin paused in front of the mirror and caught a glimpse of Kyra's pale reflection behind him. His passion spent, he contrived to achieve a more composed state when he approached her.

"Kyra?" His voice was strangely subdued as he coaxed her chin up and gazed into the exquisite glory of her violet eyes, and it unsettled him to discover that they glistened with unshed tears. One hand instinctively rose to caress her cheek while the other gently stroked her arm. "You cannot be so naive as to believe that we can carry on in this chaste fashion indefinitely. Although I pride myself on my self-discipline, I'm not made of stone. I fear the temptation of having you within my reach will not be long endurable."

Noticing that Kyra had not relaxed her rigid stance, he heaved a tired sigh and drew away from her. "You need not worry that I will ravish you—that is not my way," he drawled loftily as he strolled across the room to select a cigar from the jacket he had earlier shed.

This maneuver prevented him from witnessing the anguished look that crossed Kyra's face. But she wisely choked back the bitter denunciation she longed to hurl at him, lest she be persuaded to make a full confession of that ill-fated night they had shared aboard the *Driftwood*.

Unaware of the emotional upheaval his words had stirred

in her breast, Devlin strode toward the door. "I possess a certain amount of finesse in dealing with delicate matters. But you, my dear Kyra, would try the patience of ten ordinary men. How fortunate, my little ice princess, that *I* am not so commonplace, for the gauntlet has been cast down, forcing me to call upon all my powers of persuasion to melt your cold heart."

His blatant threat of sensual harassment thus delivered, Devlin opened the door, but paused on the threshold to favor Kyra with one final thought-provoking request. "I am going above deck to savor the ocean breezes. When I return, I expect to find you in bed and not sprawled on the floor like a servant. Do I make myself understood?"

He observed her stiff nod of acquiescence with satisfaction. "And, Kyra," he added, as though to ease her apprehension about the night yet to come, "I meant what I said about not forcing you. However, should I suddenly find myself besieged by the urge to take you in my arms, I warn you that I fully intend to satisfy the yearning. Sleep well," he called as he exited the chamber, leaving a much befuddled Kyra in his wake.

"Sleep well," Kyra repeated vaguely, then more incredulously, "*sleep well*!" She yanked the remaining items from her traveling case. "I won't get a moment's rest knowing the rogue may return to pounce on me at any moment."

Kyra cast a wary glance at the closed door and, after dismissing the notion of barricading it, she swiftly shed her dress and donned her nightclothes. It took a good while to remove the pins from her hair and brush the heavy locks into a lustrous sheen, but once this task had been accomplished, Kyra climbed into bed. She lay on her side, facing the door, the sheet pulled up to her chin, and fastened her vigilant gaze on the door, dreading the moment when Devlin would return.

"Sleep well, indeed," she muttered drowsily, unable to stifle the yawn that tugged at her mouth.

Despite her conviction that she would not enjoy one restful moment, the gentle rocking motion of the ship eventually lulled her to sleep. Though she would have steadfastly denied it, a wistful smile turned up the corners of her mouth as she drifted off to sleep, her head filled with visions of Devlin gathering her into his arms and taking her above deck to carry out all those delicious threats he had made.

Kyra's peaceful repose did not go uninterrupted, however. During the night, she was summoned from her dreams by the persistently inquisitive stroking of a hand along her thigh. At first, the soothing touch had a calming effect on her, and she rolled onto her back, her arms stretched above her head, feeling like a contented kitten. But when those fingers embarked on an exploration of her more feminine attributes, Kyra came awake with a startled gasp.

The cabin was in total darkness, but Kyra could sense that Devlin rested above her on one elbow. She could envision the roguish gleam that sparkled in his eyes and the wicked grin that broadened his sensuous lips. She swallowed the lump in her throat and found the courage to place her hand over his to cease its wanderings.

"I couldn't sleep," he murmured in his deep, husky voice, as if this explanation justified his libidinous conduct.

"But you promised." Kyra was very much aware of the hand beneath hers that had traveled up to massage the stiffened crest of her breast.

"You misquote me, forgetful wife." He tweaked her nose. "I promised only that I would not ravish you. I clearly recall warning you that I would not ignore the desire to embrace you, should I be thus inspired," he reminded her, moving his hand to her other breast. "And the compelling urge to cradle you in my arms consumed me when I joined you in bed.

"Perhaps it was the soft scent of your perfume or the fact that I cannot move an inch without coming into contact with your very nicely proportioned body." He lowered his head to nibble hungrily at the exquisitely sculptured column of her throat. Then, releasing a heady sigh, he continued, "Whatever the reason, I found the temptation too great to resist." He resumed his activity.

"I trust your urges have been adequately indulged," Kyra droned coolly, pushing aside the hand that continued to plunder her sensitive flesh.

"Hardly!" came his throaty denial. "But I am a man of honor, and I will not press you further tonight." He placed a perfunctory kiss on the tip of her nose and settled her more securely within his embrace. "However, I would offer a suggestion for when you return to your dreams." One hand found its way to the throat of her nightdress and skillfully began to undo the decorative ribbons as he talked. "You make it difficult for a man to fully appreciate your supple charms, and I want nothing to come between us when we lie in bed together." He gathered a handful of the finely spun linen in his hand for emphasis.

"Rid yourself of this bothersome gown." He chuckled as Kyra tried to pull away from him, thoroughly chagrined by his bold speech, but he held her fast and resettled her in the crook of his arm. When his laughter had subsided, he murmured softly against her ear, "Allay your fears, Kyra. I won't strip you. I merely pose the suggestion, for once you have experienced the sensation of flesh against flesh, I think you'll agree that nothing else quite compares. Sleep now." He settled himself beside her and immediately lapsed into a peaceful slumber, but Kyra stared at the ceiling of the darkened cabin, confident that she would never sleep again.

9

On the afternoon of their third day at sea, the *Windjammer* approached the island where Devlin made his home. During the voyage, Kyra had engaged her new husband in civil discourse, hoping to learn something of the tropical paradise to which he was taking her. She discovered that her new home was a British holding, a small, sparsely populated island that did not command a great deal of attention from its larger neighbors.

It was the island's anonymity that had attracted him, Devlin confided to Kyra, during a rare moment when he abandoned his resolve to torment her and actually conducted a highly animated and interesting discussion. Kyra now sat in the children's cabin, mending a tear in one of Sarah's dresses, and a little smile softened her face as she recalled the conversation.

The island, he had told her, was so small that it had never received a formal name, so the inhabitants had taken to calling it Carraba. It was named, Devlin had explained, after a tribe of fierce cannibalistic natives who had dwelt on the island until the early seventeenth century. Kyra had been fascinated by the tale as well as by his description of the cascading waterfalls, lush vegetation, and tropical forests of his island paradise. Silently Kyra conceded that she was looking forward to exploring her new home.

To her surprise, she realized that she could almost *like*

Devlin when he forgot to treat her as a plaything obtained for his gratification and instead regarded her as an equal, worthy of his regard.

If only all our encounters could be so amicable and so chaste, she thought, knowing full well the folly of harboring such an unrealistic wish. Devlin was a robust and virile man; it was only natural for him to attempt to assert his conjugal rights.

Kyra did not know how long she would be able to deny him the treasure he sought. His sensual assaults had already taken a toll on her spirit; she found herself unable to relax when he was near. And since they had been almost constantly together aboard the yacht, she had had little opportunity to rest, which accounted for her wan complexion and the weary yawn she let out as she folded Sarah's mended gown. With a tired sigh, she set the garment aside and went to join the others on deck.

Shielding her eyes from the blast of sunlight that greeted her as she emerged from the companionway, Kyra walked straight to the railing. She was suffused with excitement as she took in the panoramic view of the blue water and the diversely shaped isles that dotted the horizon.

"How do you manage to find your way?" Kyra inquired, correctly assuming the shadow that had positioned itself beside her belonged to her husband.

"It's not so difficult, especially when one has traveled these waterways as often as I have. Besides, we do have a compass and navigational charts on board," he added dryly.

But Kyra would not permit him to spoil her gay mood and, ignoring his comment, folded her arms atop the rail and lifted her face to breathe deeply of the fresh, salty air and feel the sea spray on her cheeks. "Even so," she continued after a moment, "if I were at the helm, I would be forced to stop at every island to ask directions."

"Then you must remind me never to engage you as my helmsman." Devlin laughed good-naturedly.

"Is your island visible from here?" Kyra turned a sunny smile on him, and seeing her sincere interest, Devlin answered in kind.

"Yes, but only to the keen eye." He stepped very close, leaned down so they were on an equal eye level, and pointed toward the horizon. "Do you see that speck just beyond the tip of the island there to the starboard side?"

Kyra did not favor him with an immediate reply, for she had not reckoned that his nearness would set her heart to pounding at such a feverish pace, nor had she foreseen the gooseflesh that suddenly tingled along her spine, the result of his warm breath caressing her cheek. Thus engaged in a battle to bring her erratic emotions under control, she did not yet trust herself to speak.

Blissfully unaware of the turmoil he had inadvertently caused, Devlin assumed she was experiencing difficulty in locating the island. Therefore, he found himself obliged to draw Kyra securely against him as he again pointed it out. "Now do you see it?"

"Yes!" she exclaimed breathlessly and stepped away in an effort to regain her composure. "Still so far to go? How long will it take?" Kyra glanced up, an unspoken question knitting her brow in response to Devlin's chortle.

"You are aptly called a magpie. You even put young Nicholas to shame, for he, too, questions everything."

Thus chastised, Kyra averted her gaze. "I apologize for being such a bother," she mumbled petulantly.

Kyra felt his hand on her shoulder compelling her to face him and knew that she could not disregard the gesture. But she was surprised to discover that Devlin's expression was contrite; she expected to be soundly scolded in that mocking tone she had already learned to despise.

"You must not be distressed by my every word, Kyra, else we shall never share a peaceful moment. You should know by now that I am given to saying pretty much what comes into my head. I apologize if my unguarded speech has offended you." He disengaged her fingers from the railing and tenderly lifted her hand to his lips.

After pressing a conciliatory kiss against the smooth flesh, he favored Kyra with a boyish grin and continued, "In answer to your question, if the wind stays with us, we should dock within the hour. Do you intend to remain on deck?"

"Yes, it's such a lovely day. I think I will stay here and enjoy the view."

"Excellent!" he bellowed pleasantly. "I suggest you join Biddie and the children in the shade, however." He pointed to where the maid had positioned the youngsters—out of the crew's path and away from the railing where they would be safe.

Drawing Kyra's arm through his, Devlin escorted her toward the little group. "You'll be more comfortable out of the sun, and I shall have no trouble finding you when we approach the island." He took in the question that twinkled in her eyes and explained, "We must sail around to the other side of Carraba to reach port, and in doing so, we'll pass Cauldurae. It's quite an impressive sight; indeed, there is no other view of the island that so completely captures its majesty," Devlin said proudly. He shrugged in a manner reminiscent of young Nicholas. "Anyway, I thought you might like to see your new home."

"I would . . . very much." Kyra gave him the response he had hoped to hear, and a bemused smile curved her lips as she watched him stride away.

An astonished expression crossed her face an hour later as the *Windjammer* drew nearer Carraba, permitting Kyra a breathtaking glimpse of a palatial edifice that seemed to be standing guard over the tropical isle. Kyra had surmised that Devlin was by no means a pauper and she had not expected him to take her to a hovel, but neither had she anticipated this—there was no other word for it—this palace.

The stately mansion stood atop a hill overlooking the sea.

It consisted of a central four-story brick structure flanked by three-story wings and surrounded by a low stone wall. Despite its massive size, the manse instilled in Kyra a sense of peace and tranquillity. This, she sensed, was a place where she could feel at home.

Kyra hugged herself excitedly, anxious to arrive at the mansion so that she could thoroughly investigate each and every room. Her exuberance waned considerably, however, when she heard approaching footfalls—that self-assured stride belonged to Devlin, and she was ruthlessly reminded of the events that had led her to this picturesque spot.

"I told you it was an impressive sight," Devlin said, taking up his stance at her side.

"Yes, you did. But you drastically understated the matter." Her gaze remained fixed on the object of their discussion. "It's the most beautiful mansion I've ever seen, but whatever—"

"Possessed me to buy such a monstrosity of a house?" Devlin interjected.

"Yes."

"It was the first sight that welcomed me when I approached the island some eight years ago. I was smitten by its majestic splendor and promptly decided it must be mine," he explained simply. "The stables and other buildings are behind the main structure, as are the ruins of the original house. There is a garden complete with statues, fountains, and a gazebo where I'm certain you'll be content to while away many a restful hour."

They had long since passed beyond the magnificent view of Cauldurae, but Devlin and Kyra remained on deck, talking quietly.

"Why did you decide to make Carraba your home?" Kyra asked.

His instinctive reaction was to respond with a caustic remark, in keeping with his plan to encourage a speedy return to her father. But when Devlin saw the genuine

interest in her face and the inquisitive sparkle that glistened
in those captivating violet eyes, his desire to ridicule her
abruptly vanished. Casting the sharp rejoinder aside, he
turned to face Kyra and, with his tall frame shielding her
from the glare of the afternoon sun, he rested an elbow
against the railing and began to recount the circumstances
that had led him to his island home.

"It all began during my travels through Europe," he
stated simply. "I was in Paris at the time—Lynette and I had
begun our courtship—when I met David Kincaid. He and I
became instant friends, and he accompanied Lynette and me
about Paris. We went everywhere together—to the theater,
the opera, the museums, all the places one frequents when
seeking diversion.

"As our friendship grew, David told me of his life in the
West Indies and eventually confided that he was planning to
expand his enterprise to include other nearby islands. It was
going to be a costly venture and he needed investors. I was
interested in the prospect and told him as much, but David
was skeptical—understandably so, I suppose. Still, I persisted, and on the day he left Paris, David suggested that, if
I was sincere, I come to the islands to view his operation
firsthand.

"Not one to put things off when I've set my mind on
something, I followed him within the week." A faint smile
of reminiscence tugged at his lips, and Kyra supposed he
was recalling some amusing incident from that first voyage,
and felt a little disappointed that he did not share the
memory with her.

"I fell in love with the islands the instant I laid eyes on
them," he continued, a wistful lilt softening his normally
brusque tone. "I cannot explain it, but I derive a sense of
peace and tranquillity from them that I've never experienced anywhere else."

Now it was Kyra's turn to wear a secret smile, for he had
described her exact feelings when she first beheld Cauldu-

rae in all its glory. "Yes, I know," she murmured faintly on the wind. Then, not wishing him to stop, she urged, "Please go on."

"There's not much more to tell. David and I became business partners. I purchased Cauldurae—though it was not so called at the time—and sent for Lynette, asking her to join me on the island as my bride." His voice trailed off and his pensive gaze appeared to focus on some distant spot on the horizon.

Believing that their talk had conjured up contented memories of his first wife and the life they had shared at Cauldurae, Kyra chose not to interrupt his reverie. She did, however, continue to stare at the profile of the powerful man standing beside her, and, not for the first time, she marveled at the compassion that flared in her breast whenever she caught a glimpse of the vulnerable side of an otherwise inscrutable facade. Kyra grew suddenly melancholy as she recalled her dismal situation, and though her eyes rested on the passing seascape, her thoughts were focused on the bleak future that unfurled before her.

For some inexplicable reason, her musings settled on Lynette, and Kyra grudgingly allowed that she was a little envious of the former mistress of Cauldurae. Kyra knew nothing about Devlin's ill-fated first marriage, except that it had ended in tragedy. Even though it was obvious that their turbulent relationship had fostered Devlin's misogynistic tendencies, Kyra could not believe the couple had always been at odds. After all, Nicholas and Sarah had resulted from the union.

Kyra felt the green-eyed monster tug at her heart once more, and she glanced down at her hands in an effort to repress the unbidden sensation. It was inconceivable that she was experiencing these emotions for a man who had conducted himself in an abusive and contemptible manner almost from the moment they met, the single exception being an unforgettable waltz on a spring night. Still, Kyra could not banish the fanciful notions from her romantic imagination, and her reflections returned to the young French girl who had traveled halfway around the world to be with the man she loved.

Kyra knew that Lynette must have loved Devlin dearly to leave her home and family to join him in a foreign land. She thought it unfortunate that Lynette's life had ended so prematurely and under such tragic circumstances. Before Kyra's vivid imagination could become embroiled in speculation as to the cause of the decline of Devlin's marriage, she was abruptly routed from her reverie.

"What a noble little magpie you are, allowing your bereaved husband a moment of uninterrupted silence in which to remember his dear departed loved one," he said in that mocking tone that so easily rankled her.

Kyra was startled at his choice of words and surprised that he had correctly guessed her motive. She prayed silently that her other thoughts had not been so easily deciphered.

"Tell me," Devlin went on, "will the halo you've symbolically hoisted above my head be tilted askew if I admit that I was merely preoccupied with mundane thoughts about whether my carriage will be waiting at the pier for me, what delicacies Francesca has prepared for supper, and whether my mount has been properly exercised during my absence?" he droned coolly.

Devlin ventured an aloof glance at Kyra's upturned face and was not displeased to note that the wide-eyed expression that had previously molded her lovely features had been replaced by one of truculence. Gratified that he could easily exasperate Kyra, Devlin cupped her chin between his forefinger and thumb and regarded her with approval.

"That's better," he said, chuckling before releasing her and turning his attention to the crystal-blue water that lapped against *Windjammer*'s hull. When he spoke again, his tone was more subdued. "Do not pity me my life's misfortunes, Kyra. That will be your undoing."

"Pity . . . *you*?" Kyra scoffed in disbelief. "Not likely!" She stomped her foot in a fit of pique and folded her arms indignantly across her bosom. "You are a monster to be scorned and despised, not pitied."

"Well spoken!" Devlin applauded her temerity, an action he knew would intensify her annoyance with him. "Let us hope that you always feel this way. Do not permit your resolve to weaken and begin to think that I can be wooed by your innocence and beauty," he cautioned. "I was once foolhardy enough to be seduced by a pleasing face and a coquettish manner, but I've long since rendered myself unsusceptible to such feminine wiles," Devlin said flatly. "Commit these words to memory, Kyra. Remember that I am a heartless cad, and we shall deal well enough during your sojourn at Cauldurae. We can but pray it will be a brief one."

An expression of relief swathed Devlin's handsome face as he looked beyond Kyra to find that they were sailing into port. With a curt nod, he pushed away from the railing, intending to issue last-minute instructions to his crew. Devlin had taken only two steps, however, when his progress was halted by happy shouts of "Papa, Papa!" and he turned to find Sarah toddling toward him.

Ever on the lookout for the father she adored, the youngster had spied him when her attention strayed from a game she and Nicholas were playing. With a gleeful shriek, Sarah clambered to her feet and ran across the unsteady deck as quickly as her tiny legs would carry her.

Kyra observed the scene with keen interest, expecting Devlin to disregard Sarah's plea for attention. She was surprised to see him stride over to the little girl and scoop her into his arms. But if Kyra had thought she was about to witness an affectionate encounter between father and daughter, she was to be sadly disappointed, for in the next instant Devlin thrust the child into her startled arms.

Kyra glanced up at Devlin's face and resisted the urge to shrink away from his withering look. She was determined not to give him the satisfaction of knowing how effortlessly he could instill fear in her heart. Her trepidation reverted back to righteous indignation, however, when her husband's callous accusation pealed in her ears.

"It would appear your mothering instincts leave much to be desired," he admonished and, giving his head a ponderous shake, added cruelly, "Have you no accomplishments? Did your upbringing prepare you for nothing more than a life of languishing in the shade of a magnolia, sipping lemonade with a bevy of lovesick swains dancing attendance upon you?

"Your conduct as a *wife*"—Devlin spat the word sarcastically—"has thus far shown you to be sorely lacking in the qualities that please a husband. The very least I expect is for you to keep your end of the bargain—a bargain that was of your making," he reminded her. "Nicholas and Sarah are your responsibility. See that you don't neglect them again," he cautioned, an ominous glint flickering in his brown eyes. Having had his say, Devlin wheeled around and stalked across the deck.

Kyra could not immediately give in to the rage that boiled inside her, for she now had to soothe the bruised feelings of the toddler she held in her arms. She felt a pang of sympathy as Sarah's exuberant smile faded into a dejected pout. Her blue eyes instantly filled with tears that proceeded to tumble down her cheeks, and her joyful shrieks turned into mournful wails at being so coldly ignored by the father whose attention she had sought.

"There, there, little one," Kyra whispered soothingly as she rocked Sarah in her arms.

Sarah's cries eventually subsided, and Kyra coaxed the little girl's head down onto her shoulder. Then she gently brushed aside the strands of hair that were matted against her pale cheeks, murmuring endearments against Sarah's ear as she did so. "I know, I know," she continued in a soft, mellifluous voice. "Grown-ups, especially your daddy, can be quite intolerable." She pressed a kiss against Sarah's tearstained cheek and, even though she knew the toddler would not understand her, aired her thoughts aloud.

"Poor little outcast," she cooed. "You and I have much in common." Her eyes followed Devlin as he prepared the yacht for docking. "But at least you will always have a home waiting for you with Amanda if life with your vexing papa becomes too much for you to bear, where as I—" She faltered as a huge lump rose in her throat, and she recalled Devlin's cynical remark that he hoped her stay at Cauldurae would be short.

Should he become disenchanted with the game they played and decide to send her back to Charleston, she would be faced with an impossible dilemma. As long as she was being sought for questioning in the death of Clayton Fairchild, Kyra could not return home. She had, in effect, no place to go.

Kyra looked down at the child, who was regarding her thoughtfully, and it was as if some unspoken bond suddenly united the pair. Sarah reached to touch Kyra's cheek, bringing tears of joy to her happily surprised eyes.

"Mama Keewa," Sarah purred contentedly, snuggling against her newfound friend.

"Yes," Kyra murmured, gently removing the small hand from her cheek and giving each chubby finger a loving kiss. "You and I are going to be great friends," she promised as she strolled toward the shade where Biddie endeavored to entertain her charge. "Now we must concentrate our efforts on breaking Nicholas's staunch reserve and, of course, your father's. But never fear, sweet Sarah. We shall contrive to bring them around," she vowed. Kyra returned the little girl's trusting smile and lowered her to her feet. The pair walked the remaining distance side by side, one tiny hand clasped tightly within a larger, reassuring one.

Sunset was almost upon them by the time the *Windjammer* docked and the weary travelers were told they could disembark. Kyra accepted the crewman's news cheerfully, thinking it would be good to feel the earth beneath her feet again. Her spirit faltered, however, when she emerged from the companionway to find Devlin walking toward her, a glower darkening his face.

Kyra, Biddie, and the children were just returning from the cabins where a final inspection had ensured that everyone's personal belongings had been carried on deck to be dispatched to Cauldurae. But when Kyra beheld the approaching thundercloud that was her husband, she instructed the maid to take the children and await her near the gangplank; she did not wish to subject the youngsters to the forthcoming conflict. Sarah was reluctant to be separated from her new ally, but Kyra bent down and pressed a loving kiss against the child's brow, proffered her favorite doll, and asked her to run along like a good little girl; "Mama Keewa" would join her presently. Pacified, Sarah scampered off to join her brother, and Kyra whirled to confront her husband.

"What is it?" she demanded before Devlin had an opportunity to address her. "I cannot imagine how I could be responsible for provoking you to such passion, especially since I have taken great pains to avoid you this past hour or more."

Devlin was taken aback by her candor, but his grimace gradually changed into a mischievous grin. "I assure you, Kyra," he began, his appraising gaze sweeping over her from head to toe, then returning to the violet eyes that glared at him reproachfully, "I need merely conjure your charming image to be hurled into the throes of a violent *passion*." He emphasized the last word on the off chance that Kyra might misinterpret his meaning, but he need not have bothered.

Kyra knew him well enough to correctly decipher his lusty references, but even so, she could not prevent a flush of embarrassment from flooding her cheeks. Nor could she deny her intense yearning to scratch the self-satisfied smirk off his sensuous lips, but she decided not to yield to the impulse. Rather, she tore her eyes from his smoldering stare and asked, "What do you want?"

"I believe you already know *that*" was his ribald taunt, but when Kyra refused to be baited, Devlin gave a conciliatory shrug and grudgingly returned to the matter at hand. "Very well, then," he said in his most authoritative voice. "There is a small problem I need to discuss with you."

"Yes?"

"We have arrived later than I anticipated. It's at least an hour's journey to Cauldurae, and even if I dispatched one of my men immediately to fetch a carriage from my stables, we will not arrive home till half-past ten. We can either remain aboard the *Windjammer* another night or seek accommodations at the inn. It is small but comfortable," he informed her, his displeasure with both alternatives registering plainly on his face.

"But you would prefer to travel to Cauldurae tonight?" Kyra guessed his thoughts.

"Of course, but—"

"Send your man for the carriage, Devlin," she said firmly. "Biddie and I will keep the children occupied until it arrives. Perhaps we could have supper at the inn as a way of passing the time." When he offered no immediate response, Kyra started to step past him to advise Biddie of this new development, but the pressure of his hand on her shoulder stayed her.

"You're certain this will not put you out?" he asked, suddenly perturbed and amazed that he found himself mindful of her needs.

"It will be only a slight inconvenience, I am sure. I realize I have much to learn about mothering," Kyra said for his benefit, and did not so much as flinch when Devlin guffawed at her reference to his earlier gibe, "but I believe the children have been away from home long enough, and their interests will be better served if we complete our journey tonight."

"So be it." Devlin smiled down at her, and Kyra was gratified to note that, for once, he did not mock her. "I'll make the necessary arrangements, then return to escort you and the children to the inn." He tipped his hat and began to whistle an airy tune as he swaggered across the deck, his mood obviously much improved.

To Kyra's surprise, the evening meal proved to be an enjoyable experience. Devlin secured a private room, and while Biddie attended to Nicholas and Sarah at a small table slightly removed from the couple, he regaled Kyra with tales of his life on the island and his business exploits. Though he avoided any reference to Lynette in his vivid narrative, Kyra learned many things about this perplexing man who had so completely shattered her previously idyllic existence.

She learned that the Cauldurae plantation house comprised eighty-seven rooms. "More or less," Devlin explained. "The original house is said to have had one hundred twelve rooms, but much of that structure was destroyed by fire near the turn of the century and never rebuilt. I recall one occasion in particular," he continued, as he leaned forward to refill Kyra's wineglass, "when I set out, determined to explore every nook and cranny of the place."

"What happened?"

"I became hopelessly lost."

"No!" Kyra exclaimed.

"It's true," Devlin assured her. "I spent an entire morning roaming aimlessly, desperately trying to find my way back to the main hall." He chuckled good-naturedly at his own folly. "To this day, I never venture into the west wing unless I've got my compass with me." He threw a look at her from the corner of one hooded eye to see if she believed his tall tale. She did not.

"You're teasing me," Kyra accused him, laughing despite her attempts to appear offended.

"Yes, and with such delightful results." He gazed at her fondly. "You have a musical laugh that is quite pleasing to the ear. I hope I'll hear it often while you are at Cauldurae."

Not knowing how to respond to his unexpected and uncharacteristic flattery, Kyra merely smiled and inquired about the condition of the house. He told her that the main four-story structure had undergone extensive renovations under his supervision. Apparently a few improvements had been made in the wings as well, but he explained that much needed to be done to restore the mansion to its former glory.

They continued this amiable exchange for the remainder of their stopover. Kyra enjoyed her husband's witty and knowledgeable conversation so much that she felt a little pang of disappointment when the innkeeper announced that their carriage had arrived.

Darkness had fallen when the travel-worn group made their way to the well-sprung carriage that waited to whisk them away on the final stage of their journey. When Biddie and the children had been comfortably situated, Devlin assisted Kyra to her seat and, after climbing in beside her, gave the signal to the coachman to spring the team. The adults spent much of the trip in comfortable silence with only the children's excitable chatter occasionally interrupting the stillness.

Nicholas sat in the corner opposite his father, with his sister next to him. The pair seemed content to engage in a make-believe game of Nicholas's invention. Kyra watched them with a surreptitious eye by the light of the lantern that illuminated the tiny compartment, and she was surprised to note that Nicholas did not entirely abandon his stern reserve even when immersed in play. Not until he wearied of this diversion and curled up in the corner to be lulled to sleep by the swaying motion of the coach did his small boyish face relax its normally acerbic expression.

Kyra felt a lurch in the vicinity of her heart as she studied Nicholas's profile in repose, and she suddenly yearned to cradle him in her arms and smooth back the dark curls that had fallen across his forehead. But before she could match her actions to her thoughts, she found her lap occupied by a swirl of ruffled petticoats and wrinkled muslin, prompting her to glance down into Sarah's happy face.

"Mama Keewa, play?" she asked hopefully, grasping Kyra's face between her tiny hands.

Kyra felt, rather than observed, the shocked reaction from the gentleman at her side. Devlin had obviously not expected her to be so readily accepted, and Sarah's uninhibited display of affection had caught him by surprise. A little smile of triumph spread over Kyra's lips, for she could not deny her elation at the thought of annoying the one who had, on more than one occasion, gratified himself at her expense.

Her jubilant smile quickly palled, however, when Devlin leaned close and whispered, "Do not swell up prematurely, little pet. Sarah was an easy conquest, Nicholas is made of stronger stuff. He's a true Cauldwell and will not be so easily won over."

Surprised that Devlin seemed to possess the uncanny ability to correctly read her every thought, Kyra chose to ignore him and instead devoted her attention to the child who patiently awaited a reply to her question. Kyra favored Sarah with her brightest smile and was profoundly relieved when Devlin showed no interest in continuing his taunts.

Instead he rested his broad shoulders against the back of the leather seat and stretched his long legs out in front of him as far as the cramped space would allow. Then, with a nonchalant gesture, he tilted his hat forward to shield his eyes from the glare of the lantern and folded his arms across his chest, as if emulating Nicholas. In truth, Devlin maintained an aloof surveillance of the quaint scene as Kyra tenderly clasped Sarah's hands and pressed a loving kiss on each tiny palm.

Kyra and Sarah spent the next quarter of an hour in a variety of pastimes that included the recitation of nursery rhymes and the singing of hand-clapping songs, and ended with Kyra humming a lullaby that eventually caused Sarah to give in to the sleep that tugged at her eyelids. Her arms filled with this delightful bundle, Kyra was finally able to satisfy the yearnings she had earlier been forced to suppress when regarding Nicholas's sleeping face. With a little sigh of contentment, Kyra kissed the top of Sarah's blond head and cuddled the child to her.

"There's room for de li'l one over here, Miz Kyra," Biddie whispered, indicating the space on the bench between her and Nicholas.

Kyra was reluctant to relinquish her armful, but she realized that Sarah would be more comfortable if she could stretch out. This decision made, Kyra scooted forward and gently handed Sarah over to Biddie.

While the maid settled her young charge, Kyra, thinking the light from the lantern might rouse the children, stood up and extinguished the flame. No sooner had she done so than the carriage struck a pothole and lurched violently, throwing Kyra off balance and depositing her on Devlin's lap.

Suddenly engulfed in darkness after being accustomed to a bright light, Kyra needed several moments to adjust to her blackened surroundings. But she did not have to see Devlin's face to know that he was regarding her with a singularly rakish expression, his haunting eyes sparkling with impish pleasure. This much she easily determined from the familiar way in which one brawny hand clasped her waist while the other slid beneath her arm to rest dangerously close to one voluptuous breast.

Kyra placed a trembling hand over Devlin's in an effort to discourage him from embarking on an exploration of her sensitive flesh, and her voice shook when she said, "Forgive me. I . . . I did not mean to—that is, I did not expect the carriage to lurch so suddenly. I hope my clumsiness has not caused you any discomfort."

"On the contrary. I was just wishing for a diversion to alleviate the boredom of the journey. How thoughtful of you to extinquish the light; it would dampen my ardor considerably were I expected to conduct a dalliance in full view of the ever-watchful Biddie," he murmured in the darkness, and Kyra shivered in spite of herself when she felt his warm lips tugging gently at the ear in which his ribald insinuation had been murmured. "But now—"

Devlin had no opportunity to describe his intentions, for Kyra soundly slapped aside the offensive hand that had begun to slide up toward her breast. Before he could react, she slipped out of his embrace and positioned herself as far from him as the narrow seat allowed. But his self-satisfied chuckle reminded her that, although she had triumphed in this instance, the conflict was far from over.

Some thirty minutes later, the conveyance trundled between the masonry gate posts that marked the entrance to the plantation, and Devlin's face softened as he viewed the welcoming sight. The long driveway was ablaze with light from a hundred or more lanterns, and the sentries, who stood watch at various points along the winding route, acknowledged their employer's return with hearty waves and boisterous shouts. Devlin's expression broadened into a smile when he saw that a number of servants lined the front veranda in anxious expectation of their arrival.

The carriage had barely rolled to a stop before the spacious edifice when a footman stepped forward to assist the passengers. The children were gently transferred into capable hands and carried inside, and Biddie emerged from the vehicle in wide-eyed wonder at the grand sight. When Kyra did not immediately follow, Devlin bristled, certain she meant to create a scene. However, a cursory glance inside the coach tempered his ire. Like the children, Kyra had fallen asleep.

"Poor chile, she's plumb wore out. You want I should wake her, Mr. Devlin?" Biddie offered.

"No Biddie, that won't be necessary. Go with Sally." He nodded toward a servant who remained on the veranda awaiting instructions. "She will show you to your quarters and help you get settled. You may wait on your mistress in the morning."

"But—"

Devlin suavely sidestepped the maid's protests and nudged her toward the entrance. "I assure you, I'm quite able to care for my wife's needs. Off with you, now."

With the air of one who is accustomed to having his commands obeyed, Devlin did not give Biddie a second thought as he stepped to the other side of the carriage and pulled the door open. Reaching inside, he lifted Kyra in his arms and, with her head lolling against his shoulder, strode toward the mansion. As his boot scraped the first step, he bent slightly to whisper against Kyra's cheek. "Welcome to Cauldurae, magpie."

10

The familiar sounds and smells of morning gently nudged Kyra's groggy senses, taunting her, forcing her to bid farewell to her dreams and embrace the new day. But she was reluctant to forsake the peace that enveloped her. As she lay there, suspended in that drowsy state that precedes full consciousness, Kyra gradually became aware of the mingled aroma of brewed coffee and fried bacon, and it seemed that a flock of birds had perched just outside her window, considering the cacophonous symphony that was in progress. For a fleeting instant, Kyra experienced the sensation of being safely tucked away in her room at Raybourne, for she had often been awakened in such a fashion.

Although she silently hoped that Biddie might be responsible for those delicious odors, she was not surprised to see her husband's imposing figure lounging in a chair near the window. Thinking it likely that Devlin had come to provoke her with more of his biting repartee, Kyra was determined to quickly have done with the upcoming confrontation. Thus resolved, she prepared for battle by propping herself up on her elbows, but her clever words of greeting shriveled on her tongue as her senses were overpowered by a blinding flash of color.

Her initial thought was that she must have been dreaming, for she had never seen a more ridiculous room. She blinked, shook her head, and blinked again, but the strange sight remained. All the room's furnishings, from the papered and wainscoted walls to the upholstered wing chairs, bed linens, covers, and window hangings, were various shades of pink. Pale, delicate hues were accentuated by darker tones of the color, but the bedroom was nevertheless most decidedly and hideously *pink*!

Caught up in her bemused scrutiny, Kyra did not notice that Devlin had moved from his perch by the window to stand beside the bed. Her flustered expression did not change when he pulled the pink mosquito netting aside, and she did not flinch when he bent forward and playfully chucked her chin, encouraging her to close her gaping mouth. Before straightening up, he succumbed to the impulse to press a kiss against her mouth, and still she did not react.

Devlin chuckled at her wide-eyed amazement. "It is a bit bewildering," he said agreeing with her unspoken assessment of the room's decor.

"It's so . . . so *pink*," Kyra mumbled, having at last regained the use of her tongue.

"So it is. Lynette was partial to the color."

"Lynette?" Kyra echoed. "This was her room?"

"Yes."

"Then . . . then that must mean—" Kyra stopped, her gaze settling on the door to the adjacent room.

"Yes, I fear it must. I am just next door." Devlin derived enormous pleasure in corroborating her assumption. Mindful of the grimace that darkened her face, he sauntered over to the breakfast tray he had brought into the room.

"But that simply will not do!" Kyra shouted at his back as he stooped toward a platter of delicious-smelling food. Sitting up, she extended an accusing finger at him, demanding, "And what of our bargain?"

She watched with growing trepidation as he turned slowly and strolled toward the bed. Even then Devlin did not exhibit undue haste in responding to Kyra's question. Instead, he set the tray on the bedside table, poured himself a cup of coffee, and boldly sat on the edge of the bed beside his disgruntled wife.

Eventually, he said, "Must I again remind you that I am bound by neither law nor honor to uphold any bird-witted provisos you have arbitrarily affixed to this cursed union? You are—through a lamentable act of happenstance—my wife, and as such, you must observe certain proprieties," he informed her in that haughty voice she had grown to despise. "But tell me, where would you have the new mistress of Cauldurae sleep?"

Angered by his words, Kyra snapped, "I would as soon sleep on the roof, or . . . or—"

"In the stables with the other mulish and cantankerous creatures?" Devlin suggested. "That can be arranged, magpie. However, I should imagine you would much prefer sleeping in this pink shrine to sharing a stall with a braying jackass." Devlin regretted his choice of words when he saw the twinkle in Kyra's eyes.

"That is precisely why I am averse to sleeping in such close proximity to you," she purred sweetly, fluttering her lashes in a way that made Devlin long to throttle her.

Ignoring the glare in his brown eyes and completely unaware of the alluring picture she created—what with her silken curls tumbling wildly around her and a bounteous display of cream-colored flesh exposed above the night-dress's low neckline—Kyra poured herself a cup of coffee. Oblivious to the heated stare that followed her, she stirred a generous portion of sugar into the bitter drink and selected a rasher of bacon from a china platter.

"You mustn't be so critical of yourself, Devlin." She nibbled the hickory-flavored meat contemplatively. "Although I will admit that you do a prodigious amount of braying, I would hardly be so uncharitable as to brand you an out-and-out jackass." Kyra finished off the bacon with a flourish and blew on the coffee to temper its scalding heat, then swallowed a satisfying draft.

Devlin seldom found himself outdone in any venture, but in this instance, he conceded that nothing good would come of baiting this quick-witted vixen. His cup and saucer clattered noisily on the tray as he discarded them, and muttering some obscure oath about impossible females, he met and held her implacable gaze.

"Your misgivings are duly noted, ma'am," he droned dispassionately. "However, I've decided that this will be your room, so you may as well resign yourself to that fact. But should you find the decor offensive, I hereby give you leave to change it to suit your fancy."

"Am I to understand that I have free rein in undertaking any changes I may choose?" Kyra tugged at her lower lip in studious reflection of the delightful and potentially expensive enterprise, and a wicked gleam illuminated her eyes.

Devlin nonchalantly plucked a slice of buttered toast from the breakfast tray and studied it while he mulled over his reply. He knew Kyra well enough by now to realize that her puckish expression could not possibly bode well for him *or* his money. Hoping to dash the scheme that was now being plotted behind her guileless eyes, Devlin bit into the toast and leveled a shrewd gaze on his lovely nemesis.

"Yes," he answered, startling Kyra from her reverie, "by all means, let your imagination have its way. You may chop the furniture into pieces, burn it as kindling, and replace it with mountains of satin pillows and shimmering veils. Employ servants—perhaps you could find a eunuch—to fan you with ostrich feathers and feed you peeled grapes from a silver platter." He gestured grandly while Kyra merely rolled her eyes in disgust. "Drape the walls with tapestries depicting nude couples in various stages of lovemaking, if that is your desire.

"Be as garish, as vulgar, as extravagant as you like, but be certain that you are content with your selections, for you will have to live with them. I will bear the expense of refurbishing this room but once," Devlin stated bluntly, and added alarmingly, "because there is, I fear, only one other room I am willing to make available to you."

Kyra needed no interpreter to explain Devlin's innuendo: She could either behave herself or suffer the consequences in the adjoining chamber. With a pout turning down the corners of her mouth, the result of having her scheme thwarted, she asked, "Are you always such a spoilsport?"

"I daresay I'm not, but then, I haven't come to discuss my disposition, Kyra." He tossed the half-eaten toast onto the platter, and as he wiped his fingertips with a linen napkin, his manner became humorless and businesslike.

Leery of his reply, Kyra ventured, "Why have you come?"

"Biddie."

"Biddie!" she exclaimed, disconcerted by his admission. Thinking the worst, Kyra unwittingly gripped his sleeve, and he detected the dread in her voice when she asked, "What has she done?"

"Nothing," Devlin replied, lowering his brown gaze to the fingers that trembled against his arm and placing his hand on hers in a reassuring gesture. "There is, however, a matter regarding her that requires our immediate attention."

"What?" Kyra asked, her eyes glazed with confusion.

"You recall that I explained this island is a British holding?" he asked, acknowledging her faltering nod with a gentle squeeze to her fingers. "Kyra, slavery was abolished in these islands many, many years ago. Do you know what that means?"

"I think so. Biddie—"

"Biddie must be given her freedom without delay," Devlin informed her.

"But . . . what if—"

"What if Biddie decides to take advantage of her freedom

and establish a life for herself elsewhere?" He quickly untangled her jumbled thoughts.

Kyra nodded woodenly, stunned by her husband's revelation, albeit her chagrin sprang from the dismaying thought of losing a trusted companion more than from any lofty, idealistic position on the issue of slavery. If asked, Kyra would have freely admitted that her apprehension concerning Biddie's independence was purely selfish. If the servant chose to leave her, Kyra would be left alone on an unfamiliar island with no one but a lurking, lecherous husband to taunt her and two young children for whom she was expected to act as mother, a role completely alien to her. She would undoubtedly be driven mad within the week.

"Kyra?" Devlin prodded, his stern voice dispelling the gloom that had enveloped her. "Am I to assume that Biddie is your personal property?"

Again Kyra nodded. "Father presented me with Biddie's papers on my twenty-first birthday."

"Good. That will make it all the easier, then. We are husband and wife, which means that whatever is yours is also mine, and I can dispose of your property in any manner that suits me." He noticed that Kyra stiffened at his blunt speech. "Don't poker up at me, little pet. Surely you must realize that ours is a reciprocal arrangement—you are equally entitled to my possessions. Indeed," he whispered suggestively, "I am most anxious to share *everything* with you."

Kyra was less than reassured by these terms, and Devlin's subsequent actions merely confirmed her worst suspicions. He wasted little time making it plain that his benevolence would not be limited to his worldly goods, as he lifted her hand from his arm and guided it purposefully between his thighs.

With an incensed gasp, Kyra jerked her hand from Devlin's and glared at him while struggling to ignore the sudden excited thrumming of her heart. "We were discussing Biddie," she reminded him with a saintly quirk of her brow.

Swallowing a complacent smirk—he had not failed to notice Kyra's flush of color—Devlin cleared his throat and nodded in mock acquiescence. "So we were. Shall we consider the matter settled?"

"Yes," Kyra murmured, struggling to come to terms with her ambivalent feelings concerning both Biddie and the awesome masculine specimen who was regarding her with an unnervingly sensual gaze.

"Excellent! I shall instruct my attorney to draw up the appropriate documents." He clapped his hands together like a man who had just satisfactorily closed a business transaction, then stood to leave the room.

Impulsively, her hand flew upward to catch his sleeve, preventing his immediate departure. "May I tell her?" Kyra asked hesitantly.

"Of course" was his understanding reply. He slipped a brawny finger beneath her chin, forcing her to look at him. "You may advise her that, as mistress of this hall, you can afford to pay her a handsome salary if she is inclined to remain in your employ."

Unable to endure those eyes any longer, Kyra lowered her head and muttered an obliging thank-you.

"Not at all." Devlin took her hand and, pressing a lingering kiss into the palm, executed a grand bow and inquired, "How else may I serve you?"

"The key."

"The key?" he echoed, unsure if he had heard right.

"May I have the key?" She looked pointedly at the door between the two rooms.

"Certainly," Devlin said between gritted teeth, masking the dark look that contorted his handsome features.

Without further discussion, he disappeared inside the neighboring room. Upon his return, he marched straight to the bed and tucked the requested item between her enticing breasts.

Kyra started at his abrupt action, but her shock turned to dismay the moment the fingers of that menacing hand fluttered deliberately against her skin. Then, having withstood as much of the beauty's touch-me-not manner as he cared to suffer for one morning, Devlin strode to the door. But his wounded pride would not permit him to take his leave with Kyra believing she had gained the upper hand in their battle of wits.

He paused on the threshold, his quelling glare raking over her as he said, "You should realize by now, Kyra, that a locked door will not long dissuade me from my purpose." Having said his piece, he walked away.

Kyra would reflect on her husband's dire warning at a later time, as her immediate attention had been garnered by the discovery she had just made. Having been preoccupied with Devlin since wakening, Kyra had not noticed the filmy nightdress in which she was clad until he stuffed the wretched key between her breasts. Logical deduction told her that the garment's previous owner must have been Lynette, considering it was the same cloying pink that dominated the chamber.

She remembered having fallen asleep in the carriage en route to Cauldurae. But who had carried her to this chamber, and how had she come to be thus attired? Raising her suspicious eyes with the intent to purge herself of these gnawing questions, Kyra was surprised to find herself alone in the blush-pink chamber. It was just as well, however, for Mrs. Cauldwell would not have been comforted by her husband's roguish reply.

In the days immediately following her arrival at Cauldurae, Kyra was spared a repetition of this unorthodox awakening. In fact, she saw very little of her elusive husband, for Devlin was preoccupied with plantation affairs. Anxious to determine how his business had fared during his absence, he was up and out of the mansion each morning even before the servants had stirred from their beds. The couple did share an occasional dinner, but more often than not, Kyra was already in her room and nodding off before Devlin's door opened and a bar of light appeared beneath the connecting portal.

Time and again she heard his footfalls approach that barrier, and the breath would catch in her throat as she watched the latch jiggle while Devlin checked to see if the door was locked. Despite this ritual, Kyra slept peacefully, reassured by the security of the lock—however false it might ultimately prove to be.

Kyra was to discover that, even though her husband could be the most exasperating of men, he was nevertheless true to his word. By the end of the first week, Biddie's papers of manumission had been prepared and executed. Although Kyra contrived to display a sunny disposition when she informed the servant that she was free to go wherever she chose, she could not repress her joyful cry at Biddie's response.

"Bless my soul, Miz Kyra," the servant declared, "but you know I wouldn't dream of leavin' you, not with everythin' all jumbled like it is. No one would treat me any better'n you do, and besides, I done set my eyes on Henry, a young man that works in the stables, and I can't leave yet, considerin' he ain't even had a chance to notice me." Upon that admission, the two of them embraced, and Kyra settled down in front of the mirror to be soothed by Biddie's gentle ministrations. For once, Kyra did not mind the maid's chatter as Biddie regaled her with the many virtues of her hoped-for swain.

Kyra quickly learned that her husband was a business magnate who owned sugarcane plantations, distilleries, warehouses, sawmills, and shipping companies, as well as other enterprises. She was, however, perplexed by Devlin's frequent and often lengthy absences with his business partner. She did not badger him about them, deciding instead to be thankful for the respite from his persistent ogling and innuendos. Besides, while Devlin was engrossed in his entrepreneurial pursuits on Carraba and the neighboring islands, Kyra was free to roam the estate.

Having been asleep the night they arrived at Cauldurae, Kyra was unaware of the sentries who regularly patrolled the grounds. It was not long before she discovered their existence, for she found that she could not take a leisurely stroll through the garden without encountering a heavily armed guard. Though she was naturally curious as to why Devlin ran his home like a fortress, she did not pester him about it, thinking he would merely shrug her questions aside in that maddeningly insensitive way of his and politely inform her that she need not trouble herself with the matter. Still, she wondered.

Devlin's sojourns away from home also gave Kyra an opportunity to become acquainted with the servants, especially those with whom she had daily contact.

She felt instantly at ease with Hannah Wilson, the housekeeper. The rosy-cheeked middle-aged woman was slight in stature, but her diminutive size was misleading, for never had Kyra seen a household run with a firmer hand. Mrs. Wilson was not a tyrant, but having been in Devlin's employ since his arrival on the island, she knew how he expected things to be managed. He did not tolerate slipshod work from his subordinates, and neither did Hannah Wilson.

But beneath Mrs. Wilson's rigid facade beat the heart of a truly kind woman, and her sunny smile and friendly ways drew Kyra to her each morning. In the tearoom just off the huge dining room, in the sewing room, or in Kyra's sitting room, the two women would sip coffee and plan the day's menus, confer over patterns and colors for Kyra's bedroom, or discuss other household details.

Kyra had found a valued and trusted friend in Mrs. Wilson—but her relationship with the children's governess proved to be quite another matter. Whereas Kyra had felt an immediate rapport with Hannah, she was instantly put off by the disagreeable Alice Lovejoy. Lovejoy—if ever there was an inappropriate name, *that* certainly was one! Kyra was convinced that a less loving and more joyless woman never lived.

The governess was tall and slender, perhaps five or six years Kyra's senior, with cold gray eyes and black hair pulled back in a tight chignon. The woman wore a sour expression, but whether as a result of her severe hairstyle or her natural disposition, Kyra had no way of knowing. Following her initial confrontation with the surly Miss Lovejoy, however, Kyra decided, with only a negligible pang of guilt, that it could be attributed to the latter.

For some reason, the woman took an instant dislike to Cauldurae's new mistress, and though Kyra was confounded by the governess's hostility and rudeness, she did not mention it to Devlin. Rather, she decided that, as long as the woman performed her duties and did not subject the children to her ill humor, she would not complain. Sarah and Nicholas had suffered enough turmoil; separation from the sour-faced Miss Lovejoy would not be to their advantage.

Nearly a month after the morning when Kyra had awakened to find Devlin in her room, Kyra was walking on the beach with the children, wondering why she found Devlin's cavalier treatment of her so objectionable.

Inconsistent! came the chastisement from her inner voice. *You lash out at him if he so much as looks at you, yet when he goes about his business and pays you no mind, you're still not satisfied.*

Kyra ignored this inner reasoning and continued her musing. She suspected that Devlin was involved in a romantic entanglement, but could she fault him if he was?

After all, she herself had suggested that he avail himself of the affections of women who could appreciate his charms. Kyra had meant every word at the time, so why did the image of Devlin in another woman's arms stir such fierce resentment in her breast? Before she could embark on a lengthy analysis of this, she was distracted by Sarah's squeals of delight.

Kyra glanced up to watch the child toddle in and out of the waves that lapped at her feet. A few feet farther up the beach Nicholas was diligently constructing a castle out of wet sand. His efforts were severely hampered by his little sister, who annihilated each work before Nicholas had a chance to show it off. Sarah's latest method for wreaking mayhem upon her brother was to sit forcefully on the sand structure. Surprisingly, Nicholas was not annoyed by her antics; he simply selected a new spot and began again, knowing in advance what would happen to the fruits of his labor.

Kyra smiled and returned her attention to the kite she was making, but her spirits faded when she remembered the unsmiling face of the children's governess. Kyra was still at a loss to account for Miss Lovejoy's abrupt change of heart. When she had first informed that dire lady of her intention to take the children on an outing, the governess had balked. But when Kyra further explained that she meant to take them for a romp along the beach, Miss Lovejoy had acquiesced without demur. Perhaps Kyra would have been more wary of the governess's motive had she noticed the sly grin on the woman's lips when Kyra ushered Nicholas and Sarah from the nursery.

Further reflection on the matter was made quite impossible, however, as Sarah—impervious to the wet sand that clung to her dress—flung herself onto Kyra's lap, demanding, "Fly kite *now*!"

"It's almost ready," Kyra assured the child, attaching the final cross strip to the tail with a little grunt of satisfaction.

"There." She held the kite out to survey her handiwork. Even though the spine and crosspiece were a little off-center, Kyra decided the kite would do well enough.

"You know, Sarah," Kyra began, and gazed down into the sand-smeared face from beneath her wide-brimmed straw hat, "many people think kites are only for boys. I say those people are full of bunk, and we shall all have a marvelous time once we get this contraption airborne. Up with you now." She removed Sarah from her lap and, shaking the sand from her skirts, stood up. "Run and fetch Nicholas."

The boy's embittered manner wavered when he beheld this special treat, but when his repeated attempts to get the kite aloft proved futile, his interest soon palled. Frustration and disappointment registered plainly on his face, and Kyra, determined that he should not be defeated, decided to take matters into her own hands.

"Perhaps I can help, Nicholas," Kyra offered, reaching down to take the kite from him. "If I'm successful, you may then hold the string."

"Me, too!" came Sarah's pleading cries.

"And Sarah, of course," Kyra amended. "We shall all take turns, I promise, but first I must get this silly thing up. Go stand beside your brother, Sarah," she instructed the child and, taking a moment to judge the wind's direction, turned and marched several yards down the beach.

Glancing about self-consciously, Kyra tucked her skirt hem into her waistband to improve her mobility. Then, with one hand anchoring her hat and the other extended behind her, she ran up the beach toward the children, the kite rising and dipping in the air behind her. From the children's excited shouts as they scampered about her, she inferred that she must have achieved some success, and looked over her shoulder to ascertain her progress.

Thus preoccupied, Kyra did not see the solitary figure who positioned himself directly in her path until—with her gaze still directed behind her—she plowed straight into the unyielding obstacle.

The collision left Kyra breathless, and she struck with such force that she fell backward, her backside greeting the wet sand with a thud as the kite fizzled to the ground behind her. Startled by this unforeseen incident, Kyra aimed her dazed expression up at the giant who towered over her. But when violet and sable-brown eyes melded in the morning light, her inhibitions lifted with the billowing wind.

"Devlin! You nearly frightened me to death!" she exclaimed, jamming her hands against her hips in outrage. Then, instinctively, she kicked his well-shod ankle and shouted, "Don't you ever sneak up on me again!"

Devlin's response was not immediate; he found himself affected by Kyra's disheveled and thoroughly enchanting appearance. Having just returned from a business expedition, Devlin had inquired after his wife's whereabouts and had been none too pleased with his findings. Deciding that he and his headstrong wife were long overdue for a heart-to-heart chat, Devlin had stalked from the mansion to search for his stubborn wife and errant waifs. His progress along the footpath leading from the bluff down to the beach had gradually slackened, however, as he paused to observe, almost enviously, the intimate familial scene taking place below.

Kyra was fussing with some object while the children clustered around her, and as he continued his surveillance, Devlin's irritation gave way to curiosity. It was not until Nicholas emerged from the little group and began to race up and down the sand that Devlin's puzzled frown relaxed. A kite! Kyra had made a kite for Nicholas and Sarah!

Of their own volition, his eyes settled on his wife's trim form, and he was imbued with a strange sense of wonder as he watched her shout encouragement to the little boy who ultimately lost hope of ever catching a sea breeze. Devlin's fascination became even more acute, and his handsome face underwent a series of contortions ranging from mild amusement to outright admiration, as he beheld Kyra's antics. He observed as she began to run alongside the crashing waves, much encumbered by her damp skirts and the children who dashed in and out of her path, her face set with determination.

It was then that his thoughts were ruthlessly invaded with unbidden images of Lynette, but try though he might, Devlin could not envision his first wife engaged in such playful gamboling. Lynette's memory, however, rekindled Devlin's ill temper, prompting his collision with Kyra.

Thinking that Devlin had momentarily taken leave of his senses, since he continued to glower at her in a most disconcerting way and uttered not a word, Kyra started to climb to her feet. She was stopped short, however, when he thrust a large hand beneath her nose, and she fell back in surprise.

Without thinking, Kyra slapped his hand aside and climbed to her feet unassisted, affording Devlin a view of an exposed calf and a pair of shapely ankles that he found particularly gratifying. Mustering as much dignity as the situation allowed, she flounced over to the lifeless kite and snatched it up from the sand. Seeing the children's crestfallen faces, Kyra rounded on her husband furiously.

"Look what you've done! You had to spoil their fun, didn't you?" she snapped at him, waving the kite in his face, but her courage dissolved when Devlin stepped over to her.

"You were going about it all wrong, my little hoyden," he informed her dryly, with a pointed look at her unkempt state.

"I suppose *you* could have the kite airborne in an instant," Kyra snapped crossly.

"Very likely," Devlin agreed, and as he embarked on a lengthy dissertation on the proper method for flying a kite, Kyra paid him little heed. Her attention had been diverted by the masculine hand at her waist that worked to restore order to her appearance by pulling her skirts from her waistband, allowing them to flutter back into place about her ankles. With a roguish wink, he plucked the kite from her fingers and, after running up the beach a few yards, called over his shoulder, "Let me show you how it's done, my lovely gazelle."

Kyra reddened at his reference to her unladylike gallop, but forgot her pique seconds later when Devlin's successful launch of the kite elicited jubilant shouts from the children. She maintained her distance, content to watch as Nicholas and Sarah converged on their father, begging for the right to hold the string. Kyra suddenly became aware of Devlin's befuddled expression—it was obvious he hadn't a clue as to how to pacify the excited youngsters—and with a little smile she stepped forward to help him.

She gently took the string from Devlin and handed it over to Nicholas, taking care to show him how to make the kite dip and plunge through the air. Then, instructing Nicholas not to let go and to let Sarah share in the fun, Kyra strolled a few feet away, conscious of the intimidating shadow beside her.

"You know, Devlin," she ventured softly, in a voice bereft of criticism, "if you would only spend a little more time—"

"I came here to discuss *your* shortcomings, Kyra," he interrupted coldly, "not mine! Shall we begin with this frolic on the beach in which you have stupidly exposed my children to all manner of danger?"

"What?" Kyra blurted, stiffening at his insult. "I was looking after the children. I would not let anything happen to them, and I would *never* knowingly place them in danger."

"But you have done just that," Devlin informed her coolly, taking her to task for straying so far from the house.

"But . . . how?"

"Privateers," he answered shortly. "Many of the islands, Carraba included, have been plundered by marauders in recent months. I would not care to have my children kidnapped and held for ransom or, worse, sold for profit. And as for you, dear wife . . . well, I do not like to dwell upon the possibilities, but even a tattered ragamuffin like you"—his disdainful gaze swept her from head to toe— "would fetch a handsome sum.

"Have you nothing else to wear?" he asked tersely, realizing that he had seen her in the same dress on a number of occasions since their arrival at Cauldurae.

"No," she replied, tilting her chin at a defiant angle, refusing to cringe before him. "My belongings have not yet arrived from Raybourne."

"The sorry state of your wardrobe is not the issue at any rate." Devlin dismissed the topic that he had only moments before introduced, but his manner was less abrupt when he asked, "Did Miss Lovejoy not advise you against bringing the children here without an escort?"

Kyra shook her head in response, looking beyond her husband's broad shoulder to where the children played merrily.

Devlin followed her lead, and even he could not ignore the fatherly pride that swelled in his breast as he observed their unrestrained revelry. Deciding that he would not like to be responsible for disrupting their fun, he again focused his attention on Kyra. Breathing a sigh, he said, "Miss Lovejoy will be reprimanded for her oversight." Then with a shrug, he ambled toward the footpath leading to the mansion. "I'll send one of my men to stay with you until you are ready to return to the house. And, Kyra, you can spare me a great deal of anxiety if you will have one of the guards accompany you on any future outings."

"If you insist" was her accommodating rejoinder.

"I do," he replied flatly, throwing up a hand to forestall

her ready question. "Don't—not now. I have neither the time nor the inclination to explain my actions."

Swallowing her curiosity, Kyra ran after him and caught his sleeve. "Devlin, won't you stay with us? Nicholas and Sarah would welcome the chance to play with their father." Even as she spoke, Kyra saw that Sarah had started to toddle toward them, and desperately hoping to bridge the gap between father and offspring, she whispered imploringly, "Please?"

Devlin was hard put to ignore the pleading violet eyes that gazed up at him, and he was nearing the brink of acquiescence when the recollection of a similar coquettish beauty left him cold. Lynette's haunting image dashed the harmonious mood that fleetingly burgeoned within him, and shaking off Kyra's hand, he shook his head brusquely.

"Kyra," he began tiredly, "I've had little sleep in the past few days. Therefore, I trust you will understand why I prefer the comfort of my bed to wallowing in the sand with two urchins. I'll send one of my men to you," he said with an air of finality and strode off without so much as a backward glance.

Devlin had no sooner disappeared than a burly guard appeared in his stead. The man—Jenkins, he was called—made no attempt at conversation, nor did he demonstrate any interest in the children. Instead, he patrolled the beach, his eyes constantly scanning the horizon—for what, Kyra could only guess.

In very short order, she forgot the man when Sarah's frantic wails and Nicholas's forlorn cry alerted her to the demise of the kite. As it fluttered away on the wind, Kyra instructed the children to gather their belongings and follow her. When they began their ascent up the narrow trail, however, Kyra became mindful of the guard once more; he fell in behind them, ever watchful for some unexpected aggression. With a skeptical shake of her head—Kyra questioned the need for such extreme caution—she herded the children up the path, carrying Sarah the last few yards.

When they reached the summit, Kyra thanked Jenkins for his escort, and the small party resumed the trek toward the mansion. Even though the sentry did not accompany them, Kyra could feel his gaze as she walked away. Thoughts of this latest encounter with her elusive husband were still nagging at her when she and the children arrived at the main gate, where they were hailed by an approaching horseman.

"Hello, the house!" the man shouted, bringing his mount to a halt beside them. "You must be Mrs. Cauldwell," he greeted Kyra, a smile broadening his handsome face. "I'm Dr. Joshua Fowler, your neighbor," he introduced himself, as he slid from the saddle.

"It's a pleasure to meet you, Dr. Fowler." Kyra returned his smile, positioning Sarah on one hip so she could extend her hand in a friendly gesture.

"The pleasure is mine, ma'am," he said warmly, briefly grasping her hand and doffing his hat.

Kyra felt flattered by the man's attentiveness. Then, reminded of her own tousled appearance, she smoothed back an errant curl and, suppressing a blush, explained, "Devlin just returned from an exhausting business trip and has retired to his bed."

"No matter. My business is with young Master Cauldwell," he informed her, reaching across his horse to retrieve a large basket. A smooth golden head, with liquid brown eyes and long ears protruded from the basket, as did two somewhat oversized paws. "Remember, Nicholas? I promised you one of Birdie's pups when it was weaned. Well, here she is, lad, the pick of the litter," Joshua announced, gently removing the puppy from the basket.

An instant later, the puppy was free to race about, darting between Nicholas's legs, scurrying here to investigate the leaves of a bush, there to sniff at the masonry gatepost, finally returning to throw himself at Nicholas, playfully licking the child's face. Hearing her brother's squeals and delighted giggles, Sarah scrambled from Kyra's arms. Sensing another conquest to be made, the ball of fur bounded toward Sarah and treated her to the same display of unconditional affection.

While the puppy's attention was thus diverted, Nicholas turned to the two adults who stood fondly watching the frenzied melee taking place on the emerald-green grass. "Do you mean it, Joshua? Is she really mine?"

"Yes, Nicholas," Joshua assured the child. Then, as an afterthought, he added, "assuming it's all right with your new stepmother."

Kyra knew she would never forget the look of supplication that Nicholas turned on her, and though she was eager to grant him his wish, she knew what her response must be. "I think she is a beautiful pup and you would make a fine master, Nicholas, but your father must give his permission."

Undaunted by this pronouncement, Nicholas merely whirled and ran toward the house. "Come on, girl!" he shouted over his shoulder to his new canine friend. "Let's go ask him!"

The puppy, intrigued more by Nicholas's flailing arms and legs than by his command, sprinted after him, leaving a thoroughly dazed Kyra behind. She did not remain idle for long, however, for the image of a disgruntled Devlin prematurely wrested from his sleep spurred her lethargic feet to action, and after bidding her guest a hasty good-day, she gathered Sarah in her arms and ran after the rapidly vanishing duo, her panic-stricken cries of "No, Nicholas, wait!" echoing unheeded on the wind.

11

The polished oak doors were still ajar when Kyra arrived at the main entrance, and Nicholas was scurrying up the wide mahogany staircase as fast as his little legs would carry him, the puppy a golden-brown bundle of energy at his heels. Realizing there was no time to waste and ignoring the stabbing pain in her side, Kyra hurried across the parquet foyer. She paused at the foot of the stairway, thinking her ascent would be swifter if she could persuade Sarah to remain below with one of the servants, but sensing a great adventure in the making, Sarah locked her fingers about Kyra's neck and clung for dear life, preventing any separation.

Thus encumbered, Kyra reached the second floor landing just as Nicholas flung open the door at the end of the corridor and let it crash noisily against the wall. With a groan, she sprinted down the hallway, arriving breathless and expectant in time to see the ball of fur bound onto the pine chest at the foot of the bed, leap over the rail, and scuttle up the length of the slumbering giant. Then, bracing her paws on Devlin's shoulders, the puppy proceeded to bathe his face with frenzied strokes of her long wet tongue.

"Oh, no, Nicholas," Kyra moaned, slumping against the doorjamb, dreading the coming explosion.

It came with all the fury of an unleashed hurricane when Devlin's eyes snapped open and he stared incredulously into a furry face that exuded a nauseatingly frolicsome spirit, a feeling not shared by the recipient of the wet awakening. Impervious to any pending danger, and before Devlin could react, the puppy pounced forward to nip his chin, lick his face, and yip a cheerful greeting in his ear. She then plopped down on Devlin's chest, crossed her white-tipped paws in front of her, and panted while her tail tapped a contented rhythm against his flat stomach.

"*Nicholas*!" came the ear-splitting bellow as Devlin sat bolt upright in the middle of the massive four-poster, ruthlessly dislodging the pup from its comfortable perch.

Momentarily put off by this sudden outburst, the animal backed away to reevaluate the situation, its smooth head cocked at an inquisitive angle. But Nicholas was too elated to be alarmed by his father's furious summons; he scrambled happily onto the roomy bed, following the same route the puppy had taken. Unable to curtail his exhilaration, Nicholas bounced up and down beside his smoldering father, pleading excitedly, "Can I keep her, Papa? Can I? Kyra said it was all right. Can I? Please say yes. *Please*!"

Having recovered his composure, the victim of the puppy's mauling leveled an accusing eye at Kyra. "Am I to understand I have *you* to thank for this?" Devlin inquired smoothly, indicating the scene in progress on his bed as Nicholas and the puppy engaged in a jubilant romp.

Under normal circumstances, Kyra would have been mistrustful of her husband's calm manner, but she did not so much as blink when she beheld the devilish gleam flickering in his brown eyes. Her attention had been diverted by a single word from the boy who gleefully submitted to the puppy's rough-and-tumble antics. Having grown accustomed to being addressed in a grudging little voice as "ma'am," Kyra was surprised by Nicholas's unhesitating use of her name, and in her joy she dismissed Devlin and his troubles from her mind.

Sarah soon restored Kyra's attention to the business at

hand. As she watched her brother cavorting with the puppy, she squirmed in the hope that she could take part in their sport. Thoroughly distracted, Kyra lowered Sarah to the floor and, her misty gaze fixed on Nicholas, she replied to Devlin's question as she straightened up.

"What?" she murmured distantly; then, shaking her head, she lent him her full regard. "No, Devlin, I am not responsible for Nicholas's joy—would that I were," she added wistfully. "That distinction belongs to one of your neighbors. We met him on our return from the beach and he presented Nicholas with this lively gift." She glanced fondly at the young dog who was trying to drag Sarah across the mattress by the ribbons that dangled down the back of her gown.

Kyra stepped over to the bed to prevent the child's dress from being ruined. "Nicholas wants to keep the puppy, and I told him he must discuss that with you. If I had known he meant to pester you now, I would have suggested he wait until you wakened." Kyra's contrition vanished as she disentangled dog and child.

The puppy, mistaking Kyra's intervention for an appeal for attention, suddenly lunged at her, knocking her off balance to stumble sideways onto the bed. While the puppy launched an earnest offensive on its latest victim, the children swarmed their father, their heartfelt petitions barely discernible above the pup's raucous barking and Kyra's frantic protestations.

"Can I please keep her?" was Nicholas's desperate entreaty.

"Puppy stay!" Sarah chimed in for good measure.

Even Devlin's impenetrable facade could not withstand the hopeful looks cast on him by the pair of begrimed and beseeching faces. "Oh, all right, you may keep the wretched beast," he eventually grumbled, "but—"

The remainder of Devlin's speech was preempted as Nicholas vaulted forward to embrace his father and press a fierce kiss of gratitude on his stubbled cheek. His happy cries of "Thank you, Papa! Thank you!" reverberated through the room.

Unused to such lavish displays of affection, Devlin slowly unwound the tiny fingers from his neck and set the child away from him, dashing any such reaction from Sarah by reaching around the children to pluck the energetic puppy away from Kyra. "*But*," he continued emphatically, "she is to be kept outside. You may ask Henry to build you a doghouse near the stables. And see about teaching her some manners. This undisciplined spirit is most objectionable and will not be long tolerated.

"Off with you now." Devlin thrust the pup at its new master, adding one surprising postscript. "And, Nicholas, be sure to say a proper thank-you to your stepmother before you go, for the decision to let you keep the animal was as much hers as mine."

Nicholas, who had already leaped from the bed and was running toward the door, the tireless puppy chasing after him, came up short with this command. Immediately assuming the stance of a rebellious youth—hands shoved in his pockets, eyes downcast, shoulders hunched, the toe of one shoe scraping back and forth against the thick piled rug—Nicholas muttered, "Thanks."

"You're welcome, Nicholas," Kyra replied lovingly, but when she extended a hand to ruffle his dark curls, he and Goldie, as the puppy had been spontaneously named, darted through the open doorway. With a disappointed sigh, Kyra lowered her hand and raised grateful eyes to her husband. "Thank you. I've never seen his face so completely alive."

"This may come as a shock to you, Kyra," Devlin began dryly, leaning near her to fondle a wisp of hair that had fallen free of its pins, "but I was once a child myself, and I do recollect having a dog or two in my day. Do you think me such an ogre that I would deprive Nicholas of the same treat?"

In all truthfulness, Kyra was finding it difficult to think about much of anything at the moment, for when Devlin moved forward, the sheet fell away in negligent folds on his lap. Thus permitted an unrestricted view of his muscular chest and lean stomach, she had been struck with the titillating realization that Devlin was stark naked beneath the covers. Kyra was very much aware of a hand hovering near her breast, ostensibly fingering a piece of torn lace that had been mangled by the frisky pup. His curious fingers then traveled sideways to caress an ugly scratch that marred her throat—more of Goldie's mischief—and Kyra struggled to think of something to say to prevent what she feared might happen.

In the end, it was Sarah who came to the rescue, for having grown weary of the game she had initiated upon Nicholas's departure—crawling in and out from beneath the bedcovers and pillows—she suddenly burst forth from behind a pile of bolsters. Taking in the scene before her with rapt interest, she inquired with the naive innocence of a child, "Mama Keewa, Papa—play?"

"Out of the mouths of babes." Devlin chuckled under his breath and asked huskily, "Well, Mrs. Cauldwell, shall we . . . play?"

As he became aware of the wild thrumming of Kyra's pulse beneath his fingertips, his warm gaze deepened with desire. Devlin anticipated any number of reactions, varying from righteous indignation to out-and-out acquiescence, but he was ill prepared for the word that ultimately tumbled from her lips.

"Joshua," she mumbled.

"*What*?" Devlin thundered, snatching his hand away as though it had been bitten by a wasp.

"Dr. Fowler," Kyra hastily amended. "It was he who gave Nicholas the puppy. I should have reminded Nicholas to thank him for his generosity."

Kyra watched in bemusement as the man who had only

moments earlier been so congenial was transformed into a great, hulking brute. Her puzzlement changed to outright fury, however, as she watched this behemoth whisk Sarah from the bed, set her none too gently on the floor, and gruffly advise her to seek out her brother's company. Once again spurned by the father she worshiped, Sarah toddled out of the room, her forlorn sobs slicing through Kyra with heartbreaking intensity.

Torn between her urge to comfort the distraught child and a need to confront the unfeeling monster, Kyra chose the latter. Having stood witness to similar scenes on more than one occasion, Kyra decided that she had endured enough of her husband's ugly disposition. Believing that an explanation was now due her, she marched around the bed to plant herself squarely in front of him.

"Why?" she demanded, and when his only response was to raise one eyebrow as if questioning her temerity to challenge him, she pressed on. "Why do you treat her like that? She's just a little girl. She doesn't understand— indeed, *I* don't understand."

"Nor is it likely that you ever will," he said frostily. Devlin wrapped the sheet around him as he climbed out of bed and, stepping past her, strode toward the adjoining dressing room.

"But I *want* to understand." Kyra reached out to take hold of his arm, but when he jerked free and stalked away, she ran after him. "Is it truly so very hard for you to love her?" she cried.

"Stop badgering me, woman!" he growled threateningly, but Kyra would not be put off.

"She loves you, Devlin. Can't you find it in your heart to love her back?"

"*No!*"

"But . . . but why not?" Kyra asked dejectedly, now more perplexed than angered by his bitterness.

"*Because she isn't mine!*" Devlin shouted in exasperation, and his admission having sufficed to halt her questions, he wrenched the door open and stomped into the dressing room, furious with himself for having allowed Kyra to wheedle the truth from him.

Once Kyra's shock at Devlin's startling outburst subsided, her natural curiosity returned, but the slamming of the door emphasized her husband's departure with finality, warning Kyra that, like the door, the subject of Sarah's paternity was now closed to her.

In the days following Devlin's impassioned confession, it became apparent that he would not soon loosen his tongue regarding the mystery of Sarah's paternity. Although Kyra did not plague Devlin with questions, neither did she forget the matter, resolving instead to bide her time until an unguarded moment presented itself when he could be prevailed upon to provide a full explanation. The issue was still much on her mind as she ambled along the pathway toward the stables.

Kyra normally possessed a high level of energy and enjoyed a brisk gallop on horseback now and then, but she had found herself hampered in recent days by a tired, listless feeling. Attributing her sluggish spirits to a combination of homesickness, the recent abominable circumstances of her life, and lack of exercise, she vowed to overcome this bout of lethargy, and it was this determination that led her to the stables. Although she had no riding costume, she wanted to see her husband's thoroughbreds.

Besides, she longed for a glimpse of Henry, the fellow Biddie kept talking about. With these two goals in mind, Kyra trudged on to the stables and was greeted by an unexpected surprise when she stepped inside the structure— Devlin, just returned from the village. He was preoccupied with his mount, but after handing the reins over to the groom, he approached her.

"So you've come to have a look about," he greeted her warmly.

"At the moment, *looking* is all I can do," she replied glumly, her mouth drooping into a pout that Devlin found curiously enchanting.

"Ah, yes. Your clothes have yet to arrive from Raybourne. Take heart, magpie." Devlin freely used the nickname by which Colin called her, and although he no longer purposely mocked her with it, Kyra did not miss the teasing grin that lit up his face. "I've brought you a letter from your father. Perhaps it will shed some light on the status of your belongings."

Kyra could barely contain her excitement as she watched his long, nimble fingers slide beneath his coat to withdraw a thin packet of envelopes, and she had to forcefully curtail the impulse to snatch them from his hand, such was the depth of her hunger for news of home and family. Finally the coveted letter lay in her hand, and Devlin watched as she tore open the envelope and began to read.

"Well?"

Kyra glanced up into his laughing brown eyes and, feeling a bit self-conscious that he witnessed her unbridled joy, assumed a more somber manner. "Papa says for me to expect my things shortly. He has been bedeviled by Andrew's shenanigans, and the plantation consumes a great deal of his time. I suppose that would account for the delay." She folded the letter and tucked it in her pocket.

Her disappointment did not go unnoticed by the man at her side, and prompted some unexpected remarks. "I have been so preoccupied with business matters that I have neglected to fulfill even your basic needs. However, that oversight can be easily remedied.

"There is a small dress shop in the village. The selections are limited, but Mrs. Sikes is handy with a needle and will be able to supply you with a few things until your belongings arrive. Can you handle a tilbury?" he asked, and, acknowledging her eager nod with a smile, said, "Good. Take Biddie with you—and Jenkins, of course. And may I suggest that you make your first purchase a riding habit?"

"Oh, yes!" she blurted with joy. Then, tempering her fervor, she murmured, "Thank you. I will be heartily glad to be rid of these threadbare garments. Even little Sarah has commented on my shabby appearance."

Thinking to avoid the subject of Sarah, Devlin took Kyra's arm and coaxed her to follow him. "Let me show you around. I believe I have just the mount for you."

Kyra held her tongue and devoted her attention to her husband's commentary. As they strolled through the barn, he told her the history of each magnificent steed. Kyra was impressed with what she saw, not that she was surprised by the excellent condition of his stables. She realized that in all things Devlin was a man who knew, and usually got, what he wanted.

Kyra was pleased with Nutmeg, the dapple-gray mare whose gentle disposition, Devlin told her, had often been misconstrued as listlessness. "She's a lively filly," he assured her. "A sweet goer who will give you an invigorating ride, yet you need not fear she will toss you and leave you alongside the roadway in the dust. The same cannot be said, however, of this fellow." Devlin chortled knowingly and stepped across the wide aisle.

Recognizing the animal as the one Devlin had dismounted as she entered the stable, Kyra climbed onto the bottom slat of the closed stall door and leaned forward to slide a friendly hand along the horse's sleek forehead.

"Careful," Devlin warned, slipping a protective arm about her waist. "Old Scratch doesn't take to strangers."

"Pooh!" Kyra scoffed, wrinkling her nose at him before favoring the chestnut with her full regard. "I've gentled more daunting beasts than this," she lulled soothingly, reaching out to stroke the horse's reddish brown neck and receiving an appreciative whicker for her efforts.

Devlin's bemused expression changed to one of outright admiration as he watched his loyal steed nuzzle Kyra's neck, and he was still shaking his head in wonder when she jumped down from her perch and moved toward the end of a long row of stalls. Having heard restless stirrings emanating from that quarter, she was anxious to investigate.

"What's *his* name?" she called over her shoulder, pointing toward a black stallion with a white-speckled head.

Devlin bellowed a warning and Kyra jerked her hand back just in time to avoid being nipped by a mouthful of angry, gnashing teeth.

"Are you all right, little pet?" Devlin came up behind her and placed a bracing hand on her shoulder.

Kyra nodded. "He startled me, that's all. My, he *is* ill-tempered! Are you, by chance, acting as his mentor?" she inquired sweetly.

"Mind your tongue," Devlin grumbled good-naturedly, encouraged by her remark, which implied that she had not been unduly shaken by the incident. Kyra was grateful, nevertheless, for his strong arm around her shoulder as he explained, "His name is Wildstar. I know he does not appear to be a very obedient fellow, but he can be ridden, though he is skittish and even I sometimes find him difficult to manage.

"I bought him because his previous owner said he could not be tamed to saddle, and you know I can't resist a challenge." He smiled the boyish grin that always seemed to make her heart go topsy-turvy. "He'll make an excellent breeder. Feel free to ride Nutmeg whenever you wish; Henry or one of the other hands will rig her out for you. Lynette didn't care much for riding, but I keep a sidesaddle or two on hand. Personally, I think they are treacherous contraptions, but until you ladies take to wearing trousers, I suppose you must use them. Just keep your distance from Wildstar—he's dangerous. That is not a dare, Kyra, just a friendly warning." He tweaked her chin and was near the brink of surrendering to the sudden compelling urge to press a kiss on her upturned mouth when a shout from one of the stable hands checked him.

"Damn!" The curse emerged as a frustrated groan against Kyra's cheek. "Yes, Henry, I'm coming," Devlin called back and, with a parting look of longing at her tempting lips, he walked away, only to retrace his steps seconds later as something occurred to him.

"I almost forgot to give you these," he snapped, angry with himself for allowing his passions to be so readily stirred by his wife's charms.

Ever in a quandary as to how to cope with Devlin's inconstant moods, Kyra glanced down at the envelopes he grudgingly produced. "More letters?" she asked, happily surprised.

"One is from Mother," he informed her blandly. "The other—I can but speculate. Could it be from an old beau who pines for your return to Charleston?" Devlin correctly assumed the answer to his flippant query from the look of pure disdain she directed at him. "Pity," he droned sourly.

Kyra did not dignify his taunt with a reply, choosing instead to seek a place where she could read her letters in peace. As she passed through the lavish tropical gardens on her return to the house, she spied the perfect spot for a restful pause—the gazebo on the far side of the garden.

It stood just beyond a quartet of statues of willowy maidens regally poised at the four corners of a once-grand fountain erected by the original owner. Though it had acquired its share of chips and cracks over the years, the sculpture group had withstood the rigors of time and Mother Nature.

As Kyra walked past the fountain, she found herself admiring the striking statues. The four women wore gowns that, even though cast in stone, seemed to billow in soft, cascading folds down to their sandaled feet. Each held an earthen jar beneath one arm, the vessel tipped forward to allow a stream of water to spill forth, while extending her free arm out over the shimmering water in a graceful gesture. Kyra thought it a tedious way to spend eternity— endlessly refilling the pool—but once she was comfortably settled inside the garden house, all thoughts of the statues fled as she devoted her attention to her letters.

Like a child determined to prolong a special treat, Kyra reread the letter from her father before opening Amanda's, both messages expressing many of the same sentiments. They wished her well and hoped she was getting along with Devlin.

Kyra pulled the remaining envelope from her pocket, and her brow puckered into a soft frown as she studied the unfamiliar handwriting. Though her name was scrawled boldly across the paper, she did not think it was penned by a man, but neither did the script possess the delicate, precise curves of a feminine hand. It certainly was a puzzle and, knowing there was only one way to solve the mystery, Kyra broke the envelope's seal and spread the letter out on her lap.

As she read, Kyra was consumed by uncontrollable shivers, the result of a numbing terror that gripped her heart and left her skin cold and clammy.

Kyra stared blankly at the newspaper clipping that lay crumpled on her lap. It was the article about the fire that had taken Clayton Fairchild's life. Her frightened eyes fell to the accompanying note clenched between her tense fingers. Though brief, the message was explicit. Almost against her will, Kyra read the bone-chilling threat: "I saw you leaving Fairchild's house the night he died. I can prove you were there and I'll tell the authorities if you refuse to cooperate. Instructions will follow soon."

There was no signature, only that threatening message, and Kyra shuddered as she folded the incriminating letter and returned it to the envelope. She longed for the solitude of her room, where she could gather her scattered wits and make some sense of this unexpected revelation, but her lifeless limbs would not support her. Thus she remained, until the flickering shadows of evening began to descend on the garden, signaling the approaching supper hour. Not wishing to be found moping among the flowers by an inquisitive servant—or worse, by her husband—Kyra rose stiffly and made her way back to the house.

Kyra muddled through the following days like one who had fallen under an evil spell. She became reclusive, choosing to remain sequestered in her room for much of the day, eating little and speaking only when the children, a servant, or her husband directed a comment to her. The fact that she had developed an almost obsessive interest in Devlin's comings and goings did not go unnoticed by Hannah, the watchful housekeeper.

"She's as constant as the North Star, she is," Hannah confided in her husband one morning as she poured him a cup of coffee in their cozy kitchen. "Comes creeping out of her room about noontime each day and sidles down the stairs real quietlike, as if she had no right to be there. Then she sets up a vigil at the window in the back parlor and watches until the mister comes home. The missus greets him at the door and whatever he says seems to pacify her, 'cause she's fine till the next morning when it starts all over again.

"I don't know, Jim, something strange is goin' on. I can't quite put my finger on it, but I'll get to the bottom of it—mark my word." And before the solemn little man could respond to his wife's chatter, she pecked him on the cheek and left the cottage.

Actually, there was a perfectly logical explanation for Kyra's peculiar behavior: She lived in constant anticipation of the arrival of another sinister letter, and since the back parlor afforded an excellent view of the path that Devlin followed from the stables, it seemed the best place for her to wait. Not only could Kyra observe his progress toward the house, but the entrance was just a few feet from the parlor door, allowing her immediate access to him.

If Devlin was curious about his wife's sudden preoccupation with the post, he gave no indication. In fact, he found himself more baffled by Kyra's reaction each day when he patiently informed her that he had no letters for her. Invariably she would breathe a happy sigh and walk away, leaving a mystified gentleman in her wake.

Finally, on the fourth afternoon of this perplexing ritual, Devlin, having just experienced the nastier side of Wildstar's temperament, was hard pressed to put forth a cheery demeanor when Kyra pounced on him. He brusquely reminded her that Carraba was a small island and that it was not unusual for several days, or even weeks, to pass without the arrival of a mail packet.

With this information, Kyra stopped shutting herself in her room, but she did not emerge from her sullen mood. If she was blind to the dismal aura that draped her like a shroud, those around her were not. Glancing up from his breakfast one morning, Devlin found himself both annoyed by her uncommunicative behavior and concerned about her ashen pallor.

"Kyra!" he barked.

Contentedly lost in her self-imposed misery, Kyra jumped at the unexpected sound. "*What*?" she snapped irascibly.

"Is that all you're going to eat?" He nodded at the mangled slice of toast that lay shredded on the plate before her.

"No, I'm also having tea," she replied, with an insolent quirk of her brow.

"You needn't take that saucy tone." He leaned back in his chair. A careful scrutiny of her wan complexion made him inquire, "Are you feeling all right?"

"I'm a little tired," she admitted with a gloomy sigh, "and I haven't had much of an appetite lately."

Devlin mulled over this vague reply and observed his wife's glum expression as she mechanically stirred a lump of sugar into her now lukewarm tea. "What you need," he said, "is some exercise. Have you visited Mrs. Sikes's dress shop?"

"Yes, one of your men is to drive Biddie and me into the village this morning to pick up some things she's made for me," Kyra replied distantly.

"Excellent," Devlin remarked, standing to take his leave. "Am I to assume you ordered riding clothes?"

Again Kyra responded affirmatively, this time with a detached nod of her head.

"Good. But what's this about having one of my men drive you? Are you feeling so much out of sorts that you cannot even handle the reins?" he questioned, his eyes narrowing in concern as he awaited her reply.

"No," she murmured and reddened at her forthcoming admission. "I fear there will not be room for myself, Biddie, *and* my purchases in the gig. We will require the carriage."

"Ah, I see. Oh, well, I suppose that serves me right for not keeping a firmer hold on my purse strings," he chuckled, accepting the fact that the dressmaker's till would soon be plump at his expense. "Perhaps you would care to try out your new riding habit this afternoon? A few matters require my attention, but I should return in time to accompany you," he added, though considering Kyra's abstraction, he might as well have directed his comments at the wall.

When Kyra emerged from her trance some moments later, she discovered a servant removing her husband's place setting—Devlin was gone.

Kyra's thoughts remained riveted on the sinister letter and its unknown writer during the carriage ride to the village. For days she had fretted over its ominous tidings; the

faceless tormentor had warned that he had proof and that
she must cooperate. Try though she might, Kyra could think
of nothing she had left behind that might implicate her in
Clayton's death, and she dared not speculate about what the
writer would demand of her in return for his silence.

With a little shudder, Kyra chanced a glance at Biddie
who, though she pretended otherwise, was troubled by her
mistress's brooding. Having realized days ago that the
young woman had fallen into the blues, Biddie had decided
not to badger her about it, thinking that Kyra would soon
return to her former cheerful self. But as the days passed
and she saw no sign of improvement, Biddie had become
apprehensive, prompting her to interrupt Kyra's thoughts.

"Is you all right, Miz Kyra? You've been lookin' poorly
lately."

"What—oh, I'm fine, Biddie . . . *really*. I'm a little
tired, that's all." She appeased her attentive servant with the
same excuse she had given her husband at the breakfast
table.

Suddenly mindful of the concern she had caused to others
with her melancholy behavior, Kyra resolved to set aside
her fears until they were warranted. After all, there was no
need for her to mope over something that might never come
to pass. She would deal with her nameless adversary when
and if she received another letter. After much reflection,
Kyra had begun to wonder if this might be one of Andrew's
pranks, and if it was, she knew how to deal with her
mischief-making sibling.

Shaking off her mood, she favored Biddie with her
sunniest smile and said, "I am fine, Biddie, just a bit
melancholy, but I'll be all right in no time, I promise. Now,
why don't you tell me all the news about your Henry?" As
the servant eagerly complied, Kyra turned her attention to
the passing landscape, listening halfheartedly to Biddie's
excited chattering.

The carriage trundled into the village, and the driver

brought the team to a halt before Mrs. Sikes's shop. Kyra alighted, and with a nod to the ever-vigilant Jenkins, she and Biddie entered the store. The tinkling of the silver bell was still echoing when the dressmaker appeared.

It had been Kyra's intent to collect her goods and be on her way, but the seamstress insisted that she try on the garments to ensure a proper fit. When Kyra started to protest, Mrs. Sikes ushered her through a curtained doorway and into the sewing room where an assistant was ironing Kyra's favorite purchase.

Kyra's attention was immediately caught by the exquisite creation, a lemon-yellow riding habit trimmed in white with a double row of gilt buttons. A matching plumed hat, gloves, and half-boots of tan Spanish leather completed the elegant ensemble. Kyra had known when she selected the material that it would soil easily, but she had been unable to resist the vibrant color and the stylish design Mrs. Sikes had shown her. She had, however, been more practical about her remaining choices, ordering modest dresses of gauze, muslin, and other soft materials and colors.

Against her better judgment, Kyra had allowed Mrs. Sikes to include an evening dress, on the off chance that a formal occasion would arise before the arrival of her own wardrobe from Charleston. The remaining two garments were also for riding—one of rose-blossom cloth ornamented with frogs, and another of dark blue with a blue satin stock and bow headed with cambric frill; each had a matching top hat and veil. There were, of course, the usual accessories to be considered, and by the time all the bulging parcels had been loaded into the carriage, Kyra's mood had brightened considerably.

A faint smile graced her lips as she shook the proprietress's hand and bade her a cheery farewell. But as Kyra turned to exit the shop, she ran headlong into a customer who was just crossing the threshold. She stumbled back slightly, and when a masculine hand darted out to steady her, Kyra looked up, fully expecting to encounter Devlin's roguish stare. The eyes into which she gaped were green, however, and belonged to Joshua Fowler.

"Dr. Fowler!" she exclaimed, her fingers correcting the damage done to his neckcloth. Then, recalling that she was treating a virtual stranger with unseemly familiarity in a public place, Kyra snatched her hand away. "Forgive me! If I'd seen you, I would have stood clear of the doorway."

"I was at fault, Mrs. Cauldwell," he told her before asking solicitously, "Are you hurt?"

"Oh, no!" Kyra assured him. "Only a little rattled. Are you contemplating a purchase for Mrs. Fowler?" she asked conversationally, retying the ribbons of her fashionable new hat.

"What—me? No, I'm a bachelor, ma'am. I saw you across the way and was in such a rush to give you my regards that I failed to notice you taking leave of the store," Joshua explained. "I wanted to inquire after Nicholas and the puppy and to ask you to join me at the inn for a light luncheon. By the time you arrive home, Francesca will have begun preparing the evening meal," he reasoned. "Have you had any altercations with Devlin's fiery cook?" he asked knowingly. "She can be quite . . . daunting."

Kyra recalled the one time she had innocently suggested that Francesca consider reducing the amount of pepper she used in her lamb stew. The next time a serving of Francesca's stew was placed before Kyra, it was so heavily sprinkled with the spice that a single bite had provoked the consumption of three glasses of water. Francesca's unspoken message was clear. *She* reigned supreme as mistress of Cauldurae's kitchens, and unsolicited advice was not welcome.

A laugh bubbled in Kyra's throat as she wondered what sort of skirmish this man might have had with the overbearing cook, and suddenly feeling ravenous, she accepted Joshua's invitation. Silently pooh-poohing the disapproving look Biddie sent her—what harm could there be in taking lunch with the man and fostering a budding friendship?—she placed her hand on Joshua's sleeve and allowed him to escort her to the inn.

It was early afternoon when Joshua helped Kyra into her waiting carriage. She was bubbling with enthusiasm as the vehicle pulled forward, and she eagerly anticipated their arrival at Cauldurae so that she could plan a dinner party to which she would invite Joshua and an eligible young lady. Assuming, of course, that there were any suitable unmarried ladies on the island; she would have to consult Devlin about that. Kyra had found the doctor a delightful companion, a refreshing and witty conversationalist—not unlike Devlin, she admitted grudgingly, when he was not being disagreeable.

But further thoughts of this social gathering were ruthlessly banished when the carriage rumbled out of the village onto the ocean highway and her attention was drawn by a woman's high-pitched laughter. As the carriage rolled swiftly past an impressive mansion nestled on the side of a hill, Kyra caught a fleeting glimpse of a couple whose faces would be forever branded on her memory. As the vehicle traveled on, Kyra blinked hard in an effort to blot out the painful image of a familiar man lifting an attractive brunette from an open landau and turning to stride toward the house, the woman still clasped in his powerful embrace. The most devastating blow came when the woman rested her cheek against the man's broad shoulder and entwined her fingers possessively about his neck.

Devlin. Kyra's mind screamed the name. *Devlin!*

12

By the time the carriage rumbled between Cauldurae's stone gateposts, Kyra had worked herself up into a full-blown rage, her emotions flamed by the memory of her husband locked in an embrace with another woman. Although Kyra had suspected Devlin of conducting any number of romantic liaisons, the evidence that he was indeed a brazen philanderer was a devastating blow to her pride. Her initial shock had been gradually replaced by stunned disbelief, but during the hour-long journey home, Kyra had ample opportunity to brood over this disturbing discovery, which accounted for her present stormy disposition.

"He didn't even have the decency to be discreet," she muttered miserably.

But you said you didn't care what he did, her pesky conscience reminded her.

"Forget what I said!" Kyra shouted in frustration, drawing a perplexed look from Biddie.

" 'Scuse me, Miz Kyra?"

"Nothing, Biddie," Kyra snapped, though her ire was directed toward her womanizing husband, not her faithful servant.

Before the maid could question the reason for her mistress's sudden and unexplained pique, the vehicle rolled to a stop in front of the house, and she watched helplessly as Kyra leaped out of the carriage and stalked inside the mansion. Biddie's curiosity would not have been assuaged by Kyra's actions, for the ill-tempered young lady succumbed to a genuine fit when she reached the seclusion of her room.

The slamming of the door echoed from the four corners of the chamber as she marched to the chest of drawers, carelessly discarding her straw hat and gloves in her wake. She yanked the bottom drawer open and began slinging the bureau's contents helter-skelter. Moments later, trembling with anger, she grasped a tiny brass object, and Kyra smiled with malevolent pleasure as she pulled a key from beneath a pile of clothes. Her gaze fell on the door of her husband's room, and of their own volition, her feet propelled her toward it. However, her fingers paused uncertainly as she started to insert the key into the lock—and with a sigh of indecision, she turned away from the door.

What had she been thinking? She could not simply barge into Devlin's room and vent her fury by ransacking his belongings. Kyra did not want to be taken to task for impetuous and childish behavior. Besides, what possible justification did she have for her jealous response to Devlin's philanderings?

Can it be you're falling in love with the scoundrel? ventured her bothersome inner voice.

Kyra slumped into the chair before her dressing table to consider this improbable notion, but a fleeting glance in the mirror confirmed her greatest fear. Despite everything—his disdain for her, his apathy toward the children, and his generally unpleasant disposition—she had come to love him. There was no other explanation for her jealousy.

He was arrogant, stubborn, and utterly impossible—but Kyra cared for him despite these imperfections. This unaccountable phenomenon had come about in part because she knew intuitively that beneath his crusty exterior beat the heart of a genuinely caring, feeling, and loving man. Though he would scoff at her reasoning, Kyra surmised that

Lynette's infidelity had hurt Devlin more than he would
ever admit, fostering his contempt for women. So how was
she, a newcomer to this world of men and marriage, going
to convince her cynical husband that she loved him, and that
her ardor would not pall as Lynette's had?

It certainly was a quandary, especially when she considered all the ghosts with which she and Devlin would have to
contend before they could establish a harmonious marriage.
There were at least three: Lynette, Clayton Fairchild, and
Devlin's deceased brother Gareth. For, ever since that day
in Savannah when Devlin had curtly warned her never to
mention his brother again, Kyra had suspected that her
husband was much affected by Gareth's death.

At present, however, it was not a ghostly apparition that
haunted Kyra. Instead, she was bombarded with visions of
a willowy brunette, her hands clasped familiarly about
Devlin's neck. Kyra blanched at the memory, but the color
quickly returned to her cheeks. The thought that Devlin was
at that very moment closeted with the unknown woman—
caressing her, touching her, willing her to respond to his
body's rapturous rhythm—drove her almost mad with
despair.

With renewed anger, Kyra stood up and, taking a pair of
scissors from the dressing table, marched to the door she
had faced earlier. She did not falter this time as she slid the
key into place and, with a determined twist of her wrist, let
herself into her husband's room.

Devlin did not return to Cauldurae to partake of the
evening meal, an exercise in judgment that only intensified
his wife's anger. Kyra dined alone and then adjourned to the
drawing room to await her husband. She endeavored to
concentrate on the embroidery hoop she had absently
selected from the sewing basket by her chair. That proved
impossible, what with one ear cocked toward the door
expectantly, and her eyes darting to the clock at regular

intervals. This lack of attention resulted in a series of uneven stitches, severely hampering the completion of the pillow slip she was embroidering.

Finally, when the mantel clock chimed ten without any sign of her wayward spouse, Kyra abandoned her stitching for the comfort of her bedroom. As she climbed the staircase, she decided it was just as well that Devlin had stayed away, for she would have been hard pressed to hide her irritation. She was not over-eager for a confrontation, but it might have been interesting to encounter the libertine fresh from a day of debauchery.

Could he have faced her, she wondered? Would there have been even the slightest hint of remorse in those wondrously dark and deceptive eyes?

With a sigh, Kyra resigned herself to the fact that her curiosity would not be appeased this night and pushed open the door to her room to find Biddie waiting to attend her. With a wan smile, Kyra submitted to the maid's gentle ministrations, grateful that Biddie did not seem overly talkative. When the servant slipped a white satin gown trimmed with Brussels lace over her head, Kyra became aware of a faint rumbling in the distance, and a glance at the window revealed a flash of white heat across the sky.

Tying the sash of her robe around her waist, Kyra sat down before the dressing table mirror to allow Biddie to brush her hair. But before the maid could begin this task, a tremendous crack of thunder and a brilliant burst of lightning brought Kyra to her feet with a start.

"Goodness, but that gave me a fright!" she exclaimed, pressing one hand to her breast to still her heart's erratic rhythm. "It sounds as if we're in for quite a storm, Biddie." Kyra hurried to the window to assess the force of the approaching tempest, then squealed and jumped in fright as a series of jagged lightning bolts slashed the blackened night.

"The children," she mumbled. "They must be terrified, Biddie. Let's see to them."

As she and Biddie progressed up the narrow staircase toward the nursery, Kyra admonished herself for her fear. It was merely a summer squall, nothing to be afraid of. She must work to allay her emotions in front of the children; it would not do for her to appear as frightened as they were. By the time they reached the chamber door, Kyra had managed a thin smile of reassurance, a smile that quickly faded when her slender fingers encircled the knob and twisted it. The door was locked.

Kyra blinked in disbelief and, thinking she must be mistaken, jiggled the latch once more, only to discover that she was correct—the door had been bolted. But why and by whom?

Even before the questions were completely formed in Kyra's mind, she easily guessed the culprit's identity. As to why Miss Lovejoy would resort to such a measure, Kyra had no ready answer, though she resolved that the governess would be quickly brought to justice for her irresponsible conduct.

"Miss Lovejoy? Please unlock the door," she called, rapping sharply. When she received no response, Kyra's face grew scarlet with rage, her voice rose two octaves, and her graceful hands curled into fists as she pounded furiously on the door. "Miss Lovejoy? Open this door *at once!*"

Biddie, wary of her mistress's unprecedented fury, sought to soothe Kyra by offering, "I seen Miz Lovejoy goin' in the library a while back."

Kyra whirled around, eyes blazing and chest heaving. "Are you telling me that Nicholas's and Sarah's governess has taken herself off for some leisurely entertainment after barricading the children in the nursery to fend for themselves in this storm?"

"It wasn't stormin' when she left de children, Miz Kyra," Biddie replied fairly.

"That's not the point, Biddie! Nicholas and Sarah are never, *ever*, for any reason to be locked in their room. Such barbaric measures are suited for hardened criminals and snooty governesses who have yet to learn their place, but certainly not for young children," she seethed. An angry gleam darkened her violet eyes to a deep blue as she started toward the staircase.

"Where you goin'?"

"To find Miss Lovejoy and remind her of her station in this household. Wait here," she instructed the faithful servant.

Miss Lovejoy was handily run to ground, for the unfortunate target of Kyra's wrath was unhurriedly wending her way up the staircase, humming a tuneless ditty and thumbing through a leather-bound novel when Kyra arrived at the third-floor landing to greet her. If the errant governess was surprised to find Kyra blocking her path with a hand outstretched in a meaningful gesture, she gave no sign.

"The key," was all Kyra could manage, her voice little more than a rasp as she endeavored to control the anger that boiled within her.

Miss Lovejoy had half a mind to inform the upstart mistress of the manor—as she considered her—that she could go straight to the devil, but something about Kyra's barely contained demeanor forestalled such a foolish remark.

With an acquiescent shrug, Alice Lovejoy dropped the key into Kyra's upturned palm, saying, "Why you need to fly into a dither over a silly locked door is beyond me. I could hear you squawking above that unholy din outside." The violet glint in her eyes grew a shade darker, but Kyra's expression softened from irrepressible fury to implacable self-control, and her voice was clear and unwavering when she said, "Then you will be pleased to know you won't be subjected to any more of my offensive squawks. Pack your belongings, Miss Lovejoy. You're dismissed!"

"But . . . but you have no right! You can't dismiss me!" The governess ran after Kyra who presently hastened toward the locked nursery.

"Oh-h-h, yes, I can!" Kyra said flatly, jamming the key into the lock and giving it a vicious turn.

"We'll just see about that," proclaimed Miss Lovejoy, dogging Kyra, who flung the door open and stepped across the threshold into one of the three rooms that constituted the nursery suite.

This was the common area the children used for play, and in which Nicholas would presently begin taking his lessons. Their bedrooms were located on either side of the spacious room, with Miss Lovejoy's accommodations situated farther along the corridor. A cursory inspection of Nicholas's room showed it to be empty. Without hesitation, Kyra wheeled toward Sarah's chamber with Miss Lovejoy hard on her heels, that lady's screeches highly audible above the crashing peals of thunder.

"You've got no right! Mr. Cauldwell hired me, and only he can let me go. We'll just see what he says when he comes home—*if* he comes home," Alice Lovejoy added, a knowing sneer curling her lips.

Kyra's blistering retort died on her lips when she hurled the door of Sarah's room wide open. A scene of utter chaos left Kyra momentarily speechless. In one corner of the room an uncontrollable tempest was in progress. The raging wind whipped the lace-edged curtains about convulsively, rain gushed in through the open window, and the loosened shutters banged relentlessly against the outside wall. But the sight that would be forever branded on Kyra's memory was that of Nicholas and Sarah. In the middle of the canopied bed, the young boy knelt before his sister, desperately trying to comfort her and curtail her terrified screams, though it was obvious that he was as frightened as she.

Kyra's eyes filled with compassionate tears and her breast swelled with renewed anger at the one responsible for this devastation. Although she longed to strike out at the impertinent governess, Kyra realized that assuaging the children's fears must come first. With this thought in mind, she ran to the window, and leaning out of it—encountering some difficulty against the gale and becoming thoroughly drenched in the process—she managed to secure the shutters. Then she lowered the window and went over to the bed.

"It's all right, Sarah. It's only a storm. It'll be over soon," Nicholas was murmuring, stroking her tiny hands with his own trembling fingers. When he glanced up to see his stepmother approaching the bed, for once he did not glower at her. Indeed, both children bounded forward simultaneously—Sarah to hurl herself into Kyra's arms and cling to her neck for dear life, and Nicholas to bury his face in the soft folds of her satin robe.

"There, there, darlings," Kyra whispered soothingly, kissing the top of Sarah's head and ruffling Nicholas's dark curls. "You are exactly right, Nicholas. It's only a storm; there is nothing to be afraid of, little loves," she cooed. Turning to Biddie, who had followed her into the nursery, she said, "Bring a change of nightclothes for Sarah; she's soaked through. The children will spend the rest of the night in my room." With that, Kyra turned toward the exit, only to come up short when she found the doorway filled by a totally unexpected form.

"What the devil is all the commotion about?" Devlin's voice carried just enough disdain to stir the embers of Kyra's smoldering temper.

"I'll tell you what this is about," Kyra all but shouted as she walked to where he stood, Sarah clasped protectively against her with one hand and Nicholas clutching the other. "I want that woman"—she jerked her head toward Miss Lovejoy—"out of my house by morning."

"Madam, what grounds—" Devlin began testily, only to have his inquisition ignored by the infuriated woman who swept past him and out of the room, a swirl of satin and lace and glorious indignation.

"Here's the little one's nightdress, Miz Kyra," Biddie announced several moments later when she entered her mistress's room.

"Thank you, Biddie. Come along, Sarah; I'll help you change." Kyra accepted the soft lawn garment and directed the child toward a folding screen in the corner of the room. "Did Mr. Cauldwell say anything after I left?" she called from behind the barrier, tugging the damp nightdress over Sarah's blond curls and adjuring her to stand still when she began to prance from foot to foot.

"Oh, he had a great many things to say," replied a familiar menacing masculine voice from the open doorway.

With a little groan, Kyra bristled as the fresh nightdress fell into place about Sarah's ankles. Straightening, she shooed the child around the screen and toward the bed. Sarah's face brightened instinctively when she saw her father, but whether because of his grim countenance or because she knew she would only suffer rejection from him, Sarah did not approach him, nor did the room reverberate with her gleeful cries of "Papa, Papa." Instead, she toddled to the bed where Nicholas was already tucked snugly beneath the fragrant sheets.

Chancing a glance at the simmering giant, Kyra noted with chagrin that Devlin had come into the room and was closing the door behind him. Feigning indifference to her husband, she turned her attention to Sarah, hoisting the child onto the bed beside her brother. The next moments were devoted to Sarah, whose trepidation had vanished with the fading thunder. Now that she was calm, the child was bouncing atop the sheets.

"None of that, young lady," Kyra scolded, taking Sarah firmly by the hand and coaxing her back down onto the mattress. "To bed with you."

"Mama Keewa play," Sarah whimpered, but her father's looming shadow caused her wishful look to evaporate. Flinging herself back onto the pillow, she squeezed her eyes shut.

Kyra lovingly tucked the sheet in and bent to press a kiss against the little girl's cheek. "Sarah must go to sleep now. Mama Kyra will be here in the morning."

"Kiss Nicky 'night?" Sarah mumbled, obviously intent on prolonging the bedtime ritual.

Kyra wore a hopeful expression as she shifted her gaze to Nicholas, and she continued to fuss with the bedclothes as she made her way around to him. When she leaned over to extinguish the bedside lamp, Kyra bussed his cheek. Amazingly, this act did not prove irksome to the lad, who merely rolled onto his side and grumbled drowsily, "G'night."

"Goodnight, sweet one," Kyra replied brokenly.

"My, my, what an adorable little mother you've become," droned a sarcastic voice behind her. "Charming, utterly charming. But tell me, dear wife, now that you've seen fit to fill your bed with my children, where will you sleep?"

Kyra disregarded his taunt by stepping behind the privacy screen to retrieve Sarah's discarded nightdress. After laying the wet garment neatly across the back of a chair to dry, she snuffed out the candle. Then, by way of a response to his flippant query, she sank down on the chaise longue, wishing he would go away so that she could change out of her own rain-soaked garments.

"Not so fast. I want a word with you, madam." Devlin's husky whisper buffeted her cheek.

This said, his hand encircled her wrist and he dragged Kyra to her feet and propelled her across the darkened room toward the door to the hall, which he wrenched open without ceremony. Their silhouettes were framed in the opening—one tall and threatening, the other small but resolved not to cower before the formidable man. They remained thus for an awkward stretch of time until a little voice's innocent inquiry from the shadows prompted Kyra to pull the door closed and march past Devlin to the staircase. He caught up with her at the landing, however, and his hand on her arm quickly dashed any thought of a swift descent.

"Well?" Devlin drawled in his most mocking tone. "'Mama Keewa kiss Papa 'night?'" he mimicked little Sarah.

"I'd sooner kiss a frog!" she hissed bitterly, flinching at his spontaneous bark of laughter. Kyra tried to shake off his hand, but Devlin held her fast, adding to her frustration and provoking the reckless accusation she flung at him. "You've had enough kisses for one day."

"Oh, don't look so surprised," she scoffed at his bemused frown. "I *saw* you, Devlin! I saw you with that . . . that woman!"

Devlin's expression grew contrite, and his grip loosened as he murmured, "It's not what you think, Kyra. Elyse is my business partner."

"Don't treat me like a fool!" she snapped. "David Kincaid is your business partner."

"He *was*," came the softly spoken rejoinder, and Kyra wrested herself free of his hand. "David was Elyse's husband," he explained. "They were traveling home from Cauldurae one evening about a year ago when their carriage was waylaid by highwaymen—most likely privateers who had come ashore or marauders from one of the big islands—and they murdered David. I'll spare you the details; it is a grisly tale." He paused and his eyes clouded over with the memory of the horrible incident and the loss of a dear friend.

Then, shaking off the disquieting reflections, Devlin said, "The Kincaids had no heirs, so I offered to purchase his shares, but Elyse decided to take her husband's place in the company. It was not a situation that I accepted willingly, for Elyse can be disagreeable at times—much like you, magpie," he said. It was his intention to rile Kyra, and he was rewarded by a spark of glaring violet fire. "So there you have it. It was not a lover's assignation you witnessed but rather a dull meeting between business associates."

"Don't insult me with your lame excuses, Devlin," Kyra spat scornfully. "I saw you *carrying* that woman!" She flung the words at him, completely unaware of the jealous intonation of her speech. "And her with her lily-white hands entwined about your neck, as if . . . as if—"

"As if what, Kyra?" Devlin asked with an amused chuckle. Folding his arms across his chest, he leaned sideways against the banister, his gaze never leaving her face. When it became apparent that she had no reply for him, Devlin stated, "I have no romantic interest in Elyse. Oh, there have been rumors, and I have not disputed them. Indeed, I have often derived enormous satisfaction from watching Mother turn purple with anger when she thinks I have been off cavorting with Elyse when, in reality, our jaunts have been purely business.

"The plain truth is that Elyse sustained a grievous injury during the ambush that took David's life. She was left a cripple, Kyra. She is unable to maneuver without a wheel-chair, and it is not always convenient to have one about. I was returning Elyse to her home following a meeting at the distillery construction site. I was carrying her because she cannot walk."

Kyra's lips formed a silent "oh" of comprehension, but Devlin continued before she had a chance to speak. "I am not unmoved by your little tirade, magpie. Surely you must know that I am not indifferent to you, and if your jealousy is an indication that you have suffered a change of heart and would now have me as a *real* husband, let me assure you that I am both willing and able to accommodate you." He bent forward to whisper suggestively, "Ah, yes, more than able."

"You flatter yourself," Kyra said curtly, slapping his

hand aside and adding as she wheeled around, "I'd sooner bed down with—" But the remainder of Kyra's cheeky rejoinder died on her lips to be supplanted with an ear-splitting scream of absolute terror.

Having paused on the staircase landing above the main floor entrance hall, Kyra had become so absorbed in their conversation that she had forgotten how close she was to the edge of the topmost step. When she whirled away from Devlin, her foot became entangled in the hem of her dressing gown and she was thrown off balance to plummet forward into the treacherous abyss. Only moments earlier, Kyra had silently prayed that the floor might open up and swallow her for the rash and unjust conclusions she had drawn about Devlin and the mysterious woman, and now it would seem that her wish was to be granted.

For one heart-stopping, infinitesimal space of time, Kyra was suspended in midair—arms flailing, hands groping in desperation for the elusive railing. Then, miraculously, a sinewy arm wrapped itself about her waist and jerked her away from the beckoning chasm. The next instant, Kyra was twirled about and, in that fleeting second before Devlin smothered her in his embrace, she saw that his face was an agonizing mixture of fear, relief, and something else that she could not quite identify.

The next moments were a blissful blur in Kyra's mind, and during this respite, the frantic pulsing of her heart gradually subsided. But when she lifted her head to thank him for snatching her from certain disaster, her words of gratitude were obliterated by a pair of lips that swiftly descended upon her own, rekindling her heart's erratic rhythm.

Devlin's mouth played against hers with an unsuppressed passion born of panic for someone who was nearly lost but had mercifully been spared. Kyra reveled in the ferocity of his caress, her arms encircling his shoulders to hold him as tightly as she herself was being held. They clung together feverishly at the end of the dimly lit corridor, and when Devlin's tongue deftly slid inside her mouth, Kyra accepted the intrusion willingly, eagerly, her sweet sighs of contentment serving to awaken his long-suppressed desires.

Devlin was the first to pull away from the embrace, but only to allow his lips to blaze a trail of fervent kisses, first exploring the pulse that pounded in the hollow of her throat, then traveling downward until they encountered the lace-trimmed edging of the satin wrapper. With a little groan of disappointment, he cursed the obstruction and returned to pepper her cheeks and brow with endearing kisses.

The fear-induced delirium that had momentarily enveloped Devlin eventually passed, and confident that the woman he presently clasped to his chest was no apparition and would not fly away down the staircase if he released her—oh, but he didn't want to let her go, not yet, not yet—Devlin bent his patrician head over Kyra's curls, murmuring ever so softly, "Oh, my love, my love, I almost lost you!"

This utterance served to break the trance to which Devlin had fallen victim, and as if splashed in the face with cold water, his head snapped back. Like a man awakening from a heavy sleep, he gave his head a brusque shake and glanced up and down the corridor, apparently searching for the one who had spoken, but there was no one else about. With an embittered oath, realizing that he had aired his thoughts aloud, and he flung away from Kyra.

Kyra was equally surprised by her husband's ardent admission, but she was ill prepared for his subsequent actions. She experienced a suffocating feeling of dread as she watched the transformation. She could almost see the barrier falling back into place, cloaking him with impenetrable armor, and she felt a great sadness constrict her heart. Her melancholy proved to be transitory, however, for in the next moment her whole being was set to trembling with apprehension. Without a word, Devlin claimed Kyra's hand

and dragged her back along the corridor to his room, where he flung the door wide and thrust her inside. Then, assuming a slow and deliberate stride, he followed her inside and closed the door with an ominous click.

The tension hung suspended between them like a thick fog; indeed, the room wanted only the portentous ticking of a mantel clock to perfectly dramatize the forbidding scene. Kyra stood quaking on the far side of the spacious chamber directly in front of a large gilt framed mirror. Her fretful gaze was fastened on the giant who only minutes earlier had saved her from a tragic mishap, but now seemed to be contemplating an even darker fate for the one who had guilelessly stirred his blood.

They remained silent for several nerve-racking moments until Kyra, finding her husband's brooding silence and unyielding stare even more unbearable than the consequences of her actions, ventured tentatively, "Devlin?"

Kyra underwent a sharp reversal of feelings, however, when she heard his throaty rejoinder, for the probing brown orbs had been irrevocably drawn to her rain-drenched bodice since the instant he pushed her across the threshold. The flickering candlelight gently accentuated her shapely curves and the rosy-tipped peaks straining proudly against the soft material were enough to drive even the most timid of men to distraction, such that a man of Devlin's passion found it impossible to curtail his reaction.

He walked toward her purposefully, saying as he nodded toward her nightclothes, "Remove them."

"*What*?" Kyra gasped, instinctively recoiling from him.

Devlin substantiated her worst fears by repeating gruffly, "Your nightdress and robe are soaked. Remove them."

"No!" To Kyra, her rebuttal sounded like a demented screech, but in reality, it emerged as little more than a frightened squeak. Her hand flew to her throat where she nervously fingered the delicate lace, and her violet eyes glistened with panic as she observed Devlin's approach.

Kyra actually shrank away when he reached out to stay her hand. When she showed no immediate sign of complying with his instructions, he applied himself to the diverting task of undoing the ribbons at her throat, then lowered his hands as if to undo the belt at her waist. It was here that he encountered resistance as Kyra, experiencing a resurgence of courage, angrily pushed his hands aside.

"I said no!"

"You always say no, madam *wife*," he spat the word hatefully, "but no more, my passionless little prig." He jerked her forward, oblivious to her startled cry, and allowed his fingers to resume their task. His countenance was such that Kyra dared not thwart him. "Why do you persist in hiding behind this ridiculous facade? Your actions imply you wish to be treated as the mistress of this house. You dismiss a servant without so much as a by-your-leave and order me about. I won't question your motives; you obviously believe Miss Lovejoy was negligent in her duties. Well, the governess is a moot issue. She will be gone before the sun rises. I have carried out your orders; now you shall do likewise with mine."

Devlin acknowledged the numb shake of her head by saying, "As I suspected, you demand all the privileges but will make no sacrifices. Yes," he snarled, "you're quite clever at calling the tunes to which we are all expected to dance, but you refuse to give the piper his due." Strong fingers untied the sash at her waist and impatiently flicked it aside. Devlin made as if to do the same with the satin and lace robe, then hesitated, having decided upon another, more appealing course.

His sun-bronzed hands abruptly released the fragile material, and taking a step backward, he let his brown gaze rake her from head to toe. His voice was little more than a husky growl when he said, "Do it . . . *now*!"

Kyra raised beseeching eyes to Devlin, but her half-hearted entreaty proved useless; there was no reasoning with the passion-crazed man. Stifling a sob, she lifted trembling fingers to do his bidding. A mere breath's space separated them as Kyra, very much aware of her interested observer, hesitated only a moment before opening the robe and letting it slide down the length of her arms and onto the floor.

Once again violet eyes petitioned sable-brown ones only to discover that mercy would not be granted, as the curt wave of a hand and Devlin's bluntly spoken "Go on" promptly confirmed.

Kyra swallowed hard, her skin flushed scarlet with humiliation, and hoping to preserve some scrap of dignity, she turned her back to him. She was more than a little amazed when Devlin did not ridicule this coy reaction, but the outcome of her next move explained his apathy. Kyra was shaking visibly as her slender fingers inched the material off one shoulder and down to her elbow where she pulled her arm from the sleeve; then she raised her hand to the other shoulder to repeat the action. Her movements were slow and deliberate, more from dread than from any desire to entice her husband.

In the shadowy glow of the dimly lit room, Devlin witnessed the proceedings with smug arrogance, but Kyra's unpracticed disrobing, however innocent, provoked an alarming response in him—a reaction of aphrodisiacal proportions. The velvety smoothness of her bare back shimmered in the lamplight, and the contrasting texture and color of her hair as it spilled across her shoulders and tumbled down her back made him yearn to bury his face in the brilliant blanket of gold and brown satin. But when he beheld Kyra's reflection in the mirror, his breath came in a rush, catching him off guard, nearly strangling him before escaping in a tortured groan.

Kyra heard his sharp intake of breath, but having forgotten the mirror, she was unaware of the reason for his distress until she raised her head and violet and sable-brown met in the murky shadows. She clutched the sleeves of the night-dress to her breasts in a reflex action, but as Devlin's stare intensified, her resistance withered. As if no longer pos-sessed of the will to fight, Kyra released the garment, which rustled as it fell into a crumpled heap at her feet. It took all the pluck she could muster to keep from looking away when she saw the appreciative gleam that enlivened Devlin's face, for she could feel the incredible heat of his gaze as it enveloped her in its fiery splendor.

Kyra was more than a little disconcerted by Devlin's lengthy scrutiny. Although she was grateful that he had not touched her, he continued to stare in a way that made her uneasy. As the agonizing minutes ticked slowly away, Kyra became more ill at ease until, deciding she would no longer be a bullied participant in Devlin's games, she bent to retrieve her nightdress.

"Leave it!" ordered the voice behind her.

Kyra meekly obeyed the command, stiffening instinc-tively as she saw him take a step toward her. Amazingly, he still made no effort to touch her, but she experienced a mysterious sensation in the pit of her stomach nonetheless as she became aware that his penetrating gaze had embarked upon a thorough inspection of her unclad body, and she flushed shamefully. Mesmerized by his entranced air, Kyra stood motionless and even though she quivered inside, she did not so much as blink as she watched his feverish stare blaze a searing trail down the length of her body, lingering almost reverently to gaze upon her exquisitely shaped breasts—the hardened tips baiting him in a way that he found virtually impossible to resist—before returning to hold her gaze in the looking glass.

The normally composed young woman was much af-fected by her husband's loverlike actions. Even though he had not laid a hand on her, Kyra's flesh tingled as if it had been caressed by his skillful fingers. The meticulous strok-ing of his smoldering brown gaze had caused an answering heat to stir her blood and sparked a curious sensation at the very core of her femininity that spiraled upward to embrace her. Experience had taught Kyra that she could not hope to conquer two such compelling forces—Devlin *and* her own perfidious desires—and realizing this, she felt her shoulders droop in acceptance of her fate and closed her eyes to await the inevitable.

He was close, so close that Kyra could feel his warm breath buffeting her cheek when his hoarse whisper came, "You're so very beautiful. I want you. God, how I want you!"

Kyra opened her eyes then, but she could not bring herself to confront Devlin's scorching gaze, and fighting back rapidly gathering tears, she whimpered softly, "I know."

She sensed rather than observed the arms that extended toward her, prepared to whisk her about and sheathe her in a rapturous embrace. Before Devlin could indulge his sorely tested passions, Kyra spoke again, her words delivered on a choked sob. "But that is not enough," came her forlorn admission, and as a single teardrop trickled down her desolate face, Devlin abruptly mastered his rampaging emotions and took an involuntary step backward.

When Kyra next summoned the courage to confront his discomfiting reflection, she was surprised and enormously relieved to find that it no longer hovered behind her. The sound of a door closing drew her attention from the mirror, and with a confused glance in that direction, she realized Devlin had regained control of his emotions. Kyra reacted by falling to her knees atop the pile of discarded night-clothes and promptly bursting into tears.

Kyra winced upon awakening the following morning. When she rolled to her side, stretched out her hand toward the down-filled pillow, and encountered instead the coarse texture of a tapestry rug, she discovered the reason for her discomfort. Her eyes flew open as her head filled with unhappy memories of the previous evening, and sitting up, she groaned miserably. One hand rose to push aside the tangled wisps of hair that fell across her face while the other found its way to her back where it gently massaged the stiff and sore region—the result of having spent the night on the hardwood floor among her rumpled nightclothes.

As an afterthought, Kyra let her eyes skirt the huge four-poster that dominated the room, and upon finding it empty, she released a haggard sigh. Thinking it would be wise to vacate the chamber before Devlin returned to torment her, she climbed painfully to her feet, and after pulling her gown over her head and securing the robe about her waist, she stepped into the hallway.

There she encountered the future master of Cauldurae, already up and dressed. From the looks of him, the boy had suffered no ill effects from the storm. Would that she could say the same of herself.

"Good morning, Nicholas." Kyra forced a cheery lilt in her voice.

"Mornin'," came the stilted reply.

"Where are you off to so early and so smartly dressed?" She nodded at his riding apparel.

Nicholas, not one to waste words, stated simply, "The stables." Then, overcome with excitement over his pending excursion, the child blurted happily, "Henry's gonna let me ride Pepper!"

"That sounds like great fun, Nicholas," Kyra said, smiling down at his beaming face. "Yes, it does," she repeated absently, and momentarily forgetting the little boy, she began to amble down the corridor. Then, thinking that perhaps an invigorating ride through the countryside might be just the thing to revive her own battered spirits, Kyra turned to address the child who continued to stare at her quizzically. "Nicholas? Would you be a dear and ask one of the grooms to prepare a mount for me? I think I would enjoy a ride this morning, too."

"Sure," he said, turning to run down the staircase.

Half an hour later, Kyra, dressed in the new lemon-yellow riding habit, complete with a gaily plumed hat, emerged from the house. Tugging on her riding gloves as she walked, Kyra was deep in thought as she progressed along the path toward the stables, bouncing her riding crop against her thigh. But she was yanked forcefully from her reverie when she arrived in the stable yard and, hearing a restless whicker, glanced up to see the horse that waited to be mounted . . . Wildstar.

13

The stallion galloped along the coastal highway, his hooves kicking up a trail of dust as he plodded onward, mindlessly heeding his rider's directives. They had maintained this frenetic gait for a long time and the horse's stamina was waning rapidly. His sleek hide glistened with sweat, his sides expanded and contracted with every gasping breath, the wind whipped through his chestnut mane, and still the rider showed no sign of slowing down.

A stand of trees overlooking the sand and crashing surf appeared on the horizon, and as they approached, the rider gave a signal and the mount slowed accordingly. With a graceful snort and a toss of his majestic head, the horse trotted over to the wooded area where the rider dismounted and permitted the stallion to roam aimlessly while he did much the same.

Devlin was so engrossed in thought that several minutes passed before he realized he was no longer astride Old Scratch but was sitting with his back against a palm tree, staring blindly out over the vast expanse of water, his hat dangling between his knees. He was the picture of dishevelment, what with his wrinkled coat, his untidy neckcloth, and the stubbly growth of whiskers that darkened his handsome face. His brown mane was sadly mussed as well, but that was to be expected since he had thrust his hand through the thick strands repeatedly in helpless desperation.

He was at war with himself; grappling with an inner conflict so profound he dared not delve too far beneath the surface lest he stir the dormant embers of a long-suppressed emotion that was better left buried.

Devlin had not returned to his chamber the previous evening. After abandoning Kyra to her own devices, he had adjourned to the library to try to make some sense of the tempestuous events that had transpired between them. But aside from determining that he had behaved like a contemptible barbarian and that Kyra was perhaps the loveliest vision his bleary eyes had ever gazed upon, he resolved nothing. His mind remained a blur, but whether this malady was directly attributable to his rampant emotions or to the numerous glasses of very fine whiskey he had consumed throughout the night remained an enigma.

He had drifted into a fitful sleep during the wee hours of the morning without arriving at any definite conclusion about the little firebrand he believed to be resting peacefully upon his bed. But Devlin's dreams, like his every waking moment, had haunted him with images of the one he sought so desperately to expunge from his memory. No matter how hard he tried, he could not shed his thoughts of Kyra's likeness.

She was everywhere; she preyed on his sensibilities in a way no woman ever had before, unconsciously throwing up obstructions that clogged his normally flawless reasoning. When Devlin closed his eyes, as he did now, his mind effortlessly conjured her image. He visualized her sitting across the dinner table surreptitiously stealing a glance at him when she thought his attention elsewhere, or she was tenderly nursing one of Sarah's little hurts or exchanging heated barbs with him. It was uncanny how clear the images were. Her musical laughter echoed in his ears, her fragrance overpowered him with its subtlety, and her eyes—

"*No!*" The cry erupted with excruciating force and reverberated down the precipice to be consumed by the rolling waves. Devlin lunged to his feet, awakening from his reverie in a cold sweat and shaking his head to cleanse it of the disquieting reflections. "This must not be!" he shouted, sending the fist of one hand crashing into the palm of the other.

Devlin began to pace the bluff, muttering to himself as he walked, "Get hold of yourself, man! You're acting like a lovesick bull rutting after a heifer just brought to pasture." He halted in mid-stride, and his head came up as a particular phrase vibrated in his head.

"Lovesick?" he repeated; then, with a disgusted grunt, he began to ramble again, swearing, "Not bloody likely! Oh, I want her right enough. I'm eaten up with the idea of possessing her, but *love* Kyra? *Never!*"

Again he gave his dark head a vigorous shake to purge his thoughts, and he continued in a dull monotone, "You loved Lynette, remember?"

But Kyra was not like Lynette; perhaps things would be different with her. The brooding man's conscience—or was it his heart?—tried to reason with him.

A fleeting glimmer of hope brightened his troubled eyes, but the enticing notion was summarily dashed aside before being given a chance to take root and wrap itself about his heart. "No," came his staunch conviction. "Mother's ultimatum be damned. The sooner I'm rid of the vixen, the better off I'll be," he vowed and, having arrived at a decision that would drastically alter the life of the lady in question, Devlin stomped over to Old Scratch and gathered up the reins.

"Come on, Scratch. Let's go back to Cauldurae and get you a brushing and a generous helping of oats." He almost smiled at the answering whicker of approval. "Then I'll send word to the men to make the *Windjammer* seaworthy, for I'll be whisking our little magpie back home to Papa— today if possible, tomorrow at the latest."

As Devlin was turning to mount the patient animal, he

glimpsed a splash of bright yellow and shimmering black in the distance. Pausing, he folded his arms atop the saddle and focused his curious gaze in the direction of the blur that galloped across the adjacent field. As he watched, the ebony speck gradually evolved into a recognizable image, and Devlin straightened incredulously, his hands tightening about the pommel—an indication that whoever had been so foolhardy as to remove Wildstar from his stall without first obtaining Devlin's permission would quickly come to regret his actions.

"But who would dare . . ." The question died on his tongue as he was enveloped with a nagging sense of familiarity. Devlin's eyes remained riveted on the streaking stallion and the svelte figure seated regally on his back. Heaving a frustrated sigh, he groaned a single word: "Kyra!"

Devlin's initial observation was that Kyra possessed a damn fine seat, for though she was obviously having difficulty restraining the headstrong animal, she hung on admirably. This thought was immediately followed by "Damn the little wretch! Does she want to break her neck?"

The words had barely left his lips before Devlin was given reason to fear that his offhand quip might very well become a tragic reality. In the next instant, his face twisted into an expression of unholy terror, for as he watched, the black stallion rose into the air to soar majestically across some unseen obstacle. For one incredible, spellbinding moment, horse and rider were suspended in midair against an emerald and sapphire background in a magnificent demonstration of equestrian showmanship. The danger-riddled situation impressed itself on Devlin with unnerving clarity in the succeeding moments, however. When the giant hooves again came into contact with the ground, both saddle and rider were dislodged and ruthlessly tossed aside.

Devlin watched helplessly as the fragile bundle was pitched headlong into the air, arms flailing in a futile attempt to cushion the inevitable blow. She landed with bone-breaking force a fraction of a second later, then tumbled over and over until finally she lay still . . . deathly still.

The distance separating them was so great that Devlin could not possibly have heard her, but he was keenly aware that an agonizing cry had been released. It was not until he was astride Old Scratch and racing toward the stricken young woman that Devlin realized the gut-wrenching cry of anguish had been torn from his own throat.

Kyra became dimly aware of the methodical probing of a pair of hands, starting at one ankle and progressing up her leg to her thigh. Then the hands cradled her shoulders and carefully rolled her onto her back, and after applying the same procedure to her other leg, the persistent, yet surprisingly gentle fingers subjected her arms to a similar inspection. A soft moan floated between her parched lips, and her violet eyes fluttered open, then closed again. In the hazy shadows of semiconsciousness, Kyra distinctly heard a well-known voice grumble, almost grudgingly, that it did not appear she had broken anything. She then sank into a sea of black where there were no voices or exploring hands, only soothing darkness.

When Kyra awakened, she felt as if she had been unconscious for hours when in actuality she had been asleep for only a few minutes. She was surprised not to find her husband towering over her, ready to castigate her for her foolishness, but when she propped her pain-riddled torso up on her elbows, Kyra discovered the basis of Devlin's indifference. He was preoccupied with Wildstar.

As her clouded vision cleared, she watched as he tended the animal a few yards from where she lay. He cautiously smoothed his hands along the front and back of Wildstar's powerful legs, lifting each hoof to check for any injuries. Kyra could not suppress the flush that mantled her cheeks as the faint recollection of a comparable examination flooded her senses, even though, she admitted peevishly, it appeared that he was more concerned with his horse's welfare than with hers. When Devlin was satisfied that the animal had not sustained an injury, he gave its rump a fond pat and walked over to inspect the saddle.

Kyra continued her covert surveillance until she saw Devlin hoist the saddle onto his shoulders and turn toward her, his expression grim. Certain his forbidding demeanor could not possibly bode well for her, Kyra slumped to the ground and allowed her eyes to flutter closed in what she prayed was a passable imitation of a faint. She knew her efforts to be for naught, however, when the unexpected thud of the saddle on the ground next to her ear caused her to flinch and she heard Devlin's deep chuckle.

"Open your eyes, little pet," he cajoled. "I'm not going to eat you."

Distrustful of his bantering tone, Kyra reluctantly complied.

"Are you hurt?"

"I . . . don't think so, just dazed and . . . and badly shaken." As if to lend substance to her words, Kyra's voice trembled as she gazed warily into his face.

"I'm not surprised. You took quite a tumble back there. You'll very likely be stiff and sore for a few days, but I don't think you're seriously hurt." Devlin hunkered down beside her, untied the bow beneath her chin, and deftly removed her bonnet.

One side of the stylish hat had been irreparably crushed in her mishap, and the spine of the ornamental plumage had been broken, causing the feather to wag listlessly in the morning breeze. Under normal circumstances the ridiculous sight would have provoked Kyra to unbridled laughter. Instead, her eyes welled with tears, and she sputtered, "I'm . . . I'm sorry, Devlin! I know you told me not to ride Wildstar, but I so wanted to get away for a while, and . . . and he was saddled and . . . and—" Her voice faltered, and Devlin, fearing he was about to be subject to a full-fledged crying spell, promptly interceded.

"Come now, Kyra," he scolded, cupping her face in his hands and tilting her head back. "We'll have none of that, if you please. Damm it, woman, I'm the one who should be blubbering; you nearly frightened me out of my wits! God, but you can ride!" he crowed.

Seeing that his airy dismissal of the incident had served his purpose—Kyra no longer teetered on the verge of hysteria—Devlin tenderly stroked her cheek. But his tone was somber when he added, "I am not angry with you, Kyra. My displeasure lies with the one who saddled Wildstar for you. That sorry fellow will promptly be given his notice, of that you may rest assured." Devlin withdrew his hand and, with his arms resting on his knees, studied her face, then murmured, "It's time I got you back to the house, little lady. Do you think you can ride with me on Old Scratch if I help you?"

Kyra, still stupefied by his composure, nodded stiffly.

"Good." He slapped his thigh before standing to proffer his hand. "Let me help you mount; then I'll deliver you into Hannah's care. She will no doubt tuck you into bed, serve you a cup of her special tea, and rub you down with liniment to ease your aches and pains. Unless, of course"—Devlin rubbed his stubbled chin thoughtfully and gave her a roguish wink—"you would prefer I rub you down myself." For his efforts, Devlin received a sharp slap on the arm and a scathing glare, to which he replied good-naturedly, "That's my girl. I won't have you turning meek on me just because you took a little spill."

They were standing now, and Devlin, placing a steadying arm around Kyra's waist, inclined his head toward Old Scratch and asked, "Can you walk or shall I carry you?"

"I . . . I think I can make it," she replied weakly, taking a tentative step forward.

Kyra unconsciously leaned against him as they slowly

made their way toward the grazing chestnut. They had taken no more than half a dozen steps, however, when a pain rippled through Kyra's lower abdomen, catching her completely unaware and causing her to clutch Devlin's arm in surprise.

They halted, and Devlin, glancing down, was taken aback by her appearance. The color that had only moments ago returned to her complexion had again drained from her cheeks, leaving her with a deathly white pallor. His arms automatically tightened about her, and his voice was full of concern when he asked, "What is it, Kyra?"

"I . . . I don't . . . don't know," she panted breathlessly, steeling herself against the next searing pain, and when it came, she had to bite down to keep from screaming.

"What is wrong?" Devlin demanded, gripping her shoulders, his anxious gaze sweeping her tortured face.

Kyra shook her head wildly, unable to speak. She was in agony, almost delirious with pain. She didn't know the nature of her affliction, only that something was terribly, terribly wrong! After a time the discomfort gradually subsided, as did the frantic pounding of her heart, and thinking the worst was over, Kyra offered Devlin a weak smile. She was about to suggest that they carry on when she was struck by a crippling pain of such force that it caused her to double over, and this time she could not keep from crying aloud. Kyra could not take another step. She was finding it difficult to remain standing, and clenching Devlin's arm, she slowly lowered herself to the ground where she promptly fell onto her side and drew her knees up to her stomach.

"Kyra!" Devlin cried in alarm. Forcing himself to remain calm, and feeling utterly helpless, he knelt beside her, his soothing fingers brushing aside the strands of limp hair that clung to her perspiring brow. "Kyra, can you hear me? I can't take you back on Old Scratch, not like this. I've got to ride for help."

"No!" she whimpered, clutching his hand. "Don't leave me!"

As she struggled to sit up, Devlin's gaze skirted the roadway in the distance, searching for some sign of activity. Spying a faint dust cloud on the horizon, he shook off her restraining hand. Then, after brushing his lips against her pale cheek and murmuring, "Be brave, magpie," he climbed to his feet. With Kyra's hysterical cries of "Devlin, *Devlin, please don't leave me!*" ringing in his ears, he scrambled astride Old Scratch, and within seconds horse and rider were galloping across the open meadow.

With a mournful sob, Kyra watched man and beast ride away to be swallowed by the landscape, and her mind reeled with a single, terrifying thought: *What if he doesn't come back? What if he doesn't come back?* But suddenly there was no more pain or fear, only darkness, and with the darkness came blessed peace.

The next few hours were a murky blur in Kyra's mind. Not until later that evening, long after gentle hands had lovingly tucked her into bed, did she fully regain consciousness. Her eyes had fluttered open briefly in midafternoon only to close again as the glare from the bedroom window provoked an alarming reaction in her head. But as she lay quietly, the relentless throbbing behind her eyes gradually receded to a dull thrum, and with dawning awareness, Kyra began to piece together the day's remarkable happenings.

Although she could not remember everything, Kyra had a vivid recollection of the wind billowing across her face as she bounded across the countryside on Wildstar. In her mind's eye, she saw the crevice stretching wide before her and felt the powerful animal beneath her lift miraculously off the ground. Then she had the sensation of flying through the air, helpless to prevent being thrown to the hard, unyielding earth. That, too, she recalled with glowing clarity.

Then there had been the pain—oh, how well she remembered that! But more devastating than the physical discomfort was the mental anguish of Devlin forsaking her after she had pleaded with him not to go. Perhaps his quick thinking had saved her life, but in her irrational state, Kyra could comprehend only a single, inconceivable reality: Devlin had abandoned her when she desperately needed him.

From that point forward, Kyra's memory consisted of a sketchy smattering of vague impressions. She had a faint recollection of a moment when the ground vibrated beneath her cheek, followed by a tremendous drumming of horses' hooves. The area had become a flurry of activity with one authoritative voice anxiously shouting instructions above a babble of hushed murmurs. Then she had been lifted ever so carefully into a darkened conveyance. As the vehicle trundled toward Cauldurae, Kyra recalled being held in a comforting embrace while a masculine voice whispered words of encouragement in her ear. Gentle fingers had stroked her cheeks, and lips had lovingly kissed her brow.

In her muddled state of mind, Kyra had been unable to determine the identity of the one who had treated her with compassion. Her heart naturally associated Devlin with the role of heroic protector, but even as his handsome face swam before her eyes, her brow crinkled into an uncertain frown, for there had been another voice . . . Biddie? No, it had been Hannah's disconcerting mutterings that had singed Kyra's brain, filling her with sadness.

As comforting hands had removed Kyra's soiled garments and put her to bed, she had clearly heard Hannah remark, "Poor little one . . . so much blood. It's lucky Doc Fowler happened by when he did. She might have died otherwise."

In the semidarkness, Kyra's eyes fluttered closed on a mournful sigh, for now she realized that Joshua, not Devlin, had been her valiant savior. "Joshua," she murmured sadly, a single tear trickling down her cheek in brokenhearted acceptance of a love that would never be returned.

On this desolate thought, Kyra slept, oblivious to the vigilant shadow hovering on the opposite side of the bed and the effect her sorrowful mumblings had on him.

Kyra became vaguely aware of the hushed murmurings above her. Curious about what was being said, she tried to push her way through the constricting darkness. But when her eyes flitted open to find that the glare of the window had been replaced by a glowing bedside lamp, they snapped closed again in protest against the offensive light. This reaction drew a chuckle and cajoling speech from the voice directly above her.

"Don't be so disobliging as to nod off again, young lady. I want to complete my examination by having a word or two with you to make sure you have not sustained a concussion." There came another pleasant laugh and the voice whispered confidentially, "Your husband would contend that your head is much too hard to have suffered any damage. But do not be fooled by his dour disposition: Devlin told me you were quite a sight to behold until you and Wildstar had that unfortunate parting of the ways. Come now, open your eyes."

"The light," Kyra managed weakly. "It hurts my eyes."

"That is easily corrected." There was a slight rustling followed by the clinking of a glass globe, then the sound of someone expelling a great breath of air, the tinkle of the globe being replaced, and the persuasive voice saying, "Now open your eyes, Mrs. Cauldwell."

Kyra meekly complied and was grateful to find the harsh glare had been eliminated. The remainder of the room was bathed in soft light, however, giving her a view of the chamber and its occupants. Kyra now realized that Joshua was responsible for coaxing her awake while Hannah and Biddie stood at the foot of the bed, their faces creased with worry, and a taller, more forbidding figure hovered near the French windows that opened onto the balcony overlooking the sea, his back to her.

"Devlin?" she murmured, but when those broad shoulders remained rigid and he failed to acknowledge her summons, Kyra returned her gaze to Joshua. "What happened?" she muttered glumly.

Devlin's heartless disregard of his wife's pitiable appeal had not gone unnoticed by the physician. Indeed, Devlin's indifference had so provoked Joshua that the doctor began restoring his instruments to his black leather medical bag. He reasoned that if his hands were occupied, he would be unable to beat some sense into that intractable figure who lurked by the window. But Kyra's softly spoken inquiry prevented Joshua from taking action against his friend.

Joshua stared down into the pale face that regarded him from the pillow, and his smile was reassuring when he asked in a voice that belied his anger, "Do you remember taking a tumble from Wildstar?"

"Yes, and . . . and the pain. Oh, Joshua, there was so much pain." She grimaced at the cramp that constricted her abdomen.

"Are you experiencing much pain now, Kyra?" the doctor inquired kindly, pulling up a chair and taking a seat.

"No, no . . . it was just a twinge."

"You may expect that for a day or two. It's irritating, I'll allow, but there's no helping it. That is typical with this sort of disorder. Rest is what you need if you are to recover, and rest is what you must have in the coming days, so there will be no more romps on Wildstar, if you please." He wagged a playfully admonishing finger beneath her nose.

Normally such antics would have brought a smile to Kyra's lips, but instead, a woebegone expression of misery marred her lovely face. Noting that his patient's sorrowful gaze had again settled on her husband's back, Joshua decided to clear the room and allow the couple a chance to talk privately, for it was obvious they had much to discuss.

"Mrs. Wilson. Biddie. Now that you have seen for yourselves that your mistress will recover in fine fashion, I suggest the two of you run along. You may take turns checking on Mrs. Cauldwell from time to time during the night," he told the watchful duo.

"Don't you fret now, Miss Kyra," Hannah said as she ushered Biddie toward the door. "The doctor says you'll be fit as a fiddle in no time, and me and Biddie will make sure you do what he says. We'll be goin' now, so you and the master can talk private-like." Then, poised on the threshold, she pulled a wrinkled handkerchief from her pocket to dab at her watery eyes and sniffed, "Oh, I am sorry you lost the baby."

Kyra, whose thoughts had been wandering, emerged from her woolgathering to hear Hannah's parting remark, but when she would have questioned the woman about the peculiar comment, she found that Hannah was gone. "Baby?" she echoed distantly. "What . . . what did Hannah mean by that?" Kyra asked shakily, an uneasy feeling beginning to rise in her breast.

"Kyra?" Joshua's manner was gentle as he leaned forward to clasp her hand in a comforting gesture. "Did you know you were with child?"

"No!" She jerked her hand away in denial, her frantic gaze darting toward Devlin, who had turned from the embrasure to watch with growing interest. "That's impossible! We have not even—" She faltered, horrified by the admission she had almost blurted to the doctor. Then the memory of an ill-fated night aboard a yacht in Savannah made her declare, "I mean . . . I mean, it's much too soon!"

"You were not very far along, Kyra . . . just a few weeks," Joshua began tenderly. Then, realizing Kyra did not fully understand that she had lost the child, he reclaimed the hand she had yanked away and gave it a compassionate squeeze. "You suffered a severe trauma when you were thrown from the horse, and even though you sustained no lasting injuries, I'm afraid the fall induced a miscarriage. You lost the child, Kyra."

"I didn't know about the baby. I didn't know," Kyra whimpered piteously, her violet eyes welling with huge tears for the loss of something dear and precious that she had not even known grew inside her.

"Kyra, you're strong and healthy. There is nothing to prevent you and Devlin from having other children."

Joshua was ill prepared for the trill of hysterical laughter his words elicited from his emotion-racked patient, as she shrieked, "No! You don't understand! You *don't* understand!" Then the laughter died and tears came, and somewhere amid the depths of her suffering emerged the lament, "Devlin, *Devlin!* Don't look at me like that. Please, don't hate me. I . . . I can explain! Oh, please, *please,* let me explain." She sniffed brokenly between sobs, extending her hand to her husband in a pleading gesture. But when it became apparent that her heartrending appeal would not melt his icy resolve, Kyra turned her head into her pillow and purged herself of her pent-up miseries.

"Come, now, Dev—" Joshua started to rebuke his friend for his cold-hearted treatment of his wife, but the reprimand died on his tongue when Devlin walked toward him, his expression threatening.

Devlin paused as he reached the foot of the bed and gestured toward the door, saying in a voice that did not augur well for the doctor should he be foolhardy enough to ignore the dismissal, "Thank you for all you've done, Doctor. You may leave us now. I shall tend to my wife."

Joshua stood, and with a sympathetic glance at the distraught woman who sobbed uncontrollably into her pillow, he picked up his medical bag and walked toward the door. When he reached Devlin, he paused to grip the taller man's shoulder. "Be gentle with her. She's in a fragile state."

"I know that, man! I'm not going to beat her," Devlin spat disgustedly, shaking off Joshua's hand and striding forward to pitch the chair aside in a hostile motion.

"Devlin—" Joshua blurted, then faltered, thinking it better to hold his tongue. Swallowing the blighting speech that had sprung to his lips, he said merely, "I'll leave a sleeping powder with Mrs. Wilson in case Kyra has trouble resting."

"Yes, yes," Devlin replied distractedly with a dismissive wave of his hand.

Devlin stood staring down at his wife long after the door closed behind the departing physician, his countenance grave yet strangely sympathetic. When he was satisfied that he and Kyra were alone, Devlin sat on the edge of the bed. He noted with some concern that Kyra's tears showed no sign of abating, and he leaned over and calmly but firmly pulled Kyra's hands from her face and forced her to look at him.

"D-D-evlin, I . . . I can ex-explain!" she sputtered between sobs.

"Shh, Kyra. Try to compose yourself so that we can talk, for you must realize we have a great deal to discuss." His manner was neither truculent nor understanding but rather like that of a parent reproving a naughty child.

Although Devlin had changed into clean clothes, he was still untidy. Ironically, his unshaven face, mussed locks, and stockless shirt, which hung open to expose the tightly coiled hair on his muscular chest, proved to be unusually intimidating. "Here," he said, drawing a handkerchief from his pocket and shoving it into her hands. "Try to stop sniveling and mop up your face. Once you are calm, perhaps you would explain this extraordinary turn of events—how you came to have a miscarriage when I, your husband, have not so much as—" He broke off in disgust.

His forced nonchalance vanished, and Devlin teetered on the edge of outright fury as he muttered, "I am growing weary of having my wives' infidelities flung in my face and of being expected to accept their lovers' bastards as my own flesh and blood." As he dragged Kyra forward abruptly, his voice grew threatening. "Who was it? An old beau from Charleston?"

Kyra felt the powerful fingers digging into her shoulders, but even more nerve-shattering was the look of pure loathing with which he regarded her. When she made no effort to respond to his angry inquiry, Devlin shook her, prompting, "Well, was it an old beau?"

"No," she mumbled faintly.

"Then who was it, Kyra? Someone you met on the island?" he barked accusingly, his face so close to hers that she could feel the heat of his wrath.

Although the events of the day had drained Kyra's feisty temperament, she felt an instinctive urge to fight Devlin's aggressive tactics, and summoning all her strength, she tried to pull away from him. "Leave me alone!" she commanded wildly.

"It will be my greatest pleasure to leave you alone, madam, *after* you tell me what I want to know," he informed her harshly, tightening his hurtful grip for emphasis. "Now tell me, was it someone from the island?"

"No!" she shouted.

"From Savannah, then?" he persisted, brutal fingers embedding themselves more deeply in her sensitive flesh.

"No . . . I mean . . . y-y-yes." Kyra's voice trembled in confusion, and she lifted a hand to her forehead to quell the dizziness that suddenly swept over her.

Blinded by his own impassioned purpose, Devlin was impervious to his wife's fragile state. He continued to rail at her, demanding, "Well, which is it—yes or no? You cannot have it both ways, Kyra. Who was it? *Who*?" he shouted insensibly, giving her shoulders an unmerciful shake. "Tell me, you little bitch!" he swore, and as one hand continued to dig into her flesh, the other drew back in a reflex motion.

Somewhere through the haze, she became aware of Devlin's fierce anger, and thinking he meant to strike her, Kyra snapped. "*You!*" she shouted, as she pummeled his face and chest with her fists. "It was you! It was you!" she cried over and over, tiny hands lashing out at him in a delirious rage.

Devlin, thoroughly staggered by Kyra's accusation, did not even attempt to deflect the blows she inflicted upon him. Her violent burst of temper quickly palled, however, and Kyra collapsed against the chest she had battered with such raw vengeance. The expression darkening Devlin's handsome countenance as he gazed down at the rag doll–like creature who hung limp in his arms was a mixture of horrified incredulity and denial. As the shock gradually subsided, Devlin tilted Kyra's head back to study her tear-ravaged face, but before he could respond to her indictment, the door crashed open and Nicholas charged into the room.

"I'm sorry, I'm sorry!" he cried, rushing to the bed. Knocking his startled father aside, he clambered onto the mattress to fling his arms about Kyra's neck. "I'm sorry, Mama. I didn't mean for you to get hurt. I should've told Lucas which horse, but I thought he knew no one was s'posed to ride Wildstar 'cept Papa. It's my fault! I'm sorry, I'm sorry!" Nicholas jabbered incoherently, his little face puckering into a mournful grimace as the tears began to fall.

Behind them, a frazzled and breathless Hannah appeared in the doorway. "I'm sorry, Mr. Cauldwell, but Nicholas got away from me. He's been worried sick about his stepmama and wouldn't take my word that she was all right. Had to see for hisself."

"Don't trouble yourself, Hannah." Devlin waved the incident aside. "I'll see to Nicholas. You go on about your other duties." When the door closed, Devlin again turned his attention to Kyra and the distraught child she cradled to her breast. With a bemused shake of his head, he muttered, "What a day this has been." Then, noting Kyra's pallor and weakness, he leaned forward and gently plucked Nicholas from her arms.

Turning the child toward him, Devlin was genuinely taken aback when Nicholas threw his arms about his neck and clung fiercely, still mumbling his sorrowful lament. "There now, son. There is no need for all this blubbering," he murmured soothingly. "Stop this nonsense at once. Of course it wasn't your fault. Just as you say, Lucas knows that no one is to ride Wildstar but me. Come, to bed with you now. I'll take you up to your room and tuck you in."

"But . . . but Mama—" Nicholas extended a hand toward Kyra.

"Your mama is going to be just fine, but she needs to rest now. You may come back in a day or two to see for yourself."

"Promise?"

"I promise, Nicholas," Devlin vowed, striding from the room, oblivious of the melancholy effect this heartwarming scene had on Kyra. Momentarily forgetting the tempestuous argument that had just erupted between her and this thoroughly frustrating man, and despite the pain she had endured, Kyra's brain reeled with a single thrilling realization: Nicholas had called her "Mama."

Nicholas was asleep by the time Devlin reached the third floor. With a smile, he let himself into the nursery and made his way to Nicholas's room. After tucking the child beneath the sheets, Devlin brushed back the hair that had spilled across Nicholas's brow and bent to kiss the boy's tearstained cheek before turning to leave the room.

He was about to leave the nursery when he noticed the door to Sarah's room stood ajar and the chamber was alight. Devlin stepped soundlessly across the floor and peered inside.

Biddie sat in a rocking chair in the middle of the room, humming a comforting lullaby to the child who nestled snugly in her arms. Sarah was sleeping fitfully, squirming on the woman's lap.

"I put Nicholas to bed, Biddie. Wouldn't Sarah be more comfortable in her own bed?" Devlin suggested.

"That's what I keep thinkin'," Biddie responded without looking up at the intruder or missing a beat in her rocking rhythm. "But every time I put her down, she starts cryin' after her mama . . . Miz Kyra, that is."

"I see," he replied stoically, stepping toward the chair to gaze down at Sarah.

In one hand she clutched a worn and bedraggled cloth doll while the other jutted outward rigidly at her side. On impulse, he stooped before the sleeping child and favored her with a long, contemplative look. On a sigh, he reached out to reposition her arm so it would not be stiff and tingly when she awakened and was startled when her little hand automatically enclosed around his fingers.

"Poor little thing. This has been a trying day for all of us," Devlin murmured.

"For some more than others," came Biddie's casual observation, her eyes never wavering from the child in her lap.

"Yes," Devlin agreed and, with a shrewd glint in his eye, he extracted his hand from Sarah's and stood, fastening his stare on the servant. "You don't like me very much, do you, Biddie?" he inquired candidly.

"Can't say as I do, but you is the master. I don't have to like you, just do as you say."

"Ha!" Devlin barked. "I suppose you're right about that. But tell me something, if you will, Biddie, for I'm in a devil of a mess with your mistress, and I truly would like to set things right."

"Yes, suh?" Biddie raised her eyes for the first time to

regard the brooding man, and now it was Devlin's turn to look away.

"Did . . . that is"—he coughed awkwardly, trying to sound blasé—"did your mistress have many beaux back in Charleston?"

"Oh, Lordy, yes!" Biddie crowed, aware of the sudden frown that quirked Devlin's brow. "The boys done swarmed around Miz Kyra like bees to honey, but she wouldn't have none of 'em. She's a mother hen, that one, always worryin' 'bout Master Colin or Master Andrew. Now it's the little ones she fusses after. But Miz Kyra didn't have no *steady* beau, if that's what you're askin'. Said she didn't have time for such foolishness."

"Did she, now?" Devlin mulled over this intelligence as he straightened and turned to leave the room. At the threshold, he glanced over his shoulder and said, "Thank you, Biddie."

Biddie's words continued to haunt Devlin as he slowly descended to the second story, as did the accusation that Kyra had hurled at him. His head ached with the torturous conundrum, and he longed for a glass of whiskey and the comfort of his bed. As Devlin strode along the corridor, fully intending to avail himself of those two luxuries without delay, he came to Kyra's room and, without truly realizing what he was doing, pushed the door open and entered.

Kyra was sitting up against a mountain of pillows. She was still deathly pale, but there was no evidence of the hysterical sobs that had riddled her slender body. She was staring toward the window, her face expressionless, and Devlin was wishing he had settled for whiskey and bed after all when Kyra's head lolled to the other side of the pillow, and she leveled her listless gaze at him.

"Is Nicholas all right?" she asked dispiritedly.

"Yes, he's sleeping peacefully," Devlin answered, and after carefully pondering his next words, he added, "Kyra, it is imperative that Nicholas be made to understand he is not culpable for what happened today. I . . . I would not like him to carry that guilt with him throughout his life. Understand?"

"Of course, Devlin," Kyra mumbled dully, staring down at her hands, which absently twisted the silk-edged counterpane. "Nicholas is not to blame for my stubbornness. I knew it was dangerous to ride Wildstar, and yet I chose to do so anyway. The decision was mine alone and I shall do all I can to put Nicholas's mind at ease."

"Thank you," came Devlin's grateful rejoinder and, taking a tentative step toward the bed, he added, "Kyra, I was wondering . . . will you be so good as to put my mind at ease as well?"

"What?" The gold-brown head lifted, and she regarded Devlin curiously.

For the first time in his life, Devlin found himself facing an obstacle he was unsure how to overcome. Repressing the urge to turn tail and run, he made a hasty decision. Stepping to the foot of the bed, he gripped the intricately carved footboard and, returning Kyra's circumspect gaze, said, "Kyra, that night in Savannah. You remember, the night you and I were together on your father's yacht. That's when it happened, isn't it?"

Kyra could not immediately find her voice, such was her surprise at Devlin's apparent acceptance of her accusation, but she did manage a faltering nod. Her eyes grew round with dread as Devlin pushed away from the footboard and walked around the end of the bed to sit down beside her. His manner was far from intimidating, however, as he took her hand in his, saying simply, "We must talk."

14

Several awkward minutes passed as the emotion-racked couple considered each other in the soft, flickering glow of the lamplight. Devlin's upheaval stemmed from the recently acquired knowledge that, while in the throes of a drunken stupor, he had forced this young innocent to submit to his base desires. Kyra's inner turmoil was the result of a contradictory commingling of relief and chagrin.

She was relieved that Devlin had believed he was responsible for her recent condition. Yet Kyra knew her husband would not rest until he had heard all the details of a passion-filled night of which he had no memory. But there were things about her Savannah sojourn in general, and their encounter in particular, that Kyra did not wish to divulge.

Noticing her anxious expression, Devlin said solemnly, "Relax, Kyra. I have no wish to cause you further anguish, nor will I endeavor to justify my disgraceful conduct with lame excuses. It is imperative, however, that I understand all that happened between us. As you know, I have no recollection of that night. So you must tell me." He hesitated, inhaled a fortifying breath, then asked, "Did I rape you, Kyra?"

Seeing the tortured expression that shadowed his brooding eyes, Kyra found herself in the improbable position of wanting very much to comfort Devlin. She was, however, n possession of some rather disconcerting memories of that empestuous night, and reluctant to make a full and true confession, she tried to put him off.

"Please, Devlin," she murmured, avoiding his watchful stare. "It's over and done. Can't we forget it ever happened?"

"I'm afraid not. I doubt if I can make you understand why this is important to me, but I *must* know." He raked his hand through his hair in a despairing motion. "You see, Mother and I quarreled that day and, thinking to put the incident from my head, I stopped in at a tavern where I proceeded to get ripsnorting drunk. The last thing I remember is engaging the . . . companionship"—he coughed awkwardly, aware of the impropriety of revealing one's past liaisons to one's wife—"of one of the tavern maids for the evening. She led me down a dark corridor, then—" Devlin faltered, his embarrassment supplanted by a deeper concern.

How much of the wretchedness that plagued his life and threatened his livelihood should he reveal to her?

Devlin regarded Kyra's wan face pensively as he contemplated the wisdom of telling her of his blurry recollection of having been clubbed on the head, and his nagging suspicion that his assailants had deliberately placed him on her yacht. Realizing this admission would only lead to other disclosures Kyra could not possibly comprehend in her weakened state, he said, "The next thing I remember is awakening in your cabin the next morning and finding you.

"Glory, but you were a sight to behold," he chuckled, his expression warm as it caressed her. "There you were, this breathtakingly beautiful vision, glaring daggers at me, shouting all manner of insults at my reeling head and screeching at me to get out of your cabin."

"I did not screech."

"You most certainly did! My dear, your behavior was positively shrewish," Devlin vowed, softening the accusation with a lopsided grin that evoked a similar response from Kyra.

Presently Devlin's smile faded and he grew somber once more, saying, "Kyra, ours has been a stormy relationship— from that morning in Savannah when you tumbled headlong into my arms to last night's interlude, which led to your hell-bent ride this morning. I realize I am possessed of an explosive and domineering personality and that, in all things, I am determined to have my way, but contrary to what you doubtless think of me, I do not make a habit of forcing—"

"I know that," Kyra interrupted, unconsciously lifting her hand to smooth away the tormenting frown that distorted his face. "Look at me, Devlin." Her voice sounded surprisingly strong and confident to her own ears, and she did not waver when those disturbing brown pools of simmering passion gazed at her. "As you said, you were drunk . . . hideously so, and in your confusion, you stumbled onto the *Driftwood* and—"

"And raped you!" came Devlin's self-condemnation. Then that great hulking bear of a man buried his head in his hands and moaned wretchedly, "My God, Mother was right about me!"

"No. Listen to me, Devlin. It was not like that. You mistook me for someone else. I tried to get you to understand, to make you stop, but you were intoxicated. There was no reasoning with you," she explained, leaning forward to clasp his shoulder in a way that compelled him to look at her. But when her graceful hand would have slipped away, Devlin covered it with his own, as if steeling himself for the words yet to come, and Kyra's voice trembled slightly when she whispered, "You were not brutal, Devlin, just . . . persistent."

"Kyra, I'm—"

Devlin's next conjecture was preempted when Kyra pressed her fingers against his mouth in a silencing gesture.

"Please, Devlin, let us speak of other matters, for I do not want you to agonize over the incident. Indeed, had it not been for today's discovery, I daresay you would never have found out the truth about that night," she murmured woefully, again experiencing a wave of melancholy for the child—Devlin's child—she would never know.

With a disheartened sigh, Kyra slumped back against the pillows, but before she could snuggle into a comfortable position, his hand encircled her wrist and he tugged her forward again. Cautiously, tenderly, the muscular arms slipped around her and nestled her against him, and Devlin's voice trembled with emotion when he said, " 'I'm sorry' sounds so inadequate, Kyra, but I *am* sorry for . . . well, for so many things. About the baby. You've been a wonderful mother to Nicholas and Sarah, and I know you are saddened by your loss, but—"

"Please, don't remind me of Joshua's words." Her words were muffled against his chest. "You know how it is with us. I . . . I shall never have children of my own."

"We shall see, little pet, we shall see," he murmured placatingly with a benign smile at the mass of tousled curls beneath his chin. Then, yielding to the temptation to touch his lips to the unruly tresses, he added with mock sternness, "Don't interrupt while I'm apologizing. Now, where was I? Ah, yes. I'm also sorry *and* much ashamed for the way I have acted toward you.

"I have treated you with little more than contempt ever since our chance embrace on the pier in Savannah. Indeed, I wonder that you have suffered my foul temper this long, and considering the circumstances—well, I will understand if you choose to return to your father. I can have our marriage annulled if that is your desire," he offered, wondering vaguely why this solution did not fill him with pleasure.

The lifeless face of Clayton Fairchild swam before Kyra's eyes, causing her to stiffen, and though she tried to assume a nonchalant air, her fingers tightened about Devlin's forearms, and her voice quavered despite her best efforts to remain calm. "*No*! I *cannot* go back! That is, unless . . . Do you wish me to go?"

There was a long pause as Devlin grappled with his own perplexity at Kyra's distraught reaction to his offer to send her home. Then he said, "Our marriage has gotten off to a rocky start, has it not, magpie? Ever since the day you swooped down on me at Robert's wedding, I have never known what to expect next," he added with a grin.

After mulling over a particularly vexing thought, Devlin continued, "Kyra, I cannot promise that anything will come of prolonging our arrangement. As you well know, I'm not an easy man to live with, but in answer to your question . . . no, I do not want you to go. I think it only proper, however, to tell you there are many things you don't know about me and my past—some of them not very pleasant. Perhaps if you knew me better, you would not wish to remain."

"No, I *want* to stay," she promptly assured him.

"So be it." He nodded, his expression darkening into a serious frown. "But why do you wish to stay with a man who has ridiculed you and scorned you almost from the moment you blundered into his life?"

The question caught Kyra by surprise, but before she could gather her thoughts and formulate a response, Devlin leaned nearer so that their noses were almost touching. It was impossible for him to disguise the incredulity in his voice when he asked, "Don't you hate me, Kyra? Don't you despise me for the things I've done to you?"

Heedful of the close scrutiny to which she was being subjected, Kyra swallowed before replying. "I was very much enamored of you after we waltzed together at the wedding, but then your behavior in Savannah shattered my silly schoolgirl notions. I admit I did not much care for you after that, but I don't hate you, Devlin. Indeed, I . . ." Her voice faded into silence, and Kyra, realizing she had almost blurted her true feelings aloud, pressed her fingers to her temples to quell the frantic thrumming. Brown eyes and violet mingled expectantly for a scant second before Kyra— her equanimity restored—reaffirmed, "I don't hate you, Devlin. And I don't want to leave. Nicholas and Sarah need me."

"Of course. I should have known . . . the children." Devlin sighed, and his expression grew serious as he breathed throatily, "And what about us, Kyra? If you remain, will it be as my wife?"

"Devlin, please!" Kyra looked away, unable to meet his demanding gaze. "It's too soon to talk of such things. Perhaps in time—" Her voice broke off in confusion.

"Very well, magpie." Devlin nodded in resigned acceptance of Kyra's response to his question. Easing her back onto the pillows, he tucked the sheet under her chin. "Get some rest," he said softly, and giving her nose a playful tweak, he rose and walked to the door where he hesitated to impart a final comment.

"Kyra, I will not bully you into advancing our relationship to a more intimate level. There will be no repetition of last night's shameful incident. I shall depend upon you to let me know when you're ready to have me as your true husband." From the flush that darkened Kyra's cheeks, he knew she understood his meaning. With a roguish wink, he drawled in parting, "Until that anxiously awaited moment, you will find my conduct exemplary. Indeed, I shall be a model of gentlemanly grace and charm."

Kyra could not help but smile at the preposterous image that sprang to mind, but as the door closed behind her husband, her brow creased into a frown as she recalled fragments of their conversation. "Perhaps if you knew me better, you would not wish to remain," he had said, implying there were ominous happenings in his past that would make her feel disgusted with him.

As she lay there, exhausted, hovering on the brink of sleep, her final conscious thought was of Devlin and his reaction should he ever learn her own dark secret—that she was suspected of murder and had kept the truth from him all this time. It was a confrontation she could not bear to contemplate, and on a disheartened sob, Kyra resolved that he would never learn of her deception.

By the end of Kyra's third day of convalescence, Joshua had pronounced her well enough to sit in a chair for a few minutes at a time and to take an occasional turn about the room. She was forbidden to go downstairs or, more disappointing to Kyra, upstairs to the nursery.

"You're recuperating nicely, Kyra," Joshua had explained, drawing the sheet over her as he concluded his medical examination, "and I won't have you suffering a relapse because of any foolhardy notion you might take into your head. Heed my instructions and you'll be back on your feet *and* back on a horse," he added with a friendly wink, "in no time at all."

With a glum sigh and an acquiescent nod, Kyra had petulantly agreed to the doctor's strict regimen, but an entire fortnight had passed since her accident and there had been no word from Joshua in days. Kyra was now permitted free rein of the second floor as well as the balcony, but she was still denied access to the children's rooms and the main floor. A normally sweet-tempered Kyra, accustomed to a more rigorous routine, found her patience wearing thin with those who insisted on carrying out Joshua's instructions to the letter.

"But, Devlin," she said as he led her onto the balcony and settled her on the chaise longue, "I'm fine! Truly, I am. Why can't I join you in the dining room for breakfast?"

"Because," Devlin sighed indulgently, "the doctor has not yet given you leave to do so, and until he does, you will just have to resign yourself to your limited activities. Now, be a good little wife and do as you are told." He clucked his tongue in a tolerable imitation of Mrs. Wilson. "And for God's sake, Kyra, try to exercise some discretion in your dealings with the servants, especially Francesca. You know how temperamental she is. I had to call upon all my powers of persuasion to keep her from storming your chamber yesterday after you returned your untouched dinner to the kitchen with the lofty message that you 'don't much care for putrid chicken,'" Devlin quoted his wife with a lamentable shake of his head.

"Well, I don't," Kyra informed him peevishly, snatching the book he proffered and perusing the title page with a disinterested yawn.

Kyra was bored. And, Devlin, being an astute gentleman, wisely decided the time had come for him to leave his wife to her doldrums; nothing good would come of continuing the discussion.

Giving her knee an affectionate squeeze, Devlin straightened and turned to stride to the French windows where he lingered to say, "Take heart, Kyra. After breakfast, I'll be going into the village to check on supplies and such. If I should see your wayward physician, rest assured that I'll send him for a look at his surly patient.

"Enjoy your book, magpie," he said with a wicked grin, chuckling outright at the face she pulled.

Kyra stared at the embrasure for a long while after Devlin left, his laughter echoing in her thoughts, and a whimsical smile—the first in days—curved her lips. Not for the first time she pondered the change that had come over her enigmatic husband since the night of their intimate discussion.

True to his word, Devlin had been a gentleman since that moment. He inquired after her health daily and was solicitous of her every need, often fetching her a book or glass of lemonade, once even going so far as to act as her scribe when she was too weary to write a letter to her father. The one-time quarrelsome mountain of seething passion had been transformed into a paragon of civility and Kyra—instead of being gratified by the amazing metamorphosis—found she preferred the former arrogant version.

Kyra's smile faded, and a gloomy sigh fluttered between her lips as she settled herself more comfortably on the chaise longue. *What is it now?* demanded the pesky little voice that had returned to monitor her thoughts. *What do you expect of him? First you spurn his advances; now you pine for them. There's no pleasing you.*

"I know, I know," she lamented glumly. "I *am* relieved to be free of his constant lecherous innuendos. It's just that—"

What?

"I wish he didn't treat me like a sister or, worse, like Uncle Ned, with a sort of . . . of casual deference." She exhaled a hollow breath and glanced down at the book that lay open in her lap.

"*A Treatise on the Mores of the Modern Woman*," she read the title aloud, giving a spontaneous whoop of laughter. Momentarily forgetting her pique with her husband, Kyra examined the gold lettering on the book's spine. "Volume One, no less," she chuckled in disbelief, "*and* written from a man's point of view. What rubbish is this?" she asked aloud. A thorough scrutiny of the title page disclosed the book had been published in 1765, nearly a hundred years ago.

With a curious shrug, she conceded it might be diverting to find out what yesterday's modern woman was like and, turning to the first chapter, she began to read. She had progressed no further than the second paragraph, however, when she became aware of an eerie feeling that someone was watching her. A cursory inspection of the balcony revealed no intruder, and shaking off the spooky feeling, Kyra returned to the text. She had devoted no more than two minutes to her reading, however, when she not only felt but also heard the presence of someone just beyond the door.

Closing the volume with a definitive snap, Kyra tossed the book aside and sat forward, her eyes focused on the opening. "Who is it? Who's there?" she called. "Come now, show yourself."

Thinking Devlin might have lingered to ensure that she adhered to Joshua's strict rules, Kyra was genuinely surprised when a tiny head of blond curls and a pair of vibrant blue eyes peeked at her uncertainly from behind the gently billowing curtain. "Sarah!" Kyra squealed with glee, throwing her arms wide in a welcoming gesture. "Come here, love. I'm so happy to see you! Come sit with me." She patted the space beside her and watched with interest as Sarah cast a nervous look at the room behind her before inching onto the balcony.

"Mama better?" the little girl asked hopefully, taking a tentative step toward Kyra.

"Yes! Much better now that you've come to visit me," Kyra replied with alacrity, noting again that Sarah seemed unduly fretful, almost as if she feared discovery. Then comprehension dawned on Kyra, and giving Sarah a conspiratorial wink, she said, "Ah, I see. You've given your new governess the slip, have you? Well, it was foolish of Joshua to curtail our visits, as if spending time with you and Nicholas would hinder my recovery—bah! I am heartily sick of everyone deciding what is best for me, Sarah. The time has come to take a stand against these dictatorial tactics, so come on over here, give me a great big hug, and we'll have ourselves a marvelous visit."

For her efforts, Kyra was rewarded with Sarah's sunniest smile as the child toddled happily to her, dragging a tattered rag doll behind her. After several minutes of mutual hugging, during which time Kyra was obliged to kiss the tip of each tiny finger as well as Sarah's pudgy cheeks, she lifted the child onto the bench beside her.

"Now, what shall we do until the others find us out?" she asked gaily.

"Mama fix dolly," Sarah suggested promptly.

"What?"

"Dolly hurt," the child explained, extending the toy for Kyra's inspection.

Kyra glanced down at the little girl's favorite possession. Sarah carried the doll with her from sunup to sunset. A knowing smile softened Kyra's lips as she observed its thoroughly disheveled condition.

At Sarah's insistence, she and the doll were always dressed alike, wearing gowns made of the same material with matching hair ribbons, but that was where the resemblance ended. Whereas Sarah was neatly coiffed, the doll's hair, which was made of yellow yarn, was sadly tangled. While Sarah's eyes were a brilliant shade of blue, the doll's big button eyes were dull in comparison and one was in danger of being lost altogether, for it dangled precariously by a single thread. But the defect that was of the utmost concern to the doll's owner was a jagged rent extending from the knee of one leg up the thigh, from which a considerable amount of stuffing protruded.

"I see why you are so troubled, but never fear, little one," she cooed lovingly. "I'll have your dolly mended in a second." Kyra patted Sarah's arm before going to collect her sewing basket.

When Kyra returned, she applied a few expert stitches to the damaged region, and Sarah's contented smile grew even brighter as she watched Kyra securely anchor the dangling eye back into place. "There," Kyra proclaimed, snapping the thread with her teeth. "Your dolly is all better now, Sarah," she announced, proffering the repaired toy.

With a grateful squeal, Sarah grasped the doll and hugged it to her. Kyra would have been treated to a similar display of affection had the child not spied the book lying neglected on the balcony floor, causing her to trill excitedly, "Mama, story!"

Setting the sewing basket aside, Kyra retrieved the

forgotten volume and, wriggling into a comfortable position, settled Sarah in the crook of her arm and opened the book, remarking, "Very well, love. But I'm not altogether certain this story is appropriate for your little ears. Then again," she chuckled with a feisty toss of her gold and brown head, "it is never too early to begin one's education."

Devlin returned to the mansion at midday and immediately made his way to his wife's chamber. When she was not to be found in her room, he realized she must still be on the balcony and turned toward the French windows. "Kyra," he called, barreling through the opening, only to come up short at the enchanting scene that greeted him.

Kyra lay in graceful repose upon the chaise longue with Sarah curled up against her, clutching her shabby rag doll, both of them fast asleep. A smile crossed his face as he folded his arms across his chest and leaned indolently against the window casing, content to gaze uninterrupted at the charming picture. As he watched, Kyra stirred, dislodging the volume at her side and sending it tumbling to the floor. The thud of the book against the hardwood planks served to rouse her, and as Kyra gradually relinquished her dreams and returned to the conscious world, she became aware of a tall, shadowy figure lurking near the entrance. She swallowed her startled squeak of surprise when the figure came into focus, and she recognized her husband.

"Hello," he murmured huskily, pushing away from the embrasure and lowering himself on his haunches beside her. He plucked the book from the floor, and a mischievous sparkle danced in his brown eyes as he examined the title. "You know, I selected this book for your reading pleasure because I am given to understand that Judith Tanner, the original mistress of this hall, was a stickler for social niceties. I've heard that she was especially fond of the companion volume, *On Being a Dutiful Wife*," he added with a roguish wink.

"I thought you might be curious to know how a woman's role in society was perceived in bygone days, as well as how your forebears viewed the hallowed state of matrimony," he ended on a casual note. He jerked his head toward Sarah and, in a voice rich with feigned sarcasm, said, "I should imagine, however, this material is a bit sophisticated for Sarah's tender ears."

"Actually, I made up a story and only pretended to read from the book," Kyra explained, realizing with a delicious shiver that she was being courted. Hiding a smile, she chose to withhold comment on his sly prank, saying instead, "It seemed to please her." She gazed fondly at the sleeping child.

"She didn't exhaust you, then?"

"No, Devlin," she murmured, absently stroking Sarah's cheek. "I enjoyed our visit immensely, and I've missed the children so. You and Joshua have sanctioned but one visit since the accident, and that was only to assure them of my well-being and to convince Nicholas that he was not responsible for my tumble."

"They have missed you, too, little pet. Why, Nicholas was saying just yesterday during our fishing expedition—"

"Fishing?" Kyra interrupted, hardly believing her ears. "*You* took Nicholas fishing?"

"Yes," Devlin replied dryly, obviously affronted by the incredulous lilt in her voice. "He's become quite the little angler, I'll have you know."

"That's wonderful!" Kyra exclaimed. "I'm certain Nicholas had great fun."

"Yes, he did. And his father had a tolerable time as well—that is until Goldie interfered and made me lose my best catch of the day," he grumbled.

"Ah, yes . . . the one that got away." Kyra nodded skeptically.

Devlin, who was deriving considerable pleasure from their carefree bantering, was about to take his delightfully presumptuous wife to task when a little voice intervened.

"Mama, read more?" Sarah begged drowsily, rubbing the sleep from her eyes. When the blue eyes focused on her father's imposing form, the child stiffened reflexively, and Sarah was on the verge of tears when she asked fearfully, "Papa mad?"

"No, little one," Devlin whispered, unwittingly addressing her by the endearment Kyra often used. "Papa is not mad. I cannot, however, say the same for the remainder of the household. The place is in an uproar, young lady. Seems they've been turning the house topsy-turvy all morning searching for you. Miss Peabody is quite beside herself wondering where you meandered off to. For the life of me, I cannot fathom why no one thought to look here. Well, no matter. Come, Sarah." He leaned across Kyra to scoop the child into his arms. "Let us go put everyone's mind to rest."

"No!" Sarah whined pitifully, stretching her arms toward Kyra. "Me stay, Mama!"

"Shh! None of that," Devlin gently scolded the unhappy child. "You may visit your mama later, but for now, it's off to the nursery with you," he informed her in no uncertain terms, and Sarah, suddenly gratified to be the sole recipient of her father's attention, promptly dried her tears.

"That's better," Devlin said approvingly. Turning to Kyra, he added, "I'll return in a moment to take you down to dinner."

Kyra's entire countenance brightened and she sat up, clapping her hands together. "You mean—"

"Yes," he interrupted, laughing at the amazing transformation his announcement prompted. "I stopped by Fowler's office. He's been busy on one of the neighboring islands and hasn't had time to stop in and check on you. Anyway, I apprised him of your much improved condition, and he agreed that you should resume your normal activities, with the understanding that you are to take things slowly for a while. You're not to overdo," Devlin told her sternly. "Agreed?"

"Oh, yes! Thank you, Devlin," she cried, bounding up from the upholstered bench to embrace him with fervor. Pressing a kiss to Sarah's cheek, she said, "Did you hear that, Sarah? Mama is free again!"

"And God save us all," Devlin muttered beneath his breath, wary of the vivacious spitfire about to be set loose to cut up his peace once more. With a woebegone shake of his dark head, he turned toward the French windows, a deliriously happy Sarah snuggled in his embrace and Kyra's hand tucked in the crook of his arm.

As they stepped across the threshold, Devlin recalled another piece of information that he knew would be of interest to his wife. "By the way, a mountain of trunks, valises, and hatboxes arrived for you today. I suppose they're your long-awaited belongings from Raybourne."

"Finally!"

"I sent Henry with a wagon to fetch them home for you," he informed her, adding wryly, "You and Biddie will be much occupied in the coming days with unpacking it all." They had arrived at the door, and Devlin paused to reach inside his jacket to retrieve a slim packet of letters, which he extended to Kyra. "These came for you as well. Sarah and I will leave you to your letters for now, but I will return shortly to take you down to dine."

"Thank you," Kyra murmured, her eyes transfixed on the envelopes.

She reached up to take the packet and watched with a sinking heart as Devlin let himself out of the room. Kyra walked as if in a trance to the dressing table and sank down on the stool. She shivered with dread as her eyes scanned the first epistle. She recognized the handwriting; it was her father's. The next letter was from Emily, Devlin's sister, and the next from Fanny Cookson, her childhood friend.

A single envelope remained, and Kyra bit her lip anxiously as she directed her gaze toward the paper, but she could not check the sob that sprang from her throat when she beheld the ominous scrawl. Her worst fears had become a reality. Her hands trembled as she slid the blade of her scissors beneath the flap, withdrew the letter, and began to read.

Three days later Kyra was again seated in front of the dressing table mirror. Her thoughts were as rattled as they had been the day Devlin delivered that discomposing letter. The message, like the previous one, had been brief, but this time her correspondent had provided specific instructions: "Be at the logging site at noon on Friday. Don't be late," the writer had warned, ending with a threatening "I'll find you."

"Is you all right, Miz Kyra?" The question came from Biddie who stood behind Kyra, applying the finishing touches to her mistress's coiffure.

"What? I'm fine. I was just daydreaming." Kyra's laugh sounded hollow even to her own ears, and she avoided the servant's eyes as she plucked her broad-brimmed straw hat from the table. Settling it atop her curls, Kyra attempted to tie the decorative ribbons into a becoming bow, but in her exasperation she managed to hopelessly tangle the fragile satin.

"Let me, Miz Kyra," Biddie said kindly, turning her mistress away from the looking glass. As she untangled the rose-colored ribbons and wove them into a charming bow, Biddie inquired conversationally, "Is Mr. Cauldwell expectin' you?"

"No," Kyra admitted, still ignoring the maid's shrewd gaze. "But as you know, Biddie, we have been on the island for nearly three months now and I have seen very little of Devlin's enterprises. I thought it would be fun to drive the buggy inland to where the men are cutting trees for the sawmill and surprise Devlin with a picnic lunch."

"Uh-huh," came the servant's skeptical reply.

"Really, Biddie!" Kyra exclaimed, turning her head away just as the maid finished anchoring the bow at a jaunty angle beneath her chin. "You sound as if you suspect me of some devious plot. It is only a picnic." Kyra stood to retrieve her short jacket from the bed and shrug into the garment. She collected her leather driving gloves, and her crinolines swished melodiously as she made her way to the door.

"Besides, it is not so very unusual for a wife to carry lunch to her husband in the field. Mama did as much for Papa when she was alive," Kyra informed the servant and promptly left the room before Biddie could remind her that there was no comparison between the blissful union of Colin and Rebecca Raybourne and this ramshackle marriage.

Kyra paused in the corridor to draw on her gloves. Then, squaring her shoulders, she smoothed out a wrinkle in her wide muslin skirt and proceeded down the hallway to the grand staircase. Before she had placed her foot on the top step, however, Kyra's progress was interrupted by a gleeful squeal from the opposite corridor. Turning around, Kyra saw Sarah—a swirl of pink and white checked gingham—break away from her governess and scamper toward her.

Seeing that Kyra was dressed for an outing, Sarah pleaded, "Me go with you, Mama!"

Kyra's initial thought was to suggest that it might be better for Sarah to wait and accompany her another time, but remembering Biddie's reaction to this excursion, she reasoned that Devlin might entertain similar suspicions. After all, she had exhibited no great interest in his business acumen thus far. It might serve to her advantage to bring Sarah along so Devlin would have no reason to suspect her of ulterior motives.

"Of course you may, love," Kyra announced cheerfully. "Dolly, too?"

Kyra glanced at the treasured toy—as always, Sarah and he doll were identically dressed—and nodded. "Yes, dolly, oo. But you must run and fetch your bonnet. Go on. Miss Peabody will help you, and I will wait for you right here."

A quarter of an hour later, Kyra, Sarah and her dolly, and a huge wicker basket filled with food were bundled into the buggy, and the expedition got under way. At the last ninute, the entourage was joined by Goldie, who, having been deserted by Nicholas, saw the makings of a promising adventure and decided to tag along. Kyra firmly declined he escort of one of Devlin's guards, but since the journey would take her to a section of the island she had never visited, she did ask Henry for directions.

After an hour and a half of wending their way through the thick tropical foliage and up a narrow mountain trail, they arrived at the logging camp. By this time, Kyra's nerves were on edge, for not only was she plagued by thoughts of her pending rendezvous, but she had spent the greater portion of the trip begging Sarah to sit still and had had to reprimand Goldie a number of times for yapping at the horse's heels. She nearly succumbed to tears when she drew the buggy to a halt just outside the canvas tent that served as Devlin's office, only to find that her husband was nowhere to be found.

"But I've come all this way," Kyra sighed dismally, letting the basket of food plop back onto the floor of the buggy.

"Don't be thinking Mr. Cauldwell ain't here, ma'am. He's up on the ridge with the men," the worker who had come to assist Kyra explained, doffing his hat as an afterthought.

"The ridge?" Kyra echoed, dreading the answer to her next question. "How far is that?"

"Ten minutes due north," the man replied, pointing

toward an overgrown footpath that led deeper into the forest. "The men'll be coming back for the noontime mea in an hour or so, if you'd like to wait here, ma'am."

"No, thank you." Kyra forced a smile. "The walk will be good for us after that long buggy ride. Come, Sarah"—she extended her hand to the little girl—"let's go find you daddy."

It took the pair a good deal longer than ten minutes to arrive at the work site, their progress severely impeded by Sarah who had to pause and inspect every brightly colored blossom they encountered along the way. But they finally emerged from the thick foliage into a clearing that was bustling with activity. The region reverberated with the singsong rhythm of a dozen crosscut saws and of throaty warnings that preceded the thundering of felled trees agains the forest floor.

They had not been in the clearing above thirty second before Kyra realized it was far too treacherous a place for small child, and gripping Sarah's hand, she announced, "We'll just say hello to your father and be on our way Perhaps we can persuade him to join us for lunch," she added, scanning the trees for a sign of Devlin's powerfu physique.

In the end, it was Devlin who noticed her first. He and another logger had just finished sawing through a tree, and as he turned from watching it fall in majestic silence to the ground, he saw her. At first he thought his eyes were playing tricks on him, but when the bewitching vision did not disappear, he smiled in bemusement and, plucking his discarded shirt and jacket from the ground, strode toward her.

"Kyra?" he called when he drew within shouting distance.

Kyra whirled at the sound of his voice but did not immediately acknowledge his summons. How could she when her heart had leaped into her throat at the sight of him? He was struggling into his shirt as he approached, but Kyra was permitted a glimpse of a broad chest that glistened with tiny droplets of sweat before it was concealed behind the white linen material. In her mind, Kyra could visualize the play of muscles rippling across his shoulders as he had worked the saw, thrusting again and again to drive the blade deeper until—

"Kyra?" Devlin repeated, startling her from her reverie. "Didn't you hear me calling you?"

She glanced up to find him staring down at her curiously, and one hand immediately flew to her flushed face. She watched as he shrugged his shoulders—those same broad shoulders that had so recently served as a source of distraction to her—into his jacket and eventually nodded in reply.

"Why didn't you answer me?"

"I'm sorry we came, Devlin," Kyra blurted, disregarding his question. "I didn't realize it would be this dangerous. I just wanted to see what you do with your time. I . . . I brought lunch." She concluded her rather disjointed speech and smiled at him impishly.

"Excellent! I'm starving!" he proclaimed. "Give me a moment to tell the men to start hauling the logs down the skid road to the landing and I'll join you.

"Hello, Sarah." He smiled down at the child, who as always, gazed up at him adoringly. "And, Kyra, I'm not sorry you came. You are right, however. This can be a dangerous place, but you will be safe enough if you stay where you are. Wait here; I'll be back." He winked at her before turning to run a short distance to where a group of workers mingled.

"Did you hear that, Sarah? Your daddy said he was glad we came." She squeezed the little girl's hand, albeit her gaze remained riveted on her husband's magnificent form.

"Beggin' your pardon, Mrs. Cauldwell." A man's voice invaded Kyra's whimsical musings.

Kyra whirled, half expecting to be confronted by her blackmailer, but she exhaled a sigh of relief when it proved to be one of Devlin's men.

"Yes?"

"Sorry to bother you, ma'am, but you'll have to move out of the way," the laborer said matter-of-factly.

"But my husband said we should wait for him here," Kyra protested.

"I expect he did, ma'am, but then I reckon he didn't know we had a tree ready to drop." The man gestured at a stand of trees to Kyra's right. "If you'd oblige us by stepping out of the way, me and the men can get on with our work," he said curtly.

"Certainly," Kyra replied, irritated that one of Devlin's employees should speak to her so disrespectfully.

She was about to inquire as to where he would like them to stand when, to her annoyance, she discovered that the man had taken hold of Sarah's hand and was leading her away. Biting back an angry retort, Kyra wisely decided that Devlin would know how to deal with the worker's insolence. When they had been situated, Kyra coolly thanked the man for his assistance, then turned her back to him in a clearly dismissive motion.

Kyra forgot about the surly laborer as her thoughts turned to the reason for this excursion. Where was he? she wondered. Why had he not approached her? She could not endure much more of this interminable waiting!

Kyra was lost in her frantic musings, although she appeared to be concentrating on a clump of trees. With a glum sigh, she instinctively sought out Devlin, who had just glanced away from the group of men clustered about him to steal a peek at his wife. Their eyes met and Devlin's sensuously full mouth parted in a smile for an instant before his attention was attracted to the activity on the hill behind Kyra.

Kyra, too, became aware of some commotion and the

distinctive crackling of timber and, whirling about, she froze with panic at the incredible sight . . . a tree falling directly toward her!

The air behind Kyra exploded with a hysterical shout of warning, but she was paralyzed with fright. Though her brain cried out for her to flee, her feet remained rooted to the spot. Even the scream that slowly gathered in her throat seemed destined to go unreleased, so great was the terror that gripped her. A mere instant before the deadly tree came crashing down upon her, a Herculean body barreled into her and knocked her out of harm's way.

The force of the impact caused Devlin to lose his footing, and the two of them tumbled to the ground where Devlin shielded Kyra from the treacherous limbs as they rolled toward safety. The forest floor beneath them vibrated with the thundering collision of wood and earth as the couple came to rest only inches from the would-be instrument of death. Several minutes passed before their thumping pulses subsided, and Kyra was trembling uncontrollably when she lifted her hand to the dark head that bent over her. She gave a cry of anguish when she saw the trickle of blood that oozed from an ugly gash in Devlin's cheek, and her hand flew instinctively to the injury.

"Leave it! It's only a scratch," he grumbled, hoisting himself up to brace his arms on either side of her. Staring down into Kyra's flushed and frightened face, Devlin gave vent to his passions by swearing, "Damn it, Kyra! I thought I told you to stay put!"

"One of y-y-your m-m-men," Kyra stammered helplessly, not fully recovered from their near mishap. "He . . . he told us—" Her voice broke off abruptly, and pushing away from Devlin and his angry stare, she sat up. "Sarah?" she mumbled, glancing dazedly about the clearing.

Sarah was nowhere in sight, and Kyra felt a panic like nothing she had ever known before. Clambering unsteadily to her feet, she began to stumble toward the felled tree. "Sarah?" she repeated. There was no answer, and this time Kyra's voice quavered with hysteria as she cried, "*Sarah!*"

Kyra was delirious with fear as her eyes skirted the clearing, anxiously searching for any sign of the missing child. She was cognizant of the powerful arms that surrounded her and the hushed murmurings compelling her to remain calm. "Shh, honey. She's here somewhere. My men will find her," Devlin said tenderly, rocking her gently against him.

It was then that Kyra's sharp gaze fell on the topmost branches of the toppled tree, and what she saw very nearly induced her racing heart to stop beating altogether. There, crushed beneath a mass of gnarled branches and leaves, a scrap of pink and white checked gingham was clearly visible. At first, Kyra's numb brain did not register this alarming discovery, but as the trauma of the preceding harrowing moments abated, a new understanding was born, prompting Kyra's agonized scream as she pushed away from her husband.

"Oh, God . . . no! *No!*" Kyra wailed. Running to the tree, she dropped to her knees and began clawing wildly at the twisted branches. Oblivious to the painful scratches and ugly welts that rose on her hands and arms, Kyra continued until a pair of unyielding hands grasped her upper arms and hauled her to her feet.

"Devlin . . . no! *Devlin!*" Kyra screamed hysterically, bloodied fingers stretching vainly toward the pink and white fabric. "Let me go! *Let me go!*" she cried, frantically trying to twist free of his grip.

But Devlin held her fast until her struggles ceased, and on a sob, Kyra turned to hurl herself against his sturdy chest. When he gathered the stricken young woman in his arms, Devlin's sable-brown eyes glistened with tears as he gazed in disbelief at the splash of pink and white gingham that lay in sad contrast to the lush tropical forest green.

PART III

The Treasure

15

Kyra sat on the edge of the bed gazing down at the child who lay between the sweet-smelling linen sheets. She stared wonderingly at the stiff little body, and extended one scratched hand to gently stroke Sarah's pale cheek. Kyra's eyes filled with tears, and they spilled over the stains of their predecessors.

She remained thus until the last flickering shadows of twilight had been swallowed by the night. The faint tinkling of the supper bell had long since faded when Kyra heard the nursery door open. She felt rather than heard Devlin position himself behind her, but her violet gaze remained riveted on the tiny blond head. As Kyra and Devlin watched, Sarah fidgeted restlessly in her sleep and flopped from her back to her side, one hand groping desperately for some unfound object.

"She misses her dolly," Kyra whispered on a sob.

"Mrs. Wilson has already begun stitching her a brand-new playmate," Devlin said, pulling Kyra to her feet and settling his hands on her shoulders. He grew solemn as his gaze traveled beyond her to rest on Sarah's sleeping face. "She is all right, then?"

"Yes, she is sleeping," Kyra whispered, before being overcome by a fresh wave of tears.

"Come now, magpie. Sarah is safe," he murmured,

touching her face. "Dry your eyes and we'll go down to supper together."

"No, I don't want to leave her."

"Kyra, Miss Peabody is just in the next room and Sarah's noble protectress lies but a few feet from her bed." He nodded toward Goldie, who lay on a rug near the rocking chair chewing on a large meaty bone—her reward for having lured Sarah away from the clearing just seconds before the tree had fallen. "Come," he urged. "We shall eat a bite, then perhaps take a stroll along the bluff before retiring," he suggested, placing her hand on his arm and leading her out of the nursery.

Kyra barely touched the succulent roast duckling, parsley potatoes, and array of vegetables that Francesca had expertly prepared. Her faltering appetite was the result of a combination of external influences that had reduced her innards to a quivering mass of jelly. Kyra had not completely recovered from the shock of thinking Sarah had been crushed beneath the limbs of that massive tree, nor had she been able to dispel her anxiety over the possible ramifications of her failure to make contact with the blackmailer. It was little wonder she had no taste for the evening's fare.

"Magpie?" Devlin's deep voice interrupted her reverie, and when Kyra glanced toward him, she saw that he, too, had eaten little. Though his countenance was somber, the sable-brown eyes were softly caressing as they regarded her, and Kyra had the distinct impression that he was about to say something of consequence when the butler announced that a visitor had arrived.

"Who is it, Thomas?"

"It's Mrs. Kincaid, sir. She asked if she might await you and Mrs. Cauldwell in the library."

"Very well. Thank you. You may tell Mrs. Kincaid that we shall join her presently." Devlin dismissed the servant and leveled a circumspect stare at his wife. Then with a shrug, he tossed his napkin onto the table and, standing, went to assist Kyra from her chair. "Well, Mrs. Cauldwell? Would you care to meet my business partner?"

Kyra's heart had leaped into her throat when she learned the identity of their visitor. Elyse Kincaid—the woman Kyra had seen Devlin lift from the carriage on the outskirts of the village. He had explained away the incident, but Kyra would not soon forget the memory of that attractive brunette nestled seductively against Devlin's broad chest.

Forcing a smile to her lips, Kyra graciously accepted the hand he proffered and stood to entwine her arm in his, saying calmly, if not truthfully, "I would very much like to meet her."

They walked to the library in companionable silence as they secretly contemplated each other's thoughts. Kyra's eyes glittered as she pondered the forthcoming meeting, albeit it an expression of utter sweetness molded her face. Devlin's musings were twofold, for though he quite naturally wondered at the purpose of Elyse's visit, he found himself more than a little intrigued by his wife's deceptively innocent visage. Before he had a chance to quiz Kyra about her perplexing mien, they arrived at the library and a footman pushed the door open for them.

On impulse, Devlin increased the pressure on the slender arm entwined with his own, and when Kyra's violet gaze came up to search his face, he leaned forward and tapped the end of her nose with a warning forefinger. "Behave yourself, little pet," he whispered throatily, and Kyra was left to contend with a delicious shiver that tingled along her spine as he ushered her across the threshold.

The scarlet flush that speckled Kyra's cheeks did not go unnoticed by a pair of dark green eyes that narrowed shrewdly as they witnessed the exchange between husband and wife. The contempt that glimmered in Elyse's eyes was not representative of the expression that shaped her face, however. Her lips parted in a smile and she stretched both hands toward Kyra in a beckoning gesture.

"This must be our Kyra! How pretty you are!" Elyse exclaimed, and in the next breath, she chastised her host, "Devlin, you cad. How beastly of you to hide this lovely creature at Cauldurae and not even have the decency to introduce her to your friends. For shame, Devlin," Elyse pouted. "Oh, come closer, Kyra. I do so want to meet you. I hope our Devlin has at least told you a little about me and you understand that I am unable to get about."

"Yes," Kyra said, taking an uncertain step toward the woman who sat in the corner of the leather sofa. Before she sat down, her eyes flickered up to the sandy-haired giant who stood behind the chair.

"This is John," Elyse explained, noting the direction of Kyra's gaze. "He attends me. A wheelchair can be positively tedious, you know, so I struck upon the happy solution of hiring John to carry me about. You may go away now, John." She shooed the man from the room with a dismissive flutter of her hand. "I'll have Devlin ring for you when I'm ready to leave. Now, come here, darling." Elyse motioned to Kyra with one hand while patting the space beside her with the other.

Devlin remained unusually reticent while John took his leave and Kyra took a seat beside their caller. Then, choosing a chair opposite the ladies, he met Elyse's gaze and said deliberately, "So, Elyse, to what do we owe the pleasure of this visit?"

"As I said, I've been wanting to meet Kyra for ages, but the main reason I stopped by was to inquire after our little Sarah. I heard what happened up on the mountain this morning. Is she all right?"

"She's fine," Kyra assured the older woman.

"Sleeping like a lamb," Devlin interjected. "Actually, Sarah was never in any real danger. Appears she scampered into the woods after that pup, and lucky for us she did. Kyra was very nearly struck by the tree, however."

"How dreadful!" Elyse cried, turning toward Kyra. "Are you all right, dear?"

"I was not injured, just badly shaken," she murmured, staring down uncomfortably at her hands, the ugly scratches serving as a reminder of those horrible moments when she thought Sarah was trapped beneath the deadly branches. "Devlin pushed me out of the way in time, but Sarah . . . at first we thought—" Kyra faltered on a choked sob, her apologetic gaze searching out her husband's understanding face.

"As you can see, Elyse, we have had a somewhat unnerving day." As he spoke, Devlin moved from the leather wing chair to perch on the arm of the sofa beside Kyra and draped a comforting arm about his wife's shoulder.

This endearing gesture was not lost on Elyse, who wisely swallowed a smirk and, after clearing her throat, said, "It's fortunate no one was hurt."

"Yes, isn't it?" Devlin drawled, studying the woman's face for a long moment before adding, "Elyse, is there anything in particular you came to discuss or is this purely a social call?"

"No, nothing of import," Elyse admitted. "I merely came to ask after Sarah and to meet Kyra, of course. But you look tired, dear. Perhaps we should postpone our little get-acquainted chat until another time." Elyse patted Kyra's hand and her eyes glistened when she noticed Kyra's naked ring finger. "But my darling girl! Don't tell me you've lost your wedding band!"

Kyra's immediate reflex was to cover her left hand, but Devlin masterfully forestalled the self-conscious motion by capturing her hand and raising it to his lips. "How careless of you, magpie," he said in a softly chastising tone, touching his lips to the scarred flesh. "Did you forget to put your ring back on after Biddie tended your hands?"

In truth, Devlin had never given her a wedding ring, but

Kyra found herself nodding numbly in reply to his question.

"Naughty girl!" Elyse scolded. "You'll have me thinking unkind thoughts about our Devlin if you aren't more careful." Then, summoning a thin smile, she said, "Devlin, if you would be a love and ring for John, I shall leave you and Kyra to recover from your harrowing day."

"There is no need to bother your man, Elyse. I'll carry you," Devlin said. While this chivalrous offer summoned a coquettish smile to Elyse's face, it brought no joy to Kyra's unhappy heart.

Kyra sat motionless as she watched her husband scoop the disabled woman into his arms as effortlessly as if he were lifting Nicholas or Sarah. Despite her physical disability, Kyra thought the woman possessed a remarkably domineering nature, and she had to forcibly repel the jealous urge to snatch away the fingers that Elyse entwined about Devlin's neck.

"Kyra?" Devlin's slightly agitated voice pervaded her reverie, causing Kyra to jump to her feet. "Will you walk with me to see Elyse safely on her way?"

"Of course," Kyra mumbled, feigning contrition for not properly attending their guest. In truth, Kyra had taken an instant dislike to the older woman and could not wait to be rid of her.

Elyse's attendant was lounging beside the carriage when the trio emerged from the mansion, and while the driver leaped to his station, the bigger man pulled open the door so Devlin could place Elyse inside. When Devlin stepped back, John grunted a sour-sounding thank-you and climbed inside to take a seat on the bench opposite his mistress. As the conveyance rolled away, Elyse waved a lace handkerchief from the open window and cried farewell, promising to call again.

Kyra stood on the porch step directly below Devlin, waving distractedly at the disappearing vehicle. Finally, when the carriage trundled from view, Kyra's hand fell to her side, her brow crinkled into a pensive frown, and she muttered, "I wonder . . ."

"Yes, I am inclined to wonder much the same thing," Devlin echoed her sentiments, chuckling at the bemused expression that crossed her face. "You're wondering about the precise nature of *our* John's duties as attendant to the fair Elyse," he answered Kyra's unspoken question and laughed outright as her jaw dropped in surprise.

"How do you do that? How do you always know what I'm thinking?"

"My dear, I can read your face like an open book."

"She is very pretty, Devlin," Kyra commented gloomily.

Devlin's keen ear detected her sad tone, and hiding a smile, he drawled, "Is she? I had not noticed lately." Then, stepping down beside her, he picked up one of the lanterns that illuminated the walkway and, taking her hand in his, said, "I don't care to discuss Elyse. Let us take a walk, shall we? Today's near tragedy has made me realize that you and I are long overdue for a serious chat. Come along," he said, giving her hand a gentle tug.

Left with no alternative, Kyra followed her husband reluctantly into the darkness, wildly speculating as to what the night would bring.

The myriad questions that flitted through her confused brain remained unanswered some minutes later as Kyra stared expectantly at her husband's rigid back. The lantern sat on the ground between them, and its glow mingled with the reflected moonlight off the ocean to drape the brooding man in a blanket of eerie shadows. Kyra had no idea as to the essence of his obviously troubled thoughts, but she assumed Devlin had learned of her terrible secret and the real reason for her journey up the mountain that morning.

Unable to endure the deafening silence a moment longer, she blurted, "I'm sorry, Devlin! It's all my fault."

"What?" His dark head snapped around as if he had been

jarred from a deep sleep. "What nonsense have you taken into your head now?"

"This morning . . . the tree . . . Sarah," she babbled incoherently.

"What a silly goose you are," Devlin teased, closing the gap that separated them and taking her hand in his. "There is a place where we can sit a little way from here. Lynette used to come to this spot and stare out at the sea for hours on end, so my men put a bench up here for her. Come and sit with me, magpie, and I will explain why you could not possibly be responsible for this morning's incident."

Devlin carried the lantern as they walked to the chair, and once they were comfortably seated, he again set it on the ground. After expelling a long breath, he said, "It was Miss Lovejoy."

"*What?*"

"Kyra, an experienced cutter can drop a tree exactly where he wants to," Devlin explained.

"What does that have to do with Miss Lovejoy?" Kyra asked incredulously.

"What occurred this morning was no accident," he said seriously. "The tree that nearly crushed you had been undercut so as to fall in a specific area. You were purposely placed in its path, magpie. I spoke with the men after I brought you and Sarah back to the mansion, and several of them recalled seeing Jeb approach you."

"Jeb?"

"Lovejoy's brother."

"Are you suggesting she enlisted her brother's aid to do me harm?"

Devlin nodded.

"But why would she want to hurt me?" Kyra asked, lifting her face to him, and he was hard-pressed to keep from dragging that beguiling vision into his arms to kiss away the confused look that saddened her eyes.

"Because, dear heart, it was you who persuaded me to

dismiss her as the children's governess. This is a small island, Kyra, and jobs are hard to come by. Miss Lovejoy comes from a large family that includes a shiftless drunken father with a violent temper. It seems that a significant portion of Alice's salary went to her ne'er-do-well parent while she tucked the remainder away to use one day to leave the island," Devlin explained, touching a finger to Kyra's lips to forestall the barrage of questions he knew her to be mentally formulating.

"After I dismissed her, she apparently became so out-raged at the prospect of returning to live with her ill-tempered father that she decided to seek vengeance against the one she felt responsible for her plight. That someone was you, little pet, and as you said, she used her brother to carry out her twisted plan for revenge."

"How did you learn all this?"

"By questioning the right people," Devlin replied. "There is more," he admitted reluctantly, cradling her in the crook of his arm to soften the blow of his forthcoming revelation. "Kyra, the tumble you took from Wildstar was no accident. I have discovered that the groom who saddled him for you was Lovejoy's nephew. Undoubtedly, he did not expect you to handle that crazy horse as well as you did, but just in case, he made certain you would not return from your ride unscathed."

"How?"

"By cutting the girth just enough to ensure that any sizable jolt, such as the one you sustained when Wildstar cleared that ditch, would result in a fall. I suspected the strap had been tampered with when I inspected the saddle after you fell that morning, but then you became ill and I . . ." His voice faded, but the reassuring pressure of Kyra's hand on his gave him the strength to continue. "Well, I was so distracted and guilt-ridden after we talked that I forgot about the girth until this morning. A thorough interrogation of the stable hands revealed that Lucas,

Lovejoy's nephew, was the one who saddled Wildstar that morning."

"She killed my baby," Kyra mumbled dully.

"Yes, little one," Devlin whispered soothingly. "She is surely to blame, and I would have her brought to justice, but she has disappeared, and—" He broke off abruptly as Kyra shoved away from him, but the accusing glare she leveled at Devlin was clearly discernible in the moonlight.

"Devlin, I was not the only one affected by this morning's mishap. Sarah could have been injured as well. I understand why Miss Lovejoy might want to harm me, but I know there is much you are not telling me. Your actions have been shrouded in mystery ever since you brought me to Cauldurae, what with your armed guards, your talk of privateers, and your running off for days on end with that . . . that *partner* of yours," she spat the word.

"You're quite right, Kyra," Devlin admitted, smiling inwardly at her jealous reaction to Elyse. "There is much about me you don't know. I have said as much."

"But I . . . I want to know everything about you."

"Do you?" he asked softly, again coaxing her within the haven of his sheltering embrace. With his hands clasped firmly about her waist and her head lolling against his chest beneath his chin, he began to explain. "Much of what I am about to tell you began shortly after I came to Carraba, long before Lynette's death. There's really no easy way to embark upon this discussion Kyra, so let me say simply that someone has been trying for a number of years to ruin me financially and drive me from the island."

"But who? Why? How?" were Kyra's reactive queries.

"One question at a time, magpie." Devlin bussed the top of her head affectionately. "If you will permit me, I shall answer your questions in reverse. How, you ask? My cunning adversary has employed any number of deceitful methods. My ships have been plundered, my crops have been burned, my distilleries and other businesses have been undermined, and I have been personally slandered. All of this has caused me to incur huge financial losses.

"I have endured the monetary setbacks thus far, but what is more galling is the fact that the rogue has taken to intimidating my workers. Some have sustained injuries, fires have broken out at unlikely times and under questionable circumstances, and a few of my men have received anonymous threats. The people around here are a superstitious lot. They see me as an outsider who has brought bad luck to the island. Several have quit outright, and others will follow suit if something is not done soon.

"Meanwhile, because of the reduction in labor, I have a backlog of orders that remain unfilled because of curtailed production, and I have a warehouse full of perishable merchandise that cannot be delivered because my only available ship is in dry dock undergoing repairs for damages it sustained in a recent attack by privateers. To worsen matters, I cannot lease another vessel because word has gotten out that I am a bad risk, so my goods are rotting in my warehouses while I struggle to figure out who is trying to ruin me," he concluded on a grim note.

Kyra's hands tightened protectively atop the ones that squeezed her waist. "But why are you so certain that someone is trying to ruin you? Is is possible these happenings are just unfortunate coincidences?"

"Like our meeting in Savannah?" he asked.

Kyra, wary of the intonation of that deep voice, twisted around so that she could see Devlin's face. "What do you mean? I did not purposely contrive to stumble into your arms," she said huffily before presenting her back once more.

"No, I grant you that. Like our first encounter in Charleston, it was but a happy coincidence when you toppled off the *Driftwood* into my arms. What occurred later that night, however, was not," he said frankly. "In fact, my sojourn to Savannah was instigated by someone else, someone who wanted to keep me away from the island for an extended time. You see, I had been away from Carraba on a business trip—"

"With Elyse?" Kyra interjected, despite her best effort to the contrary.

"Yes, with Elyse," he said with a tolerant sigh. "When I returned to the island, I discovered that Mother had come here in my absence and whisked Nicholas and Sarah back to Savannah with her. Well, knowing Mother, I assumed she had been snooping into my affairs again, but I was mistaken. Perhaps you can imagine my surprise when I confronted her and learned that she had received a letter from me telling her that I was to be away from Cauldurae on an extended trip."

"I don't understand." Kyra shrugged in confusion. "Why is that so remarkable?"

"Because, sweetheart, I wrote no such letter."

"Oh!" Kyra's eyes widened in surprise. "Then that means—"

"Precisely. Whoever sent that note knew I would make straight for Savannah when I learned that Mother had taken the children. As far as I can determine, my adversary wanted to keep me away from Cauldurae for as long as possible. I suppose whoever it is had concocted some grand scheme that will finish me once and for all, and the longer he can keep me preoccupied, the better his chance of succeeding." Devlin gazed down at the pile of gold-brown hair beneath his chin and bent forward to whisper, "And that is why you and I were thrown together in Savannah."

"What?" Kyra cried. "But you said—"

"I know, little pet." He chuckled at her indignation. "I'm not referring to that memorable encounter on the wharf, but to my appearance on your yacht later that evening. I've had time to reflect since that night. As you well know, I drank myself into a stupor following that fateful interview with Mother, but you don't know that I have a hazy recollection of being clubbed over the head in the tavern. Then I suspect I was dumped on your yacht. I have no proof, of course, only a keen suspicion—and the memory of a painfully throbbing head upon awakening."

Very carefully, Kyra unclasped Devlin's hands from her waist and turned to face him. "But why would anyone wish to involve me in all this?"

One lithe hand reached out to caress Kyra's cheek, and Devlin's voice was genuinely remorseful when he said, "I cannot be certain, but I believe our meeting on the pier that morning was witnessed by someone who saw the encounter as a way to keep me in Savannah indefinitely. I don't know, perhaps my unknown enemy hoped we would be discovered and I would be arrested or, at the very least, called out by an enraged relative for dishonoring you."

"You very nearly were," Kyra reminded him, remembering her father's forbidding visage.

"Yes, I know," Devlin murmured faintly, his lips parting in an enigmatic smile. As his hand slipped away from Kyra's cheek to rest on her shoulder, the boyish grin vanished and he was somber once more as he explained, "I assume our misguided matchmaker—knowing my aversion to marriage—thought I would be detained at length while I endeavored to settle the matter. Instead, I outwitted him and married you on the spot. Oh, I'm certain he believes he had the last laugh, but who would have guessed—" His voice trailed off and his penetrating gaze scanned her face in the moonlight.

Kyra, very much aware of the compelling brown eyes that seemed fascinated with a silky wisp of hair that fluttered near her cheek, swallowed self-consciously before asking, "Why would anyone want to destroy you, Devlin?"

With some little effort, Devlin managed to repulse the amorous sensations that flooded his being. Shrugging, he answered, "I have offended any number of people through the years, though I assure you that I have never used deceit or trickery to gain the upper hand in any business venture. Who is to say why a person takes a vengeful notion into his head, Kyra? Perhaps he resents the success I have enjoyed since coming to Carraba."

"But who, Devlin? Who would want to do this to you?"

Devlin did not immediately respond to this question, but stood to pace before the bench as he mulled over his reply. Then, having come to a decision, he turned to face Kyra and extended his hand to help her to her feet. His tone was ominous when he said, "I haven't been able to prove anything yet, but I'm convinced the one responsible for all my woes is the person who stands to gain the most if I default on my mortgage payments. Cauldurae is heavily encumbered," Devlin explained, adding a disturbing post-script, "If these attacks continue, I shall lose the estate, magpie. And if I lose Cauldurae, I lose everything."

Despite the sultry summer night, Kyra felt chilled to the bone by this startling revelation, and her heart went out to her troubled husband. But the comforting hand she started to extend to him fell numbly to her side when she heard his concluding remarks.

Bending to collect the flickering lantern, Devlin said, "As for who? Your friend Joshua Fowler holds the mort-gage on Cauldurae."

The initial moments of their return walk to the mansion were made in awkward silence. Kyra's thoughts were racing, for she found it exceedingly difficult to believe that the man who had treated her with such kindness since her arrival on Carraba could be capable of the malicious acts her husband had described. Yet Devlin seemed so positive, and Kyra did not think that he would openly declare his suspicion of Joshua unless he possessed some evidence to support his accusation. Kyra was on the verge of airing this insight when an unexpected occurrence abruptly thrust all thoughts of the doctor from her mind.

Kyra had fallen a few paces behind Devlin, who trudged on through the dark, extending the lantern to light their way. They were on the path high above the mouth of the river where it merged with the sea when a mournful wail split the night. Kyra was frightened by the eerie sound that echoed up the ravine to envelop her in its doleful lament, prompting her to run toward the protective shadow that loomed in front of her.

Devlin paused on the footpath. He, too, had heard the noise, and anticipating Kyra's reaction to the scary sound, he turned to her. His words died on his lips, however, as Kyra—her gaze intent on the ground lest she stumble over some unseen object—ran into him. The force of the collision knocked Devlin's feet from under him, and as the lantern went flying, they tumbled to the ground. In the next instant, a stunned Devlin lay flat on his back with Kyra sprawled breathlessly across his chest.

"Wh-what is that?" Kyra whispered, glancing nervously over her shoulder as if she expected some ghostly apparition to swoop down upon them.

"The wind," came his unruffled response. Witnessing her astonished expression by the glow of the moon, Devlin queried, "Kyra, has no one told you of the legend of Carraba?"

"No, and I don't care to hear about it, thank you," she informed him pertly as another haunting blast of air caused her to shiver and huddle closer to Devlin.

"Come, now, magpie, don't be so fainthearted," Devlin playfully scolded as he smoothed an errant strand of gold-brown hair back into place. "Even Nicholas begs to be told the tale," he baited her.

Pushing away from her husband, Kyra fussed with her skirts and crinoline before fixing him with a resigned look. "Oh, very well. Tell me your story," she snapped petulantly, though her irritation was self-directed for having reacted so foolishly to nothing more than the whistling wind.

"This is no mere *story*, Kyra," Devlin assured her as he pulled himself to a sitting position and, brushing the dust from his trousers, braced his shoulders against the trunk of a cedrela tree that stood beside the path. "It's a tale of swashbuckling pirates, hidden treasure, and . . . unrequited love," he began, emphasizing this fanciful element, knowing it would pierce Kyra's romantic heart. "Legend has it that in the days when Spanish galleons were known to frequent the waters near here, the island was inhabited by a Frenchman known as Pierre le Roublard and his band of cutthroat pirates."

Devlin smiled to himself as he noticed Kyra's involuntary quiver at the mention of pirates, and as he proceeded to spin his yarn, he casually drew her against him and settled his arm about her. "It seems that wily Pierre, as he was known, was a most resourceful and ruthless buccaneer. He and his men had amassed a tremendous fortune by freebooting Spanish ships they suspected of transporting priceless Peruvian treaures back to Spain."

Kyra, now totally enthralled by the story, interrupted, "But surely someone would have followed him and brought him and his men to justice."

"Ah, but our Pierre was a crafty fellow. He displayed his cunning by choosing Carraba as refuge, for its very anonymity made the island a virtually inaccessible lair. That, coupled with the fact he was, alas, a heartless rogue who felt obliged to sink every ship he seized."

"But what of the people on board? What happened to them?"

"Ever the compassionate one," Devlin chuckled fondly, absently reaching down to cover her hand with his. "Pierre did not believe in taking prisoners," he said meaningfully, "until, that is, Luisa caught his eye."

"Luisa?"

"Yes, Luisa." His tone deepened as he repeated the name in a sensuous murmur. "She was a beautiful Spanish maiden, and Pierre was instantly smitten, so he removed her from the ship and brought her back to Carraba."

"Was she happy here?"

"No, little one. That unnerving sound that frightened you into my arms is Luisa warning all the island girls to beware," he whispered ominously.

"To beware of what?" Kyra asked, her eyes round with expectation.

"Why, island men, of course," he quipped, handily dodging the graceful hand that shot upward to deliver a much deserved reprimand.

"Oh, you!" Kyra grumbled at his deviltry. "Be serious, Devlin. What happened to Luisa and the unfortunate Pierre? Did they marry?"

"No, even though Pierre was persistent in wooing and courting her, Luisa remained standoffish until . . ."

"What?"

"Kyra," Devlin drawled reproachfully, "Pierre was, after all, a pirate. What do you think happened?"

"The cad!" Kyra exclaimed. "He forced her?"

"I'm afraid so," he answered flatly. His next comment, however, was carefully phrased. "Kyra, a man will not wait indefinitely for that which he desires."

Kyra, suddenly mindful of the disastrous turn in conversation, endeavored to steer Devlin back to the topic at hand by asking abruptly, "What happened to the treasure?"

Devlin acknowledged her successful parry with a quirk of one dark eyebrow. "No one knows for certain, but some of it went toward the building of a massive house, the ruins of which can be found at Cauldurae."

Kyra gasped at this unexpected revelation. "Do you mean to say that—"

"Yes." He laughed outright at her stupefied expression.

"Many people speculate that what is left of Pierre le Roublard's ill-gotten-booty is hidden at Cauldurae."

"Don't you believe so, too?" Kyra stared in dismay at his indifferent shrug and demanded, "You mean you have never even looked for it?"

"Kyra"—Devlin sighed disdainfully, as if censuring a naughty child—"I have this plantation and others to manage, as well as a number of businesses. Lest you forget, I'm constantly keeping watch for clues that would lead to the exposure of an enemy who would take everything I have worked for. I don't have time to search for a treasure—a tainted treasure, mind you; the legend also warns that sorrow and misery will befall whoever prospers from others' misfortune—a treasure that in all likelihood was found by the people who built Cauldurae years ago. That is precisely why I employ a large number of armed guards—to keep would-be treasure hunters from destroying my peace and despoiling my property."

"Likelihood," Kyra echoed, thoughtfully biting her lower lip. "Then the treasure's discovery was never documented?"

"No," he answered slowly as he, too, contemplated a serious matter. Then his dark head bent toward hers and his voice deepened to a seductive murmur as he whispered against her cheek, "Let us have done with this talk of hidden treasure, for I find myself suddenly mindful of the untold riches I have here before me. A man has no need of gold or silver or priceless gems when he holds a treasure such as you in his arms," he breathed huskily.

Kyra flinched as his mouth crept purposely closer to hers. "No—" came her instinctive whimper of protest as she twisted her head to avoid the kiss.

"Shh, little pet," Devlin reassured her as he carefully lowered her to the ground and settled himself comfortably beside her. Then he coaxed her to look at him by saying ever so softly, "It is only a kiss after all. Surely you will not deny me a sweet token beneath the starlit heavens."

Before Kyra could respond, she felt the gentle warmth of his mouth against her own. The moment their lips touched, Kyra realized this kiss would be vastly different from the others she had experienced with this volatile man. Whereas his previous kisses had been full of arrogance, bitterness, and angry lust, this one—though it equaled the others in passion—was decidedly more tender and yes . . . even loving. This last thought had barely taken root in Kyra's besotted brain when Devlin lifted his mouth from her lips.

A disappointed groan warbled in the back of Kyra's throat, but she did not remain frustrated for long. Devlin had merely relinquished the honey-sweet lips so that he could explore the other treasures available to him. He then pressed a trail of kisses from the corner of her mouth along her cheek and eventually nibbled a path down the slender column of her throat. On impulse, he pulled aside the gauzy material to gain access to the silken flesh of her shoulder, and once it was exposed, he applied himself to the practiced manipulation of this sensuous region.

Devlin was very much aware of his partner's contented sigh and the fact that she trembled every so slightly against him. With a knowing chuckle, he moved his lips along the enticing flesh, his warm breath stirring up a frenzy of tingly gooseflesh. He whispered sweet endearments in her ear and gently tugged at a lobe that proved to be an irresistible temptation. And just when Kyra felt she might actually swoon from the epicurean spell he had masterfully woven, Devlin's lips returned to capture hers.

Whereas the initial caress had begun as a somewhat docile adventure, this one rapidly deepened in both fervor and desire, a fact that could be attributed to Kyra's sudden active interest in the proceedings. Devlin nearly crowed with delight when he realized that his heretofore seemingly indifferent partner was returning his kiss with a rapture he had only dreamed possible. He reveled in the feel of her soft, pliable flesh beneath him and the hands that shyly stole up his back to experience the play of hard, rippling muscles and subsequently clung to him out of feverish desire.

Kyra's lips parted briefly to allow a blissful moan its freedom, and seizing this unexpected opportunity, Devlin's tongue quickly fluttered inside to feast on the guarded bounty therein. Kyra rapidly accustomed herself to the probing invader's insistent rhythm as she reciprocated this caress as well.

In her passion-blinded state, Kyra could have been persuaded to while away the remaining hours of the night in her husband's arms. Had it not been for a sudden twinge of conscience from the gentleman in question, that very well could have happened. But Devlin was reminded of the promise he had made to Kyra the night of her miscarriage. Thus acutely aware of his rising passions, and wary of his apparent inability to curtail them, Devlin surmised that reason must prevail if he was not to break his vow.

With a regretful sigh, he pulled his mouth from Kyra's and touched his lips to the tip of her nose. His voice shook faintly when he said, "You know, magpie, you are mistaken when you assume I know your every thought. I wish you would tell me what you're thinking now." His throaty entreaty brushed her cheek, creating further havoc among her already passion-stirred emotions.

Kyra was silent as she stared up into the expectant face, and a lump gathered in her throat as her hand traveled from his back to stroke his forehead and down his cheek to linger near the corner of his mouth. She now knew how it felt to want someone, to want to give herself body and soul regardless of the consequences. As she struggled to bring her rampaging senses under control, she pondered this startling discovery.

Always before, her standoffishness had sprung from her desire to keep the events of that night aboard the *Driftwood* a secret. Her physical response to Devlin, a virtual stranger, had been shameful. Her saving grace had been the fact that Devlin had only hazy recollections of the occurrence and none whatsoever of her own disgraceful conduct. She was horrified that she had reacted with such abandon to a man whom she did not love and who treated her with such blatant disregard. Her constant fear since that night was that he would somehow seduce her into his arms again and thereby learn the extent of her wretchedness.

But that was before she had grown to love Devlin and, even though she was not wholly certain of his feelings for her, Kyra knew she would now surrender willingly to his desires were it not for her suspected involvement in the death of Clayton Fairchild. She loved Devlin, but knew in her heart that she could not give herself to him with the threat of imprisonment, or worse, hanging over her head. It would not be fair to him, and she would be little better than Lynette if she embarked upon such a deception. Kyra could not bear to hurt Devlin, but neither could she bring herself to trust him with the awful truth, for that would only make him despise her.

With tear-filled eyes, Kyra idly ran her fingers through his hair and coaxed Devlin's head down so that she could touch her lips to his in a fleeting kiss. Then she pulled away to say—

"Devlin, I want you!"

Devlin blinked, thinking he could not have heard right, for although these were the words he had longed to hear, he was perplexed by the husky timbre of the voice and moreover by the extraordinary fact that Kyra's lips had not moved.

"Damn it, Devlin! Where the hell are you?" the unidentified voice again rumbled.

As comprehension dawned, Devlin muttered a particularly vitriolic oath and climbed to his feet to confront the unhappy intruder. "Yes, Marcus, over here. What is it?" he called, extending a hand to assist Kyra to her feet.

Kyra managed to repair much of the damage inflicted upon her appearance as a result of her husband's passionate play, but Devlin's hair remained noticeably mussed. Just as Kyra reached up to brush a thick strand back into place, the man came upon them, effectively destroying any hope Kyra entertained of maintaining a semblance of dignity.

A quick glance at his employer's agitated face and the lady's flushed visage, confirmed what Marcus already suspected—his intrusion had been ill timed. Marcus's flustered gaze darted back and forth between the couple, and he doffed his cap and blurted, "Beggin' your pardon, ma'am . . . Devlin, but they told me at the house they had seen you come this way. I wouldn't have bothered you, but—well, it's important."

Never one to mince words, Devlin demanded, "Out with it, man. What the devil has happened now?"

"I've just come from the mill. There's been another accident today. The support ropes snapped after we secured a wagonload of timber, and the load shifted and tumbled off. The men scattered but when the dust cleared, I did a little investigating and found that those ropes didn't break free on their own—they had a little help."

"Was anyone hurt?" Devlin asked somberly.

"Clem busted his arm. Doc Fowler fixed him up good as new, but Old Clem, you know how he is. He raised a stink, got the men all stirred up. I tried to smooth things over 'cause we all heard what happened up on the mountain this morning, and I figured you'd be occupied elsewhere," Marcus announced unthinkingly, although he had the grace to lower his eyes. Then clearing his throat, he continued, "The men are at the mill now, Devlin, threatening to—well, all sorts of things. You better come quick. You're the only one who can settle them down and get them to think straight. I've got horses waiting." He gestured over his shoulder into the night.

Devlin's involuntary reaction was to start running toward the horses, but remembering Kyra, he halted and turned to her.

"Go on," she responded to his unspoken question. "The house is not so very far. I'll be fine."

"Are you certain? I could—"

"I can manage by myself, Devlin," Kyra said pertly. "Run along! Your men need you, and you're keeping Marcus waiting."

With an appreciative smile and a promise to explain everything when he returned, Devlin sprinted after the departing Marcus to be swallowed by the night.

Kyra stared after him for several moments, then lowered her gaze to the ground where she and Devlin had enacted that tempestuous scene. Her cheeks reddened with the memory, but before she became caught up in a lengthy daydream, the renewed mournful wail of the wind convinced her it was time to hurry home.

"Yes, Luisa, I know," Kyra mumbled, pressing her fingers to her lips, which had so recently thrilled to Devlin's touch. "You tried to warn me about island men," she sighed forlornly, bending to retrieve the discarded lantern.

The flame had long since sputtered and died, but there was no need for Kyra to be afraid, since the path was awash in moonlight. She jumped and screamed, however, when an unexpected sound caught her off guard. Then, roundly chastising herself for her fainthearted reaction to the night cry of an owl, she started for the mansion before anything else could frazzle her badly strained nerves.

Kyra had managed no more than half a dozen steps when a hooded figure leaped from behind a tree to block her path. The lantern crashed to the ground with a loud clank, and before Kyra could muster a scream, the shape bolted forward to grasp her cruelly by both arms. A hood was shoved over her head and a hand clamped down on her mouth to prevent her from sounding an alarm. Then, despite her valiant struggles, she was half dragged, half carried into the forest away from Cauldurae's beckoning lights.

16

Kyra's heart pounded out a desperate rhythm as she anticipated her abductors' next move. She had determined from
the hushed murmurs there were at least two of them—the
burly one who had accosted her on the trail and another,
who appeared to be the leader of a band of night marauders.
Kyra had no idea how far she had been carried into the
forest before she was dumped on the ground and bound to
a tree. She knew only that this waiting and guessing at their
purpose was unbearable.

While she awaited their next move, Kyra speculated
about her kidnappers' identity. Her most frightening
thought was that the privateers Devlin had warned her about
had invaded the island and intended to hold her for
ransom . . . or worse. Her second fear was that her
blackmailer had decided to confront her. Neither theory
proved comforting.

As Kyra sat with her spine pressed uncomfortably against
the tree, the frantic rhythm of her heart gradually lessened,
enabling her to think more clearly. She knew she would
never be a willing victim of their wretched crime, and she
searched her mind for some means of escape. Her obvious
course was to untie her bonds and slip soundlessly into the
forest when she was not being observed. The black hood
obscured her vision, but Kyra would deal with that obstacle
once her hands were free. With this thought foremost in

mind, she began to rub her wrists together in an effort to loosen the ropes that dug into her flesh.

"That's useless, Mrs. Cauldwell. You cannot escape," a low, raspy voice snickered above her.

Kyra grew instantly still and cocked her head in the direction of the voice. "Who are you?" she demanded. "What do you want of me? I have no money."

"I'm not interested in your money. It's your help I'm after," came the villain's mysterious announcement.

"What makes you think I would be willing to help you?" Kyra snapped.

"I have a pocket watch and reticule that belong to you, Mrs. Cauldwell—items that were taken from Clayton Fairchild's house the night he died. If you choose not to assist me, I will turn these incriminating articles over to the Savannah authorities along with the information about where they were found, or perhaps I'll give them to your husband. I daresay he will be none too pleased to learn he has been harboring a murderess these many weeks."

"I am not a murderess," Kyra protested. "It . . . it was an accident," she gasped, knowing full well that her petition fell on unsympathetic ears.

"You cannot prove that. The man is, after all, dead," the faceless voice replied bluntly.

The forest became eerily silent as Kyra pondered her unhappy situation. The alternatives at her command were less than appealing. Either she would have to do this unscrupulous person's bidding or she would face a daunting and potentially heartbreaking interrogation from Devlin.

Kyra knew that their tenuous relationship had undergone an amazing, albeit gradual, transformation in the past few weeks, but she did not yet dare to believe that he had learned to love her. Still, she sensed that Devlin cared for her in a way she had never imagined possible, and to chance losing the man she had come to love and the life they shared at Cauldurae was a risk she simply was not willing to take.

With the memory of Devlin's arms surrounding her, his laughter tickling her ear, and his kisses lightly buffeting her cheek, Kyra choked back a sob and asked, "What do you want me to do?"

"You must help me locate the treasure," the leader said.

"Treasure?" Kyra repeated hoarsely.

"Don't play coy, Mrs. Cauldwell. I overheard that romantic little chat just now in which Devlin explained the legend of the island. He's a fool to believe that Pierre le Roublard's treasure does not exist. I *know* it does and I intend to have it for myself. If you know what's good for you, you'll do everything in your power to help me." The raspy voice grew more ominous with this portentous statement.

"But why me? How can I help you?" Kyra cried.

"By finding the diary. Your husband was correct in assuming the treasure was discovered during Cauldurae's construction, but he misjudged the craven nature of those erstwhile island dwellers. Like him, they heard of the treasure's tainted legacy and therefore chose not to tempt the fates. Instead, they hid the booty in another place. The mistress at that time kept a diary in which she recorded clues that would direct other, more stalwart adventurers to the treasure. I charge you with locating that diary."

"But—" Kyra tried to object, only to have her entreaty ruthlessly ignored.

"Others before you have failed. Lynette was a spineless little mouse, and the Lovejoy woman was careless and greedy." The nameless blackmailer gave an evil chuckle upon hearing Kyra's surprised gasp at this revelation, then continued, "Yes, my quest for the treasure has been going on for some time. Lynette agreed to help me because I promised that, once the diary was mine, I'd give her safe passage off the island and transport back to France.

"Lynette hated her life here and had grown to despise Devlin. Then she struck upon the unfortunate idea of telling him of my scheme, thinking Devlin—doubtless from some sense of honor—would release her from her interminable confinement on Carraba. Well, I could not afford to let that happen. I've come too far and waited too long."

"*You* killed Lynette?" Kyra exclaimed incredulously, wishing that she could somehow rid herself of the hood in order to discern the identity of this admitted murderer.

"Suffice to say my men encouraged her to go sailing one stormy night."

"But Devlin was implicated in Lynette's death," Kyra breathed hoarsely.

"Yes," the mysterious voice mumbled wryly. "It's a pity those charges could never be substantiated. All of this would have been unnecessary, for Cauldurae would have been mine and I could have hunted for the treasure to my heart's content."

"Instead, you engaged Alice Lovejoy as your new accomplice," Kyra deduced.

"My, but you are a clever puss. That will serve to your advantage in the coming weeks. Alice, like Lynette before her, was anxious to flee the island. The promise of a sizable reward did much toward ensuring her cooperation. In her capacity as governess, she had unlimited access to the mansion, but as you well know, she proved to be a lamentable nurserymaid. I apologize for the turmoil Alice has caused since her dismissal, however. You may rest assured she will no longer trouble you."

Kyra detected the sinister inflection and, despite her instincts to the contrary, found herself asking, "What do you mean?"

"Merely that after this morning's tree-falling incident, I realized she had become a nuisance I could no longer ignore. You see, the two letters you received were written by Alice—the first at my instruction. But before I could arrange a suitable meeting, our vengeful governess took it upon herself to pen the second letter in order to lure you to the mountain and kill you. I rather imagine she assumed that, if you were out of the way, she could persuade Devlin to reinstate her as the children's governess, thereby enabling her to resume her activities for me. I daresay her ingenious ploy might have worked had it not been for your husband's quick reflexes. But that is neither here nor there." Kyra's abductor sounded suddenly bored with the tale.

"That brings us around to you, Mrs. Cauldwell. As you can see, your predecessors had much to gain in return for their cooperation, and still they disappointed me. But you, I think, are more suited for this task. You will succeed where the others failed because you stand to lose a great deal if your efforts prove unsuccessful." The cold, calculating timbre sent a shiver of fear racing down Kyra's spine.

"Do you understand what is expected of you?" the blackmailer asked gruffly.

Kyra, knowing she could not control the frightened tremor in her voice, nodded stiffly.

"Good. My assistant will take you back to the footpath. Then you may remove the hood. Please, refrain from doing anything foolish," the menacing figure cautioned. "Remember, once you give me the diary, I'll return your belongings. Your husband need never know about you and the lecherous Clayton Fairchild."

Kyra could tell by the crunching of footfalls that her unknown adversary had retreated deeper into the forest, causing her to feel panicky. "Wait!" she cried. "How will I let you know when I find the diary?"

"Never fear." The forest reverberated with a sinister chuckle. "I'll contact you, Mrs. Cauldwell."

Kyra sat in dazed stupefaction before her dressing table mirror as Biddie methodically brushed the tangles from the silky tresses. Her mind was a whirl of confusion as she mentally relived those frightening moments after her captor had released her. She had stood frozen in terror, half expecting the man to inflict some horrible injury upon her, but her worries proved unfounded; the man vanished soundlessly into the forest.

Then Kyra sprang into action. Flinging aside the hood, she had braced herself against the trunk of a tree while she inhaled huge gulps of the fresh night air. With a nervous glance over her shoulder, she began to run along the path. She ran as fast as her quaking legs would carry her along the uneven trail, pausing only when Cauldurae's lights came into view. Then she streaked down the rolling knoll, across the adjoining meadow, and through the gate. The entrance hall was empty when Kyra bolted across the threshold, and impervious to the stabbing pain that ravaged her side, she clambered up the stairs to her room. With a heaving bosom and a visibly shaken countenance, she threw open the door to find Biddie puttering about the chamber.

"Is you all right, Miz Kyra?" The servant presently repeated the question she had asked upon Kyra's arrival several minutes earlier.

"As I explained, Biddie," Kyra said tiredly, unable to meet the maid's eyes in the looking glass, "I suffered a small fright on my way back to the mansion after Devlin left me . . . that is all. I'll be fine in a moment," Kyra reassured the doubtful maid, wishing that Biddie would leave her to her thoughts.

Just when Kyra had abandoned all hope of ever being left alone to sort out her woeful plight, Biddie made a welcome announcement. "There's a warm bath awaitin' Mr. Cauld-well in his dressin' room, but he ain't 'spected back fer a while, so it'll be long past his wantin' to make use of. Why don't you go soak fer a spell, Miz Kyra? It'll help ease your mind. I laid out your night things, and there's plenty of towels," Biddie added temptingly. "I 'spect you'll be needin' some time to yourself," she said understandingly, and as she wove the mass of curls into a single braid, Biddie chatted about Sarah.

"She was sleepin' like a little angel the last time I peeked in," she informed Kyra. "Dr. Fowler done dropped by to check on her while you and Mr. Cauldwell went walkin'. Did you see him?"

"No," Kyra replied distantly.

"Well, it don't make no never mind. He said he might walk up on the bluff to greet you. I guess he done changed his mind." She concluded by draping the heavy braid across Kyra's shoulder.

The maid then devoted her attention to straightening the silver tray of hairpins, combs, and brushes. With the completion of this task, she prepared to take her leave, but her actions were momentarily thwarted when she felt Kyra's hand on her wrist. Their eyes met in the mirror, and Biddie's puzzled frown grew deeper when she observed the tears that misted her mistress's eyes.

"Thank you, Biddie. You take such good care of me," Kyra whispered gratefully.

"Aw, shucks, Miz Kyra. 'Tain't nothin'," came the servant's embarrassed reply. "You has had a rough go of it lately, that's all. I just wish you'd trust someone with your sorrows. If not me, then you should tell Mr. Cauldwell. He ain't a bad man, just a mite uppity sometimes. He'd help you, Miz Kyra, if you'd let him." Upon uttering this sage advice, Biddie quietly left the room.

The door had barely closed before Kyra retrieved the key, let herself into Devlin's chamber, and found her way to his dressing room.

Kyra quickly undressed and lowered herself into the soothing bath. Closing her eyes, she leaned back and allowed the warm water to work its magic on her aching limbs while she contemplated the evening's disastrous revelations. Even though Kyra had been saddled with the impossible task of finding a minuscule diary concealed somewhere in the vast mansion, she found the disclosures concerning Lynette far more daunting.

Devlin, she knew, was convinced his first wife had committed suicide. "Lynette preferred death to living with me," he had said, and though he had endeavored to appear nonchalant, Kyra knew he had been greatly troubled by the incident. There were even people on the island who held Devlin responsible for Lynette's demise. And here she sat, in possession of the facts surrounding her death, yet completely powerless to do anything about it. Kyra was faced with a hopeless dilemma, for she was not so hare-brained as to think that Devlin would blithely accept this information without demanding a full explanation of how she had acquired it.

In Kyra's tortured mind, she felt she had to find the diary and relinquish it to the blackmailer. Then one day, when her life had attained some semblance of normalcy, she would tell Devlin everything—when the time was right.

"I cannot tell him yet," she muttered forlornly.

"Cannot tell him what?" a familiar voice inquired casually from the doorway.

"Devlin!" Kyra shrieked, leaning forward with a noisy splash. "What are you doing here?"

"I find that a singularly preposterous question, Kyra. This is, after all, *my* dressing room," he informed her dryly, as he became mesmerized by the sight of a gold-brown braid tumbling across an alabaster shoulder to dangle alongside one agonizingly beautiful breast. Swallowing the impassioned groan that burned his throat, he added huskily, "More to the point, what are *you* doing here?"

"I'm sorry!" Kyra blurted, splaying her hands across her bosom in a frantic attempt to conceal her nakedness, a demure exercise that merely served to entice her already enthralled observer. "I did not mean to intrude. It's just . . . well, Biddie said the bath had been drawn and you would not be returning for some time and . . . and—" She faltered, suddenly wary of Devlin's unwavering stare and his apparent unwillingness to leave her to finish her bath in peace. "If you will hand me one of those towels"—she indicated the fluffy pile that lay just out of her reach—"I'll have the servants prepare you a fresh bath."

"Don't bother," Devlin murmured suavely. Then, pushing away from the door, he stepped across the narrow floor and, much to Kyra's dismay, perched his intimidating frame on a chair beside the tub. The brown eyes twinkled with mischief as he leaned forward and added, "I'm perfectly willing to share this one with you." As if to verify this declaration, Devlin trailed his hand aimlessly through the water. "Besides, you haven't answered my question. What are you not yet willing to tell whom?"

Kyra watched distrustfully as his hand flitted dangerously close to her breast. Hoping to discourage his amorous advances, she unthinkingly rested her own dripping wet hand on his sleeve. "It's a surprise for Nicholas," she said, voicing the first thought that popped into her head. "Hannah told me his birthday is next month and I want to do something special for him."

"Uh-huh," Devlin grunted doubtfully.

Taking umbrage at his obvious skepticism, Kyra snapped, "I don't understand you at all! You browbeat me into telling you my private thoughts and then do not even have the decency to believe me. Why must you be suspicious of everything I say and do?"

"Perhaps you have given me just cause. I hope you will soon realize that you can trust me, Kyra," Devlin said, but when there was no reply, he held up a towel so that it fluttered between them like a flag of truce. "Come along, magpie, I have bullied you enough. You're looking pale after your eventful day and must be longing for your bed. Come," he repeated, wagging the towel in invitation.

With a sinking heart, Kyra realized that her self-appointed attendant would not be dismissed. She was determined, however, not to let her irrepressible husband turn her bath into a peep show. Favoring him with a dour look, she turned her back to him and, gripping the side of the tub, pushed herself to her feet. Next, she deftly plucked the towel from his fingertips and wrapped it securely about her before she faced him.

"Thank you," she breathed gratefully, taking care to avoid his eyes, for she was fairly certain where that seductive brown gaze would be focused.

"My pleasure." He offered his hand to steady her as she stepped out of the slippery tub.

With an uneasy glance at his face—Devlin had assumed an expression of angelic innocence—she accepted his hand. Kyra came to regret her trust the instant she stepped from the bath, for instead of releasing her, Devlin casually wrapped his arm about her waist and escorted her to the door. Her sigh of relief proved to be premature, however, for he nudged her backward until she was pressed against the unyielding door.

"Devlin, please don't!" Kyra started to protest, but was easily subdued by his sensual tactics.

"Shh." His warm breath tickled her bare shoulder in response, as he became preoccupied with nibbling a seductive path along her throat. "Kyra?" he murmured, allowing his hand to steal beneath the open slit of the towel.

"Hmm?" came her languid reply as the inquisitive hand lightly brushed the underside of her breast, slid down her waist and across her stomach, then paused before plunging down to the warm moistness of her femininity.

"Do you remember what I told you about Pierre le Roublard?" he whispered throatily. "Like him, I cannot be expected to wait indefinitely." Devlin began stroking the highly sensitive region, promptly rendering Kyra incapable of coherent speech, much less logical thought. "Kyra?" he repeated sharply.

"What?" she panted breathlessly, the palm of one hand

pressed flat against the door behind her while the other clung desperately to Devlin's sleeve.

Devlin, who was by no means a stranger to the throes of mindless passion, realized that a complete submission could be his if he but gently forced the issue. He also realized that, if he continued his skillful seduction, Kyra would be forever lost to him. She would never trust him again, and it had become important to him to gain her unquestioning trust.

Oh, he wanted her—he was to the point of bursting with wanting her—but not just for one night and not just as a lover. He wanted her as his friend, as the mother of his children, and as his life's helpmate. He wanted her forever. Devlin was sure of that, but he remained uncertain of her feelings for him. If he was ever to know how she truly felt about him, he would have to wait. She had to come to him, freely and unconditionally.

With a regretful sigh, Devlin withdrew his hand, eliciting a groan from Kyra. Turning her toward the open door, he delivered a playful slap to her backside and pushed her across the threshold. He smiled despite himself when he beheld her thoroughly frustrated expression, which inspired his parting sally.

"Sleep well . . . if you can," he drawled smugly.

Kyra's moonstruck expression withered instantly, and she whirled to vent her fury on the insufferable rogue just as the sturdy door closed in her face. Her cheeks grew scarlet with a mixture of humiliation and rage, and she glanced wildly about her, looking for an object that would inflict tremendous pain on the unscrupulous cur. When she found nothing suitable, she contented herself with snatching up a book and hurling it viciously against the wooden door.

The leather volume bounced against the door with a resonant thud, then dropped ineffectually to the floor. In a fit of pique, Kyra stomped her foot and used the towel to dry herself with a vengeance as if she would forever obliterate the memory of Devlin's touch. By the time she donned her nightdress, however, her fiery temper had subsided, and before climbing into bed, she picked up the book she had thrown during her heated outburst.

The title of the mistreated volume was *A Treatise on the Mores of the Modern Woman*, the book Devlin had given her to read when she was recuperating. She had never read it, even though she now recalled that Devlin had said it was one of Judith Tanner's favorites. Kyra regarded the volume with renewed interest, thinking this would be as good a place as any to begin her search for the missing diary.

As she bent to retrieve the book, Kyra's mild interest changed to outright curiosity. She lifted the volume to find that the impact had caused the pages to fall open to a section where two sheets had been pasted together. A frown knitted her brow as she strode to her dressing table. Sitting down before the mirror, she plucked a pair of scissors from a drawer and deftly slid the blade between the yellowed pages. Her discovery brought a startled gasp to her lips. Her eyes grew wide with wonder as she contemplated the enormity of her unexpected find, and her gaze became transfixed on the metal object she balanced gingerly in her palm.

It was a key. A tiny gold key had been hidden between the pages, a key that Kyra prayed would unlock Judith Tanner's diary and deliver her from this hellish nightmare.

Kyra's joy at finding the gold key was so great that she forgot her annoyance with her libidinous spouse. During the following week, while Devlin went about his business, Kyra became absorbed in her quest for the hidden diary.

Since Judith Tanner had chosen to seal the key between the pages of the book, Kyra quite logically began her search by thoroughly devouring the volume, thinking additional clues might lie somewhere in the text. But after days of reading and rereading the excessively boring passages, she tossed the book aside in disgust, no nearer to her objective than when she had started.

Her initial supposition was that the onetime mistress of this vast house must have been a forlorn and disenchanted lady to have considered this drivel to be valid doctrine. Or perhaps Judith had been a droll young woman, who had placed the key to the hidden treasure in this particular book thinking that if future generations were so desperate for diversion that they were reduced to reading this rubbish, then they deserved an invigorating treasure hunt. Always one to give the benefit of doubt, Kyra chose to believe the latter.

The next stage of Kyra's search led her to the library. If the key did indeed unlock the diary, Kyra's next logical assumption was that Judith had shelved the journal in the library. Kyra had spent many relaxing hours in the Cauldurae reading room poring over romantic novels and books of sonnets. She had never truly taken stock of the immense inventory, however, until she boldly ventured into the room resolved to ferret out the diary.

Kyra paused just inside the doorway to decide precisely where to begin her search, but her determination withered as she realized the tremendous task that lay ahead. One end of the massive room exuded a homey atmosphere in which a leather sofa, matching chairs and various knickknack tables were arranged before a fireplace. Devlin and Kyra had whiled away a number of evenings in that spot reading in companionable silence or aloud to each other and, on occasion, to the children.

It was the opposite end of the long rectangular room that proved to be the source of Kyra's woes. Leather volumes in every size and shape filled the shelves. They covered virtually every topic known to man and represented a gold mind for seekers of knowledge. Nestled in the midst of this cornucopia of learning, and surrounded on three sides by shelves extending from floor to ceiling, sat a mammoth desk from behind which Devlin conducted much of his business.

Kyra looked at the thousands of volumes awaiting her inspection and, heaving a disconsolate sigh, walked glumly to the nearest shelf.

Kyra teetered precariously on the top rung of the library ladder, stretching to reach a book that was tightly wedged between two larger volumes. Several days had passed since she had first acted on her suspicion that Judith had most likely hidden her diary among the thousands of books in the reading room. But hour upon agonizing hour of searching had revealed nothing and done little more than instill in Kyra an unnatural hatred of all books. She had been on the verge of giving up hope of ever finding the blasted diary when a visit with Sarah earlier that morning rekindled her enthusiasm for the project.

Kyra had been sitting in the rocking chair in the nursery diligently repairing, under Sarah's watchful eye, the damage Goldie had inflicted on Sarah's new doll. "We have done this before, little one," Kyra had murmured, recalling the pleasant afternoon they had passed together. "Remember, love? It was the day your papa brought me that nauseating book to read, and then had the audacity to suggest I might enjoy the companion vol—" Kyra had paused in mid-utterance, thunderstruck by what she had unwittingly said.

"That's it!" she had exclaimed.

Bounding up from the chair, she had scooped a thoroughly delighted Sarah into her arms and danced about the room. This spontaneous romp lasted but a few exhilarating seconds, however, for unfortunately, Kyra had discovered that she could not recall the title of the second volume. She had scrunched her brows together in a frown and willed her memory to divulge the forgotten information.

"Think!" she had commanded herself sternly.

"Tink!" Sarah had parroted.

"Oh, it had some utterly revolting title," Kyra had muttered in exasperation. She had then taken an agitated turn about the small room, voicing her thoughts aloud as she paced. "It had something to do with being a good wife. 'Faithful'? No." She had given her head a shake and gnawed on her lower lip thoughtfully. "It was more like 'devoted' or . . . or 'dutiful.' Yes, that's it! *On Being a Dutiful Wife,*" she had cried, then wrinkled her nose in disdain at the absurd title.

Kyra had wasted little time in depositing Sarah with Miss Peabody and had made her way to the library. Even though her search had been made consummately easier by virtue of the fact that she was now looking for a specific title, twilight had descended by the time a weary and disgruntled Kyra happened upon the volume. The book was on the top shelf, just out of reach and securely fixed between two larger works. Years of disuse had combined with the tropical climate to cause the leather bindings to stick together, further impeding Kyra's efforts to dislodge the book.

She presently stood on tiptoe, extending one arm above her head as far as she could and sliding her fingers up the spine. Kyra very nearly shouted with glee when her fingers topped the backbone, and she could at last take a firm hold on the wretched book. Her joy proved transitory, however, for the volume would not budge.

She gritted her teeth, squared her shoulders, and tightened her grip; then, with a throaty "Come on," yanked with all her might. This action produced the desired result. However, she executed the maneuver with such force that, when the book popped free, Kyra lost her balance and tumbled off the ladder.

Fortunately, Devlin had entered the room several minutes earlier and, after quickly assessing the situation, promptly stationed himself beside the ladder in anticipation of what he knew would happen. Kyra did not immediately realize her good fortune, but as her startled scream died away, she opened her eyes and was gratified to find that it was a pair of muscular arms that embraced her rather than the hard parquet floor.

"You know, Kyra," Devlin drawled wearily. "I employ an army of servants to stand at your beck and call. I'm fairly certain any one of them would have gladly fetched this book for you. You need not have risked your neck."

"Thank you," Kyra returned glibly, having recovered from her near mishap. "I'll remember that next time."

"See that you do." Devlin settled her on her feet and waved a cautionary finger under her nose. He then picked up the volume that had slipped from her fingers when she fell, and nodded approvingly at the title as he handed the book to Kyra. "I hope this means I can look forward to a marked improvement in your behavior. I trust you will not ride horses that were expressly forbidden you, and I assume you will not use the bath drawn for your husband unless you are willing to share it with him," he added wickedly.

"And," Devlin continued dryly, pretending to be engrossed in studying the back of his hand when, in fact, he was watching her closely. "I heartily suggest you henceforth suppress the urge to sneak into my room, rifle my drawers, and wreak mayhem among my neckcloths."

He gave a bark of laughter when he beheld Kyra's bewildered expression, for her jaw had dropped in surprise. A lopsided grin curved his lips as Devlin leaned forward to nudge her mouth shut and tweak her nose before explaining, "I found the evidence of your tirade weeks ago. Let's see"—he stroked his chin thoughtfully—"it was around the time you saw me with Elyse and mistakenly imagined us to be embroiled in a tawdry love affair."

Kyra would have fled the embarrassing confrontation, but Devlin held her wrist fast. She opened her mouth to speak, then closed it again. After all, there was no justification for her conduct . . . at least none that she cared to voice. She was not about to tell Devlin she had acted out of jealousy.

"There is no need to feel chagrined, little pet," Devlin whispered, drawing near her. "However, the next time you take a disliking to my neckwear, I should be greatly relieved if you gave me fair warning. I would not like to think you might feel tempted to hack the garment to pieces while it was still tied about my throat."

"Hmm," Kyra murmured as if giving his ridiculous narrative careful consideration. "Now, there's a thought."

"Cheeky wench," Devlin chided playfully. "If I had time, I'd drag you over to that sofa, turn you over my knee, and give you a richly deserved thrashing. But Francesca rang the dinner bell just before I found you dangling from the bookshelves, and she will feed our dinner to the livestock if we do not make haste."

"Poor Devlin," Kyra lamented with mock sympathy as she lifted her hand to his forehead to brush a wisp of hair back into place. "How tedious it must be for you. You seem destined to suffer the vagaries of a temperamental wife and a cook who would deny you even your most basic needs."

"Hah! Not bloody likely." Devlin guffawed, twirling her toward the door. "First, I shall see to my feisty cook, and soon, magpie, very soon," he promised, "I shall see to you."

Kyra allowed Devlin to slip his hand underneath her elbow and escort her from the library. She was no longer intimidated by his threats of sensual harassment. Indeed, had it not been for the ugly scandal that hung over her head, she would have welcomed him with open arms. With a little sigh, she hugged the book to her breast, hopeful that the clue to the missing diary was contained therein and that she would presently be free of her blackmailer so that she and Devlin could begin to build a life together.

Devlin and Kyra were chatting gaily as they neared the dining room, where the butler awaited their arrival. From the look on Thomas's face, it was obvious he expected his tidings would not be well received.

"Yes, Thomas. What is it?" Devlin inquired pleasantly.

"It's Mrs. Kincaid, sir," the butler replied.

The remainder of his explanation went unheeded by Kyra, who could not suppress the jealous spark that flared in her breast when she heard the woman's name. Nor could she prevent her heart from despairing when she watched Devlin walk away from her to answer Elyse's summons.

"It was so very kind of you and Devlin to invite me to sup with you this evening," Elyse addressed her hostess across the dining room table. "I know I'm taking a chance every time I go out driving alone, but I cannot help myself. There are times when I just want to be alone. I usually manage quite nicely."

"You were fortunate your horse went lame so close to Cauldurae." Kyra forced a smile to her lips as she directed this comment to her guest.

"Yes, I was able to push the mare this far, but I did not want to risk causing permanent damage by driving her all the way back to the village. I had not intended to interrupt your evening, Devlin." Elyse turned to her host. "There is no need for you to see me home. I merely hoped you might lend me a horse from your stables. I'll send one of my men in the morning to collect the mare."

"Nonsense, Elyse," Devlin assured her, glancing up from his plate to regard her with a meaningful look. "Darkness has fallen, and you, above all, should realize the risks of traveling the coastal highway alone at night. Besides, the ride to town will give us time to discuss the Pennington acquisition."

"Ah, yes, business," Elyse sighed drearily. "It is always the same with your husband, Kyra."

Biting back a grimace as the woman's shrill laughter filled the dining room, Kyra focused her attention on her meal. She tried to do justice to the savory dishes Francesca had prepared, but the chicken was dry and tasteless and caught in her throat when she swallowed. The wine, however, did not provoke the same suffocating sensation. Indeed, Kyra discovered that, after three or four glasses of the soothing liquid, she no longer felt an urge to scratch the smug look from Elyse's face.

The meal dragged on interminably, and Kyra grew even more distracted as Devlin and Elyse engaged in familiar and often witty discourse. What disturbed Kyra more than anything was the unerring attention Devlin lavished upon the fawning woman while giving Kyra only an occasional glance. He listened intently to Elyse's boring stories, laughed at her insipid anecdotes, and squeezed her hand intimately when he found one of her quips particularly amusing. Kyra fumed with anger when Devlin, having noticed a dribble of chocolate sauce on Elyse's chin, leaned over to wipe it away and then shamelessly placed his chocolate-tipped finger to his own lips.

"I could strip naked and dance on the table and he would not notice," Kyra muttered petulantly.

"What was that, darling?" Devlin murmured in her ear.

Kyra, thoroughly immersed in self-pity, had not realized her dinner partners had concluded their meal and were preparing to take their leave.

"Nothing," she mumbled shortly, hastily snatching up her wineglass and taking a fortifying draft.

"I'll drive Elyse home now," he advised her, dropping an avuncular kiss on the top of her head.

"Yes, darling," Elyse purred sweetly. "We have many things to discuss, our Devlin and I. I fear he may be late returning to you tonight."

"You need not wait up for me, magpie," Devlin announced over his shoulder as he stepped around the table to lift the disabled woman in his arms.

Following their departure, Kyra slumped back in her chair,

thoroughly befuddled by the disastrous turn the evening had taken. Her confusion changed to rage in the next moment when she remembered the cunning smile Elyse had directed at her over Devlin's shoulder as she entwined her arms about his neck and allowed him to carry her from the room.

"*How dare he*!" she said angrily. "How dare he flaunt his dalliances before my very eyes!" Kyra's violet eyes sparkled wrathfully as her inventive imagination went to work, and she envisioned any number of painful tortures to inflict upon her philandering husband.

She entertained herself with this amusing diversion until, suddenly, in the midst of her hostile reverie, she saw the glimmer of an idea. Kyra sat bolt upright in her chair, certain she had happened upon the perfect revenge. Deciding to act while she possessed the courage—since her mettle had been acquired from a wine bottle and would in all likelihood vanish with the sunrise—Kyra tossed back the contents of her glass and, climbing unsteadily to her feet, made her way to the stables.

17

"*What*?" Joshua exclaimed, glancing up from his paperwork to find an exceedingly tipsy Kyra tottering on the threshold of his den. Thinking he could not possibly have heard her right, he admonished sternly, "You don't mean that, Kyra."

"Yes. Yes, I do, Joshua." She nodded drunkenly. "I want you to make love to me." Kyra repeated the shocking pronouncement she had made upon arriving in the open doorway.

"Shh! Stop saying that! The servants might hear you," he warned, rushing forward to pull her into the room. Joshua cast a nervous glance down the corridor to determine if Kyra's capricious speech had been overheard by his staff. He need not have bothered, however, for his unexpected guest's next announcement rendered this precaution unnecessary.

"No, they won't. I sent them away," Kyra informed him, and spying a decanter on a corner shelf, she began to weave in that direction.

"What have you done?" came Joshua's lugubrious moan.

"I told you, Joshua. I sent the servants away so that we can make love," Kyra generously answered the rhetorical question.

The clink of irreplaceable crystal against a silver tray brought the rattled doctor immediately to Kyra's side.

"No, young lady!" he said severely. "You've obviously had quite enough to drink. Come with me." Joshua resettled the endangered goblet on the tray; then, taking Kyra by the hand, he led her to the leather sofa.

"Are we going to make love now?" Kyra asked shyly.

"No!" Joshua cried in exasperation. "We're going to talk, but under no circumstances are we going to make love." He eased her onto the sofa and, taking a seat beside her, murmured coaxingly, "Now, suppose you tell me what this is all about."

"Him!" she spat peevishly.

Joshua nodded knowingly. "What has Devlin done now?" he asked indulgently.

"He went off with that . . . that hussy!" came Kyra's bitter retort.

"Ah, that would be Elyse," Joshua mumbled half to himself, but before he could offer Kyra any words of comfort, she burst into tears.

"Oh, Joshua!" she sobbed. "Why is Devlin like that? Why does he hate everyone so?"

"Devlin doesn't hate you, Kyra."

"Yes, he does," Kyra snapped unreasonably. "He *hates* me! He proved as much that day I fell from Wildstar and he left me in the meadow. I heard Hannah say that if you had not come along, I might have died. *He* did nothing to help me, just left me there when I . . . I begged him not to go!" she wailed miserably.

Joshua was much affected by this passionate speech, and he sat back and exhaled a long breath before saying, "Poor child. These have been your thoughts all this time, yet you've said nothing. You're mistaken, Kyra," he murmured. "I don't know what you heard or *think* you heard, but let me set you straight on the matter.

"It was Devlin who, half crazy with worry, hailed my carriage that day. While I rode Old Scratch back here to fetch my medical bag, Devlin and my driver took you to

Cauldurae. Devlin cared for you until I arrived," Joshua explained.

"Oh," Kyra murmured, staring down at her hands ruefully. "But what about poor Lynette? She is dead, and he still hates her for what she did to him. And his mother . . . you should see how he treats her."

"I have," he admitted; then, unable to bear her suffering, Joshua came to a decision. "Kyra, there are apparently many things Devlin has neglected to tell you. I don't like to carry tales, but neither can I stand to watch you agonize over something for which you are not to blame. Here." He handed her his handkerchief. "Dry your tears and I'll explain a few things that will, I hope, give you a better understanding of the exasperating man you married."

Taking a deep breath, Joshua began, "Perhaps Devlin has told you that I hold the mortgage to Cauldurae. You see, Kyra, there was a time when Devlin and I were friends, a time when he trusted me and valued my opinion."

"What happened?"

"Lynette," Joshua said simply. "Unlike you, she never felt at home here on the island. Oh, she muddled along well enough at first, but in time she began to miss the gay life she had led in Paris, and she came to resent Devlin for taking her away from that never-ending social whirl. In those days, Devlin was trying to establish himself in business and had little time to spend with his spoiled bride. The novelty of being married turned to harsh reality for Lynette when she became pregnant."

There was a long silence as Joshua considered Kyra's rapt face. Eventually, he continued, "I attended Lynette when Nicholas was born. It was a difficult birth. Lynette was delirious with pain and barely conscious when Devlin came to her, but she became like a wild thing when she saw him. She denounced him with all manner of vile oaths, shouting her hatred of him and vowing to repay him for the suffering he had caused her.

"Lynette threatened to take Nicholas away with her to France and swore that Devlin would never see his son grow to manhood. She even implied she would take the child's life if need be. And"—the doctor faltered, uncomfortable with his forthcoming indelicate revelation—"Lynette vowed she would kill Devlin if he ever touched her again."

Having disclosed this intimate detail, Joshua walked across the room to pour himself a glass of the brandy he had earlier denied Kyra. Taking up a stance in front of his desk, he said, "Granted, one can often attribute such ravings to the heat of the moment. After all, Lynette had just suffered an agonizing delivery, but her mental state steadily deteriorated after that, and she made Devlin's life a living hell. He employed extra guards to ensure that Lynette could not make good her threat to take Nicholas away or do the child any harm. She, in turn, withdrew into herself. The only time she displayed any real emotion was when Devlin was near.

"To this day, I believe her sole purpose in becoming pregnant with Sarah was to hurt Devlin, to show him precisely how much she despised him," Joshua said solemnly, and when Kyra did not appear surprised by this comment, he inquired, "Do you know about Sarah?"

Kyra nodded. "Devlin blurted the truth one day when I reproached him for the way he treated her."

"Did he also tell you he believes I am Sarah's father?" Joshua surmised from her thunderstruck expression that Devlin had not. "It isn't true, of course, but your husband believes it because that is what Lynette told him. She could not abide anything that gave Devlin pleasure, and he derived great comfort from our friendship. Lynette knew that, so she told him a vicious lie in order to destroy our friendship.

"You may think me callous, since I am a man of medicine, dedicated to preserving life, but I cannot help thinking that Lynette did us all a great service when she took it into her head to go sailing that stormy night."

There was a twinge of bitterness in the voice that still mourned the loss of a valued friend, and Kyra waited a moment before asking, "What about Amanda? Do you know why Devlin holds his mother in such contempt?"

"Yes." Joshua nodded grimly. "Did you know that Devlin had an older brother?"

"Uh-huh," she murmured sleepily, the wine beginning to take its toll. "I know his name was Gareth, that he is dead, and that Devlin is much troubled by the subject. He has forbidden me to mention it."

"Devlin told me the story when I happened by Cauldurae one evening and found him half drunk, wallowing in despair. I later discovered it was the anniversary of Gareth's death."

"What happened to him, Joshua?"

"Devlin was twelve years old at the time. Gareth was two years older, but whereas Devlin, as you know, is robust in both body and spirit, Gareth was cursed with a sickly constitution. The conflict between Devlin and his mother evidently began after Mr. Cauldwell died and Amanda took over her husband's businesses. It was a difficult task, and Amanda's duties often kept her away from home for weeks on end. Devlin resented his mother's long absences; he felt she should spend more time with Emily and Gareth."

"But what about Devlin?" Kyra demanded. "He needed her, too."

"We know that"—Joshua smiled at her—"but Devlin believed his brother and sister were more fragile and needed Amanda's attention more than he. In any event, she was away on a business trip when the accident occurred," he said solemnly. "Gareth had just recovered from a particularly bad bout of influenza and begged Devlin to go fishing with him, knowing full well that Amanda had expressly forbidden any such expedition."

"So Devlin naturally went fishing anyway," Kyra murmured.

"You know him well." Joshua chuckled, then added seriously, "There had been a heavy rain the night before and the streams were swollen. Gareth slipped on the wet bank, fell into the raging water, and was swept away by the current. Despite Devlin's desperate efforts to save his brother, Gareth perished."

"How awful," Kyra murmured forlornly. "And Devlin blames himself?"

"More to the point, I believe Devlin thinks Amanda blames him."

"Now I know why Devlin insisted that Nicholas be made to understand he was not to blame for the fall I took from Wildstar," Kyra said. Her head was beginning to pound with all this new information regarding her enigmatic husband. "My poor Devlin," she sighed. "He has carried all this guilt and bitterness around for so long. Will he never be rid of it, Joshua?"

"I cannot say," the doctor replied. "But if anyone can help him, I believe you can, Kyra. Devlin is fortunate to have found you." Joshua noted with chagrin that her violet eyes had filled with tears, and thinking to avoid another drenching, he stood and extended his hand. "Come along, Mrs. Cauldwell, it's time I returned you to your husband."

Devlin whistled a merry tune as he ambled down the corridor toward Kyra's room. A devious smile curled the corners of his mouth as he balanced the breakfast tray on one hand and pushed the door open with the other. He did not immediately enter the room, but paused on the threshold to gaze at the tiny figure who slept peacefully in the middle of the huge bed.

He marveled at the remarkable transformation his disposition had undergone since the previous evening when he had returned home to find Joshua's carriage in the drive.

Devlin had been livid with fury when he found Kyra asleep in a corner of the conveyance, but he had done a lot of thinking during the night, and as the mischievous grin returned to his handsome face, he slipped inside his wife's room.

"Kyra," Devlin whispered, settling the tray on the bedside table. When there was no reply, he leaned over to brush a strand of hair from her eyes and repeated, "Kyra. Wake up, magpie. It's morning."

Kyra stirred and stretched. "What time is it?" she mumbled drowsily.

"Almost noon, sleepyhead."

"Devlin?" she murmured. "What are—"

The question died upon her tongue when her eyes fluttered open to be greeted by a stabbing flash of sunlight. She was next beset by a nauseating dizziness that assaulted her head and stomach simultaneously. To compound her plight, Devlin chose that moment to perch on the edge of the bed, creating a bouncing motion of excruciating proportions. In response, one slender hand shot out to clutch his sleeve while the other flew to the pulse that thundered at her temple.

"Please, don't!" she wailed beseechingly.

Devlin gallantly suppressed the chuckle that rose in his throat and patted her hand sympathetically. "There, there, little pet. I rather suspected you might be experiencing some difficulty this morning, so I prepared something to help ease your suffering." He lifted a steaming cup of liquid from the breakfast tray and gingerly held it toward her.

"What is it?" she muttered, propping herself up on her elbows and eyeing the cup suspiciously.

Kyra's unprecedented night of drinking had left her normally radiant eyes dull and bloodshot and rimmed with dark circles. Her thick gold and brown tresses tumbled about her face and shoulders in unruly abandon, and there was a decidedly grayish pallor to her usually vibrant cheeks.

Despite her disheveled appearance, Devlin thought she had
never looked more enchanting.

"A tonic," he replied.

Kyra remained doubtful as she sniffed the unusual aroma.
"What kind of tonic?" she asked, regarding him distrustfully.

"One that will make you feel better—a sort of 'hair of the
dog,' if you take my meaning," Devlin said, tilting the cup
toward her lips. "Come, magpie, take a sip. Even Nicholas
was not this uncooperative when he fell sick and Joshua
prescribed a bitter potion for him." He grimaced in mock
horror. "Then there was the time little Sarah—"

"All right, all right! I'll drink it. Just . . . just don't
prate on so, and *please* don't jostle the bed. My head aches
insufferably."

"Little wonder," Devlin said, handing her the curative.

Kyra quickly realized her first mistake had been not
instructing Devlin to leave her chamber the moment she
awakened to find those piercing eyes staring down at her.
Her second mistake had been allowing him to goad her into
drinking the foul-smelling concoction, for the instant the
liquid passed between her lips, her mouth exploded with a
variety of taste sensations—none of which was pleasant.

Suddenly wide-eyed, Kyra sat bolt upright and glanced
wildly about in search of a receptacle into which she could
spit out the awful-tasting stuff; she was not about to swallow
it. But Devlin handily thwarted her scheme by placing his
finger beneath the cup and commanded her to drink the
contents.

"I am going to be sick," Kyra muttered wretchedly as the
last of Devlin's potion trickled down her throat.

"No, you're not," Devlin said tolerantly, returning cup
and saucer to the bedside table. "That is a natural reaction,
I'll allow, but give it a moment."

Kyra's stomach churned, rumbled noisily, then churned

again. "Trust me, Devlin. *I am going to be sick!*" she cried hysterically.

Her stomach lurched and gave one final, violent rumble, and then—amazingly—the queasy feeling vanished. Her flesh no longer felt clammy, and what was even more miraculous, the throbbing in her head began to subside. Kyra stared up at Devlin in wonder.

"That's amazing! What's in it?"

"Believe me, Kyra, you don't want to know," came his ambiguous answer. Giving her wrist an affectionate pat, Devlin stood and made his way to the washstand. "I trust this means I never need worry again that you'll try to drink the contents of my wine cellar in a single evening?" he taunted, plunging a washcloth into the cold water.

When Kyra did not dignify this remark with a reply, he wrung out the cloth and sauntered back to the bed. "Kyra, I am ashamed of my conduct last night, and I apologize if I caused you any anguish," Devlin said unexpectedly, holding the cool washcloth against her brow. "I want you to know that last evening's little fiasco was nothing more than a misguided attempt to make you jealous," came his surprising admission.

"Jealous?" Kyra blurted, pushing his hand aside so she could see his face. "Why should you wish to make me jealous?"

"Never mind that now." Devlin evaded the question, and running the damp cloth around to the back of her neck, he continued to talk in a soft, mellifluous voice while leaning forward to brush his lips against her cheek. "Elyse means nothing to me, Kyra . . . nothing. It's important you realize that she is my business partner and nothing more." His lips traveled down to her throat, and after touching them against the pulse that thrummed in the little hollow, he lifted his head to stare deeply into the violet pools that had grown drowsy as a result of his soothing ministrations.

"I think it is time we came to terms, you and I," he said

presently, his sable-brown eyes dancing impishly. "I promise never again to behave as I did last night if you promise
to begin your search in the adjoining bedroom the next time
you go looking for a man to make love to you."

Kyra sprang up in the middle of the bed, clutching the
sheet to her heaving bosom, her expression one of horrified
disbelief. This could not be happening; it was not possible
that Joshua had betrayed her confidence. *Men*, she thought
bitterly. Kyra's mouth dropped open, but before she could
rally, her door burst open and Biddie charged across the
threshold.

"Miz Kyra, you ain't never gonna guess who just drove
up the front drive!" the maid trilled excitedly. Then,
without giving her mistress an opportunity to speculate, she
exclaimed, "It's Master Andrew and his friend from Savannah, Christopher Monteith!"

With a little sigh of discontent, Kyra plucked the book
from the library table and wandered through the open door
onto the side terrace. Two days had passed since her
unexpected, and unwelcome, guests had arrived to ravage
her peace, and though Kyra had long since recovered from
the effects of her capricious drinking binge, she had thus far
managed to escape any lengthy confrontations with the
bothersome duo by pleading a headache and remaining in
her room.

Kyra was not usually so inhospitable; her standoffishness
was a result of the circumstances in which she and her
guests had last parted company. She had exchanged a few
words with her brother in Devlin's presence, and her voice
sounded stilted and forced even to her own ears. But Kyra
was reluctant to converse with Andrew privately, for she
knew she would take him to task for his despicable
treatment of her in Savannah. She likewise knew that
mention of that disastrous night could only lead to a

discussion of Clayton Fairchild, and that was a topic Kyra wished to avoid altogether.

Kyra had ventured out of her sanctuary this morning because of a visit from Devlin the previous evening. He had come to her room to inquire after her well-being and to inform her that he and their guests would be going for an early-morning ride should she care to join them. Kyra had graciously declined the invitation, and though she realized Devlin was puzzled by her less than hospitable attitude toward Andrew and his friend, she could not yet bring herself to trust him with the truth.

Poor Devlin, she thought. He endured so much and received so little in return. She remembered his disappointed expression when she had spurned his offer to go riding.

She sat down in the white wicker rocking chair on the terrace and stared down at the book in her hands: *On Being a Dutiful Wife*. Kyra clucked her tongue as she read the ridiculous title. Then, offering up a silent prayer, she slid her fingers beneath the leather cover and prepared to open the book that might hold the answers to all her woes. Just then a tall shadow fell across her lap, and she glanced up, half expecting to find Devlin smiling down at her. She was genuinely surprised, and more than a little dismayed, when she beheld the intruder.

"Christopher!" Kyra exclaimed. "What are you doing here? Devlin said you were all going riding."

"I changed my mind," Christopher drawled smugly. "Actually, I had a devil of a time convincing your husband that I did not wish to accompany them. My purpose in agreeing to the jaunt in the first place was to make you show yourself. I felt certain you would abandon your self-imposed exile if you believed the mansion to be free of uninvited guests." He sat down in a chair opposite Kyra and regarded her closely. "I've been hoping to have a private word with you ever since Andrew and I arrived, but you have steadfastly avoided me, leaving me with no recourse but to flush you out in the open."

"What do you want, Christopher? Why have you and Andrew come here?" Kyra asked point-blank.

"Why, to felicitate you on your marriage. We learned of your good fortune after we returned to Savannah from our lengthy sojourn in Atlanta. When Andrew heard the happy news, he insisted we come here immediately, so he could make the acquaintance of his wealthy brother-in-law."

"That explains Andrew's purpose," Kyra answered coolly. "But why are *you* here, Christopher?"

"I see you still believe in speaking your mind," he commented disapprovingly. "I should have thought your husband would have corrected that irritating trait by now. But no matter," he said with an airy wave of his hand, "I shall very quickly take the sting from your saucy tongue. Indeed, I look forward to the happy moment."

"I don't have to listen to this," Kyra snapped and stood as if to leave, but Christopher's next statement made her reconsider her hasty actions.

"I wonder if, through the course of all your plain speaking, you ever bothered to tell Devlin the details of your brief stay in Savannah. For instance"—he reached inside his jacket to withdraw and light a cigar—"have you told him of your encounter with Clayton Fairchild?"

Kyra's expression reflected her chagrin when she heard those wretched words. Suddenly trembling with dread, she felt her knees give way beneath her, and her hand groped desperately for the arm of the rocking chair as she sank slowly back onto the seat. Though she said nothing, her disconcerted mien spoke volumes and provided Christopher with the answer he sought.

"I thought not," he muttered, smiling to himself.

"What do you want?" Kyra demanded. "Money?"

"Money?" Christopher repeated, thoughtfully considering the back of his hand. "No, that is Andrew's game. He knows nothing of my intentions; I have something a little more diverting in mind," he offered vaguely, but when Kyra did not rise to his bait, Christopher continued, "Very well, I shall come to the point.

"Tonight, after the others have retired to their rooms, you are going to come to me," he informed her outright. "I've observed that you and your husband maintain separate chambers; it should not be difficult for you to do as I suggest. And I promise you will not be disappointed with the outcome of our little rendezvous," he whispered suggestively and would have lifted her hand to his lips had Kyra not snatched it from his reach.

Kyra felt the revulsion rise in her throat, but she forced herself to remain strong; she was determined not to cower before the blackguard. Knowing what his answer would be, she squared her shoulders and asked, "And if I refuse?"

"Then I will be left with no choice but to tell your husband all the sordid details about you and Fairchild," came his prompt rejoinder. "I imagine Devlin will wonder if you murdered Clayton before or after he seduced you." Christopher leaned back in his chair and drew deeply on the smelly cigar. "In either event, I think he will be more than a little disgruntled to learn he has taken a cold-blooded murderess to wife." A self-satisfied smirk curled Christopher's lips as he regarded his prey thoughtfully.

Then, snuffing out the cigar, Christopher stood to take his leave. "Come to me by midnight, Kyra, or I will request an early-morning audience with your husband," he warned, and without waiting for her reply, he swaggered toward the library entrance.

Kyra sat in a state of muddled confusion for several moments. Then, slowly but steadily, her bewilderment grew into an uncontrollable fury as she considered this latest development. "Threats!" she spewed bitterly. "I am sick to death of threats! First I am set upon by a ruthless blackmailer, and now this . . . this lecherous worm demands my submission. The idea is not to be borne!"

What will you do? came the logical inquiry from the little voice inside Kyra's head.

"I don't know!" she cried miserably, flinging open the book in a spontaneous gesture.

Kyra's dismal reflections momentarily took flight, as glancing down, she made a happy discovery. Apparently Devlin's sources had miscontrued Judith Tanner's interest in the volume. It appeared Cauldurae's former mistress had not thought much of this "dutiful wife" nonsense either; the better part of the text had been hollowed out; and nestled snugly within the crudely chiseled cavity lay the much sought after diary.

The evening meal proved to be an excruciating ordeal for Kyra. She ate little and drank even less; the memory of her previous experience with an excessive indulgence of wine was still fresh in her mind. Fortunately the three gentlemen appeared content to converse among themselves while the lovely lady who graced their table merely smiled at their amusing anecdotes and offered an occasional comment. When the dessert dishes were cleared Kyra excused herself, thinking that, by the time the men finished their port and thought to join her in the drawing room, she would have long since retired to her room.

Kyra avoided Christopher's eyes as she swept toward the beckoning doorway, and she would have executed a clean escape had it not been for the hand that reached out to capture her wrist. "A moment," Devlin whispered. To his guests, he said, "I do not wish to be a poor host, but if you gentlemen will excuse me, I would like to take a turn about the garden with my wife. Help yourselves to the port. I believe it to be an exceptionally fine vintage." He passed the decanter to Andrew and, standing, offered Kyra his arm, saying, "Shall we?"

Kyra gazed up into his handsome face and, finding she could not deny him this simple request, tucked her arm in his and allowed him to lead her from the room.

The couple emerged from the mansion moments later, and Devlin guided Kyra along the brightly lit garden path. Though he knew her thoughts were greatly troubled, he did not badger her about her continued reluctance to confide in him but steered their conversation toward mundane topics. They talked about the weather, Kyra inquired about his problems at the mill, Devlin asked about the children's recent antics, and they paused now and again to admire a plant in full bloom. Once, when they happened upon an especially vibrant flower, Devlin plucked the blossom and presented it to Kyra.

"A gift for my lovely lady," he said grandly.

"It's beautiful," Kyra sighed, absently fingering the delicate petals.

"Its beauty pales in comparison with yours, magpie," Devlin replied sincerely, anchoring the blossom in her hair. When he observed the lifeless cast that dimmed her once vibrant eyes, Devlin could keep silent no longer; he could not abide seeing her so completely drained of spirit. "Why so sad, Kyra?" he asked caressingly. "I cannot bear seeing you like this. Tell me what I've done to make you unhappy so I can set things right between us."

"You have done nothing, Devlin," Kyra replied wearily.

"Then who has upset you?" he demanded. "Andrew?"

"No. I'm not upset," she lied. "I am a little tired, however, and wish to go to my room now."

Devlin was not pacified by her lame explanation, but as he studied her face, he realized that continued questioning would be useless. "Very well." He sighed and turned to escort her to the house.

They heard voices engaged in lively conversation as they walked past the drawing room, and Kyra flinched instinctively when she recognized Christopher's high-pitched laughter. If Devlin noticed her reaction, he did not comment on it. In fact, Kyra was hoping her inquisitive husband would refrain from further discussion of her melancholy mood. She longed for the peace and quiet of her room where she could decide how to deal with Christopher's demands.

"Good night, Devlin," Kyra said upon arriving at her room and would have entered immediately had Devlin not stepped between her and the door. "Devlin!" she began, annoyed by his meddling. "I'm in no mood for—"

"Shh, magpie," he murmured. "I daresay things are not as bad as you think. If you would take me into your confidence, understand that I want to help . . . Talk to me, Kyra." Devlin paused expectantly, but when Kyra showed no sign of weakening her resolve, he shook his head in exasperation. "I'm here for you if you change your mind." Devlin bent down to touch his lips to her forehead, then opened the door and gently pushed her across the threshold.

Once inside, Kyra slumped against the heavy door, unaware of the dark brown eyes that observed her from a chair near the window. *What am I going to do? What am I going to do?* her mind screamed over and over. As Kyra pushed away from the door and made her way toward the dressing table, she was startled by a movement across the room.

"Biddie!" she exclaimed, sinking down on the chair. "You gave me such a fright."

"I'm sorry, Miz Kyra. I didn't means to scare you none. I was just waitin' to see if you needed me." The servant walked over to the chest of drawers and withdrew a simple white muslin nightgown.

"No, Biddie," Kyra interrupted when she realized what the maid was about. "I'd better wear the . . . that is, I prefer to wear the yellow satin nightdress with the matching dressing gown."

After Kyra had changed into the delicately flowing ensemble, she returned to the dressing table and sat down so that Biddie could brush out her hair. But when the maid would have plaited the gold-brown tendrils, Kyra interceded, explaining, "I think I'll wear it down this evening."

"Whatever you say, Miz Kyra," the servant replied with a shrug. "Will you be needin' me for anythin' else?"

"No, thank you. That will be all." Kyra dismissed the servant with a distracted wave of her hand.

The door had barely closed behind Biddie when Kyra stood to take an agitated turn about the room, the first of many she would make during the evening as she agonized over her impossible situation. Her mind whirled with thoughts of her dilemma and the choices available to her, none of which was personally gratifying.

Kyra's musings turned first to Devlin, then to the blackmailer, then to Christopher and his nefarious scheme. But her turbulent thoughts always seemed to resettle on Devlin. Finally, she sat on the edge of the bed, her gaze fixed fretfully on the hands of the clock as they steadily crept toward midnight. With a weary sigh, she glanced at the diary that lay on the table beside the clock, and her dreary mood became even more dismal.

Then the insufferable waiting was over, and Kyra was faced with the moment she dreaded. As the clock began to chime the hour, Kyra climbed slowly to her feet, and retrieving the diary, walked to the bureau. Pulling open a drawer, she started to hide the book beneath a pile of folded petticoats, but when she pushed the clothing aside, her hand struck an object.

Kyra pulled the box from beneath the undergarments and flipped the lid open to stare down at the letters and newspaper clipping she had received from the blackmailer. Next to these items lay the key to the door connecting her chamber with Devlin's. Kyra fingered the key regretfully, and at the stroke of midnight, she whirled away from the bureau, her gaze riveted on Devlin's door. Realizing that she had but one choice, Kyra exhaled a disheartened sigh and walked straight to the door.

Devlin sat in a chair by the open window in his room, idly perusing a financial report from one of his businesses. His concentration was not focused on his task, however, and after reading the same page three times without absorbing a single figure, he decided to leave the document for another time. Tossing the report onto the table in front of him, he leaned back and allowed the sound of the crashing surf and rolling waves to console his beleaguered thoughts.

Throughout the evening, he had occasionally been aware of Kyra's restless stirrings in the adjoining room. Though he longed to comfort her, he realized he could do nothing for his unhappy wife until she was ready to trust in him completely. He glanced up, genuinely surprised by the lateness of the hour as the mantel clock began to chime midnight. Draining a crystal goblet of its remaining drops of whiskey, he extinguished his cigar and stood up.

Devlin removed his jacket as he strode toward the armoire, and after hanging it inside, he unbuttoned his shirt, the muscles in his shoulders rippling as he removed the garment. He paused in mid-stretch, however, when his ears detected the grating of a key in the lock, and he whirled toward the door to find a most improbable sight.

"Kyra?" he murmured incredulously, staring in disbelief at the shimmering vision on the threshold.

"Devlin, I . . . I—" she stammered uncertainly, but before she could dash back into her chamber, Devlin hurried forward to grasp her wrist and coax her into the room.

"You've come this far, little pet. Don't turn craven on me now," he whispered, pulling the door closed behind them.

Devlin smiled down at her as he led her to the chair he had recently vacated. Easing her down onto the seat, he gave her hand a reassuring squeeze before taking a chair opposite her. "Don't look so forlorn, magpie. Half the battle is over," he said encouragingly, adding softly, "Now, suppose you tell me what's on your mind."

"I . . . I'm being blackmailed," she blurted, rushing on before she lost her nerve. "I . . . I killed a man in Savannah—by accident, I swear. But the blackmailer has some things I left behind that night, and he has threatened to tell you and the authorities everything if I refuse to help him locate the hidden treasure. Now Christopher has arrived with more threats, for he knows the awful story as well, only . . . only he means to exact a higher price for his silence . . . a price I'm not willing to pay."

Kyra had kept her eyes downcast throughout this speech; she was more than a little leery of Devlin's reaction to these disclosures. When she finally gathered the courage to meet his gaze, she was relieved to note that his countenance was remarkably composed. When Devlin calmly inquired if she would care for some sherry and then filled a small glass for her and helped himself to the whiskey, Kyra was certain he had not heard a single word she had spoken.

But then Devlin leaned back, and taking a sip of the whiskey, he crossed his legs and said, "From the beginning, little pet. I want you to tell me everything."

And so Kyra explained the ordeal she had suffered from the moment they parted ways that fateful morning in Savannah until he forced open her cabin door later that night. Devlin interrupted only now and again to ask Kyra to clarify a point in her narrative. She, in turn, avoided looking into his face throughout much of her discourse, although she did notice that his expression darkened threateningly when she divulged the role her brother had played in this incredible tale.

She went on to relate her experiences at the hands of Clayton Fairchild and how she had contrived to escape his evil clutches. Next Kyra told him about her blackmailer, about the threatening letters and the night the extortionist had abducted her and presented her with his demands. Kyra told him everything, including all she had learned about Lynette and Alice Lovejoy, and if Devlin was surprised to learn that Lynette had not taken her own life, he gave no outward indication.

As she explained about the blackmailer, Kyra handed over the letters she had received as well as the incriminating newspaper article. While Devlin perused these items, Kyra concluded her tale by telling him about Christopher and the demands he had made earlier that day. When she finished, Kyra sat back, nervously awaiting her husband's reaction to all she had said. It was not at all what she expected, for he glanced up from the extortionist's documents and gave her a sympathetic smile.

"My poor darling," Devlin breathed tenderly. "You've had a difficult time of it, haven't you? If only you had told me about Fairchild at the outset, I could have spared you weeks of emotional turmoil."

"What? What do you mean?" Kyra demanded, confused by Devlin's announcement.

Before he answered, Devlin put aside the letters Kyra had given him, and pressing his fingertips together he rested his chin atop his hands and considered her thoughtfully. "Come here," he eventually murmured.

Kyra was trembling as she forced herself to stand and step silently around the table to gaze uncertainly into a pair of unexpectedly compassionate sable-brown eyes. She did not demur when he pulled her down onto his lap, but when she would have questioned him again about his mysterious statement, he silenced her with a kiss.

When he drew away, Devlin settled her against him, and as he lovingly stroked her hair, he said, "Let me explain. Do you recall seeing another man at Fairchild's residence?"

"Yes. There was a man who opened the door and later escorted me upstairs. I don't remember his name."

"It was Jim Wilson—Hannah's husband. He works for

me," Devlin informed her, laughing at her amazed expression.

"But I thought he was working for Clayton Fairchild," Kyra interrupted, clearly confounded by this revelation.

"It gets complicated." Devlin shrugged his shoulders in a helpless gesture. "You see, Clayton used to live here on the island. I always suspected him of being in cahoots with the bastard who is trying to ruin me. With Jim in Fairchild's employ, I hoped to learn the identity of my unknown adversary."

"But was Fairchild not distrustful of Mr. Wilson? Hannah is your housekeeper, after all."

"Yes, but the pendulum swings both ways, Kyra. My enemy hoped to secure important information about me through Hannah. But as it turned out, for all my scheming, Jim found nothing, and I am no closer to my enemy's identity.

"You, however, may allay your fears," Devlin said presently. "Jim told me about the fire when he returned to Carraba. It seems he heard a great commotion upstairs, and when he went to investigate, he saw the young woman he had admitted to the house—"

"That would be me," Kyra interrupted.

"He couldn't recall your name either, little pet," Devlin said, idly running his finger down Kyra's arm. "Anyway, he saw you bolt down the staircase and vanish through the door. When Jim arrived upstairs, he discovered a thoroughly disheveled Clayton stamping out the flame-engulfed curtains which he had yanked down following your hasty departure."

"Then, I . . . I didn't—"

"No, honey, you were not responsible for Clayton's death," he whispered comfortingly. "After you left, someone else arrived."

"Who?"

"I don't know. Fairchild sent Jim on an errand before he

could get a look at the visitor, and by the time Jim returned, the house was burning out of control," Devlin concluded, retrieving his glass from the table and taking a contemplative sip. "Do you realize what this means Kyra? Your extortionist and my nemesis are one and the same. The bloody rogue has been after that cursed treasure all this time. When I think of the pain and anguish that bastard has caused, I could—" He gripped the glass so fiercely that Kyra feared it might shatter, and she reached over to rescue the fine crystal.

Setting the glass aside, she murmured, "But I have found the diary, Devlin. Surely you and your men can apprehend the villain when he next contacts me."

"Most likely," Devlin agreed, mulling over the idea. "But I won't have you involved in the capture. You've been through hell as it is, magpie; I will not risk you coming to harm. If you receive another letter from this treasure hunter, you are to give it to me at once, understand?"

"Yes, Devlin," Kyra replied meekly, absently smoothing her hand along his shoulder. Then a thought occurred to her, prompting her to ask, "What happened to Jim Wilson? You say he's Hannah's husband, yet I've never seen him, have I? I am not certain I would recognize him."

"That's what I like about him. He's a hell of a fellow, but he has the kind of face that is, well, forgettable. There have been occasions in the past when that trait has proved to be an invaluable asset. At the moment, Jim is working for your friend, Joshua." As always, whenever Devlin mentioned the doctor, his voice filled with bitterness. "As I recollect, Joshua was most eager to engage Jim's services."

"You sound as if you suspect Joshua of being the ruthless mastermind behind all this treachery," Kyra snapped.

"At this point, Kyra, everyone is suspect," Devlin said dryly.

"Well, you're wrong! Joshua is not like that. He—"

"I don't care to discuss the good doctor's qualities at this time." Devlin cut her off in mid-sentence. "I trust we can find a far more interesting topic if we set our minds to it. For example"—his voice deepened and he regarded Kyra pensively—"I would very much like to know why you came to me tonight. Why did you not go to Christopher?"

Kyra had not anticipated this forthright question, and feeling suddenly unsure of herself, she climbed down from his lap and went to stand behind the chair opposite him. Her slender hands gripped the back of the rose-patterned seat as she wrestled with the emotions that raged within her. Finally, her intense yearning overcame her fear and she raised her eyes to meet Devlin's expectant gaze.

"Because," she whispered through trembling lips, "I could not go to Christopher . . . sleep with him, when I am in love with you."

18

The room remained awkwardly silent for several moments following this emotional admission until Kyra, a sense of impending disaster creeping over her, suddenly blurted, "I'm sorry! I . . . I should not have said such a thing." As tears of humiliation and rejection began to blur her vision, she ran blindly to the door. But before her shaking fingers could find the latch, Devlin grasped her from behind and gently turned her around.

"Don't run away, Kyra," he implored, tugging her forward to enfold her in his arms. "Not when you've just told me you love me," he murmured against her hair, lovingly stroking the silky tendrils that spilled across his arm. He stared down into her distraught face and said, "You misunderstood my hesitation, for I assure you that I did not mean to appear indifferent. Indeed, I am overcome with joy. It's just I had lost all hope of ever hearing you say those words. I did not think it possible that you could love me—not after all I've done to you."

"You were not so *very* bad," Kyra sniffled brokenly.

"Hah!" Devlin guffawed. "You've grown suddenly generous with your assessment of my character, have you not, magpie?" he teased. "You have called me everything from an insensitive beast to an overgrown bully. I shudder to think of all the unkind thoughts that have been pondered inside this pretty head in recent weeks."

Kyra smiled up at him shyly and backed away a few steps to say, "I admit my thoughts have sometimes been less than charitable, but you provoked me, Devlin," she reminded him defensively. She clasped his big hand in hers, and as she gently rubbed the palm with her thumb, she tempered her accusation with "Even though I have often thought you to be arrogant and stubborn and completely impossible, I have always sensed that, deep inside, you possessed some gentler qualities."

"Such as?" A dark eyebrow lifted in fond amusement.

"Oh, I think you can be caring and understanding and . . . and loving," came her honest reply. Kyra's gaze remained trained on their entwined hands as she offered tentatively, "Devlin, I know your experience with Lynette has turned you against matrimony, and I know you don't love me, but—"

"Kyra, look at me," Devlin interrupted, and the tremor in his voice compelled her to meet his brown eyes in the dimly lit room. "I have long since realized that, with Lynette, I mistook youthful passion for lasting love. What I had with Lynette is over and done, little pet. I am sorry for what happened to her, but I am not sorry she is out of my life, for I never would have met you otherwise—never would have known what true love is." He paused to exhale a heady breath before adding hoarsely, "For I do love you, Kyra."

Kyra's heart had never known such joy, and without hesitating, she rushed forward eager to be crushed against his brawny chest. As they embraced Kyra lifted her face and their lips met in a kiss that was mutually passionate and giving. When at last they broke apart, breathless and trembling, Kyra leaned back in the circle of Devlin's arms and studied his handsome features with loving eyes.

Then, reaching up to brush the familiar stray lock of dark brown hair back into place, she murmured, "I'm ready, Devlin."

"Ready?" he echoed.

"To be your wife," Kyra explained. "I . . . I want to make love with you."

"Finally!" he bellowed, dragging Kyra forward again to bedazzle her with another fiery kiss. When he pulled away, he scooped her into his arms and strode toward the bed, a satisfied chuckle reverberating in his chest.

"What are you laughing at?" Kyra asked happily.

"I had half a mind to tumble you right there on that very expensive tapestry rug," came his shameless admission. "There will be other times to romp on the floor, however, or in the garden or on the beach or perhaps even in the stables. But tonight . . . tonight, my beautiful wife, we shall undertake the long overdue consummation of this marriage in my bed."

Devlin settled Kyra on her feet and untied the satin belt of her robe. This accomplished, his hands climbed to her shoulders, and with a deliberate motion, he tossed the elegant dressing gown aside. Pushing her down on the edge of the mattress, he knelt to remove her slippers, then added his shirt and boots to the pile of discarded clothing.

When Devlin next faced Kyra, he saw that her expression had changed, and misinterpreting her trepidation as rekindled fear from their previous encounter, he assured her, "Don't be frightened, Kyra. This will not be like the first time. This time I am going to love you."

"You misunderstand, my love," Kyra whispered, standing before him. "I'm not afraid of you. I *am* a little nervous," she admitted. "But if I appear hesitant, it's because I'm inexperienced. I'm not sure how to go about this, and I . . . I don't want to disappoint you."

"Oh, my sweet love, you could never disappoint me," he murmured huskily, fondling a satiny tendril that curled about her cheek. "You undoubtedly have a great many things to learn, but I shall endeavor to be a patient teacher."

"And I shall strive to be an exemplary pupil. Shall I begin like this?" Kyra inquired coyly, as her slender fingers slid the straps of her nightdress off her shoulders and down her bare arms. Before her newfound confidence faltered, she gave a seductive wriggle, and the yellow satin nightdress slithered down the length of her body to leave her standing gloriously naked before her husband.

"Yes, by all means," Devlin breathed thickly, his sable-brown eyes drinking in the wondrous site. The piercing orbs began to sparkle sensuously, prompting his risque suggestion, "Would you care to assist me?" He indicated his trousers, which presented the final obstruction to the commencing of their lovemaking.

Kyra lifted uncertain eyes to her husband's, and upon taking a fortifying breath, she stepped forward to carry out the intimate request. As she grasped the waistband with trembling fingers, Devlin's hands settled atop hers, and she raised her puzzled gaze to his face.

"It's all right, magpie. I understand if you're not ready for this," he answered her unspoken question.

"No, I want to," she assured him. "Just . . . just give me a moment."

Kyra exhaled a restless breath, and shaking off his restrictive hands, devoted her attention to undoing the buttons at his waist. Much to Devlin's pleasant surprise and gratification, Kyra's softly caressing hands slipped inside the waistband and set about a cursory inspection of his flesh. They spread out in opposite paths, traveling along the trim waist and around his back. Her graceful fingers flitted down over his hips and skirted the tops of his muscular thighs, coming closer to a dangerously virile region. He inhaled sharply.

When Kyra heard his gasp, she jerked away. "I'm sorry. Did I hurt you?" she asked innocently.

Devlin responded with a hearty laugh. "No, sweetheart. You didn't hurt me." Nodding toward the bed behind her, he said, "Will you turn down the sheets while I finish undressing?"

With a little sigh of confusion, Kyra turned and made short work of the task assigned her, but as she was straightening, Devlin's arm encircled her waist and he dragged her back against his rock-hard physique. Before she realized what he was doing, he slid his other hand across her belly and on downward to gently stroke down the inside of one thigh and up the other until his searching fingers ventured into the silken crevice.

"Devlin!" Kyra whimpered, shuddering as his practiced fondling sent wave after glorious wave of delicious tremors slithering down her spine. "Don't!" she pleaded. "I . . . I want to see you . . . hold you."

"And I want you ready for me. I want you to know what to expect," he whispered in her ear just seconds before his lips became hopelessly enamored on her collarbone.

"But I . . . I . . . already know," she panted, flinging her head back against his chest and giving herself up to the tumultuous feelings that pervaded her being.

Kyra was aware of his hand that gently cupped and fondled her breasts, devoting equal attention to each, lightly squeezing the nipples until they stiffened with excruciating pleasure. She was likewise mindful of an insistent length of masculine flesh pressed intimately against her lower back, and she could not ignore the hand that continued its rapturous assault on her frenzied senses. Finally, Kyra placed her hand on Devlin's to direct the maddening rhythm. Thus, she was ready when the mind-shattering eruption came, and she cried aloud with sheer delight.

As the rapid pounding of her heart subsided, Kyra slumped against Devlin, completely exhausted but sweetly fulfilled. She became aware of her husband once more as he turned her toward him and gently nudged her chin up.

"You knew?" he said.

Kyra gulped self-consciously, but Devlin would not permit her to look away. "That night on the *Driftwood*, I . . . you . . . that is," she stammered helplessly, "well, I had never experienced anything like it before or since . . . until now. I felt so ashamed that you, a complete stranger, could make me feel that way. I . . . I didn't want you to know." Her lower lip quivered, and she was on the brink of tears when Devlin leaned forward to press a kiss against those wondrous pouting lips.

"Silly goose," he scolded, climbing into bed and pulling Kyra in beside him. "Don't you realize that we were destined to be together? Wasn't our chance meeting in Charleston proof enough of that for you? I daresay that, had you not toppled headlong into my arms in Savannah, we would have met again somewhere else, for our union was dictated by a force far greater than mere mortals will ever understand."

They lay facing each other, Devlin's elbow burrowed into the pillow as he supported his head in his palm, his brown gaze warmly caressing his wife. "Put your conscience to rest, Kyra. You will never know how much I regret what happened that night, but I am determined to make things up to you, to be a good husband. As for a certain tempestuous night in Savannah, you need never feel ashamed when you've been well loved, magpie. In fact," he breathed thickly, drawing her toward him, "I want you to let me love you now."

"Yes! Oh, yes!" Kyra cried joyfully, rejoicing in his embrace and the mouth that promptly descended upon hers.

Kyra welcomed his kiss as his lips melded with hers, tenderly at first, but as the fire within began to mount so did the urgency of his caress. She did not quail when his tongue charged boldly between her lips to rummage for secret treasure; she accepted the playful visitor with enthusiasm. As tongues mated and frolicked in gay abandon, Devlin's hands became hopelessly entangled in the blanket of gold and brown satin that tumbled about them.

When Devlin finally pulled his lips from Kyra's, he saw the passion burning brightly in her eyes, and not wishing the flame to sputter, he masterfully continued to stir the smoldering embers of desire. He kissed the tip of her chin, then traveled down to taste the pulse that thrummed in the hollow of her throat. The adventuresome lips blazed a trail along her flesh, pausing to investigate the most unusual places. He kissed the bend of her elbow, the inside of her wrist, her navel, the back of her knee, sending chills racing to the spot most recently caressed. When he touched his provocative lips to her instep and his tongue flitted out to tickle the sensitive flesh, Kyra thought she would be driven mad with wanting him.

"Love me, Devlin," she moaned breathlessly, holding out her arms to him. "Now!"

A knowing chuckle rumbled in Devlin's throat, and a gleam flared in the sable-brown eyes as he stretched out above her, bracing his arms on either side of her sensually aroused body. He inclined his head toward her lips, which were still swollen from his kiss, and the hair on his chest tickled the rosy-tipped breasts that yearned for his touch. After pressing a fleeting kiss against Kyra's mouth, he averted his attention to the alluring flesh, nipping at one breast with his teeth, tonguing the other until the nipples stood proud and erect.

Then, without warning, he rolled away and upon hearing Kyra's disappointed sigh, he murmured, "You may touch me, too, little pet. I promise I won't run away."

Kyra began to gently stroke his broad chest. Her fingers fluttered upward to his shoulder, down his arm, and up again to trace the outline of his ear. She felt awkward and embarrassed upon initiating this intimate caress, but her inhibitions vanished with practice, and her movements became less constrained and more spontaneous and even, to Devlin's inestimable pleasure, provocative.

Feeling reckless, she rolled her surprised husband onto his back and sprang forward to kiss his mouth. Then she pulled away, and ran the tip of her tongue along his lower lip, leaving Devlin groaning in frustration as she directed her lips away from his demanding mouth and on to more diverting attractions. She reveled in the varying texture of his lean body—the stubbled chin, the softly curling chest hair, and the hard muscles beneath the smooth, sun-browned flesh all verified what Kyra had always known . . . her Devlin was a most remarkable man.

Kyra's lips peppered a trail of soft kisses along his collarbone and down his chest, her tongue lightly flicking at his hardened nipples, then traveled on downward across his lean stomach. Her aimless wandering came to an abrupt halt, however, as she approached Devlin's erect male member. She could not bring herself to look at her husband's face, but she remembered the unbelievable sensations he had stirred within her, and wanting him to experience that same rapture, her quivering hand inched downward. Her tremulous fingers had barely encircled the pulsing shaft, however, before an agonizing groan was torn from Devlin's throat and he lurched sideways to press Kyra onto her back.

"You're killing me," he gasped. "Oh, but it's a sweet death." He smiled down into Kyra's startled face, and positioning himself above her, he coaxed her hand back onto the throbbing scepter. "Help me love you, Kyra," he whispered thickly against her trembling lips. "Show me how."

Kyra became hypnotized by the desire she read in those probing brown eyes, and she guided the surging organ toward the sought-after prize. Devlin did not hesitate, but pushed forward to enter the moist passageway, causing Kyra to cry out in surprise.

"Did I hurt you, love?" Devlin murmured tenderly.

"No, never!" she assured him breathlessly, bracing her hands against his powerful shoulders and instinctively wrapping her legs about him. "Don't stop, Devlin! Please, don't stop!"

"As if I could." His deep chuckle buffeted her cheek. Then, slowly, deliberately, he began to move.

Devlin tried to pace himself, wanting to prolong the exquisite torture as long as possible, but when Kyra arched upward to sheathe him with her femininity, he lost all reason. Thus encouraged, he slid his hand beneath her hips and pulled her against him.

Kyra was caught up in a sensual delirium the likes of which she had never before experienced or even imagined. She concentrated on Devlin's exhilarating thrusts, each one burrowing deeper inside her, thrilling her, filling her with unexampled joy, and driving her ever closer to that wildly exciting moment when rational thought would be swept away on a wave of sheer ecstasy. There were other things to be considered as well. There were the lips that moved feverishly against her own, the hand that insistently squeezed her breasts, and the lips again as they tormented the stiffened peaks with more passionate play.

The focal point of this sensual phenomenon lay at the core of her being where, with each masterful stroke, Devlin sent another surge of incredible sensations spiraling through her, leaving her dizzy and faint with their exquisite intensity. She sensed the end was near as the sweet tension gathered, and suddenly fearful of the uncontrollable desire that engulfed her, she desperately groped for her husband's hand and cried his name.

Love-glazed eyes of brown and violet became locked in a timeless embrace, and entwining his hand in Kyra's, Devlin bent his head toward hers. "Soon, love, very soon," he murmured against her lips.

Smiling down at her, he buried himself once more between those velvety thighs and upon hearing Kyra's throaty cry he, too, found release. Kyra lurched upward to cling to him as their bodies shuddered with the force of the spine-tingling, earth-shattering eruption, and Devlin fell

forward to bury his face in her hair and bask in the glow of
liquid fire that gradually faded into a glorious memory.

Devlin eventually became aware of the emotional sobs
that racked the slender form that lay beneath him, and
pushing himself up—as far as he could, for Kyra still clung
to him—he looked down into her tear-ravaged face.

"Don't cry, little pet," he cooed lovingly, leaning near to
press his lips against her cheek. "Was it so very awful?"

"No!" she promptly assured him, one hand relinquishing
its death grip to stroke his brow. "It was beautiful," she
breathed wistfully.

"Yes, it was that . . . and more," Devlin murmured
huskily, his lips nibbling a path to a pink-tipped sphere that
always proved a source of pleasure for him. Then, without
warning, he blurted, "God, but I'm the world's greatest
fool!"

"What?" Kyra asked tentatively, wary of Devlin's unprecedented outburst.

"To have made love to you before and not remember!" he
roared. "I'm an idiot! There can be no other explanation."
His mood grew somber as he asked, "Tell me truthfully,
Kyra, did I hurt you that night?"

"No, at least not physically," she whispered, tracing his
lips with her forefinger. As Devlin playfully nipped the
graceful digit with his teeth, Kyra continued, "You were
very passionate then, but this time there was more than raw
desire, Devlin. This time there was love."

"It will always be so," he vowed, and kissing the tip of
her finger, he reached down to pull the sheet over them.
When he would have extinguished the bedside lamp,
however, Kyra intervened.

"What are you doing?"

"It's time for sleep, magpie," Devlin informed her
sternly.

"But I don't want to sleep. I want to talk and . . ." Her
voice trailed off as her fingers became involved with

drawing an abstract pattern across his broad chest. "Well," she murmured shyly, "I think I shall be ready for another lesson very soon."

"It may take me a little longer," Devlin advised Kyra, laughing at her puzzled expression. Settling himself beside her, he pulled Kyra into his arms and dropped a kiss on the top of her head. "What shall we talk about?"

"You," Kyra answered quite promptly. "I want to know everything about you—when you were a little boy, about your family—everything. Tell me," she begged.

And so he did; they talked through the night. It was nearing daybreak when Kyra showed signs of giving in to the exhaustion that made her eyelids heavy. She was on the verge of dozing off when the mattress shifted and jolted her awake. Staring sleepily at the pillow beside her, she was surprised not to find a mass of tousled dark brown hair reposing on the bolster. Sitting up, she dashed the tangled tendrils from her eyes and looked around the room.

"Devlin?" she called drowsily.

"I'm here, love."

Kyra turned toward his voice and was further dismayed to find him nearly completely dressed. "Where are you going?" she asked disappointedly.

Devlin finished pulling on his leather boots and tucked his shirt into his waistband as he approached the bed. Gazing down at Kyra, he said, "Not to worry, little one. I shall return shortly. At present, I fear we have some unwanted guests with whom I must contend."

He started to move away but Kyra caught his hand, preventing his immediate withdrawal. "Devlin, about . . . about Andrew?" she began hesitantly.

"I won't beat him," Devlin assured her, "even though he certainly deserves a sound thrashing. I don't think Andrew is truly bad, but wagering one's sister in a game of chance indicates that he is sorely in need of a lesson in responsibility. He lacks direction, Kyra, and it's my intent to give him some. Perhaps a tour at sea on one of my ships will do the trick.

"Mr. Monteith, however, is another matter altogether," Devlin growled, bending to kiss Kyra's lips. "Get some sleep, magpie. You're going to need it, for when I return we shall commence with lesson four, or is it five? No matter." He dismissed the issue with a wave of his hand. "Rest assured you will be engaged for the remainder of the day." Upon voicing this provocative promise, Devlin left the room.

Kyra smiled to herself as she sat inside the summerhouse in Cauldurae's blossoming flower garden. A fortnight had passed since she had dared to confess her dreadful secret to Devlin, and Kyra had never regretted the decision she made that night, which now seemed so long ago. Her life had undergone an amazing transformation since then. Now her days were filled with the children, creating a happy and loving home for them, and her nights were filled with Devlin. Kyra had never known such bliss, such utter contentment, and she prayed this newfound euphoria would last.

On this dreamy thought, Kyra directed her attention to the diary that lay open in her lap. Even though Devlin pooh-poohed her efforts, Kyra had become intrigued with the notion of finding the legendary treasure. While they waited in daily anticipation of the blackmailer's next move, Kyra had decided to decipher the clues Judith Tanner had left behind in her journal.

Through her reading, Kyra had learned that the woman was much preoccupied with the garden and especially enjoyed watching the fountain as she sat in the gazebo. This information led Kyra to assume that a clue to the treasure's whereabouts would be found in Cauldurae's lush tropical garden, or perhaps the treasure itself was hidden here. Of one thing Kyra was certain, the fountain was somehow involved in this mysterious puzzle. With a small sigh, she began to read the dated entries for at least the dozenth time, but a small commotion on the garden path forestalled her plans.

Looking up, she was surprised and dismayed to see Elyse Kincaid being carried up the path by her devoted assistant. Despite her disdain, Kyra greeted her guest cordially.

"Good day, Elyse," she said warmly, indicating the servant should place Elyse on the bench next to her. "I fear Devlin is spending the day at the mill."

"I know, dear. I just came from there," Elyse said smugly, dismissing her burly attendant with a casual wave of her hand. "While I was out, I thought I'd stop in and visit with you for a while."

"How nice," Kyra mumbled sweetly. "Shall I have Mrs. Wilson bring refreshments?"

"No, that won't be necessary. I can't stay long," Elyse replied casually, noting with interest the book on Kyra's lap. "What's that you're reading?"

"This?" Kyra held up the journal, though she did not offer it to the inquisitive lady. "It's an old diary I found."

"Don't tell me you've found Judith Tanner's diary!" Elyse exclaimed.

"Well, yes . . . I have," Kyra said slowly, growing suddenly ill at ease. "How did you know—"

"About the diary?" Elyse interrupted. "My dear, everyone knows about it. Treasure seekers have been searching for the diary and the lost treasure of Carraba for years, and you have found it. My, you're a clever puss."

While Elyse began a lengthy tale about some of the more colorful attempts to locate the treasure, Kyra's thoughts returned to a passage she had read just prior to the lady's ill-timed arrival. Though she feigned interest in Elyse's story, Kyra's mind raced as she endeavored to decipher the diary's hidden meaning: "A secret smile, a coquettish wink, and a graceful turn of her hand . . ."

For some reason, these phrases stood out more than any other, but as Kyra concentrated on the mystifying passage, she succeeded only in making her head hurt. Glancing up from the yellowed pages, Kyra rubbed her forehead and exhaled a tired sigh, but as she lowered her hand, her gaze settled on the four statues surrounding the fountain. Very slowly, comprehension spread over her, and with an excited squeal, Kyra—totally oblivious to her guest—scurried down the gazebo steps to the fountain. She ran from one statue to the next hastily scanning the lifeless figures, and sure enough, the face of the last sculpture held just a hint of a smile and one eyelid had been chiseled closed in a flirtatious wink.

"The graceful turn of her hand," Kyra said aloud, and she grasped the statue's extended hand and twisted. Nothing happened.

Not easily discouraged, Kyra stood back to reevaluate the situation. Recalling how Devlin had once told her that the mansion was riddled with secret passages and panels, she fell to her knees to examine the platform supporting the statue. Her nimble fingers deftly explored the rough surface, and just when Kyra's adventuresome spirit was about to wane, she happened upon a small lever in the upper left corner on the platform's rear panel. Taking a deep breath, she pulled the handle toward her.

Again, nothing happened . . . at least not right away. The statue had withstood the vagaries of time and weather, but continued exposure to the elements had rendered the mechanism sluggish. But as Kyra sat back, head cocked at a contemplative angle, a false panel in the base of the platform slid open. The orifice was not wide, but it proved adequate as Kyra reached inside the dark interior and withdrew a narrow box. Opening the lid, she discovered a roll of parchment. Her fingers trembled with excitement as they unrolled the thick paper, but a voice preempted Kyra's thorough examination of the document.

"What's that you've found?" Elyse called curiously.

"Bother!" Kyra muttered under her breath, having completely forgotten the woman during her frenetic search.

"Is it a treasure map?" Elyse persisted when Kyra did not immediately reply.

Kyra's enthusiasm prevailed in spite of the insufferable woman, and perusing the crudely drawn characters and letters, she surmised that Elyse's supposition was most likely correct. "Yes, I believe so," she said.

"Then give it to me," Elyse demanded abruptly.

"What?" Kyra's head snapped back in surprise. "Why should—" The question died on her lips, however, and her eyes widened in disbelief as she witnessed an incredible sight. As Kyra watched, completely stunned, Elyse Kincaid stood and began to walk toward her.

"I said, give me the map." Elyse snatched the paper from Kyra's fingers. "I've waited a lifetime for this moment. I am the only living descendant of Pierre le Roublard. The tales of his piracy have been handed down from generation to generation in my family. My ancestors were scandalized by the stories and wanted no part of Pierre's ill-gotten gains. I am not so fainthearted. By rights, the treasure is mine, and I intend to have it."

Elyse's attention remained focused on the coveted treasure map throughout this impassioned speech, and thinking her preoccupied, Kyra scrambled to her feet and started to run toward the mansion. But she had not anticipated Elyse's quick reflexes, or the woman's strength. Elyse's hand clamped down on her wrist, causing Kyra to cry out in pain.

"Don't be foolish," Elyse warned hatefully, her fingers biting cruelly into Kyra's flesh. "I have gone to great lengths to find this treasure. My men have hounded Devlin for months. They even stooped to dumping him on your yacht in Savannah, but my determination stretches beyond mere trickery. Besides Lynette and the Lovejoy woman, I had my husband killed when he grew suspicious of my motives. I have pretended to be an invalid to draw suspicion away from myself, and I did away with Clayton Fairchild when his obsession with gambling and women threatened to upset my plans. When I confronted him in Savannah, he unwisely vowed to undermine my efforts to locate the treasure. He said he would go to Devlin and tell him everything. Instead, I finished the job you unwittingly started," Elyse said coolly, laughing at Kyra's horrified expression.

"Now, I have nothing to gain by hurting you, but neither will I cavil at doing so if you get in my way. I need you for a while, at least until the treasure is safely loaded aboard my ship. After that, I don't care if you expose my chicanery to your tiresome spouse. Indeed, I relish the thought, for I believe Devlin will be infinitely galled to discover I have outwitted him all this time." Elyse's cold eyes returned to study the aged document.

Kyra caught a movement from the corner of her eye, and glancing up, her spirits lifted. "Jenkins! Thank God!" came her relieved exclamation.

"Yes, Jenkins," Elyse drawled cunningly, snickering at Kyra's suddenly fearful countenance. "I'm glad to see you. Take Mrs. Cauldwell along with you to the North Cove. If I'm reading this right, we'll find the treasure there. I'll return to the village and tell the men to bring the *Fleetwood* around and anchor her offshore. We'll have to wait for cover of night and load the treasure from launches. It will be tedious, but there is no help for it; I intend to be under sail by morning," she announced flatly. Rolling the document into a tight scroll, she lifted her skirt and tucked the map in a deep pocket in her petticoat.

"Off with you, Jenkins. I'll summon John and follow directly." Elyse walked back up the path to the summer-house. "Oh, Jenkins," she called, as the man grasped Kyra by the arm and ruthlessly jerked her forward. "Be careful. You're not to handle this one the way you did Lynette and

Alice. We need to keep her healthy until the treasure is secure lest Devlin discover our activities and try to thwart us. Then we shall see."

Kyra shuddered as the dire statement fell on her ears. As the evil man nudged her along the footpath toward a horse that would take her away from the home where she had always felt safe, Kyra's thoughts were of Devlin, and tears of anguish stung her cheeks as she realized she might never see his mischievous sable-brown eyes again.

Devlin returned to Cauldurae later that afternoon, having come from the mill by way of the village. It was not routine business that had prompted this excursion into town, but rather the arrival of a special gift he had ordered for Kyra. He paused on the garden path to slide his hand inside his jacket and pat the tiny bulge in his pocket. Smiling broadly as he imagined Kyra's reaction when he presented her with the token, he resumed his progress along the trail.

He had taken no more than two steps, however, when his boot struck a small obstruction and he bent down to investigate. His carefree expression dissolved with his discovery; it was Judith Tanner's diary. Devlin frowned as he studied the cracked leather binding, for he knew of Kyra's fascination with the antiquated journal, and he wondered what could have provoked her to discard the diary in such a careless fashion. His frown deepened as he drew erect and the statue where Kyra had found the treasure map came into his line of vision.

The secret panel was still ajar, and with a groan, Devlin realized Kyra must have located yet another clue in her quest for the hidden booty. "The little minx," he grumbled, shaking his head ruefully. "I won't have a moment's peace as long as she is preoccupied with that wretched treasure."

Thinking to put a stop to this treasure-hunting nonsense, Devlin strode to the mansion to seek out his wife. He arrived in the entrance hall just as the door burst open and Joshua Fowler bounded across the threshold.

"What the devil?" Devlin swore, irritated by the unorthodox intrusion.

"Devlin, come quickly!" the doctor exclaimed. "They've got Kyra."

"*What*?" Devlin demanded. "What are you talking about? Out with it, man."

"Up at North Cove," Joshua explained. "Jim Wilson and I came by there a while ago. We heard voices and a great commotion, so we climbed up the ridge to get a better look at what was going on. That's when I saw Kyra. I'm not sure what they're doing, but Elyse's men are swarming all over the place and her ship is anchored off shore."

"Was Kyra all right?" Devlin asked, his shrewd mind beginning to devise a plan that would bring his wife safely back to him.

"I think so. They had bound her hands behind her, and she didn't appear happy about that."

"No," Devlin murmured distractedly, "she wouldn't."

"We've got to hurry, Devlin," Joshua reminded the brooding man impatiently. "They may set sail at any moment. What do you want me to do?"

"First you may tell me this: Just why the devil should I trust you? For all I know, you may be leading me straight into an ambush." Devlin looked his onetime friend squarely in the eye.

"Good God, man! You're wasting precious time," Joshua shouted his frustration. "Why trust me? I'll tell you why. Because regardless of our differences, I would never harm Kyra. She's good and decent, and the best thing that's happened to you in a long while. No, I would never hurt her, but after this is over, I've got half a mind to call you out!"

Devlin considered the enraged man carefully, and with a smug grin, he drawled, "You do that, Joshua. I think, however, you will find I am not likely to believe that of a

friend. Now, let's see about rescuing my wife, shall we? I
will allow the little spitfire can be troublesome at times, but
you see, I've recently come to realize I cannot live without
her." Draping his arm about Joshua's shoulder, Devlin
directed him across the threshold, saying, "This is what I
want you to do."

Devlin slipped from Old Scratch's back and tethered the
horse to a tree before cautiously making his way up the
steep ridge. By following the directions Joshua had given
him, he was able to locate Jim Wilson's hiding place
without difficulty, although he very nearly stumbled into
two of Elyse's burly guards who were patrolling the area.
After his second near brush with discovery, Devlin crept
back onto the overgrown path. Following Joshua's instructions, he sounded the prearranged signal and, upon hearing
Jim's reply, swept aside a gathering of dense palm leaves
and disappeared amid the thick tropical foliage.

"Anything happening down there?" Devlin asked in an
undertone as he stretched out on his stomach beside Jim and
peered down at the cove below.

"Not now. They took a woman out to the ship yonder a
while back. She was kicking and screaming all the way. I
reckon that would be your new missus," he said, glancing
askance at Devlin.

Despite the precarious situation, Devlin smiled and
nodded. "I reckon it would. What do you think they plan to
do?"

"Can't say for sure, but it looks like they're waitin'
around till nightfall so they can load all them crates and
chests on the ship. It's the strangest thing, Devlin." Jim
scratched the back of his head. "I must've been in this cove
a hundred times or more, but I never noticed that cave
before."

"Nor have I."

"It's a narrow opening and it's partially hidden by that big rock, I grant you," Jim continued, still mystified by the discovery, "but you'd think someone would've found it before this. Maybe it's got something to do with the way the sunlight reflects off the water."

"Maybe," Devlin agreed, studying the activity below with rapt interest.

"What do you think's in all those boxes?"

"Offhand, I'd say you are looking at wily Pierre's treasure." Devlin completely stunned the little man with this statement.

"No!" came Jim's astonished whisper. "I thought that was just a tall story someone made up to entertain the children and womenfolk."

"So did I, my friend, so did I," Devlin said, and giving the man's shoulder a good-natured thump, he started to inch his way back toward the path.

"Where are you going?"

"Down there," Devlin replied with a brusque nod toward the cove. "I sent Joshua into the village to gather my men and bring the *Windjammer* in case we need her. But they are starting to load the treasure into those launches, and I cannot risk that ship sailing with Kyra on board."

"What'll you do when you get down there?"

"I don't know." Devlin hunched his broad shoulders. "It looks as if they could use an extra pair of hands."

"I'm coming with you," Jim announced matter-of-factly, starting to follow Devlin.

"No, it's too dangerous." Devlin motioned the man back toward the ridge.

"That's why I'm coming with you. I'll be a damn-sight more help to you down there than up here, lying on my belly watching you get your damn fool head blown off," Jim told him in no uncertain terms.

Devlin considered his friend's candid speech for a moment before he gave an acquiescent shrug and gestured for Jim to follow. The men emerged from the thick undergrowth and carefully made their way along the treacherous path that led down to the cove. They did not immediately become involved in the flurry of activity, but busied themselves by assessing the situation to lessen their chance of discovery. The cove was now pitch-dark except for a few torches scattered about the sand, and the workers were so absorbed in their tasks that they did not notice when two more joined their ranks.

In fact, the two figures—one tall, one short—blended in as they hoisted a heavy treasure chest and carried it toward the launch nearest them. When the cargo had been deposited within, Jim climbed aboard and Devlin gave a mighty heave to push the small craft into the water. Then Devlin clambered aboard, and each man took up an oar and adopted a smooth rowing motion as they steadily maneuvered the launch toward the mother ship. When they arrived at the vessel, several ropes were tossed from above, and Devlin attached these to the large chest before he scrambled up the side of the ship by way of a rope ladder. Once on deck, he helped haul the heavy box aboard, and when the laborers turned to carry the booty to the cargo hold, Devlin motioned for Jim to climb aboard.

"I'm going to search the cabins on the lower level," Devlin said in a hushed tone when Jim had joined him on deck. "Give me ten minutes. Then create a diversion in the hold."

"I'll do my best," Jim promised. After watching until the taller man had disappeared inside the companionway, he turned toward the cargo deck.

Devlin was familiar with the ship's design, for he and David Kincaid had often sailed together. He had a fairly good idea he would find Kyra in one of the cabins in the stern, and his supposition appeared accurate when he saw a shadowy figure loitering outside a door at the end of a long hallway. Devlin did not, however, expect to find Jenkins, one of his own men, guarding Kyra's cabin.

Devlin felt a rush of anger as he realized the man with whom he had entrusted Kyra's safety was the very one who had brought her to this danger, and without truly thinking, he reacted. He was on the man before Jenkins knew what was happening, and in his fury Devlin made short work of the rogue. As the unconscious guard slid to the floor, Devlin opened the cabin door and slipped inside.

He came up short, however, when a slight figure hurled itself at him from the opposite side of the tiny room. The unanticipated blow sent Devlin staggering into a small armoire. "Damn it, woman!" he swore, doubling over and gasping painfully for the breath Kyra had unwittingly knocked from him. "Is this how you welcome your rescuer?"

In response to his question, Devlin heard a series of garbled mumblings and saw that Kyra had been gagged as well as bound. Devlin grunted when he saw her disheveled state, but when his gaze lifted above the tattered rag that covered much of her face and beheld her anguished eyes, his stern mien withered. In two long strides, she was in his arms.

His fingers trembled as he untied the knot at the back of Kyra's head, but when he had tossed the constricting gag aside, and before Kyra could utter a sound, Devlin's mouth swept down upon hers. Though the kiss was fleeting, it was nonetheless passionate and ended with an abruptness born of urgency.

"I'm sorry, Devlin!" Kyra blurted as soon as her lips were free. "I heard the commotion in the hall and thought Jenkins was coming for me."

"Never mind, magpie." Devlin whirled her around to untie the ropes that bound her wrists. Once she was free, he grabbed her hand and led her toward the door. "Come on, we haven't much time."

"But, Devlin," she cried, hanging on to him desperately.

"I've got to tell you . . . it was Elyse, not Joshua. She is the blackmailer. She's responsible for *everything!*"

"I know." Devlin's hand fell upon the latch. Gazing down at Kyra, he added lovingly, "You can tell me everything later, but right now we've got to get off this ship before it sails." Wrenching the door open, Devlin came face to face with Elyse Kincaid.

"I'm afraid you're too late, Devlin," Elyse said with a snicker. "The last of the treasure has just been brought aboard and we shall sail presently. Shortly thereafter you will be dead, and your wife—" She cast a thoughtful look at Kyra, and her lips spread in an evil smile. "Who can say what will become of her when you are no longer around to protect her from my men?"

Devlin glanced down at the gun Elyse pointed at him, then over her shoulder at the ever-present John. He had begun to calculate his chances of wresting the weapon from Elyse without discharging it when a cry from above distracted them.

"*Fire!* There's a fire in the hold!" a voice shouted.

"What the—"

Just then Kyra sprang from behind her husband to send her fist crashing into the woman's chin. The unexpected assault sent Elyse's head reeling, and she fell backward into her watchful attendant. As the big man struggled to disentangle himself, Devlin threw an astonished look at his wife. Then gathering her hand in his, led her up the corridor toward freedom.

Jim was waiting for them by the railing when they burst out of the companionway. "Come on! It won't take them long to bring that fire under control. The ship's underway and there's not time to lower a launch. We'll have to swim for it."

"No!" Kyra shrieked, pulling her hand from Devlin's and backing away. "I can't." She shook her head wildly, terror filling her eyes. "I can't swim!"

Under different circumstances, Devlin would have been more sympathetic to her plight, but the clattering of footsteps in the companionway made him realize that time was running out. Grabbing Kyra around the waist, he thrust her toward the rail.

"We have no choice, Kyra," he told her bluntly. His tone softened as he quickly shrugged out of his coat, and wrapping one sleeve securely about his fist, he shoved the other into her quivering hand. "Hold onto this. Once we're in the water, I'll help you get to shore. Don't worry, love, I'm not going to lose you now." His adoring gaze caressed her as he climbed up on the rail and hoisted her up beside him. On Devlin's command, they jumped, and seconds later, the intrepid trio splashed noisily into the water below.

Devlin was the first to surface, and as he dashed the salt water from his eyes with one hand, he yanked upward with the other, expecting to encounter some resistance as he pulled Kyra to the surface. When he received none, Devlin became panic-stricken as he realized the impact must have caused Kyra to lose hold of the lifeline. Flinging the useless coat aside, Devlin bobbed up and down in the water, glancing about wildly and shouting her name. When there was no reply, he dove beneath the surface, desperately groping for a hand or a piece of clothing—anything he could cling to that would allow him to haul her to safety.

Jim had joined in the frenetic search by this time, and as the majestic ship sailed off into the night, a terrifying drama occurred in its wake. Two desperate men dove into the water repeatedly, surfacing only for a rejuvenating breath of air before submerging again. They continued in this fashion until Devlin, exhausted and distraught, inhaled a final great breath and plunged beneath the surface once more, his heart-wrenching cry of anguish echoing on the ocean waves.

EPILOGUE

Kyra suddenly burst through the watery surface, gasping and sputtering as she groped for her husband's muscular form. "Devlin!" she shouted, slapping at his arm. "You're supposed to be teaching me how to swim, not letting me sink." She wrapped her graceful arms about his neck and snuggled against him.

"I'm not likely to let that happen," he chuckled, holding her close. "Not after the last time." He silently recalled the harrowing night less than a month earlier when he thought she drowned and was taken from him forever. "I promised myself then that if God spared you, I would make certain that frightening moment never recurred. It's unconscionable that you should live on an island—completely surrounded by water, mind you—and not know how to swim. Now, swim, woman!" he commanded.

"I'm tired," Kyra said, nuzzling his cheek with her nose.

"Ah, do you have another game in mind, then?" he murmured suggestively. Devlin allowed his hands to slide down her back to squeeze the softly rounded hips, and he pulled her forward to rub against him intimately.

"No, silly!" Kyra chided, and pushing away from him, she paddled to the beach and climbed out of the water. "We don't have time for that now. Your mother's letter said she and Emily would arrive by noon," she reminded him, plucking a towel from the sand and rubbing the excess moisture from her hair and chemise.

"I don't know, honey," his doubtful voice split the air behind her, and Kyra looked up just as Devlin strode out of the water, his glorious naked body glistening in the morning sun and his manhood impatiently erect. "It seems a pity to let this go to waste . . ."

Later, after Devlin had dressed himself, he leaned back on his elbows and watched lazily as Kyra tucked the hem of her gauzy white blouse inside the waistband of her skirt. She had just concluded fussing with her hair and was bending to collect their belongings when Devlin's hand circled her wrist, and he pulled her down onto the blanket beside him.

"Devlin," she protested, "we don't have time."

"We have time for this," he said mysteriously, reaching inside his pocket to withdraw a small jeweler's box. Turning her hand over, he settled the square container on her palm. "Open it."

Kyra's quizzical gaze darted from Devlin's face to the tiny package and back to her husband's face. Finally curiosity overcame her, and she lifted the lid to find an exquisite wedding band lying on a bed of blue velvet. Her expression gradually changed to one of overwhelmed stupefaction as she stared at the diamond-studded circle of gold that glittered in the sunlight.

Finding her voice, she eventually murmured, "It's beautiful."

"As are you, my love," Devlin whispered adoringly. Lifting the ring from the box, he nodded toward her ring finger. "May I?"

"Please," Kyra replied softly as tears began to gather in her violet eyes.

She was amazed by Devlin's subsequent actions; after settling himself on one knee before her, he clasped her hands and pressed them to his heart. "I know I've done this before," he offered tentatively, "but I was a bitter man then, and I promise not to mock you this time." Exhaling a long breath, he said, "Kyra, you've brought joy and laughter and love back into my life. Indeed, my heart has never known such contentment. You will make me the happiest of men if you will agree to be mine. Marry me, my love," he concluded on a hoarse whisper, slipping the ring onto her finger.

"Of course I will, my darling," Kyra sobbed happily, flinging her arms about Devlin's neck. "Well, I mean . . . we're already married," she sniffed. "But if we weren't, I would. Oh," she cried in exasperation, flustered by her own babbling, "you know what I mean."

"Yes, I know," he said with a fond chuckle and kissed the tip of her nose. Devlin stood then to gather up the towels and blanket, but when he looked at Kyra again, he was puzzled by her suddenly thoughtful expression. "What is it, little pet?"

"I was just wondering. Weren't you the least bit disappointed that Elyse escaped with the treasure?"

"I'm more dismayed by the fact that Elyse has not been brought to justice for the senseless murders she committed," he said matter-of-factly. "As for the treasure, I told you once before that I have no need of Pierre le Roublard's ill-gotten riches. You are all the treasure I will ever need. Now, come along, magpie. We have guests to greet."

Devlin wrapped his arm about his wife's waist as they trudged up the sandy footpath. They were nearing the summit when Kyra dared to broach a sensitive subject. "Devlin, about your mother's visit. Remember, you promised there would be no . . . confrontations."

"I shall endeavor to be a most congenial host," came his reply.

Realizing she would have to be content with this vague pledge, Kyra casually offered, "Darling, I was thinking it might be nice to invite Joshua to dine with us while Emily is here."

"So you've decided to number matchmaking among your varied accomplishments, have you?" he quipped.

"Be serious," Kyra scolded. "What do you think?"

"I think you should do as you please," Devlin promptly replied. "And if the evening does not progress to your liking, perhaps I could engage the doctor in a game of cards. I have it on excellent authority that it is perfectly acceptable to offer one's sister as collateral at these betting matches."

"Oh, you!" Kyra giggled at his antics, but her laughter died when they arrived at the top of the bluff and she saw the carriage trundling up the long drive. "They're here!" she shrieked. "Amanda cannot see me like this. I look an absolute fright."

"You look delightful," Devlin informed her.

"To you perhaps, but I doubt my mother-in-law will think so." Kyra eyed the approaching vehicle with chagrin. On impulse, she snatched the blanket and towels from Devlin's arms and scurried toward the mansion. "You greet them, darling. I'll just freshen up a bit."

Kyra ran with unladylike haste across the lawn and up the front stoop where Thomas immediately opened the door for her. "Let me take those for you, Miss Kyra," the butler offered kindly, and as Kyra handed over the sand-encrusted blanket and damp towels, her gaze was drawn to the carriage that had just rolled to a stop before the mansion.

Kyra watched anxiously as Devlin helped his sister from the conveyance, and her breath caught in her throat as she anticipated the forthcoming meeting between mother and son. Then a remarkable thing occurred. After the pair exchanged casual greetings, Devlin abruptly leaned forward and kissed Amanda's cheek, and then mother and son embraced.

Kyra's heart swelled with joy as she observed the

touching reunion, and although she knew there was still much to be said between these two, at least they had made a small start toward reconciling their differences. Kyra remained transfixed on the threshold until the sound of children's voices jolted her from her reverie, and glancing up, she saw Sarah and Nicholas scamper from the side yard, the playful Goldie in hot pursuit, and run gleefully toward their grandmother.

A sob lodged in Kyra's throat as she watched Devlin swoop a jubilant Sarah into his arms and accept her soggy kiss. Then, handing the little girl into Amanda's waiting arms, he settled Nicholas atop his shoulders, and as he turned to usher the little group up the walkway, his adoring gaze settled on his wife. Kyra had never felt more loved, and completely forgetting her disheveled appearance, she blinked back the tears of happiness that stung her eyes and ran down the steps to be with her family.